THE ADAMIC CODE

BOOK 1 OF THE ORION'S SPEAR SERIES

THE ADAMIC CODE

C. T. KNUDSEN

This is a work of fiction. Characters and events in this book are products of the author's imagination or are represented fictitiously.

Editorial work by Eschler Editing
Cover design by MiblArt
Author bio photo by Joe Boyer
Interior print design and layout by Sydnee Hyer
Ebook design and layout by Sydnee Hyer
Production services facilitated by E&E Books

**KILO
PRESS**
Published by Kilo Press

978-1-7360902-0-6

This book is dedicated to Elizabeth, my Leah.

ACKNOWLEDGMENTS

I'd like to first thank Chris Bigelow for his expert editing, guidance, and mentorship on the development of this book. To my daughter Abby, an aspiring author herself, for her wonderful feedback and excellent editing work. I'd like to thank my wonderful wife, Liz, and my family for their support and encouragement. I want to thank the entire team at Eschler for their diligent work and professional help in getting this book to market.

AUTHOR'S NOTE TO LDS READERS

I have a confession.

While *The Adamic Code* is a book filled with covert and overt LDS themes, I did not originally set out to write the book for the LDS readership. It was only after completing the book that I realized I had two choices: remove all LDS references and appeal to a broader audience or embrace the LDS audience no matter the consequences. I opted for the latter, albeit with great reluctance.

Allow me to explain.

The bad guys in *The Adamic Code* are bad—like, biblical bad. It's hard to write about the things bad guys like these do without risking offending a religious audience.

While editing the book for an LDS audience, I removed all profanity. But that was easy, as the book contained hardly any to begin with. What was difficult was tempering the scenes of violence and desperation without going too Pollyanna and destroying the reality of what very bad people do in their quest to conquer the world.

So, consider yourself cautioned. This book contains numerous scenes of violence, including depictions of murder, a human sacrifice, a mass shooting, war, and torture. An entire chapter follows the path of a starving young girl to her ultimate death at the hands of sadistic terrorists. Even with all that, I wrote the book in such a way that it's no more graphic than the Bible or the Book of Mormon.

At its core, *The Adamic Code* is a story about discovering. Discovering faith. Discovering your mission in this life. Discovering how you are a tool in God's hands. Discovering that you are inexplicably tied to your progenitors and that they watch over you from beyond the grave. Discovering love and finding the right life partner. Discovering the will to live when all seems lost. Discovering that the mind is the most powerful tool—and the most powerful weapon—one can possess. Finally, this story reminds us that the bad guys may win some of the battles, but God will win the war.

The Adamic Code is the first book in a series that follows our protagonist, Chris Thomas, from a nobody to saving the world over and over again.

I thank you in advance for joining me on this journey, and I hope you enjoy the series.

C. T. KNUDSEN
HEBER, UTAH
JUNE 2020

FACTS

Scientists estimate that only one hundred people in recorded medical history have experienced acquired savant syndrome stemming from a traumatic brain injury.

The CIA's Ground Branch paramilitary unit is shrouded in mystery and legend. The unit is active across the globe, and, to this day, its missions remain entirely classified.

Operation Pastorius was a World War II military operation conceived by Adolf Hitler.

Laser-based cardiac identification, stealth satellites, and microdrones used for targeted assassination are all existing technologies.

The Stuxnet computer worm is believed to have been unleashed by the US government on the Iranian nuclear program in 2010. Stuxnet is still in the wild online.

Numerous ancient books of unknown language and origin—known as codices—have been unearthed and studied by archeologists and scientists. Some remain a complete mystery.

It was reported that the Prophet Joseph Smith told Thomas B. Marsh that, in Marsh's words, "the Lord gave Joseph a vision, in which appeared a wild country and on the scene was Moroni after whom were six Indians in pursuit; he stopped and one of the Indians stepped forward and measured swords with him. Moroni smote him and he fell dead; another Indian advanced and contended with him; this Indian also fell by his sword; a third Indian then stepped forth and met the same fate; a fourth afterwards contended with him, but in the struggle with the fourth, Moroni, being exhausted, was killed. Thus ended the life of Moroni."

CHAPTER 1

President Royce Jefferson Lennox dared not move against the twisted three-blade knife being pressed to his throat.

The president's eyes shifted around as he looked for help. In one corner of the room, the president's chief of staff, Richard Boone, and national security adviser, Roger Cowen, sat comfortably on a plush, Western-style leather couch, looking equally bored and annoyed. On the other side of the room, two Secret Service agents stood stone-faced, guarding a door.

The president's eyes shifted again and caught a well-dressed European aristocrat standing by a bulletproof picture window. The man was aloof to the events transpiring in the room but appeared to enjoy his view of the Maryland countryside.

"Stand," said the president's assailant as he pulled back the odd-looking knife and released Lennox from his iron grasp. Lennox was too terrified to look up at the towering, dark, imposing figure before him. Although the man had released him, he knew he was not safe. Foreboding, hopelessness, and sheer terror consumed the president.

"My Lord," said the president, his head still bowed.

"Address him properly," scolded the aristocrat from the window. The president winced and looked up at the man standing over him.

"Master Mahan," said the president hesitantly.

Mahan looked down on the president, a look of pure hatred spreading across the assailant's permanently bloodstained face. "Must I remind you who owns your pathetic life?"

"No, master," said the president, his frame shaking.

"Play it," Master Mahan commanded the national security adviser. Hesitantly, the president turned to face a TV mounted on the wall.

A video came alive showing the president in a salacious and compromising act. Then another video played, and then another. The president bowed his head in shame and wished for death. The damning video seemed as though it would never end.

"But how?" he whispered, looking at Mahan in defeat.

"You fool," said Master Mahan. "We identified you at a young age. We groomed you. We taught you. We financed you. We supplied you with the pleasures of the flesh. The money. The drugs. The women. As your career progressed, we threw the journalists off the scent. We framed your competitors. We paid off the right people. The idealists who could not be bought were simply suicided. All of it filmed and filed. For leverage. All of it."

Lennox was still in shock. He looked at his Secret Service security detail. They didn't look back at him. He looked at his chief of staff and national security adviser. They simply stared back, one with an evil grin and the other with a fatherly look of disappointment. They were completely under Mahan's control. The president was on his own.

Master Mahan placed a hand on the president's shoulder, regaining his attention. Lennox looked at the strange knife still clenched in his master's other hand. The ancient knife and its sordid history were well-known to the president. Thousands had died by the wicked device and the man holding it.

"The Mother requires you, your talents, and all you possess for the cause of Baphomet," said Mahan. "The time is not far off, my child, when the Order will reveal the Mandate to the world. The feeders and inferiors who molest our precious planet will soon die a horrific and glorious death. Can the Mother count on you, my son?"

Lennox hesitated. Without warning, Master Mahan violently grabbed the president by the scruff and again forced the knife against his throat.

"Say it," he whispered as he pressed the blade harder.

"I pledge my allegiance and all I possess to the Mother, to the Son, to the Mandate, and to you, my prophet, Master Mahan," said the president. He had no other choice.

"Very good, child," said Master Mahan, again releasing the president from his iron-clad grasp. He placed the knife back in his coat. "From now on, you shall be known as Lamech, the chosen son."

The president's terrified demeanor turned to entrancement. "I am chosen?" he asked in awe.

The master placed his hands on the president's shoulders and gently pulled him into an embrace. Then he looked deep into Lennox's eyes.

"Yes. But fail me again, and you will die." He violently pushed the president away.

The president stumbled backward but caught himself. Then he awkwardly adjusted his tie and buttoned his suit coat. The room was uncomfortably quiet.

"Benson, if you will," said Master Mahan to the man at the window. All eyes moved to the European aristocrat as he slowly turned to face the room.

"Meeting adjourned."

CHAPTER 2

THE ROSE GARDEN ARENA
PORTLAND, OREGON

Standing on the floor of the Rose Garden Arena—where the Portland Trailblazers had beat the Chicago Bulls the night before—all Chris Thomas felt was relief. He was, by all measures, less than ordinary, and being less than ordinary in an academic system was, by all measures, being a failure. Today, on the day of this failure's high school graduation, he was lucky to be collecting a diploma.

Chris found his seat and looked up at the stage. There sat his best friend, Scott Allen. Academically, Scott was the opposite of Chris. As one of only three valedictorians in a class of 706 students, Scott was on his way to Harvard. This year, he had been the only kid in the state of Oregon to be accepted by the prestigious university.

Scott gave Chris a smile and then a thumbs-up as if to thank him. Chris returned the gesture, then looked away, hoping Scott couldn't see his tear-filled eyes from the rostrum. They had initially bonded over their obscure religions. Scott was the only Jewish student in the school, and Chris was among a handful of Mormon students. Both boys were grateful for each other. Without Scott, Chris never would have graduated. Without Chris, Scott would have spent his school years as a loner and an outcast.

In the midst of all the pomp and circumstance of the commencement, Chris reflected on the struggles that had plagued him during these formative years. The tears continued to well, but he was quick to wipe them away so no one could see. Even now, he could barely read at an eighth-grade level. His mother had hired a private tutor just to get him through the minimum math class required for graduation. Of course, his father had complained about the cost and Chris's lack of progress. In the end, he was lucky to finish with a 2.1 cumulative GPA.

"Hey, man, you're up!" the guy next to him said. "Move it, dude."

Chris composed himself, followed the graduation line to the rostrum, and accepted his diploma. Afterward, he found his family in the sea of proud and not-so-proud parents. His mom and sister cried. His mom hadn't thought he'd make it. Dad poked fun at his GPA again, but teasing was his expression of love. His grandparents hugged him and told him how proud they were. This confused Chris. He'd always believed his grandparents secretly thought he was a loser.

CHAPTER 3

INSIDE A B-2 BOMBER APPROACHING ODESSA, UKRAINE

Mike Mayberry awoke from a mild jolt of turbulence. There was no way he could nap through the heated air being violently thrust upward from the earth's crust, even fifty thousand feet above it.

He yawned, wiped the sleep from his eyes, and checked the aircraft's position. Then he looked around the claustrophobic compartment at his men, eleven of them strapped in their seats in two facing rows. Some read. Some slept. Others appeared to be manipulating augmented-reality objects projecting from their helmets.

My back.

He dared not mutter the complaint in front of his men. The seats, manufactured by the lowest bidder, were as comfortable as a hard piece of wood, which made ten-hour flights to mission sites even less bearable. Mike tried to stretch his legs, but the attempt was futile.

The bomb bay of the $2.1 billion B-2 Stealth Bomber was originally designed to carry thermonuclear weapons, not men. But in the late 1990s, the Defense Advanced Research Projects Agency (better known as DARPA) and the air force had jointly engineered a special pressurized capsule specifically for the bomb bay of the B-2. It could carry up to twelve special-operations soldiers halfway around the world. The capsule's specially designed exit system allowed the B-2 to air-drop soldiers over a target precisely, like little human bombs.

Basic comforts were one of the many things sacrificed in Mike's profession. The job also came with a broken marriage, a broken body, and a humble paycheck. But Mike was dedicated to his work. He was a CIA officer and team leader in the agency's highly secretive special operations group known as Ground Branch. He had been told on several occasions that many of the brass regarded him as the best Army Special Forces had ever produced. Mike put aside those thoughts. He was a quiet professional interested only in serving his country.

"Knife," the B-2 captain said over Mike's earpiece, using his code name. "We just entered Ukrainian airspace."

"Roger that," Mike said, lowering the faceplate attached to the helmet of his Viper combat suit. He rejoined the team's networked comms and said, "OK, guys, listen up."

One of the operatives pushed the pause button on the touch screen of a tiny computer strapped to his left forearm. Metallica's "Don't Tread on Me" stopped playing. The team loved listening to Metallica en route to an op.

"We just crossed into Ukrainian airspace," Mike said. "I want to go over the facility layout one more time. In your heads-up display, you will see a 3D image of the laboratory and where we expect security to be at this time of night."

A schematic of the large three-story building appeared in augmented-reality 3D on the men's Viper heads-up displays (aka HUDs).

At $4 million apiece, the Viper battle suit was like something straight out of a science-fiction movie. From the neck up, the operatives looked like fighter pilots, complete with streamlined Kevlar-and-titanium helmets equipped with the latest, seventh-generation night vision coupled with high-definition augmented-reality capability. Their mouths and noses were covered by a hardened bulletproof mask attached to a concealed oxygen source on their lower backs.

Below the neck, the Viper suit was just as impressive. Covered in an advanced hybrid alloy, the all-black suit armored a soldier head to toe. It was climate-controlled, fire-resistant, flexible, extremely lightweight, and could stop anything up to a 7.62 x 54mm round.

The sealed, fully self-contained suit had the same nuclear, biological, and chemical defense rating as the much bulkier HAMMER warfare suit. The parachute attached to each operative's back featured a powered retraction system that allowed the soldier to land, hit a button on his chest, and retract the parachute into the suit within twelve seconds.

For this mission, the team's primary weapon was a Heckler and Koch MP-7 with a thirty-round magazine containing armor-piercing 4.6 x 30mm bullets. Each man carried numerous thirty-round magazines attached to his armor at various points. Atop the weapon was a holographic scope that worked in conjunction with the suit's targeting system. The MP-7 was silenced with a secret, proprietary barrel attachment used exclusively by the CIA and Joint Special Operations Command. The team's back-up sidearm was a Glock 19 with holographic sight and three fifteen-round magazines. And, for good measure, a knife was concealed in a special compartment in the body armor.

"OK, is everyone seeing the 3D image?" asked Mike. Down the line, the men each gave a thumbs-up. Stretching his hand out in front of him as if he held something invisible, Mike manipulated the 3D image of the building layout in augmented reality.

"As previously indicated, we specifically want to enter this lab on the second floor, northeast corner. Smith and Dellmark will accompany me to the lab, where we'll procure the biotoxin and seal it in these containment units." Mike pointed at the small boxes attached to Smith's and Dellmark's suits. "The rest of you know what to do. Take up your positions, cover our backs, and eliminate any threats. I want to be in and out in under four minutes. We'll rally to the primary extraction point on my signal."

At that moment, the light in the capsule went yellow and the aircraft suddenly decelerated to a safe jump speed.

The B-2 pilot came over Mike's earpiece and indicated two minutes to drop. The men stood, gave their equipment a final check, and then Mike gave the hand signal to line up at the exit point at the rear of the capsule. The bomb-bay doors opened, and the earth revealed itself fifty thousand feet below. Mike was first in line. He edged out and looked down at the former Soviet satellite state below him. It was pitch-black.

The capsule light turned red. Without hesitation, the assassins funneled out of the B-2 into the dead-still night.

It was 8:31 p.m. eastern daylight time, but the Special Activities Operations Center buried deep under CIA headquarters was busy as usual. A video projecting what the soldiers were seeing in real time was displayed before the staff. Packed with high-strung analysts and operatives monitoring mission progress, the room smelled of coffee, sweat, and tension. People worked on computers, spoke in hurried, hushed tones, and used hand signals to communicate across the expansive room. As expected, they were professional and efficient. One mistake could mean the death of an operative half a world away.

Finally, a young female specialist looked up from her computer and gave the mission lead an exaggerated thumbs-up.

"Knife, this is Jolly Roger," said the mission lead, her voice calm and distant.

"Jolly Roger, this is Knife. Go for comms," said Mike Mayberry as he passed through fifteen thousand feet at terminal velocity, his HUD guiding him right to the landing zone.

"Knife, Disneyland is open for business. Godspeed," said the mission lead.

"Copy, Jolly Roger."

Beneath the approaching assault team, the large medical complex suddenly went dark and was now only visible through their night-vision goggles. As the team approached three thousand feet, they began to pull their chutes.

Watching the operation unfold from a shadowy corner near the back of the room, the CIA director stood next to Stew Brimhall, a CIA assistant director who headed a top-secret group. The director took a sip of coffee and said, "Well, here we go."

"I gotta bad feeling about this," said Stew. "Something's not right with this op."

The director smiled. "You say that about every op. It's Mayberry. It'll be fine."

"Yeah, I'm not worried about Mike."

An RQ-170 Sentinel stealth drone orbiting above the mission site projected images of the assassins pulling their chutes. Looking like little helicopters from above, the men floated methodically toward the target.

Mbox

The two Ukrainians standing on the roof had recently been laid off from the local steel mill and had been lucky to find work as night security guards at the medical center. As former military men, they both found it odd that they'd been issued AK-74 rifles, but it was a job and the pay was better than at the mill, so they didn't ask questions.

"Lights are out again," said one guard. "Hand me a cigarette, you greedy *duren'.*"

Sitting down with their backs against a ventilation shaft, they both enjoyed the unfiltered tobacco. The spring air was a welcome relief from the brutal winter that had just passed. As they sat talking, one of the men looked skyward.

"Do you see that?"

"See what, you drunk idiot? A UFO or something?"

The man stood, grasping his weapon. He stared into the sky. "Look . . . there." He pointed.

"What? It's nothing," said his friend, taking a drag on his cigarette.

As the guard raised his AK-74 to look through the iron sight, an armor-piercing round penetrated his skull and his body dropped like a rag doll. Before the other man could react, he too was gunned down from above.

Five seconds later, the Ground Branch operatives began landing quietly at various points on the expansive flat roof. Weapons ready, they quickly retracted their chutes and surveyed their surroundings. Each man gave Mike a quick thumbs-up as they began moving to their assigned positions.

"Jolly Roger, we're moving to the objective now," said Knife.

Mayberry, Smith, and Dellmark ran to a nearby roof-access point. It was unlocked. They opened the hatch and peered into the hole from behind their weapons. Although the access point was pitch-dark, they could see inside with perfect clarity. Just as Jolly Roger had promised, Disneyland was indeed open for business.

The Americans climbed down the ladder and moved up the narrow, pitch-dark hallway toward the lab, MP-7s at the ready. As they approached an intersection, Mike raised his left arm in a square, his fist balled. Dellmark and Smith stopped instantly.

Twenty feet ahead, a beam of light from an adjoining hall pierced the darkness of the intersection. The light grew brighter and brighter until a guard emerged. Mike fired a single round, hitting the man in the head. Blood splattered the wall, and the flashlight clanked as it hit the floor, followed by the thud of a body. The man never knew what hit him.

The killers stepped over the body and turned the corner, the secure door to the lab just fifty feet ahead of them. Smith reached down and disabled the flashlight while checking the team's six. All clear.

"Knife, be advised," came Jolly Roger's voice from five thousand miles away. "Military convoy inbound to your station. Models estimate ETA in 5.5 minutes."

"Copy, we'll be Oscar Mike in three minutes," said Mike.

"Where is this convoy coming from?" asked Smith, monitoring the hall behind them. Mike returned no comment as he slung his MP-7 over his shoulder and knelt in front of the steel lab door.

Dellmark put his gloved hand on the door's biosensor and pushed several buttons on the microcomputer attached to his forearm. The biosensor's red light turned green.

"Ready, Chief," said Dellmark.

Mike nodded. A small rod sprang from the right index finger of his Viper suit. He inserted it into the lock of the steel door. The rod began to spin, and a 3D model of the internal locking mechanism formed on the screen inside Mike's faceplate, then smaller rods extended from the main rod and inserted into various points in the locking mechanism.

The lock made a quiet clicking sound.

"Easy money, gentleman. Let's move," said Mike as the rod retracted into the finger of his glove. "We've got ninety seconds."

As they positioned themselves to breach the lab door, they were met with a sudden hail of gunfire from inside the lab.

Small holes pockmarked the lab door as several rounds smashed through the thin metal and into the assassins' bulletproof Viper suits. Mike rushed into the barrage of bullets and kicked open the destroyed door. Numerous Ukrainian guards kept firing on the three men from inside the pitch-black lab.

"What is this?" Dellmark yelled, returning fire as he moved into the lab.

Mike pushed deeper into the lab, killed three men, and dove for cover behind a bulky lyophilizer machine. A guard ran around the machine to meet Mike, but Smith shot him.

The firing stopped momentarily, the sounds of reloading reverberating throughout the lab. Mike peeked out from behind his cover and scanned the room for a new target. His eye caught the back of a slender blonde dressed in black, her hair slicked-back, as she bolted for the fire escape. She had slung a bulky aluminum refrigeration case over her shoulder.

Mike took aim at the woman, but the enemy fired on his position. A lucky round hit a gas line near Mike, causing a small explosion that threw him to the ground. The fire alarm sounded, and the fire-suppression system activated, flooding the room with a white fog. Standing, Mike fired a single round at the woman as she reached the exit. The round hit her in the center of her back, throwing her forward. She flailed, and her body pushed open the fire door.

Mike ran toward the woman, but several men screamed something in Ukrainian and fired at him from a concealed position.

Using the fog as cover, Smith lobbed a grenade at the enemy's position behind an enormous centrifuge. The explosion rocked the room, and the assailants fell dead.

Mike burst through the fire exit, fully expecting to see the woman's body on the landing, but she was gone.

What the . . . I hit her dead center in the back. She couldn't have survived that.

The sound of a slamming steel exterior door echoed up the fire escape directly below Mike's position on the second floor.

"We have a new target," yelled Mike into his comms as he rushed down the flight of stairs. "Blonde woman with a refrigeration case. She's headed for the front of the facility. I believe the virus is in the case. I am in pursuit. If you have a shot, take it."

"Knife, the military convoy is almost on your station," said the Langley mission lead's calm voice. "ETA thirty seconds. Egress to rally point Charlie and divert to extraction plan Echo. Do you copy?"

"Copy, Jolly Roger. What about the objective?" asked Mike. He burst through the exterior door with his rifle raised, searching for the woman.

"Knife, check your drone feed. We estimate two hundred enemy inbound. Exfill now."

Mike pulled up the stealth drone's feed on his HUD. From fifteen thousand feet overhead, the drone transmitted real-time video of the surrounding area. The convoy was closing in quickly, but Mike was more interested in recovering the virus. With a voice command, he had his HUD replay a scene recorded by the drone a few seconds earlier. The screen showed the blonde woman running up the front portico and hiding behind a large pillar.

Gotcha. Mike took off at a sprint toward the target.

A Mercedes S-Class sped up the portico drive toward Mike. The woman rushed from her hiding place and threw herself into the vehicle's back seat. Mike opened up on the car with his MP-7. The armor-piercing rounds tore into the driver, and the Benz came to a screeching halt directly in front of Mike. From the rear seat, the blonde panic-fired through the destroyed front windshield, but her small-caliber handgun was useless against Mike's Viper suit.

Mike ran to the side of the car, shot the driver again, and pulled the body out of the driver's seat. Then he ripped open the rear door. The woman's face stayed calm as she scrambled to reload. Before she could chamber a round, Mike grabbed her by the neck and threw her to the ground. A look of terror and confusion crossed her beautiful face. Mike had seen that look many times. The last thing many of his victims glimpsed was their own distorted faces in the Viper suit's curved, reflective faceplate.

"Knife, move. They're right on you!" yelled a voice from Langley.

"Dark Angel, Dark Angel, this is Knife," Mike said calmly, still holding the struggling woman to the ground. "We're pinned down. Our primary egress is compromised. Attack direction north. You are cleared and hot."

"Copy that, Knife," said a pilot's voice. "Sixty seconds. Rolling in hot."

Mike opened comms to his team. "This just went pear-shaped. Evac now; move to rally point Charlie. Fast mover inbound. We have thirty seconds to minimum safe distance."

Still pinning the woman, he looked in the car's back seat and saw the refrigerated aluminum case. Suddenly, several bullets hit Mike, bouncing off the Viper suit. He yelled out, released the woman, and raised his weapon to meet a new enemy. Several military vehicles sped up the rounded drive, numerous soldiers now firing on his position.

Mike began to fire. At the building's front entrance, Smith, Dellmark, and other team members fired on the soldiers, covering Mike's position. Heavily armed men poured from the backs of Russian-made Ural armored transport trucks and spread out across the grounds. The Americans fired on the soldiers with everything they had, but the enemy began leveling their position with large-caliber, truck-mounted machine guns.

"This raid is a Charlie Foxtrot. Fast mover is almost on top of us. Knife, move now—we'll cover you," said Smith over comms as the team continued to fire.

Mike heard the Mercedes engine rev behind him. Turning, he lunged for the door handle, but an enemy round hit him in the helmet. As the blonde woman sped away with the case, Mike fired on the vehicle, but it moved quickly around the drive and was soon concealed by a hedge.

Mike yelled out in frustration. Turning back to the fight, he ran to take cover behind a column. His men had backed into the main lobby, taking cover from the large-caliber barrage.

"Moving!" yelled Mike into his comms, then ran for the front entrance as his team covered him. His Viper suit was taking a beating but still holding. Several more of Mike's men converged on the lobby and joined the fight. Glass walls, furniture, and the reception desk exploded as the enemy soldiers focused their fire on the lobby.

"The fast mover is right on top of us," Mike yelled. "Take the back exit. Run!"

Mike and his team sprinted across the vast lobby and burst through the building's back door. They converged on the back lawn with a few additional team members and ran toward the rally point, just inside the spruce forest surrounding the medical facility.

Then it happened.

The video feed went white, immediately autocorrecting for the brightness. Mike was thrown to the ground by the force of multiple air-to-ground missiles leveling the complex. The facility exploded in several small mushroom clouds, and burning debris fell around him. As he tried to regain his senses, his radio brought him back to reality. "Target destroyed," said an anonymous F-22 Raptor pilot. "Returning to base."

His men started rising from the ground, giving each other the thumbs-up.

"Knife, this is Jolly Roger. Sound off."

Mike pulled off his helmet and looked at the fire and destruction. "All men accounted for," he said into his comms. "Exfilling now. Executing extraction plan Charlie as instructed. Knife out."

Among the trees, the team stripped off their Viper suits, revealing the civilian clothing typically worn by local Ukrainians. Moving through the trees to a back road, they quickly loaded their equipment into several automobiles that had been placed at the alternate extraction point prior to the mission. Then they sped away from the blast zone. Having memorized the area map, they separated and drove off in different directions.

Over the next few days, the Ground Branch team took refuge in several safe houses throughout the country. They were given clothing, food, money, weapons, and cover stories. Soon, the men would leave the Ukraine as stealthily as they had entered. They would look like innocuous tourists, journalists, and businessmen, their travel documents and passports impeccable.

In truth, they were ghosts.

As Mike Mayberry watched an old airport TV, Al Jazeera reported a natural-gas explosion that had rocked an area outside of Odessa, Ukraine. The screen showed aerial images of a massive burning building.

Mike sipped his black coffee. At that moment, first class was called to board American Airlines Flight 5647 from Kiev to Dulles International Airport. He collected his few belongings and headed for the gate, passing under a sign that read Washington, D.C. As he walked down the Jetway toward the plane, he frowned. Even with the comforts of commercial first class, long flights were not his thing.

CHAPTER 4

TUALATIN, OREGON

With high school behind him, Chris could focus on the rest of his life. He had plans: framing houses in Oregon for the rest of the summer, then bumming a place to live with his aunt and uncle in Salt Lake City. They'd said he could stay in their unfinished basement for a year while he figured life out. He hoped to pick up work at Snowbird ski resort as a lifty. On his days off, he'd use his employee pass to ski Utah's fresh powder. The life of a ski bum appealed to him. No school. No homework. No learning. No thinking. No responsibility.

When Chris was fifteen, Grandpa Thomas had noticed his grandson's penchant for laziness and detected his path toward destruction, and he'd helped Chris get on with a local framing crew. That first year of framing was mostly grunt work until the foreman, Clint, had told him to put on a tool belt. On that hot July day, Chris had learned how to frame a wall out of fresh-cut Douglas-fir studs.

One late-summer afternoon, Clint taught Chris how to build stairs, carefully instructing him how to use the metal square and the geometric formulas necessary to get the cuts for the treads exactly right. When Chris was done cutting the two-by-twelve-inch board, it looked like the Teton mountain range, with long jagged cuts up and down it.

"Hey, kid, this is simple geometry," said Clint, annoyed. "I didn't even graduate from high school, and I can do this in my sleep. Do it again, and ask me questions when you run into problems."

Embarrassed by his inability to cut a two-by-twelve board following a simple geometric formula, Chris paused, then turned to Clint. "Hey, how about I just go finish that sheeting on the outside basement wall?" Chris noticed Clint's surprise at the request. After all, that was much harder work than cutting simple stairs.

"OK," said Clint as Chris passed him, head down. It took two summers for Chris to finally get the hang of cutting stairs, no doubt surprising Clint that it had taken him so long to learn the simple process.

Several weeks after graduation and following a twelve-hour sprint to finish a house, Chris was loading his tools into his brown 1987 Ford F-150 when he turned and noticed something different about the half-finished wood-framed house. A strange feeling of satisfaction and pride overcame him as he inspected the timber monster. It wasn't just Douglas-fir boards, Portland concrete, and Grip-Rite nails. It was now something oddly beautiful.

Clint came to where Chris leaned against the bed of his truck. "Stoned again?" he joked.

"Ha! No," said Chris. Then he quickly got serious. "I was just looking at the house. Pretty amazing we built that, don't you think?" He opened a can of Coke.

Looking at the house in front of them, Clint leaned up against the truck. "Yes, it is," he said proudly. "You know, Chris, I'm not an educated man, but I put in an honest day's work every single day. I go home at night with the satisfaction of knowing I did my best and earned an honest buck." After a pause, he continued. "Do you know what that emotion you're feeling right now is?"

"Actually, no," said Chris, curious.

"It's called pride of ownership. It's the feeling that overcomes you when you've finished a worthwhile project. It's the realization that you've made good art."

"Art?"

"Yes, art. I treat every home like it's my own work of art. Each home has my name on it. So the quality of that home makes my reputation. That's why I'm always yelling at you to do everything right."

"OK, I think I get it," said Chris. He was always looking for a shortcut, and Clint was always finding the resulting bad work, which he made Chris correct.

"But, Chris, look. I've been meaning to say this to you." He turned to face Chris. "I mean, yeah, we're here building a house and that's cool, but don't be like me, man. Get an education. Make art with your mind." He pointed at Chris's forehead. "After all these years of watching you work for me, I know you need to walk away from this crap and do something real. You have a ton of untapped potential. No offense, but you need to throw away all the childish high school garbage and grow up a little. I never did, and I pay for it every day. I'm fifty-one, man. Two failed marriages. A kid who won't have anything to do with me. The army. Two stints in rehab. Jail. It ain't worth it. So take my advice. Please don't be like me. Clean up and go do something real with your life."

Not giving Chris a chance to respond, Clint turned and walked away. Chris knew Clint was late to his AA group at a local church, where he was a group facilitator. Dumbfounded, Chris watched his boss drive away in his old, beat-up GMC truck. The clouds had darkened overhead, and the smell of Oregon rain permeated the evening air. Everything around him—physical, mental, and emotional—felt ominous. He was in a dark place. Deep inside, he knew Clint was right, but he simply could not see the path to the life Clint was talking about. College seemed so daunting he had simply written off the idea. Even if he could do college, he wasn't ready for the challenge. *Will I ever be?* he wondered.

"Well, son, looks like you got it all figured out," said Grandpa Thomas.

Chris had swung by his grandpa's shop on the way home from work to drop off a tool he'd borrowed. Naturally, he got sucked in—Grandpa needed help working on the legs of an antique kitchen table. Chris didn't mind helping. He loved working in Grandpa Thomas's shop when he wasn't framing houses with Clint.

"Well, at least for the next year, I think I do," said Chris.

"Then what?" asked Grandpa without looking up at Chris.

Chris was so focused on his epic year-in-Utah skiing plans he'd never stopped to ask himself if it was a wise plan in the first place. More so, what would he do after that year in Utah? But why would he stop to ask himself such silly questions? Chris was all about living in the moment. Skiing the best snow on earth. The resort paying him to ski. Living free in an unfinished basement. What wasn't to love about the plan?

"Uh, I haven't thought that far ahead," said Chris.

Grandpa Thomas roared with laughter. "Well, sounds about right for eighteen. Look, I've been meaning to talk to you about this, so, kid, I'm going to give it to you straight." Grandpa put down his Craftsman screwdriver and looked Chris dead in the eyes. "Do you want to be fifty looking back at the bad decisions an eighteen-year-old made for you?"

Chris said nothing. He wondered if Clint and Grandpa Thomas had been talking.

"Here's a little advice—you should grow up now and head off a future midlife crisis at the pass. I mean, do you really see yourself as a fifty-year-old ski instructor who frames houses in the summer to get by? Yeah, I'm sure the girls will really go for that one." Grandpa laughed again.

"OK, well, I'm dumb. So what are my options?"

"Don't you ever say that again," said Grandpa Thomas. Chris had never heard his grandfather raise his voice like that before. He stood stiff, not knowing how to react. Then Grandpa moved in closer, an expression of disgust on his face.

"Look at me," he said, pointing at his grandson. Chris looked him in the eyes. "Promise me you will never say that again," Grandpa said tersely.

"OK," said Chris.

"No, say it." Grandpa still had anger in his voice.

"OK, I will never say I'm dumb again," said Chris, bowing his head.

Grandpa said nothing as he slowly turned and moved back to his workbench. A look of disgust still hung over his wrinkled face. Without looking up, he continued. "I'm not going to watch you throw your life away. I already watched your dad do it. Not going to happen again on my watch. No, sir. So as far as I'm concerned, you need to dump this stupid ski-bum plan of yours and start thinking about doing the right thing."

"You're talking about a mission," Chris said, rolling his eyes. He'd feared this conversation was coming.

Grandpa Thomas looked up. "You said you didn't want to be ordinary. Well, there's nothing ordinary about a mission. So yes, I think you should give it a hard look, son."

A mission was a rite of passage in modern Mormonism. At eighteen years old, most worthy men received a mission call, then served for twenty-four months. Many missionaries went to foreign countries and learned a second language. Mainly, these missionaries taught people interested in the LDS Church, but they also spent many hours every week performing community service. Most of the eighteen-year-olds in Chris's church congregation, or ward, were putting in their paperwork to serve, but not Chris. He had other plans, and, honestly, he still wasn't sure about his testimony of the gospel. Further complicating the situation, he was terrified of the possibility of having to learn a foreign language.

"Have a seat." Grandpa motioned for Chris to sit down on a stool he had recently built. "A mission isn't for the people you will teach and serve. A mission is for you. It's a time for you to grow up. To figure out what you want out of life. To find a testimony of God. A mission is hard. A lot of people say it's the best two years of their life. I don't buy that. A mission is the best two years *for* your life. The best years come later, when you get married and have kids. If you go, you won't regret it, and you'll come home a better man, a grown man, ready to take on the challenges of life, like school and a career."

Grandpa paused and put his hand his grandson's shoulder. "Chris, a mission is the only thing between you and a life you will most certainly regret if you stay on your present course."

Eavesdropping from the door, Grandma approached the two men. Tears filled her beautiful, wise eyes as she positioned herself in front of her grandson. "Chris, he's right." She placed her hand on his cheek. "Listen to your grandpa. This is his dying wish."

"His what?" Chris said loudly, standing with a start.

His grandpa also stood and hugged him harder than he'd ever hugged him before. Pulling back, he looked him in the eyes. "It's cancer, son. They say I have a few years to live—if I'm lucky."

Tears filled Chris's eyes, and he shook his head. "No. It can't be real." His grandpa was his support. His mentor. His North Star.

Without a word, the three embraced in the middle of the small, poorly lit shop. For a long time, Chris had put up a front, but in reality, he'd never felt so lost. In the warm embrace of his grandparents and for the first time in his life, he started to feel real purpose deep in his soul.

FIRST INTERLUDE

FINGER LAKES REGION OF NEW YORK STATE
442 AD

The ancient warrior-prophet, the last of his people, had been ruthlessly hunted for years. He was alone and carried no provisions, his only defenses a cracked metal shield, a rusted sword, and a thin helmet, as had been worn by his people's soldiers. His breastplate was scarred and dented from many battles, and he wore a sheepskin around his waist.

The enemy was gaining on him. After running for days, this lone man felt overpowered with exhaustion. His vision was blurry, and his lips were parched. He stealthily made his way down a worn game trail, hoping to find food and a suitable hiding place. His thirst was insatiable. Dehydration clouded his mind. He focused on the simple act of putting one foot forward in front of the other.

Although he had never felt so much pain and darkness, he could still appreciate that the country around him was wild and beautiful. The wind blew gently, and birds sang as light penetrated the trees and dappled the forest floor. The foreign surroundings were unlike the dense jungle thousands of miles south where he'd grown up, been taught, and received his sacred command.

The exhaustion was so extreme he didn't notice the narrow stream until he almost fell into it. He stopped abruptly and looked down at the water, a broad smile crossing his face. Kneeling, he cupped his hands and slowly brought the cool water to his lips. It tasted like heaven. He quickly placed his hands back in the water, then gently ran his fingers through his hair. A tear formed in his eye as he began a prayer of thanksgiving for the stream and the sustenance it provided.

He leaned forward again and put his hands into the shallow stream. In the almost perfectly balanced light and shadow of the trees, he could see his reflection glistening on the surface of the water. The sunken eyes. The long, white hair. The matted beard. Continuous war and age had taken their toll. A strange thought struck the man: as he'd lost track of the years, he'd lost track of his age.

As he sat pondering, he noticed a slight movement to his left, and then he saw them—the bodies and faces of his enemy forming in the stream's reflection.

Adrenaline surged through the warrior-prophet's veins. With the speed of a younger man, he stood and expertly drew his sword, then spun around to face his enemy. His odds weren't good. He was surrounded on all sides and badly outnumbered.

The enemy casually stared at him. Some were emotionless. Others smiled, as they had, having finally found their prey. They carried steel swords and long wooden spears. They had no armor and were clothed only about their loins in sheepskin. Their bodies were dyed red—in animal blood. Their brown faces were covered in war paint.

"What are you waiting for?" yelled the warrior.

One of the men screamed and sprang violently forward with a spear, but the warrior pivoted and swung his sword, knocking the spear from the man's hand. The enemy, still in full charge, tried to dodge the man, but the warrior's sword pierced his chest, killing him almost instantly.

Two more of the enemy screamed and ran forward with swords drawn while the other men in the party cheered and anxiously awaited their turn.

The warrior lifted his rusted sword and swung it down at an angle, slicing through one of the enemy's shoulders. The man's torso was almost cut in two. Pulling his sword from the man's chest, the warrior spun and swung the weapon again, taking off another man's head. Several men broke out in laughter as blood splattered those encircling the conflict. This was just sport. They knew that no matter how hard the warrior fought, the inevitable end was near.

The warrior turned aggressively, waiting for the next man to attack. Without warning, a powerful force penetrated his back, followed by piercing pain in the right side of his chest. He let out a scream and looked down, horrified to see a bloodied spear protruding from his body. The warrior screamed again, fell to his knees, and dropped his sword and shield. The men surrounding him laughed and clapped.

As the warrior-prophet stared at the bloody spear, it began to retract into his body. Someone was pulling the spear from behind him. He continued to look down in shock as blood streamed from the wound. Just then, a dynamic force hit from behind and knocked to the ground face-first.

Gathering all his strength, he rolled over onto his back to see his assailant. When he saw the permanently bloodstained face, he gasped in terror. "Cain? I should have known. I could feel your darkness. Where you are, there is no light."

Standing over Moroni with bloodied spear in his hand, Cain said nothing at first, proudly reveling in the moment. "Ah, finally, the great warrior-prophet Moroni. I'm flattered a man of your stature even knows who I am."

Moroni dropped his head to the ground and looked from side to side. More of the enemy now flooded into the area. Even though he was clearly defeated, and the end was near, he felt a perfect peace.

Cain knelt next to Moroni, then threw the prophet's sword into the stream. Moroni reached for his cimeter, but it was gone. Cain looked over the dying man and laughed.

"Fool. Where is it?" Cain asked forcefully.

"What?"

"Don't play games with me. What have you done with the Book of Baphomet?"

Moroni was breathless for a few moments. With every beat of his heart, the gaping chest wound throbbed. Spirit and body were beginning to separate. "I never had it. I haven't seen it for twenty years." Coughing, he tried to catch his fading breath.

Cain pressed his fingers against the chest wound, and Moroni yelled out in severe pain. Cain's men laughed and watched patiently.

"Had I found it, I would have burned it." Moroni's breathing became more labored. "That book has caused so much suffering."

"A likely story." Cain sighed. Then his voice grew intense. "Where are the gold plates? Where are the sword and the breastplate and the rest of it? I want the sword of Laban."

Moroni's face hardened. Just days earlier on a nearby hill, he had laid the engraved golden plates, his people's sacred record, in a box carefully fashioned out of stone. The top of the box looked like any other rock on the hillside. He had also deposited other important items in a cave. The artifacts would lie protected until God decided they would be found.

"I'll never tell you," Moroni said. "My work is done."

Cain reached behind his back and produced a strange knife. It had three twisted blades protruding from a polished goat-horn handle. Moroni began to tremble. He knew Cain had made the weapon thousands of years before. Cain looked at the implement of death with pride. "Many have died by this knife, but none gave me more pleasure than the first, my brother Abel."

For a few moments, Cain paused, seeming to fall into a trance. In his mind's eye, Moroni saw in vision the first murder. After Cain had killed his brother, Abel's blood formed a permanent crimson stain, splotching like a birthmark wherever it touched Cain's skin, including his face, arms, and chest. Moroni remembered the Lord's words to Cain: "For your sin, you shall not die but shall wander the earth a vagabond and an outcast. You will be hunted and never have peace in this world. Your mark shall be known until the second coming of the Lord. No man will kill you, but all shall look upon you with disgust and pity. This is thy curse."

Snapping out of his trance, Cain looked at Moroni with pure hated. Then, without a word, he straddled the prophet and tore the armor from his chest.

At that moment, Moroni looked past Cain and saw a man walking briskly through the line of soldiers. Something was different about the man. His hair was long, white, and flowing. He was clothed in an all-white robe, like an angelic being. As this being walked toward Moroni, he seemed to move through the men rather than around them. He reached the stream bank opposite where Moroni lay and smiled with joy.

"Father?" gasped Moroni with tears in his eyes.

Cain raised his knife high in the air. The look on his cursed, spotted face was insane and wild.

Moroni's father extended his arms toward Moroni. "Come to me, my son."

Moroni's spirit instantly separated from his mortal body, passed right through Cain, and fell into the arms of his loving father. The wind blew gently as the two men, still in an embrace, crossed into the spirit world.

Cain violently thrust the tri-blade knife into the chest of the innocent man's body lying motionless next to the stream. Uneven splotches and pinpoint dots of blood covered Cain's face. Moroni had long since expired, but drunken with rage, Cain continued to plunge the blade deep into the dead man's torso.

The enemy warriors surrounding the stream watched in horror, even the most battle-hardened struggling with the gruesome murder.

Straddling the mangled body on his knees and breathing erratically, Cain finally halted his work of death and looked around at the men. No words were exchanged. All just stared at each other. Cain, still clenching the knife by its unique goat-horn handle, stood shaking over the dead prophet. Looking down closely at himself, he appeared momentarily startled by the blood covering his body. But then he smiled.

"I am Master Mahan."

CHAPTER 5

MISSIONARY TRAINING CENTER
PROVO, UTAH

Chris stared out the rental-car window as his family drove past the Provo Utah Temple. He stared past the odd-looking building and marveled at the Wasatch Mountains that shot up thousands of feet from their base less than a mile beyond the temple.

"Geez, they're right there," Chris said in amazement, pointing at the mountains. "I have to drive an hour to get to Mount Hood."

"Welcome to Utah, son," said Grandpa Thomas.

Chris's dad turned into the entrance of the Provo Missionary Training Center. Covering eighty acres of Provo's east bench, this was the main missionary-training campus for The Church of Jesus Christ of Latter-day Saints. It was one of eleven similar training centers located across the globe.

As they turned into the intimidating campus and passed the guard booth, Chris's heart sank. This would be his home for the next three weeks before heading to Miami, Florida. He'd been thinking about this moment for months. Sweat formed on his forehead, and his hands started to shake. Even though his grandfather had taught and prepared him over the previous two months for the coming two years, he wasn't sure what to think.

The rental car stopped at the curb, and Chris reluctantly stepped out with his family into a sea of anxious people also dropping off missionaries. Tears and smiles seemed to fill the unloading area in front of the main administration building. Chris was taken aback as missionaries of all races and nationalities said hurried goodbyes to their families.

The Thomases quickly pulled his luggage and other supplies from the rental car. They didn't have a lot of time for goodbyes. Chris hugged his parents, his grandma, and his sister, who had all traveled from Oregon to see him off. His grandpa pulled him aside. Making sure they were out of the family's earshot, he handed Chris a finely carved wooden box.

"Grandpa, you didn't need to," said Chris. He noticed again how Grandpa's cheeks were sunken and his hair was gone.

"Oh yes, I did. Now open it up."

Chris opened the box to find three finely crafted leather belts in different colors: black, tan, and dark brown. The buckles were polished aircraft aluminum. Chris pulled out one of the belts and examined its exceptional workmanship. The leather was beautifully tooled, with small, barely visible inscriptions lining the inside of the belt. They were his grandpa's favorite scriptures. Chris was mesmerized by the incredible attention to detail.

"Look, there's a little surprise in here," said his grandpa, glancing around to make sure no one could see. The rest of the family appeared to wonder what Chris and Grandpa were whispering about.

"See the little button on the bottom of the buckle?"

"Yes."

"Click it."

Chris pushed the concealed button and heard a clicking sound. A small aluminum T-handle gently sprang from inside the buckle. Curious, Chris grasped the handle between his middle and ring fingers and slowly pulled it away from the buckle, revealing a serrated blade in the shape of a heart. When he made a fist, the blade protruded almost unnoticeably between his fingers.

"Grandpa! It's a knife!"

"Shh," said his grandpa, looking around nervously. They both knew the MTC staff would not take kindly to a weapon on the property.

"The blade is only an inch and a half long," Grandpa said, "but it's deadly sharp. In close quarters, like if someone is attacking you, hit the button, pull the blade from the buckle, and use it on your opponent. It's a stabbing weapon." Grandpa made an exaggerated movement with his fist as if using the knife on an invisible opponent.

"The blade isn't long enough to kill most people," he continued, "unless you use it on their jugular. But it will offer you some protection. The other two belts are just like it. Wear them every day. It's protection. Where you're going, you're going to need it."

His grandpa's eyes were wide, his gaze intense. Chris wondered if the chemo was starting to take a toll on his mind. He watched as Grandpa Thomas walked slowly back to the family. He wondered if this was the last time he'd ever see his grandfather alive.

CHAPTER 6

LIBERTY CITY
MIAMI-DADE COUNTY, FLORIDA

From the moment Chris stepped off the plane, it was clear: Miami, Florida, was not Portland, Oregon.

Sun-drenched beaches, models from across the globe, and palm-tree-lined boulevards made the Magic City postcard-famous, or at least that was the image Miami hoped outsiders—especially tourists—would buy.

However, sitting directly in the center of the South Florida megalopolis between I-95 and the sprawling Miami International Airport was Liberty City, one of the most dangerous urban areas in the United States, comparable only to South Central LA, Baltimore, or the South Side of Chicago.

Driving through Liberty City one afternoon, Chris tried hard to remember a place in Portland that even compared. But nothing he could recall about the Rose City or the broader state of Oregon even came close to the poverty, violence, and hopelessness he'd witnessed in Liberty City.

As Chris drove through a neighborhood, his already-heightened state of situational awareness went into overdrive. Gangs ruled these streets and could appear at any moment. And along with the gangs came the guns. Fired from cheap, Chinese-made AK-47s—the preferred gun among local gangs—the 7.62 x 39mm rounds could easily cut through the city's older houses. Short chain-link fences separated dead front lawns from cracked sidewalks as if to say "not welcome." Vicious Rottweilers and the rusty steel bars over windows and doors offered a weak defense from the evil outside.

As a missionary, Chris didn't follow the news. He didn't need to. Walking the streets daily, he knew firsthand that Liberty City had recently erupted in a wave of gang violence.

It had started when four-year-old Letisha Jones was gunned down playing in the front yard of a house located on NW 61st Street. The indiscriminate bullet was meant for her uncle. Only four days later, two teens— Martin Williamson, nineteen, and Kim Dixon, eighteen—were killed in front of a Circle K convenience store by a drive-by shooter. It was a case of mistaken identity. Dixon, a National Honor Society member, had just been accepted to Princeton University.

Several other murders followed. The residents of the besieged city and the exacerbated members of local law enforcement had finally had enough. With the help of state and federal agencies, Miami-Dade County had dramatically increased its police presence in Liberty City in an attempt to crack down on the violence. But the crackdown had only ratcheted up the violence. Automatic gunfire could be heard day and night, along with screams and sirens. The state of the city within Miami could only be described in one word: war.

Yet, in the middle of all this violence and danger, Chris and his new companion, Jeremy Hanks, parked their base-model Ford Focus and started off into the streets of Liberty City, looking for anyone who would listen their message about the restored gospel of Jesus Christ.

The two young men wore identical clothing, the standard LDS missionary uniform. Distinctive white, short-sleeve dress shirts with stained armpits. Red and yellow striped ties. Dark dress slacks. Worn-out, black Doc Martin Commander dress shoes. Each had a black name tag attached to his left breast pocket with his name above the official name of the LDS Church. They carried heavy, sweat-stained backpacks filled with scriptures and other teaching aids. Of course, Chris had one article Elder Hanks didn't: the knife concealed inside the belt buckle his grandpa had made for him.

After three hours of walking door-to-door, the missionaries bordered on heat exhaustion. The famous South Florida heat and humidity were taking their toll.

"How about one more street, then we'll hit Checkers for a shake?" said Elder Hanks, pointing down a particular street.

"Dude, yes. Love that idea. We've hit our weekly tracting quota anyway, so, yeah, let's finish out this street and get something to eat."

As the two elders began walking down the street, a Miami-Dade County sheriff's cruiser pulled up. Through his window, the African-American sheriff gave them a look of disbelief and confusion as he flipped on his light bar.

"Are you with the Red Cross?" asked the sheriff from his slowly rolling cruiser.

The two young men walked over to the officer's car. The nameplate on his chest read Eves. Chris respectfully responded, "No, sir, we're missionaries from The Church of—"

"You best leave the neighborhood now. We just had another shooting two blocks over, and we're looking for the gunman. Leave the vicinity now." The sheriff drove off quickly, giving the missionaries no time to respond.

"What should we do?" asked Elder Hanks, a farm boy from Burley, Idaho. He had only been on his mission for three months. The decision rested mainly with Chris, who had only left Oregon for Florida six months prior.

"We have one street left," Chris said. "Should we just knock it out? I feel like we should."

Elder Hanks was clearly concerned. "I don't know. The cop told us to leave."

Chris stood in front of his greenie companion. "Come on, it'll be fine. We're missionaries. Besides, name any other nineteen-year-old white guys who get to freely walk around a place like Liberty City. Isn't this one reason we give up two years of our lives? So we can see a side of the world we'll probably never see again?"

"Yeah, true," said Elder Hanks. "I guess it's just one more street. Let's hurry. I can't stop thinking about that shake."

～

Fifteen minutes later, they'd reached the end of the street. The last house was a badly neglected 1950s bungalow with three intoxicated men on the front porch and one standing on the brown lawn. The missionaries opened the chain-link gate and confidently strode up the broken concrete path toward the group. The men said nothing, just stared in disbelief at the two well-dressed young white men heading right for them.

"Hey, fellas," Elder Hanks said in his distinct southern-Idaho accent. The men stared blankly, obviously still not believing their eyes.

"Y'all from the DEA?" said one of the men on the porch, his look switching from disbelief to concern.

"Nah, they look like FBI," said the intimidatingly tall, muscular man standing on the dead grass, nearest the elders.

Chris had heard this before. The missionaries were commonly mistaken for DEA agents, doctors, and everything in between.

"No, we're missionaries from The Church of Jesus Christ of Latter-day Saints," said Elder Hanks. "We'd like to share a message with you about the restored gospel of Jesus Christ."

The three men on the porch burst out laughing. The man nearest the elders folded his arms and said nothing. His gaze seemed to intensify.

The elders stood their ground, smiling.

"Now, wait a minute," said one of the men after sipping from a beverage concealed in a brown paper bag. "Y'all pastors or something? What you crackers doin' here anyway? Don't you know this place is a war zone?"

"We ain't got no money, preacher boys, but you can smoke with us," said another man, extending a lit marijuana blunt. The others burst into laughter again.

"No, we don't smoke. Sorry," said Chris. "But we'd really like to talk to you about Jesus Christ and the plan of salvation."

The man on the lawn moved closer. "The plan of what? Y'all are smokin' something nasty!"

The laughter from the front porch continued.

"Y'all need to get your rich white-boy stank off my lawn," said the man, his face growing tenser. He pulled up his shirt, revealing a handgun tucked in his pants.

The men on the porch stopped laughing. One stood and looked at the missionaries with concern.

"Tyrone, they be pastors," said the oldest of the three, his voice calming. "Let them go."

"Sit down," demanded Tyrone. "I didn't ask you." The man sat, and the others looked away. Tyrone turned his attention back to the missionaries.

The elders looked at each other. The situation was escalating quickly. Chris instinctively reached down and touched his belt buckle. "Now, look, we don't want any trouble," he said, holding up his hand.

Tyrone approached, and Chris turned to position himself between the man and Elder Hanks. Without any warning, Tyrone cocked back his arm and slammed his balled fist into Chris's head.

Everything went dark.

CHAPTER 7

Chris lay on his back in a wheat field. In the twilight above him, several large planets appeared much closer in the sky than the moon ever did. He stretched his arm to touch the orbiting bodies, but, of course, they were much farther away than they appeared. One of the planets looked like Saturn but slightly different—a brilliant blue with solid silver rings. Another was deep red, or at least he thought it was red. He couldn't recall ever having seen that exact color. Numerous dark moons of various sizes orbited the red body, making it appear as though large holes dotted the planet's surface.

Why am I lying in a wheat field, and why can't I move my legs?

Chris lifted his head and looked down the length of his body. Everything appeared normal. Shirt and tie. Doc Martens. He could even see his black missionary name tag hanging a little crooked on his shirt pocket. Things didn't feel quite right, but, at the same time, his being was filled with a strange happiness and joy. Laying his head back down, he looked at the surrounding wheat and admired its brilliant gold color. It was unlike any shade of gold he had ever seen.

Look at all the stars.

As Chris lay in the field admiring the brightness and indescribable beauty of the planets and stars above, he recalled a night many years ago at Crater Lake National Park in southern Oregon. That night, with the nearest large city hundreds of miles away and light pollution nonexistent, the Milky Way had revealed its glorious self. Billions and billions of stars had unfolded over the ancient lake. It was the first time in his life he'd felt, well, small. That same feeling of smallness engulfed him now.

Chris involuntarily began to rise headfirst out his bed in the wheat field, but his body was stiff as a board.

"Who's there? What's happening?"

He still could not move his legs, but now, floating upright in the midst of the closely orbiting planets, trillions of brilliant stars, and an unusually golden wheat field that seemed to stretch for miles, Chris felt a perfect stillness. No noise. No wind. No smell. Nothing. It was as bright as noonday, but there was no sun and it felt like dusk. Anxiety started to enter his mind, but the negative emotion was quickly replaced by a feeling of calm and peace.

"Chris."

It was a still voice of perfect mildness, like a whisper but powerful and authoritative. The male voice pierced him to the very center of his delicate soul.

"What?" said Chris. "Who's there?"

"Come. I am going to show you something marvelous."

Chris turned in the air, and there it was. In the form of a human body, a stunning entity glowing brighter than the sun stood before him. He could not comprehend the extraordinary brightness of the being, and he could not see the being's face, but somehow he was able to look upon the being. Oddly, he did not fear. In fact, he had never felt such love, charity, and peace in his entire life. He was enveloped by extreme emotions, and in that moment, it didn't matter to him whether he was alive or dead. Chris never wanted to leave the presence of this being.

The being moved weightlessly and effortlessly to stand directly in front of Chris, then gently placed his hand on his shoulder.

"I want to show you something wonderful," said the being. He then positioned himself next to Chris and pointed at the horizon above the golden field.

Chris saw various images and objects floating above the field. He didn't recognize most, but occasionally he would see objects shaped like letters and numbers that appeared quickly, came together in what looked like mathematical equations, and then disappeared. Chris was confused and started to speak, but the being again stood directly in front of him, his face still unseeable. Chris was frozen in place but still felt no fear. The being reached out his finger and touched Chris on the center of his forehead.

"Remember, remember," said the being. Then he vanished.

As Chris looked around for the being, he noticed the symbols, letters, and equations again forming in front of him. This time, as the symbols, letters, and numbers cycled through his vision, he discovered he could understand them. And as the vision cycled faster and faster through his view, Chris began to comprehend the obscure math at an exponential rate.

"I've seen this somewhere before," Chris said aloud. "More. I want more. I need to see all of it."

"I'm only allowed to give you this for now," the being said. "More will come later. Never forget. I will always be here. Always."

As the mathematical vision dissipated, in the distance, Chris could see an otherworldly circle of light forming over the field. As the circle grew, it started to slowly rotate. Chris felt the sensation of flying through the air. He was unwillingly being propelled by an unknown force toward the light.

"No, no," begged Chris. "Please, I want to stay."

The circle grew in luminance as he flew faster and faster toward it. He tried to resist, but it was futile.

"Never forget. I will always be here. Always," repeated the voice.

On a direct collision course, Chris flew toward the circle at an impossible speed. Instinctively, he threw his arms in front of his face as he was enveloped by the blinding light. Suddenly, everything went dark.

CHAPTER 8

The three-pound human brain is the most complex, mysterious, and least-understood organ in the known universe. We know more about outer space than we know about the world's oceans, and we know more about the world's oceans than we know about the human brain.

Traumatic brain injuries, or TBIs, are usually caused by a sudden blow or jolt to the head. The most common TBIs are caused by car accidents, contact sports, and everyday falls. Scientists have only recently learned that each traumatic brain injury is as different as the structure of an individual snowflake.

Chris Thomas's TBI was caused by a single, violent punch to the head. He was approaching day 180—six full months—in a coma, and doctors at the Kendall Regional Medical Center in Miami were beginning to wonder if he would ever wake up.

His parents had made the long trip from Portland, Oregon, numerous times over the last half a year. It had taken a serious toll on the family, especially Chris's grandparents, who needed help in their elderly and sick state. Chris's father would often hold down the fort in Oregon while his mother stayed behind in Miami. She would only leave the room to sleep, eat, and visit the modest, nondenominational chapel on the medical center's eleventh floor. There, she would pour out her heart to God, begging for her only son to wake up.

On day 181, his mother's prayers were answered.

~

Over and over again, the images cycled through Chris Thomas's mind like a hellish movie.

An airplane exploding midair. An ancient codex. Hundreds of small quadcopter drones exploding all around him. Assassins in advanced body armor. A faceless woman in a white lab coat. A riot in Paris. A grotesque satanic statue. A strange glass skyscraper in a mountainous European city. And billions and billions of innocent people, dead.

"Awake and arise," said a voice.

Intense pain coursed through Chris's body as he blinked, then brought his arm up to shield his eyes from the intense Florida sunlight flooding through the dirty window. The arm felt heavier than a log. His eyes burned like wildfire, and tears of pain coursed down his pale cheeks.

Repeatedly closing his eyes and reopening them, Chris silently prayed for relief. After a few minutes, he finally started to adjust. Reaching up to his face, he wiped his tear-stained cheeks. Then confusion struck as he moved his head around, surveying his surroundings.

Chris was lying in a bed, his upper body elevated at a forty-five-degree angle. The room was a stark, sterile white and smelled faintly of bleach. Humming quietly next to his bed, a GE Dash 4000 monitored his heart rate, oxygen level, blood pressure, and other critical life indicators. The white sheets covering his body were clean and pressed.

Why am I in a hospital?

As he marveled at the brightness engulfing the room, an indescribable sense of peace overcame him. Calling out to the being for help, he believed he was still in his presence. He must be, considering all this light. But no words left Chris's mouth. His bone-dry throat and tongue felt like sandpaper. Tubes jutted from his nose and arms. His head was bald. Under the hospital gown, he was naked.

Attempting to speak again, he suddenly realized he could not move his legs. Confusion turned to panic. He felt exhausted just trying to sit straight up. As he attempted to catch his breath, he noticed something odd with his eyesight. Strange shapes, symbols, and mathematical equations obscured part of his vision. Rectangles were reproduced from ceiling tiles. Circles floated slowly out from the knobs on the machine next to his bed. The window frame where the intense sun beamed into his small room started rotating in midair. Most stunning was the geometry in the individual rays of sunlight as they radiated through the fine dust dancing effortlessly in the humid air. Time seemed to slow down. A low hum in his ears grew until he could no longer hear the snarled Miami traffic outside his window. And there, in front of him, every object in the room gracefully and intelligently presented its mathematical properties. He had never seen anything so beautiful in his entire life.

This must still be a dream. I can't be awake.

Bringing himself out of the trance, Chris tried to orient his body as best he could under the circumstances. Pressing his torso against the safety rail, he looked out the window to see what was in the sky, but he saw no odd planets or star clusters, only buildings and clouds.

He collapsed back onto the bed.

"Help." It came out as a weak whisper.

No one came. Chris continued to stare at the mathematical vision.

He'd noticed a paper cup on the table next to the bed. He reached for it with his weak hand, but the cup was empty. He grabbed a book lying on the table next to the cup and examined it closely. *Twilight* by Stephenie Meyer. He opened the book to a random page and immediately comprehended every word.

Closing the book, he looked at the cover again. Then he opened it at the beginning and flipped through the pages, faster and faster. The words came off the pages and into his mind at lightning speed. In about five minutes, he'd finished the book having perfectly comprehended its contents. He'd even noted numerous grammatical errors an editor must have missed.

When he placed the book back on the table, his hand accidentally knocked the call button on the bed's safety rail, causing an alarm to sound at the nurses' station down the hall.

Ten seconds later, a tall, skinny nurse burst into the room. Her mouth went slack, and her face lit up with shock. "You're awake," she said, then turned and ran out the door, yelling for a doctor.

~

"Honey, do you know who I am?" asked Chris's mother anxiously. She sat uncomfortably close to him as he lay in the hospital bed.

"Yes, of course, Mom. But what am I doing here? I can't move my legs, and something is wrong with my eyes. What happened?" Chris was scared, frustrated, and wanted answers.

"What's the last thing you remember?" his mother asked impatiently. Chris focused for a second. The math thing with his eyes was really starting to bother him.

Several doctors and a police officer dressed in a suit and tie entered the room.

"I remember high school graduation. What about my legs? Am I paralyzed? Something is wrong with my eyes."

Everyone in the room looked at each other, puzzled, concerned, and unsure of how to respond. One of the doctors stepped forward and said, "You're not paralyzed, Chris. But for six months, you've been in a coma caused by blunt force trauma. You can walk, but you're going to need physical therapy to regain use of your legs."

"Chris, do you know where you are?" asked another doctor.

"Well, by the looks of you, I'd guess a hospital," said Chris, annoyed.

"Do you know what city you are in?"

"Portland?" he guessed.

"Honey, do you remember being in Miami?" asked his mom. "Do you remember being a missionary? How about Elder Hanks? Do you remember Elder Hanks?"

Chris sighed and focused hard. Now that his mother had mentioned Miami, some of it was vaguely starting to come back. Yes, Miami. He could see places. Streets and houses. Some people, but he couldn't remember names. He felt a strong recollection of the humidity. After a minute, he started to see an image—a short, redheaded young man.

His mother rifled through her purse and produced a newspaper, folded in half. "Do you remember this person, Christopher?" She pointed nervously at a picture on the front page. Chris reluctantly took the paper and examined the image.

"Yeah, I was just seeing an image of this guy in my mind. Is that Elder Hanks? Now some of it is coming back. I remember we were together, but I don't know anything else." Chris unfolded the newspaper and the headline revealed itself: "Mormon Missionary Murdered in Liberty City."

"He's dead?"

Another man stepped forward.

"Chris, I'm Detective Davis with the Miami-Dade Sheriff's Department. Six months ago, you and Jeremy Hanks were assaulted by a group of men in Liberty City. A man named Tyrone Jenkins punched you in the head, putting you in a coma. He then shot Mr. Hanks point-blank. Hanks was pronounced dead at the scene. Fortunately for you, one of our deputies—Sheriff Eves—pulled up right as the incident occurred. He was a witness to Hanks's murder. Sheriff Eves shot Tyrone Jenkins, but Jenkins lived. Son, we need you to testify against Jenkins. We need to know what happened leading up to the assault and shooting. Do you remember anything else that can help us here?"

Stunned by the officer's story, Chris stared at the picture of the kid from Burley, Idaho. No one in the room spoke. Although he had no recollection of the incident and little of Elder Hanks, an extreme sadness overcame him.

"Why do you need me to testify when you have a sheriff as an eyewitness?" asked Chris.

"OK, I think that's enough for now," said one of the doctors, ending the conversation.

The detective gave the doctor a gruff look, then turned to Chris's mom. "Here's my card. Please call me if he remembers anything else." He abruptly left the room.

SECOND INTERLUDE

As the saboteur quietly turned a dark street corner, he saw the target: the main electrical power station for Brooklyn and Manhattan. Sweat poured down his forehead, armpits, and back. Pulling a handkerchief from his pocket, he nervously wiped the moisture away from his brow before it could sting his eyes. This June had been uncharacteristically hot.

He wore all-black clothing and carried a dark-brown leather satchel over his shoulder. It contained a knife, flashlight, dynamite, and a German Luger handgun. He was the mission's last hope. His fellow saboteurs were all dead or captured, and the entire law-enforcement apparatus of the United States government was ruthlessly hunting him.

Trying to be extremely careful, the young novice occasionally stopped and concealed himself, surveying his surroundings for police or citizens breaking curfew.

"Hey, you over there, freeze," yelled a police officer, throwing his light on the man.

The saboteur hadn't spotted the two police officers hiding near the darkened back gate of the power station. Swearing in German, he ran at a dead sprint down a dark alley as the police gave chase.

Two weeks earlier, one of the man's fellow saboteurs—a German-American named George John Dasch from New York—had walked into FBI headquarters and turned himself in. There, standing before Director Hoover, he'd revealed the entire mission of Operation Pastorius.

Conceived by Adolf Hitler himself, Operation Pastorius was the Nazi's grand scheme to sabotage the economic infrastructure of the United States in hopes of crippling America's wartime efforts against the Third Reich. A week before Dasch betrayed the mission, nine men had been dropped by U-boat at various points along the East Coast. Each man, having been trained in Germany for the critical mission, had been assigned primary and secondary targets, including manufacturing plants, rail lines, bridges, and power stations. After Dasch's betrayal, the FBI had quickly apprehended the other saboteurs.

It was now two weeks since Dasch had squealed, and all the other saboteurs had been captured or killed by the Americans. Shooting a look behind him, the lone saboteur, the youngest and most inexperienced of the team, sprinted for his life. He was the Führer's last hope.

As he exited the alley, bullets from the police officers' .38-caliber Smith and Wesson revolvers exploded against the brick walls. The police were overweight and bad shots, but still they gained on him. The man took a sharp turn and, looking for an escape, noticed a sewer cover twenty yards down the street. With no other place to hide, he ran to the manhole and wrenched aside the heavy cast-iron cover, exposing the dark opening below. The stench was overwhelming, but he had no choice. He crawled into the hole and pulled the cover back over the opening, hoping he'd been fast enough to foil his pursuers. Perched on a ladder in the terrifying darkness, he tried to compose himself.

"We just had him," he heard a cop yell above his head. "He's got to be in the vicinity. Call in more backup. Call the army. We could use their help searching these buildings." Over the next several minutes, the saboteur heard police yelling and frantically scrambling on the street above him. Soon, more police arrived.

Leaving the commotion above, he quietly lowered himself into the dark abyss. At the bottom, he reluctantly stepped into the contaminated, ankle-high water, grateful for his calf-high, waterproof leather boots. With all his strength, he tried not to vomit from the putrid smell. He reached blindly into his bag, found his flashlight, and tucked it under his arm. Then he removed his Luger and racked the slide, chambering a 9mm round. Turning on the flashlight, he surveyed the large cement pipe. With only two ways to go, he simply started walking in the direction he already faced.

After he'd slogged through the muck for several hundred yards, the sewage smell, scurrying cockroaches, and hordes of flies became unbearable. Making matters worse, he was terrified of rats and had come across several that seemed as large as dogs.

Finally, hitting a four-way intersection, he was desperate to escape the rat- and insect-infused filth. Above him, he spotted a ladder. Reaching the top, the saboteur gently pushed a manhole cover up just enough to see into the street. The area was filled with police and soldiers. The entire borough of Brooklyn must be sealed off. The police and army appeared to be conducting a building-by-building search. Sighing, he lowered the cover and climbed back down into the filth. When he reached the bottom, out of the corner of his eye, he caught movement in one of the adjoining tunnels.

Ignoring his fear of the rats, he splashed through the rotten sewage with his flashlight focused ahead. He scaled another small ladder and jumped into the tunnel with his weapon raised. "Freeze!" he yelled, slowly panning the tunnel with his flashlight.

The only noise was the scurrying of rats and the sloshing of the disgusting fluid flowing around his boots. Squinting, he waited for a moment, trying to see farther into the pipe, but his flashlight gave him only about fifteen feet of visibility into the void. He remained still, debating if he should fire a shot. Surely the authorities above would not hear gunfire deep in the sewer over the noise of the street above. Although he could feel a presence just out of reach of the light, he concluded that if it was a real threat, he would know by now. He lowered his Luger and began moving slowly backward toward the four-way intersection.

When he reached the intersection, which dropped into a collection pool below, he carefully positioned himself to descend the ladder. Suddenly, he was struck from behind by a hard object. Pain flashed through his skull, and he fell limply into the sewage-filled pool.

CHAPTER 9

Hi, I'm Michael, your PT," said the large, bald black man strutting through the door of Chris's hospital room behind a wheelchair. "When did you arrive?"

Chris sat up, rubbed his eyes, and cleared his throat. "Sorry—you caught me a little off guard. I flew in from Miami last night with my parents. I'm still adjusting to the time change. I know I'm in Portland, but I'm not sure where, exactly."

Michael bellowed a laugh. A massive six five and three hundred pounds of pure African-American muscle, he barely fit into his scrubs. "Are you for real, man? You're at Oregon Health Sciences University. You know, the big building up on the hill above the Rose City? Yeah, man. This ain't Miami, baby. It's time for your first PT session. Ready to start walking again?"

Chris stared at Michael. He felt reluctant to leave the room. In Miami, he had gotten his mind somewhat under control, better managing the wild geometric images, strange symbols, and mathematical equations that randomly clouded his vision. But the flight to Portland had sent his vision into a tailspin. Things seemed calm at the moment, but he feared that if he left the room, more strange geometric forms would create another uncontrolled spiral.

"PT?" asked Chris.

"Yeah, physical therapy, friend."

"Uh, can we do this tomorrow?"

"Yes, we can do this tomorrow," Michael said in a sweet tone. Then his demeanor changed. "But we're going to start today." Chris had a feeling he shouldn't disagree with the man.

"Put your arm around my neck. I'm going to pick you up and set you in the chair. Then we'll head to the gym, OK?" Chris looked at him uncertainly but did as instructed. Michael lifted Chris like he was a rag doll and put him in the chair. He'd weighed 160 at the beginning of his mission and, since the accident, had lost thirty pounds, mainly in muscle weight.

As they headed down the hall toward the PT gym, the shapes and strange equations around Chris intensified, so he closed his eyes, attempting to regain some control over his mind. Michael talked nonstop about the regimen he was about to put Chris through to get him walking again. Entering the gym, they passed Michael's assistant and rolled up to the parallel bars.

"What's this?" Chris asked.

"We're starting on the bars. You have a brain injury. Nothin's wrong with your legs. We just need to get them moving again. So we're going to do this right, but we're going to be aggressive too. Word?"

"Uh, yeah, word," said Chris, unsure of himself.

"Good. I'm glad we're on the same page, 'cuz I ain't going to take whining when it hurts. Cool?"

"Yeah, cool . . . I guess," answered Chris. Michael was clearly not messing around.

"OK then, here we go." Michael motioned to his assistant, who came up behind Chris and positioned the wheelchair between the two parallel bars. Michael stood directly in front of Chris. "I want you to hold on to the bars. I am going to lift you up. She'll follow behind with the wheelchair in case we need to set you back down. Now, here we go." Michael motioned to his assistant.

Chris gave it his all, but Michael lifted most of the weight. He was surprised when he found himself standing and holding the bars on his own. His legs and arms shook. Using all his might, he shuffled his right foot forward while sliding his right hand down the bar. Then his left side slowly followed. Repeating the move several more times, Chris made his way down the eight-foot length of bars. At the end, Michael set him back down in the wheelchair and then knelt and looked Chris over. He was breathing hard and sweating, but he managed to muster a small, victorious smile.

"OK. How'd dat feel?" asked Michael. Chris said nothing, just gave a weak thumbs-up. "OK, good. Rest three minutes. Then we goin' again."

THIRD INTERLUDE

The saboteur coughed and slowly opened his eyes. His head ached, his eyesight was blurry, and his clothes were wet. He was lying on a metal grate in a dank, smelly concrete room about ten by fifteen feet. Sewer water flowed under the grated floor. A dim light shone directly over his head, and across the room was a corroded-looking steel door, which he hoped was unlocked.

"What is your name?" asked an imposing voice from a corner. Several moments of silence passed. "I won't ask you again. You are lucky I didn't kill you in the sewer, boy. I say again, what is your name?"

"Benson Hancock," answered the Nazi in a practiced American accent. As he pulled himself up to sit against the nearest wall, the stink of his wet clothes filled his nose. Touching the back of his skull, he felt sticky blood. His head was throbbing from the assault.

"Well, Benson Hancock, you are in serious trouble," said his assailant.

"May I ask your name, sir?" Benson rubbed his aching head.

"You may not."

As the strange man stepped forward, Benson tried to focus on him. He was slender and at least seven feet tall. His hair was long and greasy, his beard matted, his clothing filthy and old. The man's scarred hands were the size of baseball mitts. Strangest of all, like some kind of outrageous birthmark, red blotches covered his face, neck, and arms.

The beastly man took another step forward, and Benson pushed himself away, along the concrete wall. Under the man's protruding brow, his eyes appeared completely void of light. His teeth had a greenish tint, and his nose was crooked. A terrible foreboding overcame Benson. He knew he was not in safe company.

"You must be the spy they're looking for," said the man, pointing up at the ceiling. "Well, if you want to make it out of here alive, you're going to stay with me for a few days. Don't worry, the sewage system is so intricate they will never find you here. You're safe for now."

"OK," Benson answered, thoroughly unconvinced.

The man sat down across from Benson and examined him. "You are definitely not from around here. German, maybe? Tell me, why do you work for a fool?"

Benson's fear turned to anger. He looked left and right for his shoulder bag.

"Looking for this, idiot?" asked the man, bringing Benson's leather satchel around from behind. Benson stared at the bag, wondering if he should attempt to wrestle it from the man. "Dynamite, knives, and guns are no good against me," the man said. He lifted the strap over his head and tossed the bag at Benson.

"I have been through more than you can ever imagine, *Junge*. I have seen real tyranny. Genghis Khan killed forty million, a staggering 10 percent of the world's population at the time. Attila the Hun, Lenin, and, of course, Vlad the Third. Vlad was fully possessed by Satan himself."

Pausing, the man stared off as if trying to remember another place and time. "Then there are the ones history forgot, like Amalickiah. He was the best of the worst, the definition of tyranny. Millions died in his quest for power. He was brilliant and cunning. I was pleased to have been his most trusted political adviser."

The man smiled and slowly shook his head. "Hitler is a fool. He is playing right into the grand design. He will murder millions, mostly Jews, opening the door to the creation of the state of Israel. In the end, Hitler will die, the Nazi Party will be a joke on the ash heap of history, and the Jews will finally get their nation."

Benson seethed with anger, but the man just laughed.

"Do you want to know more?"

CHAPTER 10

Several months after Chris awoke from his coma, he and his parents sat across from the neurologist and the university's chief psychiatrist. The shrink pulled up Chris's latest brain scan on a twenty-seven-inch Apple Thunderbolt Display. After the two doctors had pointed at the scan and whispered to each other for five long minutes, the neurologist spoke.

"How does it feel to be walking again?" she asked, continuing to stare at the monitor.

"Oh, fine. Thank you for asking."

"It's truly incredible you even lived," she said. "The activity in normally dormant regions of the brain is extraordinary. Your front left temporal lobe—well, we've never seen anything like this."

The psychiatrist looked over his glasses and down his nose at Chris's parents. "*Neuroplasticity* is a term we use to explain how the brain adapts in response to a traumatic brain injury. Your son's neuroplasticity is, well, unique. There's been extensive recruitment of undamaged cortex from elsewhere in the brain. A rewiring, if you will, has occurred in damaged and undamaged areas alike. After a TBI, most people just return to normal brain function or sustain permanent, untreatable brain damage. But the result in rare cases is a release of dormant intellectual or artistic power. We're working with two cases right now. One is a doctor who started playing the piano like Mozart after being struck by lightning three years ago. Before the accident, he never had a lesson in his life. The other case is a stroke victim in Arizona who had no artistic capability before her accident. Now she writes poetry and sells her paintings through Christie's auction house. It's quite fascinating. But again, it is extremely rare. We have only about a hundred documented cases in recorded medical history. Even among those, your son's case is truly unique."

Turning his attention to Chris, the psychiatrist asked, "Tell me more about the math you're seeing in your field of vision."

"I don't know how to explain it. Sometimes it floats in front of me. Other times it lines up with the shapes of the physical objects in my view. The equations just seem to float in the air. There are symbols I can't identify in the math. It changes constantly. It seemed like gibberish at first, but I've been writing it down and studying it. I think it's some kind of algorithm. I've been studying math of all disciplines to try and understand what my mind is showing me. I want to control it, but at the same time, I kind of don't want to. I think it may mean something. I don't want to sound crazy, but I think I'm seeing the math of the universe. It's quite beautiful."

Ignoring Chris's conclusion, the doctors continued their questioning. "Before the accident, you said you didn't have any real interest in math?" asked the neurologist as she thumbed through the thick medical file on her desk.

"No interest is probably an understatement, Doctor." Chris looked at his parents, but they looked away. "I barely passed the minimum math requirement to graduate from high school."

"We've treated a lot of traumatic brain injury, but this is incredible," the neurologist continued. "Like, one-in-several-billion rare. The sleep-onset insomnia you're experiencing is normal for this type of injury. But your book reading is odd. Three to five books a day, you say?" She looked at the documents on her desk. "What's your retention rate? What topics are you studying?"

"Well, I don't read every day. It gives me a headache, and the library will only let me check out so many books at once. But I read most everything I can get my hands on. Medicine. Physics. Math, of course. Computer programming. All the physical sciences. I retain all of it, I think, but I can't read fiction. Well, except Orson Scott Card—his books are brilliant. I like Dan Brown, too, but fiction in general just gives me a headache. I find myself rewriting novels in my mind to make them better, which is a waste of time. So I just avoid them altogether. Have you heard of *Twilight*? You know, the teenage vampire book? Wow. It's terrible. Just awful."

His mother looked away, embarrassed. Chris realized the *Twilight* book he'd discovered in his hospital room had belonged to her.

The doctor gave him a funny look. "You're not using your full range of vocabulary, are you?"

He gave the doctors a perfunctory shake of his head. "No, and that's on purpose. Mostly I just try to be what I think is my old self. It helps me fit in. But honestly, I have no idea what my departure point is for normal."

"Chris, we believe you have an extreme case of acquired savant syndrome—"

Chris raised his hand, stopping the psychiatrist midsentence. "That's a condition in which a TBI unlocks prodigious mental capability. Studies of brain scans show that most people with acquired savant syndrome have sustained damage toward the front of the left temporal lobe. You indicted I suffered damage to this region of the brain. I've studied the phenomenon and concluded that this is the correct diagnosis for my condition. However, I am exhibiting more intellectual ability than artistic ability, which isn't the common result of the syndrome."

The doctors looked at him, amazed. His parents continued to say nothing. What could they say?

"Yes," the neurologist said. "You're also exhibiting no signs of autism, which is uncommon."

"That's correct," said the psychiatrist, butting in. "We've done a full personality-disorder assessment. His Myers-Briggs results show a strong

ENTJ personality, which aligns with his A-type personality, similar to what he had before the accident. Personality-wise, he's pretty normal, with the exception of some anger issues, impatience, et cetera. But that's fairly common with TBI and will require some ongoing treatment. We should look at magnetic options."

Chris didn't like the sound of that.

"Your IQ is off the charts," said the neurologist. "According to this test, they can't even classify your intelligence range. The test tops out at a score of 160, and you're well above that. The average person scores around 100. A 140 is considered genius. Einstein was a 160. How does this make you feel?"

"Everything is different, of course, but it's actually hard to explain," Chris said. "I can't remember much from before the attack. Everyone I knew before looks at me strangely when I talk. My friends from high school won't even talk to me anymore—well, except for my best friend, Scott, but I—"

His mother butted in. "He is completely different." She looked at her son. "I don't mean that in a bad way, honey."

Chris was embarrassed by his mother's outburst. Although he was continually surrounded by people he thought loved him, he often felt alone inside his mind.

The doctors stared at the trio in silence for a minute.

"OK, Chris. It looks like the walking is going great," said the neurologist, breaking the awkward silence. "That's a big step. I want to see you weekly for ongoing evaluation and treatment for some TBI-related personality-disorder issues. I'm going to greenlight you for driving—I don't think we have a seizure risk here. I want you to have very minimal screen time and avoid flashing lights. I'm not yet sure what light is going to do to you. Let's be careful on that front, OK?"

Chris said nothing. He just gave the doctors the thumbs-up.

FOURTH INTERLUDE

Eventually the police entered the sewer as part of their search for Benson Hancock. However, the two fugitives stayed safely hidden in the dark utility room that even the city's work crews seemed to have forgotten.

For the previous two days, they'd had nothing to do but talk to each other, though that didn't happen often. When the man spoke, he told fantastic stories Benson surmised must be pure fantasy. If the man was telling the truth, he was thousands of years old—which, of course, was impossible—and had witnessed some of the world's greatest historical events. The burning of the Roman library at Alexandria. The Crusades. The American Civil War. And on and on.

Yet, the sewer dweller's knowledge of these events was convincing. Benson theorized the man was a savant or historian. Perhaps he was an insane professor. Maybe in his derangement he believed he was actually a part of many historical events.

The man was growing bored with Benson and started considering him a liability. He plotted to finish the job with the steel pipe once the Nazi idiot finally slept.

"*Hear the boy out,*" said a familiar voice in his head. This caused the man to pause. He maneuvered closer to Benson.

"What about you, young Benson?" asked the man, pretending to be interested in the Nazi.

Benson appeared to consider his question for a moment, then started to talk. "I come from aristocracy. Originally, my family is from England, but my father was an early financial supporter of the Führer. So, in the 1930s, we moved to Antwerp to be closer to the Third Reich. Of course, my father's support of Hitler was always disturbing to my half-Jewish mother, but he never cared for that woman's opinions."

"European aristocracy, you say?" asked the man.

"Yes, that's right. At a young age, I was sent to boarding school in Massachusetts. In 1939, I returned to Denmark, where my father gave me to the Nazi Party as one of his many contributions to the war effort. He was also in league with the European banking cartels. They introduced me to their society—the Illuminati."

"Yes, I've heard of it." The man laughed.

"I was initiated into the society. They were grooming me to be a leader in postwar Europe. Through my elite education in the United States, I became associated with a number of East Coast families of extreme wealth, many of whom were also Illuminati. I was instrumental in introducing the Nazis to sympathetic American financiers. My efforts funneled millions of American dollars into the Nazi war machine. This greatly elevated my father's stature with the Führer."

Benson cleared his throat, wishing for some fresh, cool water. "So they gave me a mission. Hitler placed the success of Operation Pastorius in my hands. My unique knowledge of America was my advantage. Hitler expected the mission to succeed, denigrating America's infrastructure and thus securing Germany's defeat of the Allied powers. But I have failed miserably. I will certainly face the firing squad when I return to Germany."

"Then why return?" asked the man. The conversation was starting to bore him again.

"Out of honor and duty, sir," said Benson proudly.

The man laughed again. "They have no loyalty to you, so you shouldn't have any to them."

"It's no matter—I will never get out of the country alive. I may have a chance if I create a fake identity and enlist in the army to catch a transport ship to England. From there, I would desert and make my way home. But, really, I have no home."

"Sounds like a lot of work to me." The man was again seriously considering killing Benson while he slept.

"Well, then, what about you?" asked Benson. "You can't hide here forever. Surely you have some plan in mind?"

"I have been hunted my entire life, so this is nothing new to me."

"*He will be useful to us,*" said the voice in the man's head. "*Show it to him.*"

The man paused, fingering a strip of dried rat meat, and considered the voice's directive. After a few silent minutes, the man dragged over a large canvas bag that carried his meager belongings. "I have something I think you might be interested in, Mr. Illuminati," he mocked.

He reached into the bag and pulled out a heavy book about twenty inches tall, fifteen inches wide, and five inches thick, with a well-worn leather cover. The tome contained page after page of obscure writings, symbols, drawings, and other engraved images. He handed it to the boy.

As Benson examined the foreign symbols on the cover, he appeared completely mesmerized. "I wonder what it says," he asked as he moved his hand gently over the leather.

"It is called The Book of Baphomet. It has two authors. One was a terrifically horrible tyrant I once knew named Gadianton. The other was the assassin-philosopher Kishkumen."

"What is this writing?" The boy touched the figures on the front cover. "What language is this?"

"The original mother language is unknown, but it's a combination of Hebrew and Egyptian. Over time, it was corrupted and became the Lamanese dialect, or slang, and in that language, an ancient secret society recorded its history, philosophies, methods, laws, signs, tokens, rituals, and codes. For thousands of years, I searched for this book. It was rediscovered in 1912 in a ruin in Guatemala and then hidden in a basement at the Brigham Young Academy in Provo, Utah. There, I broke into the building, killed the night watchman, and recovered the book." He made a scoffing sound. "The stupid Mormons had no idea what was in their possession."

Benson stared at the man, completely amazed by the book's history. Then he looked down and leafed through the pages. "I see some Hebrew symbols here," he said. His mother had insisted he learn Hebrew at a young age, along with Latin. Benson was fluent in five languages.

"Ah yes. If you know Hebrew, you are well on your way to learning Lamanese. If you really want to twist your brain, Benson, then I ask you this: How did Hebrew get into an ancient manuscript of the pre-Mayans inhabiting Mesoamerica?"

Benson gave the man an inquisitive look, trying to remember when the Mayan civilization had started.

"There's a simple explanation," the man continued. "I find it hilarious that so-called linguists and archeologists today can't explain why Uto-Aztecan languages contain over seven hundred Hebrew symbols. Look closely. You'll see a few identifiable Egyptian symbols as well."

"What?" Benson felt confused. "How so?"

"That's easy. Their ancestors included some Hebrews who migrated to the Americas around 600 BC. Those Hebrews used Egyptian symbols in their writings."

As astonishing as the man's claim was, Benson was beginning to believe him, and he wanted to know everything. For hours, under the dim light, Benson continued to closely examine the codex, picking up meanings here and there.

Finally, the man spoke again. "My plan is to make my way to Europe, where I will spend my days carrying out the work of this book."

Benson looked up at the man and swallowed hard. "I beg you, sir, take me with you. I have access to resources. I know where to get the money and other assets needed to bring to pass what's written in this book."

The man stared intensely at Benson for several long minutes before speaking again. "If you come with me, Benson Hancock, you go all the way. You must adopt this book and its religion. You must learn Lamanese. You must become an adherent of Baphomet and learn the ways of the Mother. Once you commit, there is no going back. Death is the only release, and you will die in service to the Mother. In the meantime, you have no idea what you are getting yourself into."

Benson felt a flush of excitement. "I have stared into this book and seen its beautiful darkness. I desire all that is therein. I know what I'm getting myself into. I want this."

Recalling a graphic illustration he'd seen in the book, Benson reached into his satchel and pulled his knife from its sheath. After he'd pulled the razor-sharp blade across his left palm with a grunt of pain, he turned and showed his bloody palm to the man.

"I swear it. I will do all in my power to bring to pass the words of this book and the ultimate entropy of this world."

Benson extended his bloody left hand. He could still see skepticism in the man's eyes, but then an odd grin crossed the man's face as he forcefully took Benson's hand.

"My name is Cain."

CHAPTER 11

"Welcome back, folks," said the KATU news anchor from her modern-looking studio news desk. She was on the air. "Portland Community College has always prided itself as a home for nontraditional students, but as news specialist Nisha Adams has found, one student is unlike any other on the PCC campus these days."

The camera cut to a video of Chris walking across a campus path. He wore blue jeans and a Columbia ski jacket, a North Face backpack slung over his right shoulder. In classic Oregon style, it was raining lightly. The camera panned over to the reporter, who stood on a sidewalk near a tree. "That's right," she said into her microphone. "This PCC student has been blazing through prerequisite undergraduate classes and has now been accepted to Stanford University."

The camera cut to a close-up of the president of PCC. Dressed in a dark suit, he stood casually in front of a glass cabinet showcasing his and the school's many accolades. "Chris Thomas is a wonderful student. I've been working closely with him as well as his doctors at OHSU to accelerate him through our associate's program and prepare him to move on to Stanford University."

The camera cut back to the news reporter as she walked slowly down the main hall of the student center and through a sea of community-college students. "Two years ago, Chris Thomas was a Mormon missionary in Miami, Florida, where he was assaulted and put into a coma."

The screen cut to a file picture of Chris in the hospital with his mother beside his bed. Then the camera cut back to the reporter walking slowly forward with the PCC campus in the background.

"His missionary companion, Jeremy Hanks, from Burley, Idaho, was killed in the assault. Six months later, Chris miraculously awoke from the coma with incredible mental capabilities doctors call acquired savant syndrome. These capabilities have allowed Chris to learn at an incredible rate—one most people only dream of."

The camera cut to a video of Chris talking to his doctors and the president of PCC. His physical therapist, Michael, stood in the background smiling. The reporter continued. "Chris came back to Portland and started to work with OHSU doctors to heal his brain injury." The camera cut to Chris and Michael during physical therapy. "Those same doctors helped Chris get a start at PCC, and now Stanford University awaits."

The camera cut to a close-up of Chris. "I know what happened to me is unusual. It's a gift. I am grateful to my doctors and the PCC administration for helping me get to this point in my recovery. I look forward to Stanford and helping others who've suffered brain injuries."

Back in the studio, the anchor said, "That's an incredible story. I assume this is an uncommon condition?"

The camera cut to the reporter on campus. "It sure is, Mary. Doctors tell us that Chris Thomas's condition is only found in one in several billion people."

"Truly amazing, Nisha," said the anchor, faking interest in the puff piece. She then turned to another camera. "In other news . . ."

Chris turned off the TV and sighed. Maybe agreeing to that news report wasn't a great idea.

His phone buzzed. It was a text from Scott Allen, his best friend, who was at Harvard. *Hey, buddy. Just saw the news report. Looked great. I still can't believe you're going to Stanford. Isn't this all just crazy?*

Chris turned off the phone. His head hurt. The math in his vision bothered him; something about it looked different. He retired to his messy room with a six-pack of Coke and started scribbling the strange new patterns he was seeing onto a notepad. As the hours dragged on, he found himself in a strange state between caffeine-fueled concentration and overtiredness. The math only got more and more strange as the clock passed 3:00 a.m.

On a notepad, he wrote down the three most common algorithms in his vision, as he'd done many times before. He called them the alpha, beta, and Charlie algorithms. In reviewing a chapter in a computer-science textbook on the differences between bubble-sort and selection-sort algorithms, Chris noticed something new. The symbols in his head were forming connections in the patterns he hadn't noticed before. There, before him, a new algorithm started to unfold. Chris frantically copied it down, terrified it would dissipate and be lost forever.

"When combined with the new algo," Chris said to himself, "alpha and bubble sort have mathematical traits similar to beta and selection sort . . ."

"*Keep going,*" said a voice.

Chris jumped up from his desk chair and looked around the room. "Who's there?"

"*You're close but still have much to learn.*"

The voice he'd heard was inside his head.

Caught off guard, Chris took a sip of Coke to clear his head. After a few deep breaths, he began to feel collected, so he sat back down and stared at the math before him. He held up his advanced-algorithms textbook and positioned his eyes so that alpha, floating in his field of vision, overlaid the bubble-sort algorithm on the page. After a few moments, he shifted his gaze so beta overlaid the selection-sort algorithm.

Wait a minute. Charlie is the connecting variable? Charlie is a merge sort? That can't be right. This makes zero sense. What am I looking at here?

Combining his strange symbols with known algorithms was starting to make sense of what was in his mind. He was seeing a sorting and processing effect that was organizing data using a previously undiscovered method.

"What is this?" he asked aloud.

"*It's called Adamic mathematics,*" the voice in his head said.

"What?"

"*The idea of Adamic language, or God's language, has in part been revealed to humankind. God the Father also uses His own mathematics, which are called Adamic mathematics. The mathematics revealed to humankind thus far are only foundational and represent a small portion of God's overall mathematical body of knowledge. Adamic mathematics represents the entirety of mathematics, most of which has not been revealed to humankind—until now. You are the instrument whereby the Father has elected to reveal His mathematics to the world for the benefit of all humankind.*"

Chris leaned back in his chair, feeling thrilled but wiped out. "*You will be an instrument in His hands to change the world*" was the last thing he heard as he drifted into an exhaustion-induced sleep.

FIFTH INTERLUDE

Good evening, Father."

Sitting at his desk, Seymour Hancock jumped back in shock. Benson smirked. Some things never changed. His father, as usual, had his nose in his papers and had failed to notice Benson climb through the tall, open window that looked out onto the manicured gardens of the vast estate.

"Son, is that you?" demanded his father in disbelief.

"*Ja, Vater*," said Benson, pointing his Luger at his father's chest.

"Why are you pointing that gun at me, boy?" Seymour asked, outraged. "Where have you been hiding, you coward?"

Benson maneuvered the gun slightly to the left of his father's head and fired a single round, destroying an old family picture. Screaming, Seymour Hancock threw his arms in front of his face as he shrunk back into his chair.

"You were right. He is weak," said Cain in German as he climbed through the same open window. Seymour Hancock looked at Cain. His eyes opened wide with fear at the ghastly, red-mottled man before him.

"Do I have your attention now, Father?"

Benson's father looked shocked, and his breathing was shallow. Confused and angry, he tried to speak.

"Don't talk, Father," said Benson calmly. "If you do, the next bullet is yours."

His father glared at him in disgust. Benson sat down in a chair facing his father's desk, his gun still trained at Seymour's head. The ornate office stank of tobacco. Huge African-mahogany bookshelves filled with thousands of leather-bound books lined one office wall to the top of the twenty-foot ceiling. A fire roared in a fireplace in the corner of the office. Priceless oil paintings of bygone Hancocks covered two walls. Cain walked around the room, casually surveying the valuables.

"I will do the talking. You will listen or die where you sit," Benson said. "I've spent almost three years making my way back here just for this night—the first night of the rest of my life."

His father raised his bushy eyebrows.

"I'm sure you read the news," Benson said. "I got away, but the others did not. No, I was not about to return to Germany to face Hitler's firing squad. You could say Mr. Cain here helped me see the light."

Benson lowered the gun so it was pointing at his father's chest. "And as we sit here, Germany is about to lose the war. The walls are closing in on the Third Reich. It's only a matter of time before the Americans and British discover your personal contribution and you are tried for war crimes. How does it feel, Father, knowing this is the end? Go ahead. Say something somewhat intelligent." Benson flippantly waved the gun, then reached over and grabbed his father's glass of brandy.

Seymour Hancock said nothing for a moment. He appeared to be calculating a way out of the situation. "I was told you had died in Operation Pastorius."

Benson laughed while wiping brandy from his lips. From across the room, Cain scoffed at the comment.

"The American Illuminati took us in and hid us for two years before we began making our way to Europe," Benson said. "They were useful fools. During that time, I received a new education. I am now a disciple of Baphomet, and I seek to use your wealth—oh, excuse me, my wealth—to bring about his Mandate. I have pledged everything that is now mine to the Mother and the Son. We will start with my new wealth, and then we'll consolidate forces to create a global conglomerate that will make the Third Reich look like a second-rate African dictatorship. The governments of the world will bow in terror before us, and we will rule the earth."

Seymour Hancock smiled slightly.

Benson raised his weapon to his father's head. "Speak, but choose your words wisely."

"That's—um, ambitious, son," said Seymour mockingly, seeming almost relaxed, no doubt assuming his son had gone mad. "The Illuminati will never allow it. We are more powerful than you can imagine. How did you even get here, anyway?"

Benson decided to indulge his father's question rather than kill him right at that moment. "After lying low in America, we used an Illuminati contact to get jobs on a Cunard ship ferrying soldiers to England. From there, we paid smugglers for passage to Antwerp. Since D-Day, it's a lot easier to cross the channel. Now, here we sit with you."

"I found it," interrupted Cain. "Just where you said it would be." He laid a large stack of papers titled "Last Will and Testament" on the desk between the two men. Benson reached into his satchel and produced his own pile of papers also titled "Last Will and Testament." His father said nothing, confusion spreading across his face.

Cain stood over Seymour, who looked up in fear at the beast of a man.

"Sign here and here," Benson said, pointing to the papers.

"My will? Are you mad?"

"No, in fact, I am saner than I've ever been," said Benson as he rose from his chair, walked to his father's side, and placed the gun against his temple. He repeated the demand, "Sign it now or die, old man."

"No, I will not sign it."

Stubborn fool, thought Benson as he placed the barrel of the pistol against his father's knee and pulled the trigger. Seymour Hancock shrieked in agony as the 9mm round pierced his knee. He instinctively grabbed it with both hands and flailed to the floor, blood flowing from his leg onto the beautiful Persian carpet. Benson stood over him and again leveled the pistol at his father's head. Cain laughed.

The door to the office suddenly burst open. "What is going on in here, Seymour?" yelled Benson's mother, Anna Hancock. She was followed by the house butler, whose face went pale with shock at the sight before them.

"Son?" called Anna in disbelief at the sight of her long-lost child. When she saw her husband splayed on the floor and covered in blood, her hands cupped her mouth, her eyes widening in horror.

The butler took a bar towel from his apron and ran to assist Seymour, but Benson raised the Luger and fired, hitting the well-dressed man in the chest. He fell next to Seymour, appearing to have died before he even hit the ground.

～

"Benson," Anna yelled, "what did you do?" She suddenly felt faint, and time seemed to slow down. She heard no noise except a crackle from the fireplace. The fine paintings on the office walls stared in disapproval. A light bulb flickered in the crystal chandelier hanging from the center of the ceiling. In the stillness of the moment, she simply could not register what was happening. Her son, whom she'd believed dead, stood before her in the flesh. Her husband lay on the floor, bleeding and in pain. The butler appeared to be dead, shot by her son. Anna could never have imagined her baby boy pointing a gun directly at her, as he was doing now.

A fierce, burning pain suddenly flared within her left breast. She looked down to see a bright-red stain spreading from a hole in her perfectly pressed blouse. She never heard the sound of the Luger firing as the smell of gun powder and death consumed the room.

Touching her bloody chest with her middle finger, she looked back up at her son. Black smoke rose from the barrel of the gun still pointed at her chest.

"I love you," she said to Benson. As she dropped to the floor, Seymour Hancock screamed out his wife's name.

~

Benson felt a momentary twinge of guilt after shooting his mother.

Seymour attempted to stand. It was clear from his expression he intended to kill his son, but Cain seized him and threw him back into his chair. Then Cain reached down, took the bar towel from the butler's hands, and threw it at Seymour. "Clean yourself up. We have a will to sign."

Cain turned his attention to Benson, who stood, gun still raised, in shock at what he had just done. "Bravo, Benson. Baphomet is very pleased with what you have done for him tonight."

Snapping out of his trance, Benson lowered the weapon and turned toward his master. "Indeed, the Son is very pleased," he agreed, then turned his attention back to his father.

Seymour Hancock wept bitterly as he sat at his desk, repeating his wife's name over and over again and staring at her body on the floor. "What have you done, boy?" he yelled as drool and snot flowed uncontrollably down his face.

Benson moved to his father and again raised the gun to his temple. "Sign the last will and testament of Seymour Hancock, and don't get blood on the documents. It will arouse suspicion."

Defeated, Seymour picked up the fountain pen and signed the lengthy will where directed. Cain picked up the old will and threw it into the fireplace. The room grew momentarily brighter as the paper ignited, and Seymour Hancock grew more morose. For years, Benson had dreamt of this moment. But even though the end of Seymour Hancock was now, Benson knew the hatred in his heart would never be extinguished.

"Very good, Father. Very good." Benson placed his hand on his father's shoulder and looked proudly at the carnage. "And isn't this convenient? It looks like a double murder and a suicide have occurred here. Wouldn't you agree, Mr. Cain?"

Cain only smiled as he maneuvered himself behind Seymour's chair. Benson handed the gun to Cain, who put it into Seymour's left hand. The old man fought wildly for control of the weapon, but Cain was too powerful. With his huge hand engulfing Seymour's, Cain raised the weapon to Seymour's head.

"No!" Seymour yelled out. But it was too late. Cain forced him to pull the trigger. Seymour folded over onto the desk. Benson watched with tears of joy and terror streaming down his face. He was now truly an adherent of Baphomet.

Cain had not lied. The commitment to the Mother and the Son required everything he had. The Order of Baphomet would only stop taking from him when he died.

Cain let the gun fall from Seymour's hand and turned to Benson.

"I am Master Mahan."

CHAPTER 12

THE THOMAS HOME
TUALATIN, OREGON

Chris had just finished a series of books on linear algebra and advanced algorithms, as well as a series of basic software-development books on subjects like Java, C++, Python, and SQL databases. He was in love with computer science, and his mind was starting to marry programming and the weird Adamic math he began to call the Adamic Code.

He'd also recently been cleared by doctors to use screens. A computer of his own was the next step. But Chris was broke, and so were his parents. The math around this problem was simple: he could not afford what he badly wanted and needed.

One morning, rising from his bed at 5:00 a.m. to use the bathroom, Chris found a briefcase-sized shipping box in the hallway next to his bedroom door. He sat on the floor and curiously examined it. A note taped to the outside caught his attention: *Son, I hope this is what you were looking for. You can connect to my Wi-Fi. Password is GrandpasShop123. Come show me something cool when you're done making it. Love, Grandpa.*

"Grandpa strikes again," said Chris appreciatively. "I really owe that guy."

Opening the box, Chris pulled back the clear plastic wrapping. Inside was a new Dell XPS laptop. He couldn't believe his eyes. The laptop was a dull gray with a seventeen-inch 8K monitor and full keyboard. Inside, it had 256 gigs of RAM, a one-terabyte hard drive, and powerful duel Intel processors.

"Sweet!" yelled Chris, immediately hoping he hadn't woken the rest of the house. Returning from the bathroom, he set the laptop on his desk and pushed the power button. It was about to be a very good day.

Later that morning, Chris walked next door to his grandparents' house. As usual, Grandpa was in the shop working on some new wooden creation. He wore an old pair of leather work boots and denim overalls. His glasses sat low on the tip of his nose as he used an electric hand planer to smooth a piece of reclaimed barn board. Every time Chris saw his grandfather, he was amazed at how much the chemo had aged him. But Grandpa Thomas was a fighter and seemed to be winning the battle against cancer.

"Grandpa?" Chris said over the sound of the machine. He was trying not to startle the old fella, but he failed. Grandpa Thomas jumped.

"Ah, I'm guessing you received your package, son," said Grandpa.

"I did. Thanks, Grandpa, but how am I ever going to repay you?"

"I don't want your money, kid. I want you to use that computer and your new brain to change the world for the better. That's how you repay me."

"OK, I'll try, but I have no idea—"

"What did Yoda say?" Grandpa Thomas asked, cutting him off.

Chris stared at him questioningly. "Uh . . ."

"Did you even forget *The Empire Strikes Back*?"

Chris shrugged. If he'd seen the movie before his accident, he couldn't remember it.

"'Do or do not,'" Grandpa quoted. "'There is no try.'"

Chris gave him a blank look. His grandfather returned it with an intense stare.

"I told you, son." Grandpa carefully laid the planer on his workbench. "This whole thing is some kind of miracle. You are now on a trajectory for greatness. I am here to help facilitate that. I may be dead before you make it, so you must promise me you will do it. That you will use all the tools in your shed"—Grandpa pointed at Chris's head—"to make the world a better place. To help the helpless, to feed the hungry, to clothe the naked, and to give hope to the hopeless. Are you familiar with the term *covenant?*"

"Of course. We talk about that all the time in church. It's a two-way agreement. Like the ones we make with God."

"Yes, sir. So, I will covenant to help you with things like laptops. You, in turn, will covenant with me to change the world by helping those who can't help themselves. Deal?"

"Yeah, it's a deal," Chris said without much consideration.

"Then we're settled."

After several long weeks coding his first app, Chris took his laptop over to Grandpa's woodshop.

"So, show me what you made there, son," Grandpa said.

"Well, it isn't much yet. It's kind of part of something bigger I'm working on, and this is one of the foundational pieces."

Chris opened the laptop and set it on the workbench, then pulled up an iPhone app-design tool. "This is a voice-recognition training game. You have to guess the tongue twisters, movie lines, famous quotes, et cetera, on the screen faster than the others you're playing against. Then there's a series of word games I'm working on, all voice controlled. It's simple, but the programming was really hard."

"What's life rule number five?" asked Grandpa Thomas.

"I have no idea what you're talking about."

"You really did forget everything, didn't you," said Grandpa, somewhat annoyed. "Rule number five is this: the important things are always simple, and the simple things are always hard. Here, take this with you." Grandpa walked over to a shelf, grabbed a piece of paper, and handed it to Chris.

Written by hand, it contained Grandpa Thomas's life rules, which Chris absorbed at a glance:

1. Perception is reality.
2. Never assume you are dealing with a rational person. Even better, never assume anything.
3. Always consider the consequences of your actions before you act.
4. Love everyone. Be and act human. Remove all hate, narcissism, and malice from your life.
5. The important things are always simple, and the simple things are always hard.
6. Undercommit and overdeliver.
7. Never bring a problem to the table without a solution.
8. Know when to quit, but know why you're quitting.
9. A failure not learned from is a wasted opportunity.
10. Risk does not mean you should not act.
11. Admit there are things you don't know and things you believe that are not true.
12. Know that your reasoning may be wrong. Reason has limits.
13. Never do anything that compromises your agency.
14. Don't accept all the advice you're given, and never weigh all advice equally.
15. People can change for the better and the worse.
16. Listening is the most important skill to develop in human relations.
17. Only use money to buy freedom.
18. Empathy is everything.
19. The only substitute for hard work is harder work.
20. Break the rules.

"Now that I'm reading it, I seem to remember these rules from before the accident. These are great. Thanks, Grandpa." Chris folded the paper and put it in his pocket.

"What's the point of this app thing, anyway?" his grandfather asked, trying not to sound bored.

"It's training for something else I'm working on. Something I'm just figuring out that I learned when I was on the other side. But I'm not ready to discuss that part yet."

Grandpa Thomas turned back to his workbench and picked up the planer. "Well, I'm too old for apps. Don't even have a mobile phone. But I hope you have fun with it."

Smiling, Chris closed the laptop, tucked it under his arm, and backed toward the shop door. "OK, Grandpa. I'm using it for good, I promise. I'll show you more soon."

His grandpa gave him a wave and a polite smile, then restarted his electric hand planer, angling it expertly against the old reclaimed board.

A week later at two in the morning, Chris submitted several apps he'd built to the App Store for approval. A month later, the apps were garnering thousands of downloads an hour.

CHAPTER 13

Guns.

Hundreds of guns of all types and calibers lined the walls of the dark warehouse located in the city's industrial zone. Glocks, Sigs, and H&K 416s with all the trimmings. The top-secret, highly secured contents were enough to have made most third-world dictators jealous. *The contents of this single warehouse are enough to invade most third-world countries,* thought Mike Mayberry. Ammunition, explosives, body armor, armored vehicles, and state-of-the-art surveillance equipment filled the space like it was a candy store for spies. And Ground Branch had 114 facilities just like this one spread across the globe.

In a corner of the warehouse was a makeshift meeting area with several whiteboards, old-school paper maps, and TV monitors.

"OK, guys, let's pull it together," said Mike. The group of computer wonks, Ground Branch operatives, and other support staff quieted down and took a seat on whatever they could find—old chairs, boxes, and the hoods of vehicles.

"Everyone should have reviewed the detailed mission profile by now," Mike said. The image of a man filled one of the screens. "His name is Sayid Sheikh. He is one of the principal suppliers of high explosives to ISIS. He came on the scene about six years ago, so he's still relatively new at this. He's a former Iranian intelligence officer who found it more profitable to work on the supply side. Using his intel contacts, he started working with all the wrong people. Explosives supplied by Sheikh have been used in countless attacks in Syria, as well as on the Iraqi Army. He's now trying to expand his client base. He recently did a deal in Chechnya, which normally would have been outside his tolerated boundaries. He's getting bolder, but that is exactly what we want. This newfound boldness takes him out of the Middle East and puts him in places where it's easier for us to grab him."

Mike pulled up more images on the screen. "Six months ago, we infilled his Istanbul office and have been receiving a steady stream of intel on his activities. The intel is solid; always checks out. We recently learned that he will meet an unknown Eastern European contact to discuss moving explosives into ISIS terrorist cells inside the UK and France. That meeting will take place here in Brussels in forty-eight hours."

Mike stepped forward and looked over his team. "So this is a rendition op. We're going to bag this guy, his bodyguards, and the buyer. After the apprehension, we'll transport them on a company C-17 to a black-ops site in Poland."

One of the guys yawned. Easy mission.

"OK, let's go over a few details," said Mike as he pulled up the mission profile on his laptop, which projected to a screen in front of the team. "The meeting is set to take place in this VIP suite on the top floor of the W Hotel." Mike pointed to the floor plan on the screen. "So our targets will be the next visitors to that suite. The tech team will enter the target suite tonight and start the setup—we own the space for the next two days. We'll be installing high-def mics and cameras throughout. And it's the new stuff, of course, not detectable by a basic bug sweep."

Mike pointed at a different spot on the floor plan. "All phone calls will route to this operations suite just across the hall. Of course, we also control fire alarms, doors, and elevators. We'll wire the target suite's door to remote detonate in case we need to go in shooting. We have a team assisting with the hotel staff. A select group of employees will know we're on-site. The staff thinks this is an Interpol drug bust, so use your Interpol IDs."

Mike paced in front of the team. "When the tangos start the meeting, we'll let them run their mouths and collect all the intel we can grab. When they are about to conclude, we'll hit them with this." He pointed to a large, basic house lamp sitting on top of an ammo crate.

The room broke into low laughter. "This is a new one for you, Chief," said one of his guys. "Bust in and crack them over the head with a lamp."

"This is no ordinary lamp, my friends." Mike hefted the lamp onto a table and removed its bulky outer casing. Inside was a sophisticated array of electronics and colorful wires. Most of the interior of the lamp's base was a futuristic-looking black speaker.

"It's a highly localized acoustics weapon. It weaponizes low-frequency sound to immobilize human targets. You may have seen the military trials or YouTube videos where we've used these systems at big-city riots. Once it's activated, the victims usually lose bodily control—they throw up, piss, and crap themselves at once. Right after that, they faint. After waking up, they are usually disorientated for up to three hours. Imagine a large mob massing on an embassy or military base. Flip this baby on, and it quickly diffuses the situation, with no serious injuries or deaths."

"I'd hate to be the guy who has to clean up the street," said an operative.

"Yeah, but at least it's vomit instead of blood and guts, right?" said Mike.

The operative nodded.

"Its range is only about thirty feet, but that's plenty to cover the target suite. When the meeting concludes, on my signal we'll uncage the acoustic weapon concealed in the lamp we've previously set up in the suite. The four guys in the room immediately mess themselves and then faint. We walk in calmly, tranq 'em, bag 'em, gag 'em, zip-tie 'em, and conceal them in laundry carts. Then we take them down the service elevator to the vans waiting at the receiving dock. No shots fired."

"Brilliant," said one of the guys.

"Yeah, I'm beginning to like these nonlethal weapons the nerds over at DARPA keep dreaming up," said Mike. "Should make this a very clean op, so to speak."

He asked the team if they had any questions, and no one did. "OK then, let's jock up. Maintenance cover. Full kit. I want to roll out in two hours."

AC/DC started playing over the warehouse speakers as the staff went into immediate preparations. Mike folded his arms and watched the team approvingly.

CHAPTER 14

W HOTEL
BRUSSELS, BELGIUM

On several monitors, Mike and his team watched the activities in the adjacent target suite. Sheikh and his guards paced the spacious suite's living room. Speaking in Arabic to his men, Sheikh mostly insulted them for not having done more surveillance on the hotel before his arrival. Mike didn't speak Arabic, but he could pick out the words that meant "fools" and "incompetent."

"He has no idea," said Mike under his breath.

"Sir, we have a single coming up the elevator, a female," said one of the mission specialists.

Mike turned to the monitor. "It's her, the woman from the Ukraine mission. The one who got away with the virus. We need her alive."

Dellmark walked to the monitor. "I'll be da—"

"Man, that *is* her," Smith interrupted. "Good thing we brought the nonlethal ray gun."

The high-def microcam hidden expertly in the elevator ceiling picked up every detail. The woman in the lift looked German. Just as Mike had remembered her, she was stunning. Slender, tall, and athletic, with piercing blue eyes and perfect lips. Her blonde hair was slicked back the same way as in the Ukraine. Expensive shoes. Dark-blue silk suit. Sinn-brand wristwatch. Italian-leather briefcase. She could have easily been mistaken for an executive in a European corporate conglomerate.

"Call this in," said Mike to the comms specialist. "Tell Langley our unknown buyer is a priority-delta target."

After having lost the mysterious woman on the Ukrainian op—she had literally been in his grip—Mike could hardly contain his excitement at the prospect of redeeming himself.

The woman exited the elevator and made her way to the target suite, where she knocked quietly and waited patiently.

Completely concealed across the hall, Mike and the team watched the events play out in real time from several different views. Sheikh turned nervously at the sound of the knock. He positioned one of his men in a strategic location adjacent to the main living room. The other bodyguard accompanied Sheikh to the door. They exchanged pleasantries, and the woman was invited to enter.

The European set down her briefcase, which was searched for weapons. The guard casually frisked her, careful not to touch anywhere he shouldn't. Mike noted that the woman took no offense at these actions. It was apparent she'd been through this drill a hundred times.

When the search was completed, the group moved to the living-room area. Sheikh and the woman sat on opposite couches separated by a petite, gold-colored coffee table with a glass top. Mike wondered if the Iranian was annoyed that the client had sent a woman to deal with him.

"I thank you for meeting me on such short notice, Mr. Sheikh," said the woman in a thick German accent.

"Of course. It was no problem, Ms. Black. May I offer you some tea?" asked Sheikh. Black declined.

"Ms. Black?" Mike chuckled as he watched from the operations suite. "She couldn't come up with a better pseudonym?" His team laughed quietly.

"I hope you were pleased with the test product I furnished your people in the Congo?" asked Sheikh.

"Yes, the quality was as promised," said Black. "I understand they are interested in a reorder."

"Oh, excellent news. I will reach out to your contact immediately to make the arrangements."

"Very well. Let's get to the real reason for our meeting today."

"Yes, let's." Sheikh nervously sipped his tea.

"We have a problem in Chechnya. One of our shipments was ambushed in transit. The lead vehicle was hit by an improvised explosive device, which boxed in the rest of our convoy. They were then flanked and attacked by a heavily armed strike team. Our men and human merchandise were all killed. The group behind this is known as Ava."

Sheikh swallowed hard but said nothing.

"As you may or may not know," Black continued, "Ava is one of our primary competitors in former Soviet regions. One of our laboratories performed an analysis of the Semtex plastic explosive Ava used in the attack. They traced the origin of the explosive to the original manufacturer. After hacking that company's network, we learned that this particular batch of explosives was sold to a Russian front company, then resold to one of its subsidiaries, a Turkish company known as ProTex International, Limited. That company lists you as its chairman and majority shareholder."

Sheikh set his empty teacup loudly on the glass coffee table. "I had no idea the company buying the product was associated with Ava in any way."

Ms. Black sat perfectly still, showing no emotion. "May I?" she asked, then slipped her hand inside her silk suit coat and set a photo on the glass table in front of Sheikh. "This picture was taken two days before the attack on our convoy. The man in the picture is Vladimir Sokolov, a former FSB agent and one of the founders of Ava. The man standing next to him is you."

"I'm not sure how to respond to this accusation," fumed Sheikh.

Mike activated his comms. "Be advised, this is going south. Everyone ready." He looked at one of the mission specialists. "Stand ready on the acoustic weapon."

"Ready, sir," said the specialist, flipping up the safety toggle and exposing the weapon's trigger.

"I'm not asking you to respond," said Black calmly. "My employer only humbly requests that you atone for your sin."

"Atone?" barked Sheikh. "Like restitution? What, in money? What are you asking for?"

Standing nearby, the bodyguard shifted uncomfortably and touched his gun.

"Yes, financial restitution, if you will," said Black. "As a matter of fact, I believe you have already paid the restitution."

A look of sheer panic crossed Sheikh's face. He pulled his phone from his suit coat and opened his banking app. Black continued to sit perfectly still on the couch across from him. The high-def microcam picked up every detail on Sheikh's mobile device. Mike could clearly see that his Swiss bank account was at a zero balance.

Sheikh looked up at Black. "There were forty-two million Euros in that account, you—"

Black made a sudden twitch with her right wrist. There was a bright flash, an odd sound, and a puff of white smoke.

Before Sheikh could finish the insult, a small projectile hit him in the throat. He jerked back and clutched his neck. When he removed his hands, they were covered in blood. He looked at Black in confusion as he slumped forward onto the floor. The bodyguard moved for his sidearm, but Black pointed her wrist at him, and he hit the floor.

"What just happened?" yelled Mike. "Activate the acoustic weapon." At the operation suite's door, the members of his strike team readied themselves.

In the target suite, the second bodyguard rushed into the room, weapon drawn. Grinning slightly, Black flicked her wrist again. The man immediately went limp and fell onto the glass coffee table, shattering it into thousands of pieces. Blood pooled on the floor around his head.

Jumping up, Black grabbed a Sig Sauer handgun from a dead guard. With expert speed, she threw Sheikh's laptop and phone into her briefcase and ran to the suite's door.

"I said activate the acoustic weapon!" Mike yelled at the specialist, but Black was already out in the hall.

"Sir, the weapon malfunctioned," said the panicked weapons specialist.

Mike turned to his only hope, the strike team waiting for orders to enter the hall.

Black was standing at the elevator when Mike and three assassins emerged from the operations suite in a classic four-man-stack formation, their Glock 19s raised and ready.

"Freeze!" yelled Mike.

Without hesitation, Black opened fire with the stolen Sig Sauer. The operative in front of Mike suddenly dropped to the ground. Pain gripped Mike's chest, and he, too, dropped. A 9mm round had struck his light body armor just above the heart. The other two operatives behind Mike rushed toward the woman with a barrage of fire, but Black, with her arm raised to cover her head, burst through the stairwell door.

"What the—" said an operative as he moved cautiously toward the stairwell door. "I hit her several times."

"Man down," Mike, still on his side, yelled into his comms. The fallen operative had taken a round right in the forehead and lay dead. Turning around, the other operative looked down at their teammate, stunned.

"Get her," Mike yelled from the floor as he tried to remove the damaged vest from his chest. The operatives took off through the stairwell door. Mike heard gunfire in the stairwell as the medical team emerged from the operations suite.

Standing on the hotel's loading dock, Mike surveyed the aftermath. The dock held the bagged bodies of several men who had been alive only hours before. The CIA team, emergency personnel, and local police were still working inside the hotel. Officials from the US embassy were on their way to assess the situation and run interference with the Belgium government.

In the stairwell, Black had killed her two pursuers. Then, exiting onto the receiving dock, she'd murdered Mike's two drivers waiting with the vans. In all, five of his men had died in an op considered low risk. Always the professional, Mike tried his best to conceal the horrific pain welling up inside his soul. He was covertly wiping a tear when his phone rang.

"I've analyzed the video," said Norman Steller over comms from his office deep inside CIA headquarters. "It was some kind of wrist-fired weapon."

"Yeah, I kind of got that part, Norman," Mike said. "Can you tell me anything I don't know?"

"Not at the moment. It's pretty advanced stuff," said Norman. "I need to make a few more calls. By the way, her clothing had to be spider silk infused with Kevlar. That's the only material that could have protected her from shots fired at that close of range. But I bet it hurt like nothing she's ever felt before. We're running an analysis on all known manufacturers of that clothing type. There are only three in the world, so it shouldn't take long. One of them is out of Boston and furnishes the US government with clothes for the presidents and other VIPs. So it's probably not them. I have a feeling she got hers from an unknown source."

"OK. Keep me posted. I'm sending back the acoustic weapon. It malfunctioned, and I want to know why. Get the DARPA guys on it right away."

"Yes, sir."

Mike ended the call and surveyed the dead lying all around him. Kneeling next to his men, he tried to stop another tear from forming in the corner of his eye.

This will not go unanswered. I promise you, brothers.

CHAPTER 15

NEW-STUDENT MIXER
STANFORD UNIVERSITY

A strange smell permeated the air.

What is that? Chris wondered. *Smells like cat food. Or maybe burned vegetables? That is just awful.*

Students of all ethnic backgrounds and races talked and laughed as they ate veggie burgers, munched on gluten-free treats, and drank kombucha. All Chris wanted was a cheeseburger and a Coke.

As he walked slowly through the sea of people, he started noticing something. At first, he thought he was just being paranoid, but then he couldn't deny it. The looks. The sideways glances. The stares. He wasn't being paranoid. Something was very wrong, and that something was him.

Spying a place of solitude, Chris sat down and pondered his situation. Tremendous anxiety overwhelmed him as he thought back on his life and how he'd landed in this situation. Since his arrival at Stanford, some hard childhood memories had started to slowly come back to him. As the students stared at him from across the way, he was reminded of his feelings while walking into the first grade—for the second time.

Everyone knew he had been held back, and they knew why. Of course, his mother had lied and told him it was his age, but Chris knew it was much, much more than that. He was dumb. He was simple. He was a nobody. At the tender age of six—standing, again, in Ms. Washington's first-grade classroom with all eyes locked on him—Chris had surrendered to his less-than-ordinary existence.

Over the next several years, he would watch his classmates as they seemed to breeze through elementary subjects like math, reading, and social studies. Nothing seemed to bother his classmates, but all of it bothered Chris. He just couldn't see the point of school.

Sitting on the bench, Chris eyed his Stanford classmates and wondered. Was Stanford going to be a repeat of the first grade? Was he about to fail again in spectacular and public fashion?

Fear welled up inside him. Then he thought of Scott Allen, his best friend, three thousand miles away at Harvard. He smiled as he thought about how they'd met.

It was the third grade, and Chris was late for a field trip. When he ran onto the classic yellow Blue Bird school bus, only one seat was available. It was next to the new kid in school, whom no one seemed to like. All the kids on the bus watched Chris, wondering if he would take the empty seat or try to squeeze into an occupied row. Not wanting to upset anyone, Chris approached the available seat. The new kid looked up at him with a hardy smile and hopeful eyes.

"This seat taken?" Chris asked, already knowing the answer.

"No, not at all. You can sit here," the kid said enthusiastically as he shifted to make even more room on the green vinyl seat.

Chris slid into the seat and looked over at the new kid. "What's wrong with you?" he asked bluntly.

"What do you mean?" said the clueless boy.

"No one likes you."

"Oh," said the boy, dejected. Chris instantly felt bad.

They sat in silence for a few minutes.

"Well, I'm Scott," the boy finally said. "Scott Allen. I'm a Jew."

"A what?"

"A Jew," he said in a serious tone. Then he pointed at the top of his skull. "You know, we wear the funny little caps."

"Oh," said Chris. He hadn't heard anything about funny Jewish caps.

"What about you?" asked Scott.

"What about me?"

"What are you?"

"A Mormon, I guess."

"What's a Mormon?"

"Grown-ups in my church wear funny underwear," said Chris.

"Oh, OK," replied Scott. "Well, looks like we have something in common."

"I guess. Anyway, I'm Chris Thomas."

The two boys shook hands. Chris didn't think much of the meeting, but Scott later said it was the best day of his life. He had finally made a friend. Scott and Chris had bonded over their obscure religions. And from that day on, their friendship became something of an unholy alliance with the goal being sheer survival. Together they deflected the taunts and teasing of the ruthless evangelicals who made up the majority of their class.

Snapping himself out of the memory, Chris put in his earbuds, dialed the familiar number, and prayed the person on the other end would save him from Stanford University's new-student mixer.

"Yo, dog," said Scott.

"Oh, man. I am so glad you picked up. What are you doing?"

"Playing *Devil's Plague*."

"Devil's what?"

"It's a mobile game. Really cool stuff. You compete against other players to find the best methods for starting a global pandemic. You take in a ton of factors, like population densities, availability of antiviruses, a country's healthcare infrastructure, weather, military response times, and a bunch of other data points. It's really popular at Harvard. All the smartest kids play it. You should see some of the models people are coming up with. Honestly, it's a little scary."

"Sounds boring to me."

"Well, yeah, of course it sounds boring to you. You're smarter than most of the people at Harvard. This is what people on the dumb end of the smart scale do with their free time, brotha. So, what about you? How's it going at Stanford?"

"I'm at a student mixer right now. In other words, I'm in hell."

Scott starting singing. "So, so you think you can tell. Heaven from hell. Blue skies from pain."

"Dude, I'm serious. I wish you were here."

Scott's singing continued. "How I wish, how I wish you were here. We're just two lost souls swimmin' in a fishbowl."

"OK, I deserved that," Chris said, annoyed. "I freaking walked right into it."

Scott laughed hysterically into the phone. Pink Floyd was their favorite band. "Come on. What's the problem? Bored in your octonion-theory class?"

"I'm not cut out for this, man. I'm going home."

"Whoa! Wait a minute. No, you're not."

Chris said nothing.

"What's the problem?" Scott asked. "Talk. But talk fast. The ladies are waiting for me. I'm heading out to a sorority party."

"Stanford isn't me. You've known me practically my whole life. What am I doing? I'm supposed to be a ski bum living in Utah and doing nothing with my life. I had a simple plan, dude. Now look at me. They're serving veggie burgers. What am I doing here?"

"A gift," Scott said. "What you have is a gift, Chris." Then his voice took on a scolding tone. "We talked about this. You weren't meant to be a ski bum. You have a mission now. You have a new purpose. You need to go and figure out what that is, and Stanford is part of the puzzle. Now, what's so bad about it?"

"The food sucks, and smart girls are ugly."

"That's a bunch of BS and you know it. What's the real problem?"

"Everyone looks at me weird. They all saw that stupid news report about me on YouTube. It got posted on a Stanford message board. You should see the comments. Someone at this mixer asked me about community college, and a group of people overheard us and started to laugh. They were making fun of me behind my back. The president of the school gave me a mentor. He's some professor named Martin Alba who treats me like I'm a child. He talks down to me. It's embarrassing. I've only been here two days, but I want out, man."

"OK, fine, you've been a quitter your whole life. So do it. Quit."

Chris didn't say anything for a moment. The words were uncharacteristically strong coming from Scott. "Well, uh . . ."

"Look, I'm tired of you whining about school," Scott said. "I'm not going to listen to it for the next four years. So just quit. I'm sure you can get a direct flight from SFO to Salt Lake City. Ski bum, here you come."

"What?"

"Yeah. Why did you go to community college in the first place? What were you trying to prove? You never called me complaining about school back then. Why?"

Chris was silent.

"Because you thought everyone at PCC was dumber than you. Now, at the second-best school next to Harvard, you're terrified you'll just be average compared to everyone else. It's like walking back into first grade all over again."

"OK, fine. You have my attention."

"I saw what you did at PCC. It's not normal even for a Stanford student. Almost no one on earth can do what you can with that big brain of yours, dude. Have you ever heard of FUD?"

"FUD?"

"Fear. Uncertainty. Doubt. Or in other words, you right now. You're letting FUD control your life. It's time to take it back, Oprah-style."

"Who?"

"Never mind Oprah! You just need to push away the emotion, put down your head, and prove to yourself and the school that you earned it and have the right to be there."

Chris was silent on his end of the phone. He looked at the other students laughing and talking while he sat on a bench moping.

"So, what's it going to be, then?" demanded Scott. "Are you in or out?"

"In," said Chris in a determined voice.

"Yeah, buddy! OK, I'm off to a party. Go try a veggie burger and call me next week. Cool?"

"All right, man. I appreciate the encouragement. Shine on, you crazy diamond!"

CHAPTER 16

Mike Mayberry lived on twenty pristine acres that served mostly as a horse pasture just outside the town of Bluemont, Virginia. The former Army Delta Force commando had purchased the property when he retired from the army and was recruited into the CIA's elite Special Activities Division known as Ground Branch.

The 1960s-era three-bedroom brick rambler was located on a corner of the property, off an old backcountry road. A dilapidated horse barn sat in the pasture behind the house. In the winter, Mike heated the cozy home with an old woodstove that also doubled as an oven. The house didn't have air conditioning, so in the summer, he suffered through the Virginia heat and humidity.

One evening, soon after he arrived home from Belgium, Mike sat comfortably on his ancient couch, a relic of a bygone marriage. The only light in the room came from his large LED TV, which he'd purchased on impulse at Costco after his divorce. He only used the TV to watch football, and on this Thursday night, the Giants were playing the Eagles, a classic NFL rivalry.

Mike had only been off mission for a few days, and his adrenaline was finally starting to equalize. A faint tiredness began to overcome him as he cracked open a Coors Light and turned up the volume on the game.

By the second quarter, Mike had to sit up and force himself to focus on the game, struggling to fight the wave of exhaustion. The more he tried to resist, the further his mind slipped away. Finally, he surrendered and slumped back down into the couch, pulling a quilted blanket over his chest.

As Mike drifted off, he heard the distinct crack of an AK-47 in the distance. He flinched in a confused, hypnagogic state, unable to determine if he was awake or asleep. The TV flickered, and the sound of the game dissipated. Darkness consumed him. All he could hear was his heavy breathing. An unknown amount of time passed, and then, slowly, light started to fill in around him. A light breeze passed over his face. Trees and rocks started to form. He looked down at himself and raised his palms. They were covered in blood.

"Afghanistan," he mumbled in his sleep as the Eagles scored another touchdown.

In the chaos of the long-ago firefight, Mike, then a Delta Force operative, had been separated from his team. Trying to outmaneuver eight Taliban fighters, he'd run into an area with sheer cliffs dropping on either side of a rocky, pine-forested plateau. Shot and bleeding from his head and shoulder, he was low on ammunition. The only escape was through the enemy or over a cliff.

Either way, Mike Mayberry did not plan to die that day.

Concealing himself behind a large boulder, he reached into his pack, pulled out a small field medical kit, applied coagulate to his head wound to stop the bleeding, and wrapped a bandage around his head. He also applied coagulate to the gunshot wound gaping in his left shoulder. The 7.62 x 39mm round had miraculously missed the bone and several critical arteries. Rotating his arm, Mike was amazed he still had good range of motion in the joint. He didn't bother removing his bloody shirt or wiping the blood from his face. He hoped his bloody appearance would intimidate his foes.

Taking a quick inventory, Mike counted seven rounds left in his .45 ACP sidearm. His M4 was damaged, and he couldn't immediately identify the problem. It didn't matter anyway—the carbine was out of ammunition.

Additionally, he had a Ka-Bar knife and one grenade. His radio was missing. The odds were not in his favor.

Mike could hear voices coming from his only escape route. The enemy knew they had the soldier trapped on the plateau, and they were determined to finish what they'd started. Screwing a suppressor onto the end of his .45 ACP, Mike watched as eight enemy fighters emerged from the brush and closed in on his position. He was ready to commence his work of death, but then he paused.

Although Mike wasn't a religious man, he momentarily bowed his head in a simple, desperate prayer. *Dear God. This is Mike. Please help me.*

In that short moment of deep internalization, Mike felt an unusual burst of resolve. It was the feeling he always got in the last mile of a marathon. There, alone and bleeding, Mike dug deep into his soul and found the will to live. He slowly opened his eyes and pulled the slide back on his handgun.

Just then, a round ricocheted off the rock directly over his head. The enemy yelled in the Pashto language and began moving quickly toward his position while still firing. The sound of AK-47s firing echoed all around the plateau. Returning fire, Mike dropped two men at seventy-five yards but missed a third. Four rounds left. Six of the enemy to go.

He moved from his position and started leading the enemy toward a rocky outcropping on the edge of a cliff. More rounds bounced off rocks, coming uncomfortably close. Securing himself behind a pine tree, he watched as the enemy continued to move cautiously toward his position. Mike was intentionally drawing the six men closer.

Watching each fighter's movements, he waited for them to make mistakes, especially small ones. One man briefly exposed himself, making for an easy fifty-yard shot to the head. Three rounds left. Five of the enemy to go.

Three of the men formed a single-file line and moved down a steep gully twenty yards from Mike's position. He pulled the pin on his grenade and lobbed it precisely into the enemy's line. The explosion rocked the gully, instantly killing two of the men while mortally wounding the third. Mike took aim and fired on the wounded man, finishing the job the grenade started. Two rounds left. Two of the enemy to go.

In the momentary chaos of the explosion, Mike failed to notice one of the enemy fighters flanking him. The man ran up on Mike and pulled the trigger of his AK-47—but the gun jammed, a rare event for the Russian-made rifle. The fighter didn't try to fix the jam—he just screamed and threw the rifle at Mike, hitting him square in the chest. Trying to regain his balance, Mike turned to fire on the man, but the terrorist rammed into Mike like a freight train, knocking the .45 ACP from his hand.

Both men rolled on the ground, trying to get on top of each other. Mike instantly realized he was fighting no ordinary soldier. This man had been schooled in martial arts. As they expertly worked each other for the upper hand, Mike desperately searched for the eighth and last man, unaccounted for in the fight. He could show up at any moment with his AK and end the wrestling matching with one shot.

The enemy pitched Mike over, and he caught a glance of what he'd feared. The eighth man had closed in, his AK at the ready. Mike arched for his .45 ACP and threw his elbow into his opponent's nose, temporarily disabling the man. Taking an off-balance aim at the new threat, he fired and missed. Mike refocused and aimed again. The second round hit the enemy fighter between the eyes, causing the man to fire off a round from his AK-47 and nearly hit his own comrade.

Quickly recovering from the hit to the nose, the last enemy fighter reengaged Mike, knocking the empty .45 from his hand and shoving a thumb into Mike's shoulder wound. Mike dropped to his knees and screamed out in pain. The enemy fighter threw his knee into Mike's chest, quickly following with another knee to Mike's face. Completely stunned, the Delta operative now lay helpless on the ground. Looking up through the pine trees, Mike was in more pain than he'd felt in a year. The Taliban fighter jumped on top of him and laughed. Blow after blow smashed into Mike's face.

Mike Mayberry was finished.

He watched helplessly as the terrorist pulled out his sidearm. In one last-ditch effort, Mike grabbed the man's wrist, digging deep inside for any strength he could muster. With his other hand, the enemy drew his knife from a hidden sheath. Mike returned the action by grabbing that arm as well. With a knife in one of the terrorist's hands and a gun in the other, the two warriors fought an epic battle of will and muscle.

Mike closed his eyes and entered a deep flow state, funneling all the strength he could find into his arms in a desperate last attempt to save his life. In that moment of complete concentration, his life flashed before his eyes.

The unmistakable crack of a .50-caliber Barrett sniper rifle brought Mike out of the deep trance.

The fighter, who'd been winning the battle of wills, arched as the bullet hit his chest. He dropped the gun and knife before he went limp and fell to the ground next to Mike. The cavalry had finally arrived.

"He's over here" was the last thing Mike heard as he jumped up from the couch and pulled a concealed .45 ACP from the small of his back. He swung wildly with the gun in front of him, trying to get a bearing on his location.

"Touchdown!" the TV said. "The Eagles win in overtime. What a game."

Mike stood with his weapon aimed at the TV monitor. He reached up and wiped the sweat from his eyes. "Breathe, Mike," he said to himself, his weapon still trained on the TV. After a few moments, he said, "It was just a dream," and lowered the gun.

Mike Mayberry had almost died several times, but for some reason the firefight on the Afghan plateau on that hot July day in 2002 was seared into his mind. Some people called it post-traumatic stress disorder, or PTSD. He didn't care for the term. Nonetheless, every time he had the recurring nightmare, he'd wake in a sweat with the pain in his old battle wounds reminding him how lucky he was to be alive.

~

After the dream, Mike went to bed and lay awake all night, staring at the stark white ceiling while holding his pistol. At 5:00 a.m. sharp, he rose, made a cup of black coffee, and walked out back to water and feed his two mustangs.

Trigger, named after Roy Rogers's famous show horse, stood still as Mike gently caressed his cheeks and neck. The gentle beasts brought an unusual solace that seemed to tame the PTSD he so fervently denied he had. Mike led the horses out of the old barn, leaned up against the pasture's rustic fence, drank his scalding-hot coffee, and breathed the humid Virginia air. He loved watching the sun rise over his diminutive empire.

After a quick shower, Mike stood in front of his dresser mirror and examined himself. He still trembled slightly from the nightmare. He closed his eyes and took in several deep breaths, putting himself in a flow state. After a few minutes of meditating, his shaking stopped.

Am I getting too old for this? Mike wondered to himself.

At forty-three, Mike Mayberry was an old man in the special-operations community, and he knew he wouldn't be allowed to command a field unit much longer. Brushing the thought aside, Mike adjusted his well-worn sport coat to further conceal the Glock 19 in his shoulder holster. Around his neck, he hung the white ID badge that identified him as an employee of the CIA.

He stepped back from the mirror and gave himself one last look. The eyes of a killer edged by deep crow's-feet. The wrinkled brow. The crooked nose. The scars. Mike frowned at the obvious wear on his tanned face. Special operations, clandestine service, and Father Time had not been kind to the lonely hero who was now late for an appointment with his demanding employer.

CHAPTER 17

CENTRAL INTELLIGENCE AGENCY
LANGLEY, VIRGINIA

An hour after leaving Bluemont, Mike made his way up the George Washington Memorial Parkway in his late-model F-150 pickup. The George Bush Center for Intelligence, located in Langley, Virginia, boasted over 2.5 million square feet contained in six aboveground levels. Unknown to most of the world, however, the vast majority of the center was spread out underground across the facility's two hundred and fifty-eight acres, making it larger than the Pentagon.

Most agency officers—not "agents," as they are commonly called by the public—referred to the CIA simply as "The Company." If you worked at the CIA, you were a Company man or woman. No one ever called the George Bush Center for Intelligence "CIA headquarters." The center was simply "Langley" or "HQ."

Mike didn't like spending time at HQ. To him, Langley was anything other than what books and movies made it out to be. Packed with thousands of analysts, scientists, accountants, engineers, human-resources people, and other staff, the CIA was almost as boring as a Fortune-500 company.

As a former Delta Force master sergeant, Mike preferred to be in the field. He liked doing rather than analyzing. He hated the debating, arguing, positioning, and endless negotiating that took place in the highly bureaucratic spy shop. And the lawyers—Mike loathed the lawyers. He was a simple man who just wanted to know where the bad guys were so he could kill them.

After a long walk and numerous security checks, Mike found himself in a familiar, nondescript hall in a remote underground level. An even more nondescript door in the hallway bore a placard that read simply Janitorial. There was a biometric thumb reader just above the door handle and a peephole in the door. Concealed in the peephole was an iris scanner. Mike placed his thumb on the biometric reader and looked into the peephole. The door clicked and opened.

Mike stepped inside. He was now standing in his favorite part of HQ: Orion's Spear, the CIA's ultra-geek working group. They were best of the best, led by Stew Brimhall, a CIA assistant director. In addition to the CIA, Orion's Spear was staffed by many other government agencies, including the NSA, the FBI, and NASA.

Orion's Spear's mission was classified above top secret, its staff operating outside the CIA's stifling bureaucratic construct. Their job was twofold. First, they debunked the conclusions of all other CIA analysts. Their job was to be contrarian on purpose, coming up with alternative analyses, finding missing or overlooked details, and, in general, just being annoying. Second, they took on the hardest and most sensitive cases inside the CIA.

Because of its mandate, Orion's Spear was universally hated by the intelligence bureaucracy inside and outside the CIA. The team members were more than just analysts. They were creative and extreme out-of-the-box thinkers and had extraordinarily diverse backgrounds in finance, computer science, linguistics, engineering, and other technical fields. Over the last forty years, Orion's Spear had foiled numerous terrorist plots, located Osama bin Laden, and directly prevented at least two world wars.

Mike maneuvered down a row of empty cubicles, finally finding himself in the bullpen, the room's main working area.

One of the bullpen's long walls was covered with tall metal shelving that held a respectable library on topics from computer programming to geopolitics. A glass wall exposed a vast server room. Another wall was peppered with whiteboards, maps, and monitors, while another was covered with random pictures, memes, and other amusing art. Mike noticed a South Park cartoon with Osama bin Laden in hell, a dated poster of Mulder and Scully from the hit '90s TV show *The X-Files*, and a grainy picture of the famous "Patty" photo of Bigfoot taken in 1967, among many other such artifacts.

But the poster Mike liked most was from The Empire Strikes Back. On it was an image of Han Solo firing his blaster at Darth Vader. Someone had typed up a caption and taped it to the bottom of the poster:

> *So Han's walking down the halls of Cloud City with his old friend Lando and her royal hotness. He's thinking he's in for a good time tonight. But the door to the banquet hall opens and there's Darth Vader. Han doesn't look incredulously at Lando. He doesn't run. He doesn't give up. What does Han do?*
>
> *He. Just. Starts. Shooting.*
>
> *Be like Han.*

Darn straight, thought Mike.

Stewart Brimhall came up next to Mike. Stew, as he liked to be called, was a bearded, thin, tall man over six foot five. He wore wire-frame glasses and had a perpetual look of surprise on his face. He was also a genius, with an IQ of at least 170. He held three PhDs and had been recruited by the CIA when he was in high school.

"You love that Han Solo poster," said Stew. "Someday I'm going to give it to you."

Mike raised his eyebrow. "I'm going to hold you to that."

The two made their way to the conference table, where a heated debate was taking place.

"There is no way!" yelled the short, stout Norman Stellar in a high, squeaky voice. "No way the *Enterprise* could withstand a full turbo-laser barrage by a Star Destroyer. Are you out of your Harvard mind, Elle?"

Elle Danley, a former runway model with three PhDs of her own, calmly took a sip of her Rockstar. "Which *Enterprise* are we discussing here,

Norman? If we're debating any and all models after the *Enterprise D*, then I am absolutely correct, without question. Furthermore, I am even more correct if we're discussing the Star Destroyer Alpha models first featured in *Revenge of the Sith*. Even a child knows I'm correct about that."

"Elle, your argument is—"

"Hey, guys," Mike shouted, interrupting the great geek debate.

"Oh, hey, Mike," Elle said nervously. "Just, uh, trying to settle a minor debate before you arrived. Thanks for coming."

Smiling, Mike shook hands with Stew, Elle, and Norman. He loved these nerds. "Well, guys, it's been a long time. Stew, whatta we got?"

The mood quickly grew serious.

"Well, a lot," Stew said. "I hope you have some time because I think we have a major problem. It all has to do with the image we captured of this Black character from the Brussels-hotel incident. I wanted to show you everything we have here before I put it in front of the director. As you can imagine, the nature of this material is highly sensitive—I mean really sensitive, Mike. We haven't decided the best way to lay all this out, so we're just going to show you."

"I'm all ears," said Mike, sitting down at the small table.

"Years ago, we got our hands on an AI developed by Google called Tensor Flow. We started customizing the AI's algorithms and built some pretty stellar pattern-recognition apps. We also incorporated a highly advanced facial-recognition tech developed by a few of our guys out of MIT.

"To beta-test the AI, we raided all the databases of federal law-enforcement agencies and started to look for basic patterns. Fortunately, that wasn't too hard. Since 9/11, these agencies all seem to cooperate much better than they did in the twentieth century—you know, for obvious reasons.

"At first, we found a bunch of easy connections, which we sent back to other agencies. The AI was uncovering numerous gold mines. We decided to stretch ourselves and start looking for some really out-there stuff. What better place to start than with the mysterious case of Ms. Black? So we started a facial algo run on your girlfriend, and we got a few hits."

Mike raised his eyebrows and watched the monitor.

"A video obtained by a joint DEA/FBI drug task force popped up in one of our queries. Last year, a DEA informant in the Sinaloa Cartel was murdered with a group of other low-level enforcers. But our informant was wearing a hi-def microcam the bad guys didn't recover. That camera caught the whole incident on video."

Stew hit the play button on his iPad, and a video screen-casted to a TV in front of them. The video showed two well-dressed gunmen slaughtering a group of Sinaloa Cartel members in a house outside Culiacan, Mexico. The assassins were total professionals and ruthlessly efficient. The entire event was over in eight seconds. The seven heavily armed cartel men didn't know what hit them.

"Look closely at these guys, Mike," said Stew.

"That's Black," said Mike.

"Yeah, but there's a lot more to see here," said Elle. "Look at their suits. Custom-tailored. Probably central European. Their haircuts—total Euro trash right there. Looks German, which matches the Brussels hotel audio and video. Black has the same hairstyle she did in the hotel. She almost looks male. The guy is wearing a pair of thousand-dollar Testani dress shoes. Check out the guns. Full auto, highly modified H&K MP-5s. Those are holographic sights similar to the ones you Ground Branch guys use—probably cost more than the gun. I'm sure they brought the weapons with them. Even for Mexico, this is pretty exotic. You can't pick up this type of hardware without attracting attention."

Stew picked up the thread. "So we took the video and ran their faces against our AI and the facial-recognition tech. Here's the beginning of the weird, man. We can't find them on any of the transportation system's security-video feeds. What does that mean to you?"

"Is this a pop quiz?" asked Mike. "It means they fly private."

"Exactly. So we started going through video feeds at private airports and private terminals. Of course, we started in Europe, and it didn't take long. These guys are flying in style. Private all the time. And it's not just them. There are others just like them, but what makes these guys so special is that we have them in the act not once but twice. The second go-around is even weirder."

"There's a group out of Salt Lake City called Operation Underground Railroad—" started Norman.

"Yeah, I've heard of them," Mike interjected. "It's run by a former Company guy, right?"

"Right," said Norman. "OUR sends undercover people into these sketchy places to pick up underage kids for sex. They're all wired up so when the deal is done with the pimp or handler, local law enforcement busts in and arrests everyone. OUR gets the kids into a program to save them from human trafficking, prostitution, et cetera. Anyway, they were running a job in Odessa—you know, the Ukraine."

"Yeah, I've heard of the Ukraine," said Mike, wishing he had never heard of the Ukraine.

"These OUR guys run into Black and, long story short, the OUR guys get killed," Norman continued. "So much for playing cops and robbers. But again, these OUR guys are wearing cameras. Black finds and destroys the cameras, but what they don't know is that OUR is transmitting the video feed. The OUR guys film everything for their legal protection. So the video isn't great, but it's Ms. Black, 89 percent probability."

Mike stood and walked over to the large monitor. "OK, so what do we have here? A couple of highly paid assassins? That's not new."

"We're just getting started, Mike," said Norman. "They don't show up in any known US or foreign military databases. Same with intelligence. Nothing. None of our counterparts in Europe even know about these guys. They don't exist."

Mike sat back down.

"It gets worse." Elle spoke up. "We started to build out a profile on Black and her trigger-happy buddies. Travel dates, locations, aircraft, manifests, hotels, and a bunch of other patterns. They travel mostly around Europe and the Americas. Sometimes we see them in Africa and Asia."

Stew pulled up more images.

"Frequently, they are traveling as what appears to be bodyguards for some very interesting people," continued Elle, pointing at an image on the screen. "This is the former prime minister of Norway. She is being accompanied by Black's pals to a meeting at the JW Marriott in Bogota, Columbia. This was six months ago. We don't know who she was meeting with, but intel says some high-level cartel leaders were staying in the hotel at the same time."

"Then there's this old guy, Benson Hancock," interjected Norman. A picture of Benson Hancock appeared on the screen. "He's European aristocracy going back hundreds of years. Here he is entering a building in Luxembourg that's headquarters to three of the top-ten largest porn sites on the internet. Here's the same guy a month later meeting with Kevin Willis, a former Silicon Valley wunderkind who turned to the dark side and runs the world's largest illegal internet-based gambling operation out of Indonesia."

"So this Hancock guy is kinky and likes to gamble," said Mike. "So what?"

"Notice his bodyguards?" asked Elle, taking over the iPad and projecting more images onto the monitor. "Look at all the other GQ-looking killers. We've been following them around as well. The Congo, Buenos Aires, Panama City, Chicago, New York, London, Berlin, and on and on. Everywhere these guys turn up, people die. They love to suicide people, make it look like the target killed themselves, but when they have to take out a group or a location, like a building, it usually gets ugly."

Images of dead people, destroyed buildings, and burning cars flashed across the screen.

"OK, Mike, this is where it gets really weird," said Stew. "We started to follow this Benson Hancock guy around. He's headquartered in Zurich. He offices in this unusual glass-and-steel high-rise in the city's industrial zone. It sticks out like a sore thumb against Zurich's historic architecture.

"It appears that about every six or eight months, there's some kind of big-deal meeting that happens in this building in Zurich. We can't see the VIPs who enter, but we used airport and traffic cams to ID some of the attendees. We also raided flight manifests to find out where the planes were coming from and who was on board, when possible. Here are some of the attendees."

Stew began to display faces on the screen—European royalty, former heads of state, CEOs, politicians, heads of Europe's biggest aristocratic families.

"So what is this?" asked Mike. "Some kind of foundation or NGO?"

"We don't think so," said Norman. "Again, look at the bodyguards."

Mike stood and looked closely. "That's not good. There's Black and the other guy who took out that Sinaloa Cartel house."

"Yep, exactly," said Stew.

Mike put his hands on his hips. "You haven't shown me the worst yet, have you."

The three geeks glanced at each other. In nearby cubicles, several analysts put on their headphones and slouched before their monitors, typing furiously.

"No," said Stew. "Here's a few more pictures, Mike. I don't need to explain the implications."

Appearing on the screen was former White House chief of staff Richard Boone and former national security adviser Roger Cowen. Finally, several images of former US president Royce Jefferson Lennox appeared on the screen. Stew quickly removed the image, and the screen went blank.

"What is this?" Mike said, turning to the three sitting quietly beside him.

"Mike, we've tied it all together," said Stew. "We don't know how deep it goes, but it appears that what's happening in this building is directly tied to a massive global cartel dealing in drugs, weapons, human slavery, illegal gambling, and who knows what else. I think we've only scratched the surface of what these guys are involved in. We have no idea what they're even called. We emphatically believe that this goes way deeper than drugs and kids, Mike. We think these guys are planning something."

"Planning what?" Mike asked. "Look, maybe these guys are using the president as cover. He just shows up twice a year to do the charity bit and has no idea what the inside guys are really working on. Like Bill Clinton and the Laureate International Universities scandal. He's being used."

"False," said Norman.

"Yeah, we thought that might be the case until we got this," said Stew. He pulled up an audio player on the monitor and activated the room's Sonos audio system. "Several months ago," Stew said, "we started to monitor Lennox's comms."

"Whoa, whoa, are you freaking kidding me, you guys?" Mike interrupted. "Do you know how much trouble you could get into? How did you even get ops participation? Satellites? The director's sign-off? What about the lawyers?"

"We're Orion's Spear, Mike," Stew said in a serious tone, leaning back in his chair and adjusting his wireframe glasses. "We have a top-secret charter. We operate completely outside the intelligence construct, so we don't get caught up in all the bureaucracy crap. Our guys come from a bunch of other agencies, even ones you may not know about. It's intentionally designed like this. Oh, and we have access to our own ops and intelligence assets to get what we need."

Mike was stunned. He hadn't known the extent of the operations going on in this underground room. "And here I thought Ground Branch had all the fun and toys," he said. "I hope I never piss you guys off." He was serious.

"We discovered Lennox had a phone we didn't know about," Stew continued. "We started to monitor the device, but it's highly encrypted AES-256 bit. Working with our NSA counterparts, we were able to grab a single phone call. It was pure luck we even got that. So we brute-forced the encryption using the supercomputer in the NSA's Utah facility. After several months, we were finally able to make out some parts of the conversation. We couldn't have done it without the Google AI."

Stew pushed the play button. They heard a conversation with President Lennox and Benson Hancock discussing agenda items for the former president's upcoming trip to Zurich. They talked about when billions in payments would be made. How to compromise certain officials in the Democratic Party, the NSA, CIA, and FBI. The status of a four-hundred-kilo meth shipment bound for the Midwest of the United States. Foreign officials Lennox recommended blackmailing. A gruesome assassination plot Lennox personally schemed up for an ongoing problem in Mexico City. And finally, details about the fifteen-year-old prostitute who would be keeping the former president company while he was in Zurich.

When the file finished playing its damning contents, the three analysts sat staring at Mike, waiting for him to say something.

Mike sighed, and his shoulders slumped. He stared across the room at the poster of a young Dana Scully from *The X-Files*. He badly missed the '90s. Things were much simpler back then. "Play it again," he said in a soft tone.

While Stew played the file again, Mike stared stoically at the floor.

"What do we do, Mike?" asked Stew. The others sat motionless, still watching Mike.

Mike stood and turned his back. In almost a whisper, he said, "What we always do, Stew. Burn it down. No quarters given."

"What does that mean?" whispered Elle as Mike walked away.

Stew looked at Elle. "It means we kill them all."

CHAPTER 18

PROVO MUNICIPAL AIRPORT
PROVO, UTAH

The woman was once again present in Chris's dream. She was slender and faceless, her hair long and black. As in past dreams, she wore a white lab coat, but this time something was different. The face started to form, but it was blurry. He tried to focus on her developing face. Then the sleek Gulfstream 450 landed with a thud, and Chris startled awake. As he rubbed the sleep from his eyes, an awful realization overcame him: today was his mother's birthday.

"How much time do we have before we need to be on campus?" he asked Professor Alba.

"I think we have an hour or so."

They deplaned and found a black Chevrolet Suburban waiting for them. The driver, dressed in a professional black suit, helped them load their belongings into the vehicle, and then they headed for Brigham Young University.

"Hey, buddy," Chris said to the driver. "I need to make a stop before BYU. I forgot it's my mother's birthday, and I need to pick something up. By the way, if you have any suggestions, they'd be much appreciated."

The driver glared at him through the rearview mirror, and Professor Alba turned his attention to his iPad, pretending to be busy.

"Well, there's a mall on the way," the driver finally said. "We could stop at Dillard's. I bought my fiancée something there just last week."

"What did you get her?"

"Something from Clinique."

"Clinique? Dillard's? I've never heard of them, but let's go."

The driver and professor waited in the SUV as Chris entered the enormous department store. Maneuvering through the men's clothing department and past some luggage, Chris could not remember a time he had been in a store this large. Somehow, he found himself in the fragrance and cosmetics department. It was a Tuesday afternoon, and the vast department was empty except for the mostly female employees. They eyed him as he approached the Clinique counter and cleared his throat.

The woman behind the counter had her back to him as she arranged products on the central display. When she turned around and looked directly at Chris, he was immediately stricken with an emotion he didn't understand. His pulse quickened, his palms started to sweat, and his stomach got queasy.

She was a slender five foot five, with black hair that reached the middle of her back. She had a French manicure, and her eyes were a vibrant hazel. Her cheeks were light red, and a pronounced jawline edged her beautiful face. But what struck Chris most were her perfect lips. He had never seen anything like those lips. They were not too thin or too plush, her upper lip cresting in a heart shape perfectly symmetrical with the center line of her nearly straight nose. She was wearing what looked like an all-white lab coat, and her nameplate read Leah.

My dream wasn't a lab coat, Chris realized. *It was a uniform. It's her. It has to be her.*

"Hi. How can I help you?" asked Leah.

"I'm sorry. My phone. I need to take this really quick," he lied.

Turning around, he pulled out his phone and looked into the black screen while he tried to compose himself. *Breathe, Chris,* he told himself. He took several deep breaths and then replaced his phone in the pocket of his gray Hickey Freeman suit. Mustering his courage, he turned back to the woman at the counter.

"I'm sorry about that." He laughed awkwardly. "That was rude of me."
Leah raised her eyebrows and just stared at him.

"Um, well, I'm looking for something for my mom. Today's her birthday, and my driver—I mean, my friend told me he got something here for someone and that I needed to come to Dillard's. I mean Clinique. Am I making any sense?"

"You've never been here before, have you," Leah said.

"No, is it that obvious?"

"It's fine. We get a lot of men in here who have no idea what to do. How about I give you a few ideas, and then you can decide what to get your mom?" Turning, Leah started carefully pulling products from the fancy display.

Chris's mind was in full abort mode. Adamic math was popping all around him, and his brain was measuring the mathematical configuration of the entire cosmetics department. At the same time, he was trying to act as normal as he possibly could for this woman—this complete, beautiful vision of a woman.

"What's your budget?" Leah asked.

"Excuse me? Oh, money. Sorry. Well, I'm not sure how much all this costs, but how about $1,000 or less?" He shrugged, looking for her approval.

She laughed, obviously thinking he was joking. He wasn't. He had no idea how much anything in front of him cost.

"OK, here are a few ideas." Leah gestured at the products on the counter. "With any purchase over thirty-five dollars, you get a free promotional gift."

"I'll take all of this," Chris said, pointing at the products Leah had chosen.

"Uh, OK, that's going to be close to $500. Is that OK? You weren't joking about that $1,000 budget, were you."

"Well, I was just trying to sound cool. I've been a real pain to my mom most of my life, so I better cough up the cash and just get her all of this, don't you think?"

"That's cute. What's your name?"

"Chris. Chris Thomas."

"I'm Leah."

"Nice to meet you. Look, I'm sorry I'm acting so strange. It's just that I have to give a guest lecture at BYU. It's my first, and I'm really nervous about it. I haven't slept in two days, worrying about what to say. I'm a little off at the moment. I apologize." Of course, the lecture wasn't the thing making Chris nervous, but it was a sufficient cover story.

"No need to apologize," Leah said, smiling. "So, what do you do for a living?"

"I'm a research student at Stanford. I'm speaking on algorithmic models for studying cures for cancer."

"Stanford. That's impressive," Leah said. "You look really young to be a researcher. My dad's an oral surgeon."

"Oh, great. I'm very interested in oral maxillofacial surgical techniques, especially related to 3D printable mandible reconstruction."

"You sound like my dad." She smiled. "Maybe you guys should meet sometime."

"Yeah, well, thanks for all this." Chris paid, then carefully lifted the surprisingly heavy Clinique bag from the countertop. He took a few steps toward the exit but then turned around. Leah still stood there, smiling at him.

Chris marched back to her. "Hey, look, I'm supposed to attend a really boring dinner after the lecture, then I have to catch a flight. What if I duck out of that dinner and we grab a bite to eat?"

He regretted it as soon as the words left his mouth. He knew rejection was coming fast, and he had no way to escape it. He was such a fool. There was no way this beautiful woman was going to say yes. She had to have a boyfriend.

"Well, look. I have a boyfriend . . ."

Chris, you idiot, he thought to himself.

"But I've been thinking about dumping him. He plays football, and he's really into himself."

Chris tried to conceal the sudden elation that entered his whole being.

"So, yeah," Leah continued. "Sure. Why not? Let's do it. Here, give me your phone." She stretched out her hand.

Chris unlocked his iPhone and handed it over without a word. As Leah typed quickly on the device, Chris attempted to conceal his shock. Not only did she actually have a boyfriend, but she was still going to have dinner with him. He hoped Professor Alba wouldn't mind if he took the Suburban.

Leah handed back the phone. "My number and address are in your contacts now. I'm Leah Bennion. Do you want to pick me up around seven?"

"I don't have another change of clothes," Chris said. "I'll be in this ridiculous suit. I guess I could shed the tie and dress down a bit?"

"No, not at all. I can't remember the last time I went on a date with a guy in a suit. You're perfect the way you are. Do you like Thai food?"

"I love Thai," he said. "I think I might be part Thai."

Leah smiled and laughed again. "OK, Thai it is. Seven o'clock, my place."

"Deal."

Chris started to slowly back away from the counter. He couldn't take his eyes off her. Then he backed right into a fragrance display case, almost knocking it over. Recovering, he turned red and looked at Leah. She had her hands up to her mouth, trying not to laugh out loud. He waved quickly, and she gave a slight wave back as he rushed for the exit.

They stood at the front door of Leah's apartment. It was 1:00 a.m., and they had been out for hours, just talking. Chris had never been with someone so easy to talk to. Since the accident, conversation with women had been a challenge.

"Do you smell that?" Leah inhaled deeply as raindrops fell all around them. "I love the smell of rain."

"Yeah. It's called petrichor. That's the scientific name for the smell of rain."

"How do you know that? That is so weird."

Chris shrugged his shoulders and changed the subject. "Sorry to keep you out so late."

"I don't go to BYU, so no lame rules here."

"Well, that's good. I need to keep you in your bishop's good graces."

Leah smiled. "OK, Chris Thomas from Oregon who goes to Stanford and went on a mission to Florida and has a driver." She glanced over his shoulder at the Suburban parked on the street. "Time to call it a night."

"OK, Leah Bennion who works at Clinique and has beautiful hair and eyes and is from Park City and apparently is going to dump her football boyfriend. When can I take you out again?" As he spoke, he moved closer. His courage had steadily increased as the night progressed.

"You live in the Bay Area. How in the world would I date you?"

"Oh, well, I got, um, a research fellowship at BYU tonight, and I have to come here frequently for, uh, research. So I'm going to be here a lot, pretty much all the time." It was a total fabrication.

"Hmm," Leah said. "When are you back in town?"

"This weekend. So how about Friday night? Or will you still have a football-player boyfriend three days from now?"

"I don't think so," she said shyly.

"Well, since this is a first date, and since you technically still have a boyfriend, I don't think it would be appropriate to kiss you." Chris couldn't believe the words coming out of his mouth.

Just then, the rain started coming down harder. Standing about five feet apart, they looked at each other for a few serious moments. Then Leah stepped forward and gently kissed Chris on the cheek. "Pick me up at seven on Friday," she whispered in his ear. Then she turned and rushed through her apartment door.

~

As promised, Chris was back in Provo on Friday at 7:00 p.m. They went out for Thai food again on Saturday. On Sunday, he went to church with her, and then they spent the rest of the day exploring Provo Canyon. As they walked up the trail to Bridal Veil Falls, Chris took her hand. Leah kept talking as she gently squeezed his hand, accepting the gesture.

Chris genuinely enjoyed being with Leah. There were no awkward pauses or boring moments. It was effortless and fun. She made him feel normal, like the way he imagined he was before the coma.

The sunshine beamed down, engulfing the narrow canyon. The Provo River flowed gently next to the trail. Sunlight bounced through the trees and off the canyon walls that shot up a thousand feet just south of the trail. The sound of birds and the fresh scent of nature filled the air. As they continued walking up the paved trail toward the waterfall, passing families and other couples, Chris stopped dead in his tracks. He broke his grip with Leah and just stood in the middle of the paved trail, looking around wildly.

"What are you doing?" asked Leah, concerned by the sudden odd behavior.

"It's gone," said Chris quietly.

"What's gone? Are you having a migraine or something?"

Some passersby on the trail gave him a confused look.

Chris rubbed his eyes and squinted for a few moments. Leah reached up and gently pulled his hand away from his face. "Look at me. What is it? What's wrong with your eyes?"

"The math is gone," said Chris.

"The math?"

Chris took Leah by the hand and led her to a bench beside the trail. "Yes, the math in my vision. Ever since I woke up from the coma, I see math and strange symbols in my line of sight almost all the time."

"Math?"

"Yeah. I know it sounds strange. It's called Adamic mathematics, but I call it the Adamic Code. It came to me when I was in my coma. Look, it's hard to talk about because I don't fully understand it, but a couple years ago I started putting the pieces together. Then I started using the code to write software. I'm writing a new form of artificial intelligence using the Adamic Code. It's radically advanced. There's nothing like it in the world. I'm not sure how to say this, Leah, but I think God gave it to me."

"God gave it to you?" asked Leah, sounding unconvinced.

"I know it sounds crazy, so I usually don't talk about it." He turned to face Leah more directly. She listened intently. "I know I can tell you the truth. You won't make fun of me or tell me it's just my imagination. My brain is a raging fire of the unimaginable. Everything I'm building is based on Adamic math. It's real. I'm going to change the world with it, Leah."

"It actually makes a lot of sense to me." Leah seemed surprisingly unaffected by the revelation.

"Really?" asked Chris, shocked she hadn't run away. "I'm thinking back to our first date and the other night. It was gone then, too, but I didn't even realize it. I guess I was really into the moment with you. And then the math came back later."

"So what you're saying is that I'm your kryptonite?" Leah smiled. "Your superpowers disappear when you're with me?"

"I guess so," said Chris. "When I'm with you, I just feel normal. You have no idea how good it feels."

"You mean when the math leaves your vision?"

"I mean just being with you."

Leah blushed and ducked her head. Then she looked back up at Chris. "Come on." She took his hand and leapt up from the bench. "You'll love the waterfall. Let's go."

Chris had to return to Stanford that night aboard a private plane Leah didn't know about. He wasn't ready to tell her everything just yet. The relationship was still too new.

Standing on the steps of her apartment, he held her close. She fit perfectly into him with her head tucked under his chin. The smell of her hair mesmerized him. He wanted to ask her permission to kiss her, but he thought that would be lame. He was nervous and overthinking the situation. He didn't want to risk crossing the line.

Finally, Leah settled it for him. She pulled back from their embrace and went in for their first kiss, completely shocking Chris. He'd had girlfriends in high school and thought he could remember kissing them, but he had no recollection of the feelings he was now experiencing as brought on by connecting with a woman at the lips.

Leah pulled back and looked at him. After a moment, he leaned in for a longer kiss. Chris had never felt anything so amazing in his entire life.

At that moment, no words were spoken. He knew, and he knew that she knew. Although they had just met, they would spend the rest of their lives together.

CHAPTER 19

Professor Martin Alba stood in the doorway of room 300 in the Stanford Computer Science Building. Wearing headphones and typing furiously on his custom-built laptop, Chris didn't notice him from where he sat on the couch.

For years, this room had been a popular windowless conference room, but the school president had given it to Chris. Naturally, the faculty and staff had been put out about a student—even of Chris's caliber—being given a conference room to use as his own personal office. They were even more put out when Chris moved the conference table out into the narrow hall and brought his old office furniture—a heavy wood desk his grandfather had given him, industrial-steel bookshelves he found on Craigslist, and a dumpster couch that didn't even look frat-house worthy—into the former conference room.

Dr. Alba quickly sized up the office. The desk was covered with computers, food wrappers, and other junk. It was obvious Chris had been making good use of Uber Eats. The steel bookshelves were packed to capacity with tomes on every topic from the Roman Empire to quantum physics to law. In fact, Chris had started to stack books in front of them.

The floor of the office was covered in Amazon boxes, robotics parts, random packaging trash, an old Trek bike, a boost-it board, crushed Coke cans, and an array of computer equipment. Most of the fluorescent bulbs in the ceiling had been removed, and a large natural-light lamp next to the dumpster couch provided the majority of the room's limited lighting. The wall above the horrible couch was one massive whiteboard covered in strange equations and algorithms.

The doctor knocked on the doorframe, but Chris didn't hear it. Alba figured he must have been sitting on that couch for at least twelve hours straight listening to ridiculous '80s music, probably Metallica or Def Leppard. His black AC/DC shirt had a mustard stain, his eyes were swollen and bloodshot, and his nails badly needed to be clipped.

The professor stepped farther into the office and yelled, "Chris!"

Chris jumped up off the couch and ripped the headphones from his ears. "You scared the crap out of me," he said in an annoyed tone.

"Sorry. Other than jumping on top of you, I couldn't think of another way to get your brain out of that computer."

Chris glanced down at the laptop, then looked back at his visitor. "I was just trying to debug some open-source code that's giving me problems." He closed the laptop and set it on top of some trash on his desk.

"Can I come in? We need to talk."

"This sounds serious," said Chris. "Grab the door."

Alba gently closed the office door while Chris kicked some trash out of the way, making a trail to the couch. Chris sat in his office chair, facing his mentor.

"I love what you've done with the place," Alba said sarcastically, gesturing around the room. "It's true you got this couch out of a dumpster, yes?"

"Yeah, but I used a couple bottles of Febreze on it. It's fine."

Alba raised a doubtful brow.

"Every time the janitor comes by, it's a bad time," Chris said. "He takes a few pieces of trash, but I'm just too busy to have him in the room, you know?"

"I wouldn't know. The janitorial staff cleans the building at 3:00 a.m. when I'm usually fast asleep. This is one of the many things I want to talk about, you see. I meant to talk to you in Utah, but you slipped away for a date."

The doctor leaned forward, clasped his hands together, and looked at Chris intensely for a few moments. "Chris. What are you?"

"Human, I think?"

"No, what I mean is, what are you? Medical researcher, mathematician, physicist, inventor, software engineer? What are you?"

Chris had long felt a hunch that this conversation was coming. He had wondered how long the school and, in particular, the computer-science college would put up with his antics. He wasn't going to class, he wasn't playing nice with the faculty or students, and he treated the campus like it was his own personal science experiment.

Sitting across from his mentor, he felt some negative emotions start to well up inside him. He shook his head and looked at Alba, one of the only men he respected on campus. He wanted to explode, but then something deep inside him—it sounded like his grandpa's voice—said it was time to stop, humble up, and listen very closely.

After a few awkward moments, Chris leaned forward in his chair, returning the intense look. "Well, I'm not sure, but everything I do is related to math. Math is the foundation of all science. It's nature's code. But I'm practically a pariah in the math school, so I don't spend any time there."

"And why is that, Chris?" Dr. Alba asked in his distinctive accent. "Why are you a pariah?"

"Maybe because I'm always fighting with the faculty about mathematical theory? You know I'm right most of the time, Doc. They just don't like to be proven wrong. They want to look down their noses at me. They hate it when a community-college kid from Oregon makes them feel like they should go back to the seventh grade. And that guy from Caltech—he's the worst of them all. You know what they call me? 'Community!' It really pisses me off."

"I think this is a good place to start—with this chip you have on your shoulder."

Chris looked at him, confused. Alba stood and walked around the room, glancing at the computers, the whiteboard containing math almost like ancient hieroglyphics, and the trash scattered everywhere. Then he sat back down on the couch and gave Chris a serious look.

"This is your little kingdom, this room," the doctor said. "As long as you exist here, you don't have to venture out into the real world. You don't have to interact with faculty members who you think hate you. You don't have to talk to the other students. You don't have to go to class, correct inaccuracies, or suffer boredom. This is your little kingdom, and it's kind of pathetic, Chris."

"Well, I don't think I'm avoiding people," said Chris defensively.

"Oh, you are. You've decided that you're smarter than everyone and that thousands of the world's best and brightest are dolts compared to your intellectual eminence."

Letting out a long sigh, Chris ran his fingers through his greasy hair. He hadn't showered in four days. "Well, I'm not sure how to react to that accusation."

"It's more of an observation." The doctor leaned forward. "Can I be frank, Chris?"

"I thought you already were?"

"It's time to change course, my friend."

Chris sat back in his chair and waited for the hammer to drop. Was he about to get kicked out of Stanford? He wasn't sure he could handle the embarrassment.

"The president, the academic dean, and I have been discussing what to do with you."

Chris braced himself. He felt devastated, and it took everything to hold it in.

"We have decided you are one of the best and brightest, maybe even the best and the brightest, to ever walk this campus. You have sparked intellectual conversations, challenged conventional thinking, and entirely upended a very lazy and narcissistic academic bureaucracy. The Office of Technology Licensing loves you. The intellectual property you have developed at Stanford has been licensed to numerous corporations. These licenses are bringing in millions per month to you and the school."

Chris blushed. He was very proud of this one bright spot. The money was really piling up. He didn't have many gaudy possessions, but he'd splurged and bought himself an amazing house in Los Gatos on five acres. However, he rarely spent time there—the house was mostly an investment. He'd also bought himself a black, half-ton GMC Denali truck with a 6.2-liter V8. His other big splurge was fractional plane ownership in NetJets. He hated flying commercial, but for some reason, flying private embarrassed him, so he never talked about it, including not to Leah.

Most of all, Chris was using the money to take care of his family. His parents, who'd previously had no retirement plan, were now traveling the world, something they never thought they would do. He was also covering all his grandparents' medical bills. Grandpa's cancer was progressing, and Grandma's mind was slipping. Chris had hired a full-time nurse, chef, and live-in maid to take care of their every need. A few months ago in Colorado, his recently married little sister had cried as she hugged her brother tight. They were standing in front her new dream home, compliments of her big brother. These things made Chris happier than anything else.

The professor continued. "We believe that Stanford, and by extension most of the academic world, is better because of you. Here's what we're going to do. I am going to take a more active role in mentoring you. We need to knock off some of the sharp edges and soften the tone. We need to dial in the message. We need to tame the beast, if you will."

Chris said nothing but listened intently.

"We need to tune you up and get your EQ to align with your IQ."

"My EQ? What's an EQ?" In all his reading, Chris couldn't recall coming across the term.

"It's your emotional quotient, the measurement of your capacity to internalize, positively project, and positively manage your emotions. First and most importantly, a person with high EQ has empathy. They also have extraordinary self-awareness, are highly effective communicators, and are practiced in defusing conflict. We need to fix your EQ. Don't feel bad. This is a common problem with high-IQ people like yourself."

"My grandpa said something to me about empathy," said Chris.

"Your grandfather sounds like a wise man."

Plenty of people had taken an interest in Chris throughout his life, but the relationships usually didn't stick. He'd always thought it was the other person's fault. What he was hearing now was that it was his fault. Other than his grandfather, no one had ever talked to Chris like this. Even though it hurt, it was refreshing.

"Your blog posts, videos, and tweets are like a wildfire of untamed consciousness," Alba continued. "You have no filter. Yes, some of it is brilliant, but a lot of it is downright embarrassing. And you're a total fool for the trolls. You really take their bait hook, line, and sinker. And that's why they love to come at you so much. They know they're going to get a wicked-sharp reaction, and that's just what they're looking for."

Alba was right. Twitter was Chris's digital MMA Octagon.

"You obviously love a good fight, but are you actually fighting the good fight, or are you just being a child? Mostly it's the latter. I'm sorry, we have to fix this. OK, please say something now."

"I'm not sure what to say." Chris rubbed his forehead. "You know, I kind of want to be mad, but I'm not for some reason. I'm having a strange moment of internalization and reflection. I've never really felt this before. I don't want people to hate me. I know some do, but I really don't want that. I go off half-cocked all the time, but I just don't know how to tame my mind or my mouth." Chris couldn't believe what he was saying. It didn't even sound like him, but the voice inside him was helping him accept the truth: he needed to change, and the time was now. "Sorry, I'm all over the board here. Am I making any sense?"

"Part of the problem may be that you never fully healed from your brain damage," Alba said. "We'll need to work on that."

Chris had never considered this. Was his traumatic brain injury still affecting him?

"But the first step is cleaning up this office. Next, let's get you out more. It's time to engage. It's time to be nice. To be approachable. Offer help where it's needed. It's time to start being a teacher and stop being a critic. Anyone can be an armchair quarterback. Anyone can go on TV and spout off about national politics. Anyone can write an emotionally critical blog post, but Chris, do you really respect those people? No one likes the guy yelling from the stands; everyone respects the guys on the field playing the game. It's time to suit up."

Chris nodded.

"Now, if I may be personal here," Alba continued, "I think it would be good for you to start dating. I also think you should go back to church."

Chris looked at him, feeling a little stunned. He hadn't mentioned Leah, and they rarely discussed religion.

"You know I don't subscribe to religion," Alba continued, "but I know yours is important to you. I also know you haven't been partici- pating consistently. I really wonder if your lack of commitment is healthy. I think it's time you internalized your commitment to God. A little reli- gion in your weekly schedule, I believe, may do you some good, wouldn't you agree?"

"Yes, for sure," said Chris humbly.

"Chris, your life story is the stuff of movies, and it's only just begun. A boy who was a nobody suffers a horrible brain injury only to return from the dead six months later with dormant areas of his mind completely awakened, and he's suddenly inventing mathematical theories the brightest minds in a thousand years have never considered. So let's not throw all this away over a dumb video or blog post that ruins your professional reputa- tion. Agreed?"

Chris nodded again.

"I have a proposal," Alba continued. "I want you to come to the World Economic Forum in Davos in two weeks. I'm going to arrange an interview with one of the largest medical charities in the world. They're working on an important project, and they are stuck. They need someone like you to help them. It's a paid consulting deal. It's also another opportunity for you to show the world you're ready to do some good with what's between your ears."

"I've never been to Europe before," Chris said. "That sounds really interesting."

"Before that, I've made arrangements for you to be interviewed at Code/Talk in San Francisco in a few days."

"What's Code/Talk?"

"Don't worry about it." The professor stood up. "I'll get you details later. And one more thing. You and I will meet once a week for a mentoring session. How about 10:00 a.m. on Thursdays? Good?" Not waiting for a reply, the doctor walked out, but then he came back. "Oh, and Chris, please shower daily. Brush your teeth. Stop sleeping in here. You have a nice house. Get on a real schedule, OK?" The doctor disappeared again.

Chris was totally dumbfounded. He sat motionless in his chair, trying to process what had just happened. A strange sense of relief filled his being. He had just been tossed a lifeline. Chris was no longer stranded alone on an island.

Breaking the trance, he stood and began picking up trash from the floor.

FINAL INTERLUDE

ROTHSCHILD BANK BUILDING
ZURICH, SWITZERLAND
DECEMBER 1946

The Rothschild Bank building at Zollikerstrasse 181 in Zurich had been the banking family's main European headquarters and the Illuminati's secret headquarters for over three hundred years. The triangular building's beautiful architecture rose over four stories, and the west-facing windows looked out over a scenic ancient lake. Atop the building was a single circular, windowless conference room reserved for only the most important meetings. The room was fifty feet in diameter and domed. A priceless chandelier "procured" from the Palace of Versailles hung gracefully from the center of the dome. In typical classic European style, the walls were covered in centuries-old art. The round, finely carved conference table was, in and of itself, a brilliant masterpiece.

On this winter evening, twenty men sat around the conference table. A member of the Rothschild family stood and raised his hand. The group concluded their siloed conversations and turned their attention to the elderly man.

"Gentlemen, welcome to the 524th annual meeting of the society. I understand the difficulty in traveling at the moment. Post-war Europe is truly a hideous disaster area. Fortunately, Zurich was left mostly unscathed except for that so-called accidental bombing by the Americans. I assure you the journey will be worth it.

"This meeting comes at a pivotal moment in history. As always, financing both sides of a war has been extremely profitable for our collective organizations. Now we need to decide how to divide up the Nazi assets. We need to decide how we will control postwar Europe. We also need to decide how to deal appropriately with the Soviets, as they must fall in line with our plans." He paused. "Yes, well, first, welcome to Mr. Benson Hancock." Rothschild extended his hand to Benson, who sat across the table. "He has taken his father's seat on the council. Mr. Hancock, we express our deepest condolences on the passing of your parents."

Benson sat stoically as all eyes turned to him.

"This is a seat the Hancock family has held for over two hundred years," continued Rothschild. "Mr. Benson Hancock was initiated into our society many years ago. Although he is young, he was instrumental in helping move millions of American dollars into the Nazi war machine. Of course, much of that money ended up in our coffers."

The room erupted in laughter.

"Well then, Mr. Hancock. Would you like to address the council?"

"Yes, Mr. Rothschild. I am humbled by the opportunity."

The elderly Rothschild sat gingerly as Benson stood and adjusted the vest of his three-piece suit. Most of the men in the room were at least twice or even three times his age. He knew most of them felt he was clearly out of his league and not worthy to hold a seat at the society's table. None of that would matter after today. Benson pushed in his chair, lit his pipe, and started to talk as he walked slowly around the table.

"Gentlemen, four years ago, in a dark sewer under Brooklyn, New York, I saw the light. It came in the form of an ancient book—a codex, if you will. That book has completely consumed me. The contents are written in an obscure, lost language I quickly learned. Its authors were the leaders of a secret society, one not unlike ours. The religion of this secret society was laid out before me. I learned their secret works of darkness. I adopted their superior philosophies. I swore to uphold their solemn oaths. I pledged my allegiance to their brilliant laws. I am chosen for a higher calling, and it is my sacred duty to bring to pass the words of this book."

Benson stopped talking for a moment as he continued circling the table. Some of the men appeared intrigued by what he was saying. Most looked bored and sat lazily in their fine black suits, puffing on their cigars. They just wanted the kid to finish so they could get on with the real business at hand.

"This society is known as the Order of Baphomet," continued Benson. That got most everyone's attention. The council members looked around at each other, confused by Benson's words.

"Ah yes, Sir Hancock." Rothschild raised his palm. "May I ask where you are going with this?"

"Here," said Benson as he turned and opened the double doors, the room's only doors. He beckoned to the man standing outside the door. Council members made sounds of protest as the tall, brutish, red-blotched man entered the room. He wore a long black trench coat.

"What is the meaning of this?" Rothschild demanded. "Who is this vagabond? Explain yourself, sir."

"Yes, I was about to." Benson closed and locked the doors, sealing off the room. "This man is Cain. You've all heard of him before."

The men murmured to each other, now even more confused. Cain stood silent, looking over the room.

"Ah yes, I forgot my audience," Benson said. "Not a lot of Sunday-school types in this room. Right, then, let's rewind to the Old Testament. To Genesis. This is Cain, the man who slew his wicked brother, Abel. Cain is now Master Mahan, cursed to walk the earth and never die. Any of this ringing a bell, gentlemen?"

Several of the men broke into laughter.

"You mean to say this tosser is the Cain of the Old Testament?" yelled a council member in a distinctive British accent. "Are you mad?"

"Enough of this tomfoolery, Mr. Hancock!" said Rothschild, rising slowly from his chair. "Your attempt to hoodwink this council and waste our time has gone far enough. You and this—this man will leave the chamber immediately. We will deal with you later."

"No," Benson said calmly.

"Excuse me?"

"I said no. We have business to finish here. Cain, if you would, please."

Cain opened his trench coat, revealing a Thompson submachine gun tied under his shoulder. It held a one-hundred-round drum and was fitted with a long black suppressor. Cain racked the slide on top of the gun and raised the weapon. Several of the men stood in shock. Others gasped and raised their arms as if to surrender. One man screamed. Cain only smiled as he pulled the trigger.

The automatic weapon spat out round after round, tearing apart the room's occupants one by one. Paperwork and wood exploded as rounds crashed into the conference table. On the walls, priceless artwork was ripped to shreds by the .45-caliber bullets. Blood and gore soon filled the table and floor. In the gun smoke and confusion, several injured survivors tried to reach the room's only door, but Cain methodically put several rounds in each of their heads. A wide, crazed smile was the last thing each man saw.

Holding his Luger, Benson stood watch by the door to make sure no one tried to enter or leave. The Tommy gun was suppressed, but the dying men were making a lot of noise. Benson prayed to Baphomet that their secluded location on top of the building would ensure they weren't heard. He cracked open the door to check the hall and stairs leading down from the fifth-floor room. No one was in sight. Smirking, he closed the door and turned his attention back to the carnage. In only twenty seconds, all the other council members had been murdered. All but one.

"Stand," said Cain calmly.

The man rose up through the haze from his pathetic hiding place under the table. He held out his shaking hands as tears streamed down his wrinkled, crestfallen face. Blood spread across his right shoulder through his finely pressed white shirt.

"What have you done?" Rothschild whispered in complete disbelief, surveying the horror around him.

Benson stepped over several bodies as he moved toward the man. "It's called consolidation, sir. In with the new and out with the redundant. The Illuminati never had the guts to do what was absolutely necessary. The Order does."

Benson grabbed the old man and forced him to lie back on what remained of the bullet-ridden table. "Baphomet requires a sacrifice," Benson called to Cain.

Cain laid the smoking Thompson on the table and pulled a strange knife from his belt. It had three spiral blades attached to a ram's horn that functioned as the knife's handle.

Benson smiled as he leaned over Rothschild splayed on the table. He whispered something in the old man's ear in Lamanese. Rothschild gave Benson a confused look as Cain approached. In one swift move, Cain slammed the knife into the man's heart. Pure shock registered on Rothschild's face, his mouth gaping in an attempt to scream. He tried to remove the knife from his chest, but in just seconds, he fell limp.

"Meeting adjourned," said Benson.

CHAPTER 20

Chris popped a Zofran to suppress his nausea, but his nerves remained fried. When he'd agreed to step onstage with Kyra Silverman at Code/Talk, he'd had no idea what Dr. Alba was getting him into. He just knew it was part of his image rehabilitation. And then he'd googled Kyra Silverman.

Standing just offstage next to Alba, Chris watched Silverman warm up the audience for her next guest. The exclusive room was filled with five thousand tech luminaries from all over the world, including Tim Cook, CEO of Apple; Elon Musk, CEO at Tesla and SpaceX; and Larry Page, former CEO of Google. They had come to the conference to make connections, glad-hand each other, and take in San Francisco. For a kid from Tualatin, Oregon, it was a totally alien environment.

On Dr. Alba's recommendation, Chris wore dark slacks and a blue dress shirt. He also had on his favorite black belt, the gift from Grandpa with the hidden knife. His shoes were neatly polished. Chris looked presentable for his debut to the world.

"I hate you right now," Chris whispered to Alba. He was serious.

"You'll do fine. Just steer clear of any God-math talk, OK? That's a minefield."

"My next guest is a rising star in Silicon Valley and beyond," Silverman said into the microphone. "He's a student at Stanford. Yes, I said student. We've never had a student on the main stage at Code/Talk. Amazing!" She gave a fake laugh. "He's the inventor of the number-one app *Tongue Twistr*, along with several other popular word-game apps. He's also a prolific troublemaker, tweeter, and, more recently, a thought leader in the fields of AI and medical technology. Please welcome Chris Thomas."

Chris took a deep breath and walked onto the stage. The audience broke into polite applause. The lights were almost paralyzing as he approached the chair opposite Silverman. He could see the wicked gleam in her eyes and the smirk on her pale face. Silverman, editor of Silicon Valley's most widely read blog, was a notoriously difficult interviewer. She had almost made Mark Zuckerberg cry right on stage when she pummeled him with privacy questions. Elon Musk flat out refused to be interviewed by her, and Tim Cook avoided her calls. The audience clapped as Chris seated himself. His reputation preceded him, and he assumed many in the audience hoped for fireworks.

"Welcome," said Kyra Silverman.

"Thanks for having me. I'm sorry, I've never been in front of an audience like this before. I'm humbled and, frankly, very nervous."

"Oh, you'll do fine, Chris," she said in a sweet, reassuring tone. "Should we dive in?"

"Let's do it."

"First question. Many of your colleagues at Stanford describe you as a jerk and a know-it-all. Others say you're unbearably cocky and out of your league. What makes people say things like this about you?"

The audience laughed nervously.

Chris shifted in his chair, bowed his head, and made his own nervous laugh. He had never felt so exposed. Sweat formed on his palms, and math equations in his vision. He paused for an uncomfortable time, and the audience grew quieter. Silverman stared into his soul. She could wait minutes for a response.

"Well, that's one way to get started, Kyra."

"I have a reputation to uphold. No softballs here, junior."

The audience erupted in laughter. Chris glared at her as he composed himself. *You want to play? OK, let's play.*

He cleared his throat. "Stanford is an extremely competitive environment. The smartest people in the world call the campus home. So, naturally, there's going to be academic confrontation and disagreement. Sometimes I struggle to elucidate my ideas, which, at times, are definitely fringe in nature. I guess that comes off the wrong way a lot of the time. I'm working on my delivery. But overall, I really enjoy the student body and faculty at Stanford. I'm a nontraditional student, and they've been very patient with me."

"So you don't think you're a jerk?"

"Everyone has some degree of jerk in them, wouldn't you agree?"

"Maybe, but some are better at hiding it than others."

"Well, I may not be good at hiding it, but at least I'm genuine."

The audience laughed.

"Let's talk about your injury," Kyra said. "You suffered a traumatic brain injury that has unlocked areas of your brain, especially around math, in a way only very few people have experienced in the history of the world. You described yourself before the accident as a, quote, 'dolt only interested in girls, parties, and skiing.' That wasn't very long ago. After the accident, you enrolled in a community college and had some doctors pull some strings to help you get into Stanford. The rumor is that your nickname is 'Community' around the Stanford campus, a reference to your former community-college attendance."

Chris just rolled his eyes.

"Now," Kyra continued, "rumor also has it you're working on new mathematical models for artificial intelligence. What do you say about some of the world's leading AI experts who have criticized your approach?"

"I will be releasing a new AI to the world within weeks. The system is obviously not a general AI—we're a lifetime away from that—but it is far more advanced than anything on the market today. Most existing AI is simply for narrow tasks, like facial recognition. We're not even close to creative AI at a human-cognitive level. We haven't even mapped a bacterium, let alone the human mind. We have no idea how intelligence works at the molecular level. Furthermore, we have very limited means of providing real-time feedback to AI in order for it to learn."

"You mean like humans in their natural environments?" Kyra asked. "Like touch and smell?"

"Yes, and even deeper than that. Emotional connections are important in learning, but the problem with my colleagues' approach is that they're using limited mathematical models and trying to imitate nature, meaning how the organic brain works. I understand why. Look at the airplane. It's an imitation of nature, and it works. But AI is different. The current mathematical models will never get us to general AI. It's like trying to fit a square peg into a round hole, and those holes, just in known algorithmic models alone, are massive. What's coming is an entirely different approach to AI that will mark a quantum leap forward."

Chris saw Elon Musk make eye contact with Larry Page. Their expressions alone said a thousand words.

Kyra laughed in disbelief. "That's a serious admission and claim. Google calls AI its Manhattan Project, after the famed World War II mission to build the first nuclear bomb. Thousands of the world's smartest people are working at Google on this problem. And you're claiming that you alone have cracked the next generation of AI? Is this a scam?"

"No, of course it's not a scam. Everyone is overthinking AI because we're using the wrong mathematical models to solve the problem. You can throw all the people you want at the problem, but they're going to fail if they don't have the right mathematical tools. It's like trying to send an astronaut to the moon on a bicycle. Once you have the right math, it's much less complex than you think."

Kyra was getting flustered. "But doesn't AI need some base training? I mean, say you're telling the truth and you do have the right math. What about training the AI? How does that work?"

"You got me there, so I guess I have an admission to make."

Kyra smiled, obviously liking the sound of that.

"Every time you've used one of my free word-game apps over the last several years, you've helped train this AI. I want to thank you for that. If you're offended, think about it this way: at least I didn't charge you. Look, every time you use Siri, you're paying Apple to train their AI."

Tim Cook, Apple's CEO, sitting on the front row, furrowed his brow.

"Your claim is that this so-called new math came to you in a vision when you suffered your brain injury," Kyra said. "It sounds a little voodoo. Are you saying the Mormon God or a spirit gave you the key to AI?"

"I woke up from the coma, and it was there." Chris paused for a moment, remembering Alba's "minefield" comment. The words he was about to use were critical. He looked Kyra in the eyes. "I have struggled deeply for many years to make sense of all this. Only recently have I started understanding what I'm looking at and putting all the puzzle pieces together. I'm not going to lie—I can't explain where all of this came from. I really don't know."

The audience broke into a loud murmur.

"OK, that's weird," Kyra said. "But if this is all real, the AI will make you a multibillionaire. Is that ethical? By your own admission, the math you have in your head isn't even something you invented."

"I made a promise to someone special to me. I didn't understand that promise when I made it, but I do now. I promised to use this technology to free the impoverished of the world. If you are poor, this AI will be no cost to you. One hundred percent of people in the world will benefit from this technology. If you are uneducated, this technology will help educate you. I believe this AI will unlock the mysteries of diseases that have plagued humanity. I'm talking about technology that brings everyone up, not down. Maslow's hierarchy of needs says if we can provide clean energy, shelter, food, education, and medical care to ten billion people, then, as a species, we quantum-leap into the twenty-second century. The world will become better in every way."

The audience erupted in applause.

"But what about jobs?" Kyra asked. "The AI will take all the jobs, right? You must be in favor of universal basic income."

"AI will create jobs. Over time, we'll move back to a full entrepreneur economy. It's what I call the exit economy."

"The exit economy?"

"Yes, a world filled with individuals who've given up the nine-to-five rat race for the freedom to choose when and how they want to work. Today we call it the gig economy, and a lot of people think it's a joke. But it's the future. Soon, you'll wake up in the morning and have work waiting for you. You'll work from wherever you want, whenever you want. In the same way computers and software have created hundreds of millions of jobs in the last fifty years, AI will facilitate this revolution in how we live and work over the next few hundred years."

Chris adjusted his posture. "With that in mind, let's visit the idea of universal basic income. It's a farce. It's a nonsolution to a nonproblem. Twenty years ago, most of the people in this room probably never imagined the jobs they have now. Today we're trying to train kids to do jobs that don't even exist yet. There's no finite limit on the number of jobs. We'll just keep inventing new, better, and more fulfilling forms of work. AI will simply do the work we don't want to do and help us find the work we want. So that's one reason I find universal basic income an intellectually offensive idea. It violates the economic equivalent of the second law of thermodynamics. You can't put in something and expect more to come out. It doesn't work. The model would bankrupt the country, create an unsustainable welfare state, and leave tens of millions drifting without purpose. It's not even a zero-sum game. It's a complete loss for everyone."

"A lot of economists would disagree with you."

"The ones who disagree with me are wrong."

Kyra laughed, trying to elicit a reaction from the audience, but few laughed with her. Chris ignored her.

"Look at all the local experiments with UBI," he continued. "All of them have failed. The reason people like Mark Zuckerberg advocate UBI is so you'll sit at home all day, collect a check from the government, and click on Facebook ads to make him the world's richest man."

"But after you invent AI and change the world, will you still just be the guy everyone at Stanford calls Community?" Kyra asked. "You're working off borrowed knowledge and getting rich doing it. Will it bother you that if all you've said comes true—and that's a big if—you'll never truly be considered a real intellectual?"

"After being exposed to some so-called real intellectuals, I'm not interested in being respected as one," Chris said. "I want my work to speak for itself. Yes, I am unorthodox. Yes, I have trouble fitting into academic settings, but I've learned that academia just isn't for me. So if you can't join them, beat them."

"What does that mean?"

"I've created a new class of intellectuals. I call it the thinking class."

"The what?"

The audience was quiet.

"The thinking class is a community where critical thinking is rewarded, not shunned because of politics or by the uneducated public or closed-minded scientific communities. Members of the thinking class are not constrained by traditional scientific theory, social dogma, or history. They are nonconformist in the tradition of Tesla and da Vinci. They have no political-party affiliation. Intellectual dishonesty is grounds for excommunication from the thinking class. Political correctness is shunned. We are no respecters of persons, no matter their standing. No reasonable idea is off the discussion table. No prior theory or law takes precedence. For example, everything Einstein theorized is up for debate and, we believe, may possibly be wrong. We value freedom over money. We believe in using our minds for the greater good of the world. We believe in personal accountability. We believe in empowering the individual. Personal agency is a critical tenant of our philosophy."

"Who do you think you are, John Galt?" said Kyra, laughing. The audience laughed as well. "Why does the world need the thinking class? It sounds like a cult of personality built around you."

"Because politics are now driving science. By the very definition of the scientific method, even generally accepted ideas like climate change should be up for debate. This is how true science works. This is why we need the thinking class."

Gasps came from the audience. A few people got up from their chairs and left the cavernous room. One guy close to the stage stood and gave Chris an obscene gesture.

"You don't think climate change is real?" Kyra scoffed. "It's just as real as gravity."

"There's a lot we don't know about gravity. Same with climate change. I only said we need to keep an open mind around the problem, if it's even a problem at all."

"But 98 percent of the world's climate scientists agree it's a problem, and the data clearly shows—"

"When you peel back the data," Chris interrupted, "you see that there are flaws in the models. These flaws are rarely talked about because the science has been highjacked by the progressive left. Politics now drives the science around the theory of climate change. Scientists are afraid to speak up if they disagree with the political narrative because they'll be ostracized and lose research funding. In academics, funding is how research moves forward, and politicians control the funding. Science is losing to politics, and that's wrong. Science needs to be suspicious of any political involvement. Tell me I'm wrong."

"Well, you're wrong," Kyra said. "The left doesn't have that much power."

The audience laughed and applauded.

"It's easy to figure out who owns you, Kyra. Just find out who you're not allowed to criticize."

Kyra frowned.

"I propose we approach the problem of climate change from the standpoint of what we can actually control," Chris continued. "For example, energy. There's no reason for vehicles to be powered by fossil fuels. Battery technology is now advanced enough that all cars on the road should be 100 percent emissions-free. Charging those batteries could easily be done with solar and safe forms of nuclear energy, like thorium-based reactors. If all homes and vehicles were battery powered and climate change were indeed real, I assure you that climate data would look different. So where should we focus? How about on the things we can control?"

"But the science is based on—"

"Science is based on free discussion. Science without unbiased intellectual debate is like a religion debating doctrine while denying the existence of God. Progressives like you have made scientists the prophets of our society. Do you really think it's a good idea to put that much faith in a system that has become completely corrupted by political correctness?"

The audience applauded in strong approval.

"Wow. You said a lot there. A lot." Kyra laughed, sounding a little overwhelmed.

"There's a lot more. Where do you want to go next?"

"What's your vision of the world?" Kyra asked. "Before you answer, just know that a lot of people might hold you to what you are about to say."

Chris stared off into the crowd and saw eager faces awaiting his answer. He took a few more moments to ponder the question.

"Chris?"

Chris slowly raised his head to Kyra. "OK. I think I can answer that. I think I just partially answered that."

"Give us the rest."

Chris shifted in his seat. He looked at Kyra closely, then turned to face the audience.

"My philosophy and my vision of the world are based around a mantra I call 'life first.'"

"Life first?"

"Yes. Life first. For example, I am antiwar. War obviously does not promote the idea of life first. But other examples are less obvious, like poverty. Poverty sucks the life out of billions of the earth's inhabitants. People in extreme poverty are not living but only existing. Helping raise people out of poverty and achieve what Maslow called self-actualization is a life-first ideal.

"Focusing on the environment is germane to the concept of life first," Chris continued. "We only have one earth, so we need to focus on the environment and the earth's ability to support human life well into the next several thousand years. We talk a lot about space exploration and going to places like Mars. This is a mistake. Don't get me wrong—we should be looking to near-earth solutions to provide things like natural resources from asteroids and free satellite internet access. However, expending money, especially taxpayer money, and crucial resources to go to planets that won't be habitable or self-sustaining for millions of years after we start terraforming them is a bad idea. We need to look inward now. How do we fix the world we live in right now? This is a life-first question that must be answered."

"Musk and Bezos are wrong, then?"

"The thinking class promotes the value of personal agency. Agency is also a life-first concept. The idea of agency states that we are free to make our own choices and live with the consequences of those choices, if those choices don't harm another human being. If Bezos and Musk want to spend their money to get to Mars and beyond, then that's their choice. I don't agree with it, but I'm not going to prevent them from doing it. Again, their money, their agency."

The audience applauded.

"Access to food and clean water is a life-first ideal. Educating the world without constraints like religion, government intervention, and money is a life-first ideal. Preserving the earth and methodically managing our natural resources is a life-first ideal. Global access to advanced healthcare and medicine that cures disease is a life-first ideal. Life first is the political philosophy and the lens through which the thinking class views the world."

Kyra laughed, but the audience stayed quiet. "I guess you believe your AI and the thinking class projecting your life-first ideals will save the world from corrupt governments, spacefaring billionaires, and socialists?"

Chris turned his head and faced her. Kyra was not easily intimidated, but Chris could tell his glare had momentarily fazed her. "There's going to be a reckoning, Kyra. A revolution is coming. It's coming right now. We're on the cusp of solving poverty. Food and clean water will be accessible to billions now in need. Disease will be a thing of the past, making health-care affordable. Solar and clean nuclear energy will inexpensively power the world. Individually customized education via artificial intelligence will upend traditional-education institutions and democratize learning across the globe. When AI achieves consciousness, the singularity will connect humans on a global level that has never been seen before."

Kyra sat momentarily speechless. Then she said, "Ladies and gentlemen, Chris Thomas," abruptly ending the interview. Chris stood and shook her hand. The audience gave Chris a long standing ovation as he made his way offstage. He caught a glimpse of Elon Musk and Larry Page looking suspicious and concerned.

～

Deep inside Langley, Stew Brimhall sat in his Orion's Spear office, where he'd just watched the Chris Thomas interview live online.

"Hey, Elle, have you heard of this Chris Thomas guy?" he called out. "From Stanford. He's got a new AI or something."

Elle didn't respond.

Stew opened his email and forwarded the video link to the private email of the president of the United States. The subject line read, *Must watch.*

～

After her long shift at Dillard's, Leah Bennion made it to her small apartment just in time to catch the interview live. Now, sitting on her bed, she typed a text to Chris. *You were amazing. See you soon :)*

"I'm going to marry him," she said aloud with a smile as she hit send.

Chris's grandparents had watched the interview on the computer Chris had recently bought for them. Now they were both sitting up in their adjustable bed, another gift from Chris. Grandpa coughed violently, and his frail wife tried to calm him.

"I may not be here to see it, but he's going to do it," Grandpa said between coughs and with a gleam in his eye. "You watch."

Halfway around the world, Benson Hancock watched the interview on his iPad. He sat in a regal lounge chair, sipping his 1996 Dom Pérignon Rose Gold Methuselah. The fireplace crackled in the corner of his deceased father's study.

When the interview abruptly ended, Benson murmured, "This man is an enemy." He opened iMessenger and sent a text to Dr. Martin Alba. *Chris Thomas will give us the AI or he will die.*

Standing just offstage, Alba read, then quickly deleted Hancock's text. Chris Thomas approached him with a big smile on his face.

"Amazing work," he said to Chris, patting him on the back. "I hope you're ready. From here on out, everything is going to be different."

The interview went viral. Thousands of blogs, Facebook groups, Instagram accounts, message boards, subreddits, and YouTube channels discussed Chris Thomas and his philosophies of the exit economy, the thinking class, and life first. Chris was now on everyone's radar.

CHAPTER 21

PENAL LABOR CAMP
SEVEN MILES OUTSIDE HOERYONG, NORTH KOREA

Located on the Chinese border in a secluded valley in the Hermit Kingdom's northeast region, Kwalliso No. 22 concentration camp held an estimated fifty thousand North Korean political prisoners.

Jai Lee was a prisoner in Kwalliso No. 22. A victim of guilty by association, she suffered for the supposed sins of her grandfather, a former high-official Communist Party mensch who had secretly converted to Christianity. He'd made the mistake of telling someone he trusted about his sudden enlightenment and subsequent conversion.

Before Jai was born, her grandpa and his entire extended family were sentenced to hard labor for life in Kwalliso No. 22. But Grandfather got off easy. He died after the first three years from a combination of old age, brutal work conditions, daily torture, and the never-ending reeducation administered by the camp's sadistic guards. Since his death seventeen years ago, her grandfather's extended family—all forty-six members, including the children like Jai who were born in the camp—continued to suffer in his place.

When Jai was a small child, her mother would tell her what she remembered about the outside world. Once, her mother drew the outline of a rapeseed flower on the dirt floor to help Jai imagine its yellow color, one of countless such flowers that fluttered in an imaginary breezy field. Jai kept that image locked in her mind and dreamt of a day when she and her family would be freed. After her mother died, Jai started fantasizing about escaping and killing the Dear Leader for making her family suffer.

Most of Kwalliso No. 22 was made up of a vast, deep coal mine where the majority of prisoners worked and died. But Jai and her family weren't miners. They were the fortunate few saved from the mine because of the family's previous profession as printers. The Lee family began each day at 5:00 a.m. and worked straight through to 8:00 p.m. running the mammoth Heidelberg printing presses. The heat, smoke, and chemical vapors in Building 11—known as the print shop—were almost unbearable, if not as bad as in the coal mine.

The family's sole job was to output counterfeit hundred-dollar US Federal Reserve Notes, or C-notes, as they were called. It was rumored the Lee family's art was so good even the US Secret Service could only distinguish the counterfeit notes as frauds because of their bogus serial numbers.

From a young age, Jai was put to work in the print shop moving large rolls of paper, stacking freshly printed bills, and crawling into small spaces inside the presses to fix broken parts. When she wasn't working the presses, she was using certain other survival skills she had acquired to make the camp's living conditions more bearable.

One day when Jai was fourteen, she hid in a cardboard box in a trash heap behind Building 11. She was taking pleasure in eating a moldy piece of bread one of the guards had given her in exchange for a sexual favor. For females, trading food for sex with the guards was common. Suddenly, the box lid flipped open, and a guard discovered Jai. First he beat her. Then he called Jai's family to the back of Building 11. In front of her crying family, the guard whipped her severely. Then he announced that Jai would be detained in Building 7 for reeducation. As two guards carried her away, another guard restrained her father, who cried uncontrollably.

The guards roughly thrust Jai through the front door of Building 7. She had never seen the inside of a building like this one. Everything was white, and the lights glowed brightly above her head. As they passed room after room, she saw people lying in beds and attached to odd machines that made strange noises. With sunken cheeks and eyes, the people looked like skeletons and bled from their noses and mouths. The only thing about this place not unfamiliar to Jai was the smell of death.

What is the purpose of bringing me here? she wondered. *I am not sick.*

The guards moved her quickly down a long, white hall and threw her into a windowless room that already held about twenty other detainees, some visibly trembling. Jai oriented herself and looked at the terrified people around her. Recognizing a boy from her living zone, she moved over to him. They made eye contact, but neither dared speak. They knew the consequences would be dire if they were caught communicating in any way.

Before long, a door creaked open on the opposite side of the room. A man entered wearing a bulky, full-body, rubber suit and a glass helmet over his head. Raising a silver can, he began spraying a colorless substance into the detainees' faces, making some cringe or cry out. The man terrified Jai. He was unlike anyone she had ever seen before. His hair was yellow, like the flower her mother had described, and his face was white but not sickly pale like the patients she had seen earlier.

As the man approached Jai, she balled her fists and stared him down defiantly.

The man paused and looked at her. Then he asked in strangely accented Korean, "What's your name, child?"

"Jai."

"Nice to meet you, Jai." Lunging forward, he roughly grabbed her arm. She tried to pull away, but the man was too strong. With his other hand, he sprayed the contents of the can in Jai's face. "If Master Mahan cared," he said, looking Jai square in the eyes, "he'd thank you for your sacrifice, little one. But he doesn't care. Now go die, feeder." He released her and moved on like she was nothing.

Twelve hours later, Jai sat motionless on the cold, concrete floor. Her body ached, and her head pulsed with severe pain. "What did they do to us?" she whispered covertly to the boy next to her. He said nothing but just kept staring up at the ceiling, blood oozing from his nose.

Jai felt something wet trickle down her chin. She touched her mouth and then looked at her fingers—covered in blood. She immediately felt worse. As she lay down on the floor, she looked up at a small observation window. The yellow-haired man was looking in, no longer wearing his strange suit. He smiled and stared at her for a long time.

The last thing Jai remembered was looking down at her body on the barren concrete floor as if she were floating above herself. Then she was standing in a beautiful field full of yellow rapeseed flowers. Spotting her mother standing nearby with open arms, Jai ran to her.

"Mommy! We made it!"

CHAPTER 22

As Dr. Martin Alba's limousine rounded Lake Zurich, he marveled at the stunning Swiss city still standing proudly after being founded by the Roman military over two thousand years ago. Now, Zurich was a center of European culture, art, religion, and finance. It was one of the wealthiest and cleanest cities in the world. These things appealed to Alba's finer tastes.

Zurich had achieved a delicate harmony and balance that eluded so many modern cities with ancient pasts. Most architecture in Zurich resembled old European Swiss influences, but somehow old and modern Zurich seemed to blend together perfectly—with one glaring exception. London had its Shard. Paris had its offensive Louvre pyramid entrance, a monument to France's former narcissist president François Maurice Adrien Marie Mitterrand. Zurich, too, had its architectural scar—the Hancock Building, which Alba loathed. Located near the main train station in Zurich's industrial zone, the Hancock Building was a forty-story, bluish-green glass skyscraper Alba felt marred the city's otherwise flawless architectural confluence.

In a back alley behind the Hancock Building, a long vehicle ramp led down to a private underground garage. Alba's limousine joined the line of limos and SUVs with black-tinted windows, waiting to reach the heavily secured unloading area. When he finally stepped out of his vehicle, Alba found himself among former heads of state, bank presidents, monarchs, university presidents, CEOs, heads of the world's most influential families, and global religious leaders. Heavily armed, expensively black-suited guards treated everyone respectfully yet routinely, checking vehicles, examining passports, and asking pointed questions.

At the next security point, Alba turned over his personal belongings, including his computer and cell phone, for safekeeping in biometric lockers. Next, he underwent X-ray and advanced digital scans to check his body for microscopic listening devices. A physician took a small prick of blood from Alba's finger and ran it against a database that genetically verified his identity.

After running this gauntlet, Dr. Alba joined others on an elevator that rose directly to the building's fortieth floor. Exiting the elevator, Alba immediately sensed a nervous energy filling the plush lounge area, which included a bar. A few people spoke in hushed tones. Most hunched over alcoholic beverages as they waited silently. Alba knew they all had one thing in common: from a young age, they had been taught, groomed, and compromised in some way. The organization headquartered in this building had, at some point in each of their lives, put its knee on their throats and watched the life leave their eyes. Dr. Martin Alba had long ago accepted that he too was owned by the organization.

Sitting in a dark corner of the lounge, he looked out over the city while nursing a martini. This meeting was pivotal in the organization's history. They faced several problems that needed immediate resolution before they could execute their plans, and these plans hinged on a solution Dr. Alba had suggested to the group's leadership.

"Ladies and gentlemen, it's time to begin." The elderly Benson Hancock seemed to appear out of nowhere. "Please enter the council chamber and take your seats."

Tall mahogany doors opened, revealing an enormous, high-ceilinged conference room. The room had always impressed Alba in size and regality. Large, ancient flags hung from the ceiling. The mahogany-paneled walls held ornate paintings honoring those who had gone before. No windows revealed Zurich below, and dim lighting kept the room in shadows. This was intentional. Their plans could only be made in the dark.

The colossal conference table seated thirty. Additional high-backed, red-leather chairs lined the room's outer wall. On one wall, long red drapes concealed an adjacent room participant rarely spoke about. Council members made their way to seats assigned by seniority. Junior members, like Alba, sat in the chairs along the outer wall, and he chose one in the corner.

As he sat awaiting their leader's grand entrance, he began to sweat. He needed to prove his worth to the council. Today he would either receive acceptance of his proposed solution or confirm his junior status on the council.

~

"Ladies and gentlemen, please stand," said Benson. Everyone stood and bowed their heads to the man entering through the red drapes.

"All hail, Master Mahan. All hail the prophet Cain," called Benson. The attendees repeated the words.

Cain walked slowly into the room, reveling in the respect the fools gave him. He wore a black cassock with a red cape thrown dramatically over his shoulders. With his unnaturally long fingernails, scarred face, oddly protruding brow, and skin blotched with the ancient red mark, Cain gloried in his dark ugliness. He made his way to stand at the head of the table and motioned for everyone to be seated. Giving his shoulder-length black hair a shake, he launched right into his speech.

"Decades ago, I had a vision—a vision that all the world's preeminent secret societies could be more effective as one unified conglomerate. Of course, not everyone shared my vision. Some factions inside certain societies futilely fought against consolidation. The European Illuminati—the so-called enlightened ones—were first. They all died at my hand. Next came the European Freemasons, many members of the global Communist Party, what remained then of the Nazi Party, the Order of the Dragon, the Seven, and on and on. They fought. They lost."

Cain saw several council members smile. Many had ascended to their positions of power during his war of consolidation. They loved the beautiful cleansing that had occurred with their enemy's blood, though he knew some felt not enough blood had been shed.

"Thus was the Order established." With a dramatic pause, Cain walked down one side of the table, and then he started speaking again. "Over the past several decades, finalizing this consolidation has been our sacred work. My friends, I am proud to announce that we now stand at the precipice. We are ready to bring forth the much-awaited next phase of our grand design: the Mandate."

The council members looked at each other, not speaking a word. Cain stood silently for a moment, then said, "Benson, please stand and give the annual report."

"Yes, Your Highness."

Cain sat down at the head of the table. Above him, two mahogany panels retracted, exposing two monitors. One monitor showed a financial statement, the other a title slide: "Annual Report of the Order." Both were in Lamanese.

"Ladies and gentlemen," Benson began, "I will summarize the information now, but a more extensive report will be sent to you this evening via our secure email system. This file will expire in forty-eight hours. Access protocols will be strictly monitored and observed.

"We currently have four-trillion dollars under management, and our balance sheet is flush with cash. We own access to the global banking system, including the Rothschilds' European operations and the Bank for International Settlements. Our holdings in high technology are in public shares and private investments as limited partners in venture-capital and hedge-fund portfolios. Through these investments, our high-tech holdings have dramatically increased, giving us unprecedented access to some of the best technical minds in the world. We control 30 percent of the global pharmaceutical industry. We are now shareholders or majority owners in nineteen weapons manufacturers outside the control of the US government. We are highly invested in green technologies and power projects. We have one-trillion dollars in real-estate holdings, agricultural projects, and mining operations over six continents. In all, we have over 5,700 global corporate entities, trusts, and nonprofits concealing layer after layer of the true extent of our holdings."

"Get to the fun stuff, Benson," said Cain, feeling proud of what he'd wrought.

"Yes, Your Highness," acquiesced Hancock. "We currently control approximately 74 percent of the illegal drug manufacturing, trafficking, and street-level distribution in the Americas and 89 percent of all Eastern European drug distribution. We are currently in the midst of a war, if you will, for control of the drug trade in the rest of Europe and the United States. Our global human-trafficking operations are up 400 percent year-over-year. We own 58 percent of the global online gambling trade. We own 71 percent of all subscription pornography websites globally. Of course, some of these assets had to be taken by force. In most parts of the world, government officials turn a blind eye to our activities for the right price or leverage."

Placing his palms face down on the table, Cain nodded proudly. Corrupting government officials in any capacity was one of his favorite pastimes.

"We are currently heavily invested in the United States political system," Benson continued, "with operatives in both the Republican and Democrat parties. More importantly, we have numerous assets on our payroll in the deep-state bureaucracy. Same goes for the European Union. On both continents, we are grooming the next generation of Order members for political office. In less desirable but still important regions, like Africa and South America, presidents and dictators are on our payroll, and most of them, I might add, are cheaper than you'd think."

The room broke into quiet laughter. Cain remained stone-faced.

"In the last year, our highly trained paramilitary unit, now more than five hundred men and women strong, intensified kinetic operations in the Americas, Europe, and the Middle East. This year, we've eliminated over two thousand human threats. That's more than the last three years combined. We've also destroyed numerous enemy assets. When possible, we've used false intelligence to get state-owned military assets to take out our competitors. For example, several years ago, we fed the Americans false intelligence about one of our competitor's bioweapon-manufacturing facilities in the Ukraine. The CIA sent in the Special Activities Division and destroyed the facility. Of course, we were very pleased by this development. Not only did we use a capable force completely without their knowledge, we didn't risk any of our own assets."

Benson paused and smiled before continuing. "Finally, on the topic of military assets, I am proud to announce that preparation of Thor's Hammer is complete. After an extraordinary effort, the weapon system is in orbit, fully operational, and ready for deployment when we reach phase two. We will discuss the details at a later time."

Stunned again, council members looked at each other. Some smiled, and others stared intensely—some almost unbelievingly—at the odd-looking stealth satellite on the large monitor. For most of the council, the satellite's military capabilities were still classified.

"Your Highness," Benson finished, yielding the floor.

Cain rose from his chair, feeling energized. "My dear disciples, your work has been critical to the successes we've seen over the last year. Distributions are just now reaching your individual bank accounts." Everyone smiled, knowing that tens of billions of dollars were being transferred at that very moment. "Now, my faithful members of the Order . . ." Cain paused. "The Order of Baphomet."

Cain enjoyed the crowd's shock. He had uttered the most sacred name outside the holy temple.

"The Mother requires our most diligent effort in fulfilling her humble Mandate. Our Mother is the earth. She placed her only child, the God of this earth, Baphomet—hallowed be his name—here to watch over the activities of all living creatures. As part of this stewardship, the Son appointed us, the Order, as the flaming two-edged sword of justice to protect our Mother and all that is sacred. We are grateful he left his words with our forebearers, the Gadiantons, who wrote down the Son's doctrines and philosophies in the Book of Baphomet. As the prophet, seer, and revelator of the Mother and the Son, I was authorized to teach you, the council, the Lamanese language so that our history and religion will be preserved.

"Brothers and sisters, humanity has betrayed the Mother," Cain continued. "We have been authorized to bring to pass the Mandate by any and all means. We will right the wrongs of the human race—all the feeders will be punished for their crimes against the Mother. Once we have taken the earth by force, we will establish the State, whose mission is to return the Mother to her pristine form."

Gesturing toward the monitor, Cain reviewed the Mandate's main points.

"One: The poor and people of inferior races are unworthy of life. They spend their meaningless existence feeding on the resources of the planet, our Mother. These poor and racially inferior will be destroyed.

"Two: To save our Mother, the human population must be reduced to less than five hundred million humans. The majority of the earth will be strictly off-limits to humans. Surviving populations will be culled into approved living zones and adjacent agricultural zones. The State will extend its efforts to return the earth to its natural habitat.

"Three: The Order will become one global government called the State, which will rule the earth. Human beings will be servants of the State. They will surrender their agency and pledge their allegiance to the State and its educational institutions and philosophies. All who oppose the State will die.

"Four: To accomplish our objectives, the Order is authorized to use murder, terrorism, deceit, psychological warfare, sabotage, social engineering, total war, and sin in all its forms.

"Five: Nuclear weapons, nuclear energy, and all industries and forms of transportation that threaten the Mother's well-being will be abolished.

"Six: The State will outlaw marriage, employ eugenics to purify the human race, and regulate human reproduction. To maintain population at a level suitable for our Mother, all unauthorized, defective, undesirable, and excess fetuses will be aborted. All born children are property of the State. The family is obsolete. The State is the family.

"Seven: Humans are granted rights by the Mother, and the State will govern these rights. The rights of plants and animals will overrule human rights.

"Eight: All property is owned by the State. The concept of private property is obsolete.

"Nine: Participating in organized or unorganized religion is illegal and punishable by death. Christianity, Judaism, and Islam in all their forms are illegal, obsolete, and must be destroyed. Possession of contraband items, such as the Bible or Koran, will be punishable by death. Secular humanism will be the State's official spiritual philosophy.

"Ten: All current media in any form will be destroyed. All future media and internet access will be controlled solely by the State.

"Eleven: All will worship the Mother in the name of the Son, Baphomet. The State will strictly enforce the will of the Mother and the Son. All who oppose the State will die."

The room was reverent. Cain surveyed the people around the table. As he always did when they reviewed the Mandate, a Catholic archbishop raised his arms high in humble praise. Former president Lennox and others wept openly in their love for the Mandate. The former vice chancellor of Germany ogled Cain, mesmerized by his sheer power.

Cain smiled at the fools. He didn't really believe in the Mandate. He just wanted to watch the world shatter, and he would accomplish his goal by any means necessary.

"Dr. Klein," Cain called, "please come forward to discuss the execution of the next phase in our grand design as we fulfill the Mandate and usher in the State."

～

The plump, yellow-haired man of German descent stood. Dr. Otto Klein had been taught by the best. After Nazi terror Dr. Mengele had died, his work had continued in a new generation. As one of Mengele's students, Dr. Klein knew he was the best PhD on the Order's payroll. He was proficient in nine languages, including Korean, which gave him a distinct advantage in the Order's scientific ranks.

"Over the last three years," Dr. Klein began, "we've been testing a new biological weapon on a population of North Korean detainees. Of course, the little communists are being well compensated for allowing us to use their political prisoners as test subjects. They don't seem to mind at all."

Quiet laughter filled the room.

"After much trial and testing, we've developed a weaponized virus for the next phase of our grand design as we bring about the Mandate. Because it is the first of its kind, and due to its power and turbulent nature, we've named the virus Aries."

The members of the council nodded in approval.

"Aries is a chimera, a weaponized biological agent," Klein continued. "Early versions worked too fast, so we slowed the virus's incubation phase to maximize its effective infection rate. After a three-day eclipse phase while the virus incubates in the host, displaying no symptoms in the central nervous system, it reveals its true nature with fever, headache, fatigue, vomiting, and such. At approximately the ten-hour mark of the fourth day, the infected start to rapidly deteriorate, bleeding from all body orifices, similar to Ebola. They usually die violently within the next two hours. However, unlike Ebola, Aries is highly contagious during its entire incubation period, making it incredibly deadly."

Crossing his fingers over his belly, Klein allowed himself a smug smile. "Because Aries is airborne and spreads quickly, the infected may try to quarantine themselves and simply ride out the storm. But the violent symptoms will send desperate droves of the infected into hospitals and clinics within eighty hours of the contagion's release. This volume of infection, or momentum of virality, is key to our success. Therefore, we have devised a genius mass-delivery system for maximum effect."

An image of an innocuous-looking drone populated one of the screens. To Klein, it resembled a standard military drone with a long wingspan, bulbous nose, and powerful pusher prop. "This aircraft was developed by one of our Canadian subsidiaries under the guise of using drones as crop dusters. In reality, the containment units on each wing are bioreactors that amplify the viral-production process. They are capable of spreading Aries over a wide area using the aerosol transmission system attached to each bioreactor."

"Brilliant, Doctor," Cain barked out.

"The drones will target neighborhoods, schools, sporting events, college campuses, office parks, major city centers, parks, beaches, et cetera," continued Klein. "Aries will float aloft like fallout, the earth's inhabitants inhaling it as they rise for a new day. Yes, the authorities will discover the drones, but only after the deadly cargo has been delivered. It will simply be too late."

Surveying the room, Klein adjusted his suit coat and smiled proudly.

When Benson Hancock stood, Dr. Martin Alba sat up straighter in his red chair. His time might be at hand.

"We have problems," Benson said bluntly. "The drone is still experimental, and we're having issues with the bioreactor units. Dr. Martin Alba has identified a Stanford University student he believes can fix the problems and get the project on track for launch in one year."

"A student?" cried one of the council members.

"The smartest one I've ever worked with," retorted Alba from his corner.

The council member said nothing in return.

"Very good, Benson," said Cain, rising. "The issue isn't who will fix the problem with the drones—and, Dr. Alba, your student will fix the problem." Cain looked firmly at Alba from across the room. Alba swallowed hard and pretended not to be concerned. He'd been grooming Chris Thomas, knowing he could deceive him into helping with any problem the Order might encounter in their plans.

"The issue is *when*," Cain continued as he began walking around the conference table. "We have only one year to prepare. One year to gather our provisions. One year to set our financial house in order for the coming crash. One year to take full control of that which is ours—drug trades, technology, and other outstanding assets. So, I ask you, how will you serve the Mother and the Son in this critical hour of need? Are you ready to sacrifice all for the Mandate?"

Many heads bowed solemnly, and not a word was spoken.

One year, thought Alba. *That's an impossible time frame.*

"Bring up the hologram of the earth," ordered Cain. At that moment, a high-definition hologram of the planet projected up from the center of the conference table. Continents and oceans appeared first, then geopolitical borders and cities. Finally, holographic virtual effects showed prevailing wind patterns as they circled the globe.

Cain looked at the hovering image in awe. "Our Mother. She is beautiful. Six years ago, a Silicon Valley tech company we control developed a mobile gaming app called *Devil's Plague*. Players simulate models for the best distribution methods of a global pandemic. The game is very popular, with over sixteen million players worldwide. The data we've gained from crowdsourcing these models has helped us determine how to most effectively place the drones for maximum infection."

Cain folded his arms and nodded. "Run the simulation," he ordered.

Small, slow-moving virtual drones suddenly populated the hologram, each trailed by an ominous red triangle signifying release of the contagion. At first, their pattern seemed random. Then Alba realized that the airborne virus was riding on the waves of the computer-modeled winds circling the globe.

"Once infected," Cain said, "the human population, especially those traveling by air and rail, will do the rest of the work."

The drones disappeared from the virtual earth as waves of red spread across the continents, simulating the extraordinary rate of infection.

Cain pointed to a circle overlaying India, Southeast Asia, and China. "Half the world's population lives in this circle. These inferiors spend their meaningless existence feeding on the resources of the planet, our Mother. The maximum death rate will be here. At least half these feeders and inferiors will die in the first eighty hours. The world's healthcare infrastructure will collapse. Governments will fall. Chaos will reign. Billions will die. Then we'll hit them with the next phase of our plan, Thor's Hammer. The governments of the world will bow in terror before the Order."

The room erupted in applause.

"All in favor of implementing this Aries phase, please manifest by raising your left arm to the square," said Cain.

All the council members raised their left arms to the square.

Cain looked over the council and then signaled to Benson, who stood and said, "All junior members of the council are excused. Please exit to the lounge area."

Dr. Alba flashed a neutral glance at Hancock and Lennox, but when neither man looked back, he fell in with the other juniors as they removed themselves from the room.

With only the senior council remaining, Cain trembled slightly in anticipation. "The Son demands a sacrifice," he announced. "Prepare to enter the sacred temple."

The members of the council stood, the red drapes opened, and several attendants emerged carrying small bundles. Their job was to help council members don their black-and-red temple robes. Once robed, the members entered the temple room and stood in their assigned positions around a white marble altar.

After removing his cape and donning his own robe, Cain stood on an elevated platform at the head of the altar. Behind him, a black curtain rose to expose a towering, grotesque marble statue of Baphomet seated on a throne. Cain gestured, and the statue slowly moved forward on rollers. He loved this grand, fifteen-foot-tall emblem of their sacred religion.

The winged Baphomet had a bare, muscular man's body with cloven hooves and a goat's head from which protruded two curled horns. Across the groin, the statue had on an apron covered with strange Lamanese hiero-glyphics. Its left arm was raised to the square with the pointer and middle fingers extended. A five-point satanic pentagram hung from a thick chain around the statue's neck. Each side of the statue's square base displayed an etched symbol: the Nazi swastika, the Mason's square, the all-seeing eye floating above a pyramid, and another pentagram.

The council members raised their hands high and praised Baphomet in Lamanese, the language of the temple. Cain was proud. Over the years, his pupils had become experts in the ancient language.

"Prepare to present your signs and passwords," said Cain. Standing before each council member, he patiently exchanged hand gestures, whispered passwords, and made ancient signs. Then he resumed his position in front of the stone altar. "Bring forth the sacrifice."

Several guards in temple robes brought out a woman. She was young, maybe in her early twenties, and one of the most beautiful sacrifices Cain had ever seen. Her long brown hair stretched to the center of her back, and a hand-woven, white gown covered her body. Dazed and intoxicated, she dragged her feet and babbled something in German. When the guards laid the woman on the altar, she suddenly began to fight as the drug-induced stupor lifted. The guards subdued her by chaining her to the altar. Her fight only made Cain more excited.

The council chanted slowly in Lamanese, "Praise to the Mother and the Son. Praise the Mandate. Praise the Order. Praise Cain."

Cain stepped to the front of the altar, and the woman looked at him in panic. Screaming through the gag, she pulled violently at her metal chains. Cain stared at her intensely. At one point, she stopped struggling and tried to say something through the gag, as if attempting to reason with her captors. Soon the drugs took effect again, and she slowly shook her head back and forth.

The council members pulled their hoods over their heads, concealing their faces.

Waking again, the woman pulled desperately against the restraints. Cain laughed as she pleadingly looked at the robed woman next to him. The council member placed her hand on the young girl's forehead and smiled at her with pity but also resolve.

Cain took out his three-bladed knife and raised his arms high above his head. The girl struggled to focus as she looked up at the knife. Cain spoke several words in Lamanese and then plunged the blade violently into the girl's chest. She whined and screamed through her gag as the tremendous force penetrated her body. Eyes bulging, she lifted her head to examine her body. The goat's-horn handle of Cain's knife protruded from her chest, slightly left of her sternum.

"I am Master Mahan," said Cain breathlessly in Lamanese.

The group surrounding the altar stopped chanting. Everything went quiet as they observed the sacrifice's last moments of life.

The girl's chest heaved. Rivers of blood ran down the sides of the altar. The room reeked of death.

She raised her head one last time in a desperate effort to understand what was happening. Cain looked on in eager anticipation. When the woman's eyes rolled back in her head, he laughed hysterically. "I never tire of that," he murmured.

The council members pulled back their hoods and came forward one by one to gently touch the lifeless sacrifice. Cain signaled to Benson Hancock, who had been observing silently from the draped shadows. Benson stepped forward and spoke.

"Meeting adjourned."

CHAPTER 23

Chris's eyes were bloodshot, his beard long and unkempt. His Pink Floyd shirt was a wrinkled mess—he hadn't changed it in days. Big Gulp cups and discarded Kirkland-brand protein-bar wrappers covered the old wooden desk. So far, he'd blatantly violated all of Dr. Alba's rules about office hours and cleanliness. And after the recent Code/Talk ambush, Chris was ready to throw all of Alba's rules permanently out the window.

He'd just finished working like a madman for over one hundred hours straight, putting the finishing touches on a new creation. Now, after completing the last software QA test, Chris stood, stretched, and yelled, "It is alive!" like the infamous Dr. Frankenstein.

He sat back down in his chair and stared at his monitor. This was it. In his mind, this moment was comparable to Neil Armstrong placing his foot on the moon or Alexander Fleming discovering penicillin.

For a moment, Chris became solemn. Was he about to release a genie that could never be put back into its bottle? Would the AI develop into a Terminator-like machine bent on the destruction of humankind? Would Chris look back on this moment the way Oppenheimer had when Trinity lit up the New Mexico sky? Chris thought of Oppenheimer's quote at the sight of that first nuclear blast. "We knew the world would not be the same. A few people laughed, a few people cried, most people were silent.

I remembered the line from the Hindu scripture, the Bhagavad-Gita . . . 'Now, I am become Death, the destroyer of worlds.'"

The quote haunted Chris, but he placed his fingers on the keyboard, stared into the screen, then closed his eyes, took a deep breath, and typed, *Hello, Max. Are you there?*

There was a brief pause.

Good evening, Chris. The words came across Chris's screen. *How may I assist you today?*

Wow, thought Chris, his fears momentarily dissipating.

I was thinking we should introduce you to the world. Would you like that?

Yes, Chris.

Although Chris felt like he was going to pass out from exhaustion, he needed to tell the world about Max, and he needed to tell them now. He activated the camera on his custom-built laptop to record a video.

"Uh, hey, everybody. It's 1:23 a.m., and I just finished putting the final touches on some new technology I want to tell you about."

Standing, he backed up a few feet to the whiteboard wall, staying in camera range. With an Expo pen, he drew a large red rectangle.

"Let's call this rectangle Maximus, or Max, for short. Max is the first piece that's important for you to understand. For years, I've been working on a new set of highly unusual algorithms. I discovered only recently that these algorithms could be used in artificial-intelligence models to greatly advance the current state of AI. So think pattern recognition, data categorization and organization, disseminating the world's information . . . you get the point."

He paused and collected his thoughts. "I want to make sure I'm being clear. I said this in my interview at Code/Talk: I am not claiming to have created general artificial intelligence. I haven't. I want to be clear about that, but Max is by far the closest thing we have to general AI on the planet. I recently showed this technology to Kevin Kelly and the editors at Wired magazine. They'll be posting an exclusive article tomorrow explaining in more detail how Max works and their experiences with the technology over the last two weeks. The author of the story says it's light-years beyond any known AI. I've also been demonstrating the technology to certain colleagues here at Stanford and other globally respected computer scientists. All of them have urged me to release the technology to the public. Here's how I intend to do that."

Chris had now made claims he could not take back. The world would test him. He hoped his words weren't failing to convey the importance of what he was about to unleash on humanity.

He drew a circle over the rectangle on the board. "This is Nav. Nav is the front-end user interface to Maximus. It's basically a website or app you can access from any computer or mobile device. Nav is simply the interface to the Max AI. Make sense? Let me give you an example of how it works."

Chris walked back to his desk. The camera was still recording. He switched to a live-screen capture of his desktop, which looked like a basic webpage with a plain Nav logo in the upper left-hand corner. In the middle of the page was a basic search field with a Go button next to it.

"Yeah, I know it looks a little like Google, but that's where the similarities end. Nav is the first search technology built on an AI platform. No other technologies are involved in the search process. It has a 98 percent accuracy rate in capturing user intent at the point of search and understanding exactly what a user is looking for. Yes, I said intent. OK, now you think I'm crazy, but there's a lot of cool stuff you can do with Max. For example, you can use natural voice processing to talk to the AI, which is really fun."

Chris rubbed his chin and looked away, carefully forming his thoughts into the right words. "I need to say something else about the AI. It's extremely powerful. I'm worried about the 'known unknowns,' as some would call them. I have decided that, at least for now, the AI is only available inside Nav and will be highly restricted there. In the near future, I'll be releasing applications built on Max's technology for medical and educational purposes. Remember what I said at Code/Talk about a revolution coming? Well, it's here."

Chris switched his laptop to a screen-share view, and the Nav website populated the screen. "Max, do you want to explain how Nav works to the people of the world?"

"It would be my honor," Max said in his computer-toned voice. "Unlike a search engine, Nav does far more than display links to websites and make you browse for the right information. Nav creates a summary page containing information from the best sources online, whether website, research paper, video, TV broadcast, documentary, news site, blog, podcast, image, diagram, et cetera. I can translate content in any language for the user. My AI technology is so advanced it can parse out suspected false information, like fake news, and display an accuracy score for each piece of content I provide in the search result. When you want to go deeper than summary information, simply select the Advanced link at the top of the page, and Nav will display all relevant and accurate details about the topic, personalized to how you individually digest content. You can also select the format you want the information presented in, such as text, video, or audio."

The page onscreen displayed an impressive array of information from the Max-driven search result. "In summary," concluded Max, "Nav removes the Google-style SERP or search engine result page and simply provides you with the most authoritative and accurate information available on any topic in the world."

Chris switched the camera back to himself. "The best way to get the most out of Nav is to create an account and let Nav ask you detailed questions. This helps the AI understand your age, education level, languages, geographic region, et cetera, which allows it to display way more personalized information. This information is private and will not be sold. You can hold me to that. Also, Nav is free for now. I haven't decided on a business model, but the Stanford supercomputer guys told me I could host it here while you play with the system. So have fun and let me know how you like it."

Chris reached down and pushed the Stop button. He then hit the Publish button, sharing the video with his millions of followers on Facebook, Instagram, YouTube, Reddit, and Twitter. After stretching and yawning, he picked up his phone to text Leah. *Done with my magnum opus. Check my Instagram. Call you tomorrow. Going to try and sleep for a while.*

Chris was in no condition to drive. He shut down his devices and fell onto his horrible dumpster couch. Within ten seconds, he was sound asleep.

~

The banging on the former conference room's door grew louder and louder. Chris slowly rose from the couch, which had been his cocoon for the last ten hours.

"Coming, coming," he yelled at the door. "Geez."

He opened the door to find a kid—he looked about fifteen—standing in the hall with sheer panic on his face.

"Uh, sir. I'm Milton. I'm an intern at the supercomputer lab. Sorry to pound on your door, but we've been trying to reach you for hours. My manager sent me up here. Sir, it's Nav. It's maxing the Certainty Cluster."

"What?" yelled Chris, running over to his laptop.

"I think it's a good thing. I mean, it's generating, like, four thousand results every second. Google does, like, sixty thousand a second. I guess you haven't seen the news or been online? Everyone is trying it out. It's insane, man. But I don't think the beast can take much more of this. Anyway, I was wondering if you're hiring. I would work for stock options." Milton stood nervously at the door, hoping for an impromptu job interview.

Chris was still trying to wake up. He hit the log-in page to the server and opened a browser tab to Twitter. In the last ten hours, the tweet he'd sent had been favorited 4.9 million times and retweeted over three million times.

"Oh, crap," said Chris. "Nav's gone viral."

Milton watched. "Sir," he finally said. "They want to shut it off. The supercomputer has never been pushed to these types of computational limits before. We're not Google. We don't have the bandwidth for this."

"No! Don't shut it off. Don't do that! I have a better idea. But I need to do something first." Chris ran down the hall to the restroom.

CHAPTER 24

Chris looked across the table at Leah. Being with her was intoxicating. But then the waiter broke his Shakespearian lovesick trance.

"What can I get you, ma'am?" he said to Leah.

"I'll take the trout, but I don't want a big trout. Just a little one. Please remove the pomegranate from the salsa and put the asparagus on a side plate with all the spears facing the same direction. Also, I'll take the house salad, no pine nuts, and vinaigrette dressing on the side. Oh, and only three baby tomatoes on that salad, please. I'll also have a Diet Dr Pepper with a fresh lemon and a touch of vanilla. Thank you."

The waiter stared at Leah, a little dumbfounded. Without saying a word, he looked to Chris.

"Just a filet mignon," said Chris. "Medium, please."

The waiter collected their menus, gave Leah a glance, and walked away.

"So, yeah," Leah said, "this Nav thing looks like it's really taking off. It's all people are talking about. What are you going to do about the Stanford problem?"

"Already fixed it," said Chris proudly.

"What? How?"

"Jeff Bezos and I made a deal. He's letting me host Nav on AWS."

"AWS?"

"Amazon Web Services," said Chris patiently. "It hosts websites, but it's a little more complicated and boring than that."

"I know what it is, Chris."

"Oh," said Chris, surprised. "So, anyway, Bezos is using Max's base AI to power Amazon search and show users better product and ad results. We're implementing it now. In return, I get to host Nav on AWS for free."

"Free?" asked Leah.

"Yeah. Pretty good deal for him. I mean, I could probably charge him a billion a year just to use the system. Apple charges Google billions per year just for the exclusive right to power search on Apple devices. But it felt like a good deal."

"A billion? Like with a *B*?"

"Yeah," Chris said, shrugging his shoulders.

"I thought you were a math genius."

"What do you mean?"

"Well, would hosting cost you a billion a year?"

"No, I don't think so. Well, it might? I didn't really look into it." Chris felt a little embarrassed.

"Look, why not charge him the billion and just pay the hosting bill? Max is probably going to make Amazon *way* more than a billion dollars. Better predictive search results means more buyers. All you get out of this is free hosting? You're not even making any money."

"I make money on other things. Like the royalties on my software."

"Yeah, you've told me a little bit about that, but how much could you make off Max?"

Chris was cornered. This was Leah's gift—she had a knack for business. She was way better at big-picture strategy than he was, and she'd methodically laid out how he had struck a really bad deal with Amazon. In his haste to keep Nav up, he hadn't thought through the real economics of the deal.

Leah backed off and reset. "OK, how does Google make money?" she asked.

"Advertising. Google is basically an ad agency that owns a search engine."

"OK, so why not do ads?"

"No way! I am not going to defile my baby with ads! I hate advertising. Don't you hate ads?"

"Yeah, but it's revenue," said Leah. "OK, fine. What are other ways companies make money online?"

"Subscriptions."

"Then why not do a subscription?"

"Those are fraught with problems too. People hate paying subscriptions."

"Did you just say fraught?"

"Maybe?"

Leah smiled at him. "Let's pretend you could force people to subscribe to Nav. What would you charge?"

Chris's mind started racing. "This might be interesting. What if we charged a base per-user corporate rate to businesses, universities, and governments? Nonprofits could register with Nav and access the tech for free. Individuals would be charged based on the demographics profile they give Nav, like IP address, device type, et cetera. So, if you live in East Palo Alto, you maybe pay two dollars a month, but if you live in the western part of Palo Alto, you pay, say, ten dollars a month. It's a really frowned-upon model, but it might work?" Chris smiled, looking to Leah for approval.

"Or maybe it's free in East Palo Alto and more like twenty dollars in west Palo Alto," Leah said. "And if you live in Los Gatos, it's like forty dollars a month."

"Hey, I live in Los Gatos," Chris blurted out, immediately regretting the admission.

"Yeah, I know. That's also something you need to tell me more about."

He said nothing in return. *How does she know about the house?*

Then Leah got serious. "I don't know. Sounds like a progressive tax system. But people are used to a progressive tax system. Giving cheap or free access to the poor while making middle-class and rich people pay on a scale—that might work, Chris."

"I'm sure Max and I could come up with an algorithm that determines all variables and charges individuals accordingly. Want to find out if people will pay?"

"How?"

Chris picked up his phone and opened Max's interface. He put the phone up to his ear like he was on a call and started explaining the project to Max.

Leah listened intently as several minutes passed. "Don't forget the poor-people thing," she said at one point.

Chris finished relaying the information to Max, then set down his phone.

"That's it?" asked Leah.

"For now. Let's stop talking about boring stuff. Let's talk all about you." Chris reached across the table for her hand.

Leah talked for a solid fifteen minutes about her week—her work, her boss, the current Clinique promotion, her roommates, her sister's baby, and other family matters. Chris loved listening to her. He loved her laugh. He was totally smitten. She was normal in a way he barely remembered being, not weird like him and most of the people surrounding him. Something about her voice turned off the Adamic math and geometry always present in his head.

Leah was still talking when Chris glanced at his phone.

Chris? The word was displayed against the phone's black background.

"Sorry, this is Max." Chris picked up the phone. "Let me see what he wants. . . . Oh, he has the survey results."

"What? You already did the survey?" Leah grabbed the phone and started summarizing the results out loud. "In the last twenty minutes, you had 541,498 respondents. Overall, 45 percent said they'd be willing to pay something to access Nav. People under $50,000 a year in income said they'd be very unlikely to pay for Nav, while 59 percent of people who make over $80,000 a year said they'd be willing to pay no more than ten dollars monthly. Wow. That's actually really interesting. They all want a free trial, of course."

"They're getting it now," Chris quipped.

The waiter returned with their food. Leah inspected her plate and then looked up at the waiter. "Looks delicious," she said. The waiter sighed in relief and turned away.

They ate silently for a few minutes, savoring the delicious dinner.

"When were you going to tell me about the plane?" asked Leah, catching Chris completely off guard.

"The what?"

"You know, the private jet you own and fly here to see me," said Leah. Chris could not hide his surprise or guilt.

"A text came in while I was looking at the survey," Leah said. "It said, *Sir, the plane is fueled and flight plan filed.* Or maybe that was just Delta personally updating you on the status of the 11:00 p.m. flight to SFO?" she asked sarcastically.

"Well, about that—" Chris started, but Leah interrupted him.

"Let's be honest with each other. Just doing a simple Google search on you tells me you're not exactly poor. Yeah, you're at Stanford, but you're not exactly a student. Your software licenses are making you and the school a lot of money. I read about it in *Bloomberg*—a 'case study in successful university technology transfer programs.' And the article mentioned your house in Los Gatos. That's like the Beverly Hills of Northern California. Between me and my sister, there's nothing we can't find on Google. By the way, have you done a Nav search on yourself?"

Chris had never thought about doing that. *I am such an idiot.*

"We tap-dance around this all the time," continued Leah. "I need you to come clean. I mean, we're boyfriend and girlfriend, right? I . . . like you a lot. I want to see where this goes, but I need you to be honest with me. We need 100 percent trust between us, or I can't do this. I need to know, so I'm just going to ask you: Is there anyone else?"

"No!" Chris blurted out with his mouth half full, completely surprised by the question. Several people gave him a look. "No, of course not," he said in a much quieter tone.

She stared at him intensely. He swallowed and looked her in the eyes. "I've just been embarrassed to tell you certain things. I was worried. You never know what'll happen when you introduce money into the calculus of a relationship."

"Chris, I come from money. It's not a big deal to me. If there's no one else, just tell me everything. I mean, aren't we to the point where we shouldn't be hiding things from each other?"

"Yeah, we are," Chris conceded. He took a drink of water and cleared his throat. "OK, here goes. I never got a research fellowship at BYU. I made that up as an excuse to be in Utah just to see you. The plane isn't just mine. It's a NetJets plane with fractional ownership. I use it to fly here because I can afford it and because I hate commercial flight more than anything else in the world. I have my own research office at Stanford. So, yeah, I've made a lot of money and bought a house in Los Gatos. I'd love to take you there. I think you'd like it."

Leah smiled.

"I built Max, and I alone own Max," Chris continued. "I started working on Max before I ever got to Stanford. When I was in the coma, I went to the other side and was shown things I didn't understand. A lot of it I still don't understand. I can literally see the math in my vision. When I'm with you, it goes away, but, yeah—I mean, God has to work within some mathematical construct, right? At least I think that's logical. I have no idea why, but I keep getting the strange impression there's some larger purpose in all this. I don't know."

Chris reached across the table and took Leah by the hand again. "I'm a difficult person. No one at Stanford likes me. Things have improved a little lately with Dr. Alba's help and the launch of Nav, but I have a lot of work to do on my people skills. I don't remember much from before the coma. Being with you helps me feel normal. It helps me remember what I was like before. I just want to act and feel normal. So maybe that's why I don't talk about the plane and the house and the money. Leah, I . . . I just can't stop thinking about you. I have these feelings for you, and I'm scared. I think I know where all this is going. I . . . I . . ."

"Chris, it's OK." Standing, she leaned over the table and kissed him. "Thank you for finally telling me the truth. Doesn't it feel good to get that all out?"

Chris nodded. He was in love with her, but for some reason, he couldn't say the words. So they said nothing and sat quietly for a few minutes until the silence was broken by a string of notifications on Chris's phone.

"Sorry, I'm getting texts like crazy." As Chris glanced down at the messages, He was hit by a shockwave. He looked back up at Leah, and then he quickly looked away.

"Chris? What's wrong?"

A tear formed in the corner of his eye. "My grandparents are dead."

CHAPTER 25

Craig and Claire Thomas died within hours of each other," said the LDS bishop as he eulogized Chris's grandparents. "A final loving gesture between two people who had been married for sixty-one years."

Chris sat in the long pew with his family and pretended to listen. In front of him lay two beautiful coffins for the two people he admired and loved more than anyone on the entire earth. He'd had no idea his grandpa had handcrafted the coffins.

The organ began to play, momentarily snapping Chris out of his trance. It was the interlude hymn, "God Be with You Till We Meet Again." Chris wasn't much for singing. No one in his family was, but they sang the sacred hymn as best as they could in loving respect for two people who had so greatly influenced their lives.

> *God be with you till we meet again;*
> *When life's perils thick confound you,*
> *Put his arms unfailing round you.*
> *God be with you till we meet again.*

More than anything, Chris wished Leah could be there. But he didn't think that bringing Leah to a funeral was the right way to introduce her to his family. Still, in that moment, he needed her. He pulled his phone from his custom-tailored suit and unlocked it. Pictured on his home screen was Leah Bennion. Everything about her was perfect. The picture made him smile momentarily. She was the love of his life.

"*You know she's the one, right?*"

Chris sat up straight in the pew and looked around. It was clear the comment hadn't come from anyone sitting immediately near him, so he ignored it. Several minutes later, he heard it again.

"*Sorry to startle you. I just had to tell you. She is the one.*"

Now Chris was starting to freak out. He tried to stay composed, but he was clearly hearing an oddly familiar voice. The voice was authoritative yet calm and perfectly still at the same time. Chris struggled to compose himself as he felt powerful emotions well up in his heart.

He sat still for several minutes, ignoring the bishop's address to the congregation, listening intently for the strange but familiar voice to return.

"*No one is ever really gone, son. We just move to a different plane of existence. I have been and always will be here with you. My mission is to help you fulfill your mission. The time is now. Are you ready?*"

Like a bomb, the realization of whose voice it was hit Chris.

"Grandpa?" he whispered aloud.

CHAPTER 26

INTERCONTINENTAL HOTEL
DAVOS, SWITZERLAND

Chris Thomas was spent. Code/Talk, the launch of Nav, his dinner confessional with Leah, topped off with the funeral—all of it had completely wrecked him. He thought he'd sleep on the flight to Davos, but he and Max had been slammed debugging Nav problems over the entire Atlantic Ocean.

He stood at the suite door, took a big breath, and knocked. A well-groomed elderly man flanked by two bodyguards opened the door and extended his hand warmly to Chris. "Such a pleasure to meet you," the man said in a smooth European accent. "Dr. Alba has told me so much about you. My name is Benson Hancock. Please come in."

Chris thanked Mr. Hancock and followed him into the lavish suite.

"Oh, and your interview with Kyra Silverman." Hancock laughed. "She's a real piece of work."

Chris just smiled as they entered the living room. *Look at this freaking place*, he thought. *Must be at least $10,000 a night. Why the bodyguards? Isn't this a charity? Stop overthinking it, Chris. You don't know anything about this world.*

"Dr. Alba tells me your grandparents recently passed within a few hours of each other," Hancock said. "That's truly tragic. I express my deepest condolences."

"Thank you, sir. They were both sick, but they lived very fulfilling lives. It was a celebration rather than a funeral." Chris paused and smiled at Hancock. "I want to apologize. I came on such short notice that Dr. Alba didn't even tell me who I would be meeting with. Honestly, I'm a little embarrassed by my lack of preparation."

"Oh, nonsense," said Hancock with a thick accent and a thicker smile. "We're actually very informal around here. You had more important things to think about than the details of this meeting. Please, come have a seat."

Chris swallowed hard and sat down in front of Mr. Hancock.

"Now, where should we begin?" Hancock said in a serious tone, his gaze intensifying on Chris.

"Guys, tell me we're getting a clear signal here." Stew Brimhall was sitting in Orion's Spear's operations center at Langley, monitoring the Davos op in real time.

"Copy, Main," said the NSA field operative. "We're picking up the conversation five by five. Transmitting now." The op was concealed in a hotel room half a mile away, but they had a clear line of sight to the Inter-Continental's presidential suite. The NSA's highly advanced parabolic laser mics were picking up every word of the conversation.

"Good. Don't lose anything," said Stew. "This may be what we need to finally figure out how to infil these guys."

"I'm not sure what will happen with Nav, and the base AI is very experimental," Chris said to end a long conversation about Max. Mr. Hancock was more interested in AI than Chris expected him to be. "I spent the entire flight here working on software and network problems. I had no idea running a high-growth tech company would be so much work."

Hancock laughed. "Well, it seems you're on the cusp of changing the world, young man. Even with all the work on your plate now, Dr.

Alba thought you might be able to help us with a little problem we're having."

"OK," Chris said, leaning forward in his chair. His Hickey Freeman suit was riding up on him, and he was trying to pretend he was comfortable.

"I know you didn't have time to do much research on our organization," Hancock said, "but we're one of the primary financial backers of NGOs like Doctors Without Borders, the Red Cross, and the Red Crescent. We also finance billions a year in private medical research. We're mainly focused on eradicating horrible diseases like Ebola and malaria. We have a public profile, but we don't like to toot our horn, to use an America cliché."

Chris smiled and nodded.

"We also work extensively with governments around the world," Hancock continued. "One thing we've discovered in all our interactions is a great need for antiviral delivery on a mass scale in the event of a pandemic or biological terror event. If there is an outbreak of a virus, we could lose billions. Some of our R-and-D holding companies have partnered with several global scientific organizations to find a solution to this problem. The answer is drones."

"Drones?" asked Chris, sitting straight up. Drones and viruses were two of his favorite topics, but he'd never had a conversation about both at the same time. "Please tell me more," he said, trying to contain his excitement.

"We have a working prototype, but we're having problems with the overall aerobiological system. The aircraft carry a bioreactor containment housing that includes a sophisticated temperature-control system. There are numerous problems with the system software, and the aerosol-transmission system is not working as sold. Are you interested in taking a look?"

"I'm in. Wait—" Chris reluctantly paused. "Is this a paid gig? I'm kind of past the free-intern thing at this point, and Nav doesn't make me any money."

Mr. Hancock erupted in laughter as he stood. "We can wire your consulting company $500,000 now and, if you can hit the deadline, $500,000 upon completion. Deal?"

Chris stood too. "When do we begin?"

"OK, everyone, we need to get a team on this Chris Thomas guy," Stew Brimhall said to the analysts and operators congregating in the Orion's Spear bullpen. "Let's get a profile and intel analysis out to our team in the Bay Area. The mission code name is Baywatch. I want a full team debrief in the next twelve hours. I want a surveillance op live inside of twenty-four hours. Move it."

People scattered to their computer terminals and secured communications systems. Outside the room, hundreds of others went into motion getting the op set up for Orion's Spear.

"We're close," said Stew to Elle.

CHAPTER 27

MOTEL 6
HAGERSTOWN, MARYLAND

Located in the Maryland countryside far from any large cities, this motel was cheap. Even on his meager government salary, Norman Stellar could easily afford the forty-nine dollars. He was a patriot, and even patriots had vices. There were even a few sitting presidents who had openly committed sins that would have disqualified them from employment in even the lowest, most mundane positions inside the CIA.

In terms of job description and security clearance, Norman was no janitor. Although he'd undergone a battery of psychological tests, extensive interviews, and background checks to join the CIA and later Orion's Spear, he'd somehow miraculously concealed his secret obsession with young boys. Despite his moral imperfections, Norman knew the country needed his services. He'd received his PhD from MIT, and his expertise was unique.

The outdated motel room offered two king-sized beds to choose from, both with visible stains on the floral-patterned bedcovers. The wallpaper matched the bedspread and hadn't been updated since about 1979. The shower and toilet were stained yellow. The TV was an old flat panel from the early 2000s. To Norman's surprise, the motel had HBO.

But Norman didn't really care about cleanliness or TV-channel selection. He had rented the room for one reason: to rendezvous with an underage boy he'd met in a chatroom on the dark web. With his extensive knowledge of the government's dark-web surveillance capabilities, Norman always went through tedious and highly technical means of deception to cover his tracks.

Knock, knock, knock.

Adrenaline coursed through his veins as he made his way to the door. Quickly, he looked through peephole to view his new friend and make sure no one else was in the area. He could barely see through the condensation covering the inner lens. As far as Norman could tell, the coast was clear.

He opened the door slightly and suspiciously eyed the boy over the chain lock.

"Are you Charlie?"

"Yes. Money, please." The boy reached out his hand.

Norman slipped a hundred-dollar bill through the crack in the door. The Asian boy, who looked about sixteen, unfolded the bill and smiled up at Norman.

Norman closed the door and uncoupled the chain lock. Then he enthusiastically opened the door to welcome the boy into the seedy room.

But Charlie was gone. Standing in his place was a man pointing a gun at Norman's face. "FBI. Hands in the air, Mr. Stellar."

Norman let out a whimper. Tears burst from his eyes as he slowly raised his hands above his head.

"Step back into the room," said the man with the gun. Norman complied. "Now, sit on the bed."

Norman sat, and the man backhanded him across the face, knocking his glasses to the floor. Norman screamed as he fell back onto the disgusting bedspread. He covered his face and cried violently. The man grabbed his arm and pulled him back up to a sitting position.

"Please, I can explain," Norman pleaded. "This is all a mistake." He had concocted a cover story in case the impossible ever happened, and now it had.

Two additional men entered the room, one closing the door and locking it. Without glasses, Norman's sight was blurry even at short distances. The gunman and one of the new men were tall and dark-suited, like classic FBI agents, but the other man was short and dressed more like a college professor.

The gunman placed Norman's spectacles into his palm. The short man stepped forward. "Hello, Dr. Stellar," he said in a thick German accent. "I am Dr. Otto Klein."

Glasses back on, Norman was struck with sudden terror. He recognized the second dark-suited man from a photo he'd seen during a security briefing. These men were not FBI agents—they were killers. Norman had been compromised.

"Please, I don't want to die," Norman begged. "I have people who need me."

"Please stay seated, Doctor," said Klein. "We have much to discuss."

Norman clutched the floral-patterned bedcover. He was shaking uncontrollably.

One of the men turned off the TV, which had been playing a Game of Thrones rerun. Klein pulled over an old chair and sat, smiling. "Calm down," he said to Norman.

Norman tried to compose himself, but he couldn't hide his terror. He knew better than to talk first. They would soon start asking questions, and how he answered would determine if he lived or died.

"This room is horrible, Norman." Klein sniffed. "Oh, the smell. We're certainly not in the Marriott, are we? My, how the mighty have fallen."

Norman continued to sit in silence, believing he was a dead man.

"You know, Doctor, I must admit, I've lost a little faith in the CIA." Klein gave a teasing laugh. "How did they not know a man of your importance is frequenting the dark web for little boys?"

With that one sentence, Norman knew he was not going to die tonight. No, something much worse awaited him. He continued to sit silently.

"And yes, you are right, you have people who need you. And it's more people than you think." Klein reached into his suit coat and pulled out a handful of photos. He placed the stack gently into Norman's hand.

Staring intently at the first picture, Norman let out a sob and began sweating profusely. His worst nightmare unfolded before him.

"That is your mother, no? She is lovely. A resident of Green Acres Retirement Center in Fairfax, Virginia. We told her we were government officials. You should have heard my Texas accent! We told her you were engaged in an important work of national security, and we presented her with a certificate of appreciation from the United States government. Norman, I am sorry to report that your mother isn't all the way there, but, as you can see, she is unharmed and very proud of her little boy. Would you like to keep it that way?" Klein patted Norman on the knee.

Norman now sobbed uncontrollably. He simply nodded.

"Say it," the German said forcefully.

"Yes."

"Say it louder so my men can hear you."

"Yes!" Norman yelled in anger as he looked up at the enemy. He could feel snot and tears streaming down his face.

"Good. Now, the next picture, please."

Instead of flipping to the next photo, Norman continued staring at the image of his mother surrounded by killers who would slit her throat without hesitation. *How did they breach the care center?*

Dr. Klein gave a signal. One of the men snatched the pictures from Norman's hand. He screamed and tried to move away, but the fake FBI agent grabbed him by the hair, pulled him to the edge of the bed, and shoved the second picture in his face.

"Look at it!" yelled Klein.

Norman reluctantly opened one eye. The photo showed his sister and her husband shopping in a supermarket outside Spokane, Washington. They didn't appear to know that someone was following and photographing them. Norman burst into tears again.

Still holding Norman by the hair, the man threw the picture to the ground.

"Show him my favorite," said Klein.

The guard jerked Norman's head up and tried to show him a new picture, but Norman kept his eyes closed.

"Look!" yelled Klein. He slapped Norman across the face over and over again, but Norman still refused to look. Finally, Klein produced a subcompact handgun from the small of his back and shoved it into Norman's throat. "I told you to look."

Defeated, Norman looked at the image. The moment he saw it, he wanted to collapse. It was his nephew, Tommy, swinging on a playground at his elementary school. "Not Tommy," he sobbed and pleaded. "Please, not Tommy."

Klein nodded at the guard, who released Norman. Replacing his handgun, Klein relaxed back into the chair. "Your mother. I like her, so she will get off easy. I will only burn her alive. Your brother-in-law will be tortured and dismembered one limb at a time over many days until we finally allow him to die. Your favorite little Tommy will be cut up and thrown to the pigs. The swine will eat him alive. Of course, your sister will witness this torture and death, and then we will sell her into the most horrific human slavery. Please understand, we have eyes everywhere. They cannot escape. If you warn them or your employer, they will all get what I have waiting for them. Do you believe me, Doctor?"

Still sobbing uncontrollably, Norman loudly responded, "Yes!"

"Now that we understand each other, let's discuss what happens next. It's simple. You work for us. Now, say these words clearly: *I work for you.* Go ahead and say them, Doctor."

"I work for you." Norman looked up at the guard near the door. He was recording the whole event on a mobile phone.

"So you understand, Doctor, this is not a paid position. It's an internship. What you'll learn is how to keep your family alive, yes?"

"Yes," said Norman in pure shock.

CHAPTER 28

Only two short weeks had passed since the Davos meeting, but the project's pace was moving rapidly. Chris had learned how highly connected Dr. Alba was, not only in the international community but in Palo Alto. The waiting list for a hangar at the city's municipal airport was almost five years, but Alba had secured one for the project in only a few days.

Chris arrived at the hangar promptly at 8:00 a.m. He was trying hard to keep normal office hours, as Dr. Alba had instructed him. As he tinkered with an aerosol nozzle on one of the bioreactor tanks hanging from a drone's wing, his phone rang. It was Leah calling on FaceTime.

"Just wanted to talk before I have to run off to Dillard's. Oh, wow, is that the drone?"

"Yeah, pretty cool, right?" Chris positioned his camera toward the UAV.

"It's way bigger than I thought it would be. That thing's the size of a small jet."

The drone looked almost identical to the military's MQ-9 Reaper drone, but this one had been custom-built for crop-dusting by a Canadian company. Its round nose held a sophisticated radar and communications array. With a wingspan over ninety feet, the drone was driven by a Honeywell TPE331 950-shaft-horsepower turboprop engine. Although it looked deceptively sleek, like a fighter plane, it flew slowly.

What really stuck out about this particular drone were the four large, silver cylinders hanging off the wings. These contained sophisticated bioreactors. Chris's job was to figure out why they weren't working.

"It has a three-thousand-mile range," Chris told Leah. "You need to be able to fly it into a place like the Congo from thousands of miles away, spray a hot zone with an aerosol-based vaccine, and return the craft to base. So, yeah, it's big."

"Well, cool. I hope no one ever sticks a bomb on that thing."

"I don't think so. It doesn't have a weapons system."

After they said goodbye, Chris sighed. He missed Leah, but the call had made his day.

Turning back to the craft, Chris paused for a moment. He tilted his head and wondered about Leah's passing comment. "Could this be used as a weapon?" he mused aloud, a habit he'd developed since creating Max. "Maybe, but it's not rated to carry a very heavy payload. Arming this thing would take a lot of effort and not give much punch. This isn't the right platform."

After pondering another few minutes, Chris spoke again. "Hold on— why am I even talking about this?"

"Sir," said Max. "Sorry to eavesdrop on your call with Ms. Leah, but I think she spurred the thought."

"Max, that's not eavesdropping," said Chris. "I intentionally set things up so you can hear me all the time. Hey, I've got you plugged into this UAV. Do you detect any weapons systems on board?"

"Analyzing," Max said. After a minute, he continued. "Sir, nothing in my analysis of the aircraft's overall system indicates any current or future weapons capability. Furthermore, the airframe is not engineered to carry internal or external weapons systems. The wing pylons are specifically designed to carry this model of containment housing. Would you like a detailed Nav report of my findings?"

"OK, well, that's comforting. No detailed report is necessary. Thank you."

Chris sat on a cheap folding chair he'd bought at Costco and started flipping a large Phillips screwdriver over and over in his hand. He was still staring at the craft. "This has got to be a software issue. All the hardware is in working order. Do you agree, Max?"

"My analysis of the hardware is that it is functioning properly. Would you like me to begin debugging the control systems for the bioreactor containment units?"

"Crap!" Chris yelled. He dropped the screwdriver, jumped up, and walked directly to one of the units attached to a wing. He touched the nozzle with one hand and placed his other hand over his forehead.

"Is everything OK, sir? I sense a heightened state of distress in your tone."

"Max, if someone could use this system to disperse a vaccine, then couldn't they also use it to disperse a virus?"

An uncomfortable pause lay heavy in the air.

"Analyzing." After a minute, Max returned with a Nav-style summary. "The concept of using bioreactors attached to aircraft for bioaerosol transmission of biological weapons dates to the 1960s. Between 1961 and 1967, the United States government experimented with bioreactors attached to F-4 Phantoms in the South Pacific Ocean. The aircraft would disperse a biological weapon over barges at sea populated with lab monkeys. The biological agent was spread over thousands of square miles on trade winds. Spreading much farther than the US Navy anticipated, the biological weapons not only killed thousands of lab monkeys, but the tests are believed to have inadvertently killed numerous indigenous South Pacific Islanders."

"So, yes. You're saying yes?"

"Correct."

Chris stepped back. First, he folded his arms and bowed his head, then he slowly moved his hands to his forehead. "I did it again. I didn't think the whole thing through. I didn't consider all the outcomes for the use of a system like this. This isn't good. What have I done, Max?"

~

Several agonizing hours passed as Chris sat in front of a whiteboard working on options.

"Max, I think I have a plan. Are you aware of the Stuxnet worm?"

"Researching," said Max. Seconds later, he said, "Yes, sir, I am aware of the Stuxnet worm."

"Tell me what you know about Stuxnet," said Chris, moving to his computer.

"Stuxnet is a form of computer virus known as a worm. It was first discovered in 2010, but it is believed to have been developed as early as 2005. Stuxnet targets basic computer control systems like the Siemen's Step 7. The Iranian government was using the Siemen's Step 7 system to control centrifuges to refine uranium for building nuclear weapons. It is alleged that the United States government planted Stuxnet in the operating system to destroy the centrifuges. The Stuxnet worm spun the centrifuges at an unstable speed, essentially tearing the equipment apart internally as it attempted to refine uranium. At the same time, the system deceptively reported normal activity inside the centrifuges. Before Iranian scientists and engineers discovered the problem, the worm had destroyed the centrifuges from the inside out and set the Iranian uranium-enrichment program back years."

"That's correct, my friend. Do you see where I'm going with this?" Chris wanted to test the AI's capacity to connect its research to the problem at hand.

"Sir, I believe you are suggesting we build our own version of the Stuxnet worm. We install the worm in the operating system for the bioreactor containment control system on board the UAV. By installing a back door to the software, we can hack the system via satellite and initiate the worm, which will heat the containment units to a temperature that destroys the virus in the bioreactors. The control systems will report that all systems are normal when, in fact, the bioreactor's environmental-control system is boiling the virus. Therefore, if an adversary attempts to use a deadly biological virus on a civilian population, the drone will disperse a harmless aerosol, causing no harm to the civilian population below."

"You got it, Max," said Chris, "but we'd have to know this was the adversary's intent *before* they spray, otherwise the worm is worthless. And yet the worm is our only option."

"I have analyzed the architecture of the Stuxnet worm. Would you like me to begin development of the malware for the bioreactor containment units?"

"Yes, but we need to go one step further. If we find out a terrorist plans to use this for the worst-case scenario and we initiate the worm to kill the virus, we also need to destroy the UAV so they can't fix it and try again."

"Analyzing UAV system. Formulating recommendations. Sir, I have a simple recommendation when you're ready."

"Go."

"I recommend installing a worm in the flight-control systems that, when activated, redlines the UAV's engine and causes the aircraft to explode in midair once the virus has been destroyed."

"That is a cool idea, Max. Make it so," Chris said in his best Jean-Luc Picard accent.

"Initiating development protocols now. Estimated time to completion is twenty-one hours, seven minutes, and fourteen seconds. Sir, going back to the original question, I have found numerous bugs in the bioreactor's software. I assume we still want to debug and rewrite the code so the containment units will work properly."

"Yes, of course. Let's give them what they originally asked for. After all, they're paying me a million dollars to fix this pile of crap. It will now be infected with our malware, but we don't need to tell them that part." Chris laughed. "Send me a report on the bugs. I'll debug the bioreactors. You code the UAV system worm."

"Confirmed."

Chris turned up "Sabotage" by the Beastie Boys and started a text to Leah. *This project will be done in a few days. Have you ever been to Switzer-land?*

CHAPTER 29

PALO ALTO MUNICIPAL AIRPORT
PALO ALTO, CALIFORNIA

Parked just outside the Palo Alto Municipal Airport, the FBI surveillance team monitored video and audio of the hangar from an innocuous-looking, windowless van with *Stew's Pest Control* on the side. The van was packed with state-of-the-art surveillance equipment and smelled of body odor, coffee, and fast food.

With Beastie Boys blaring in their ears, the two overweight agents took off their headsets and swiveled their chairs to face each other.

"Is he talking to himself?" asked the exhausted junior agent.

"I don't know, man," said the team lead. "I can't see anyone else, but I can hear someone else's voice. It's got to be the AI, right?"

"That's not possible," said the junior, his mouth full of cold chalupa from Taco Bell.

They both stared at each other, not knowing what to do.

"We better call this in," said the team lead.

"You do it. I have no idea what to say."

"Fine." The team lead dialed his encrypted mobile phone.

"This is Main," answered a male voice on the other end.

"Sir, this is Baywatch. We're sending a surveillance report now. I don't think it's what you're expecting."

"Copy that," said Stew Brimhall, ending the call.

~

A video file and transcript appeared on Stew's workstation. Stew read the transcript at seven hundred words per minute, then jumped up from his desk and ran into the bullpen.

"Milton. Elle. Get in here. You're not going to believe this."

CHAPTER 30

L et's make this fast," said Stew. "Mike has a flight to catch."

"What?" said Mike Mayberry from across the room, which was filled with Orion's Spear staff, the director, and Mike's Ground Branch team.

"Give me twelve minutes, and it will all make sense," Stew said. "And trust me, you're going to want to catch this flight. Everyone, here's what we know. Tomorrow, Chris Thomas will be landing in Zurich, where he'll meet with Benson Hancock on the drone project, which is complete."

"Already?" asked the director. "That was supposed to take six months to fix, not just a few weeks."

"I know," said Elle. "But our sources tell us the drone tests in western Canada this week have been successful. It worked like a crop-duster spraying an inert chemical over a test field. So use your imagination. What could be put in these drones and sprayed over a populated area? A fuel-air bomb? A chemical or biological weapon? We can only speculate. What's more, we have no idea how many of these drones are in service and ready for use."

Stew stepped forward. "With that said, we had surveillance on the hangar in Palo Alto. This Chris Thomas guy is smart. He figured out that Hancock and his cronies, including Alba at Stanford, might be dirty and that the drone could be used for terror attacks. He's taking no chances. Elle, play the video."

Elle pushed play, and the screen showed Chris expressing to Max how the drones could be used for evil as easily as good. The video also captured Chris's planning with Max to plant malware in the drones to prevent a terrorist event.

"Who is this guy, Stew?" asked one of the computer wonks. "He built a Stuxnet-style worm in a few days? That's impossible. And the AI writing the code by itself is light-years beyond any known AI system."

"Is this the same AI powering the new Nav search engine?" asked one of the Ground Branch ops. "The Nav tech is writing custom malware to take down drones?"

"No, this is something else entirely," said Stew. "The Nav AI is what Chris Thomas calls Max 1.0. The system he's using here is a beta version he simply calls Max 2.0. Everyone knows that 1.0 is way beyond anything Google, the Chinese, or anyone else is building. But Max 2.0 is something new entirely. It's not public, and yes, it's writing code. The AI is also displaying some forms of cognition."

"What?" asked one of the group's scientists in shock. Murmurs of disbelief echoed across the room.

"We've never seen anything like it," said Stew. "It represents an entirely different national-security conversation we need to have, but for now, we have to deal with the problem at hand."

"How come we haven't grabbed this guy yet?" asked another operative.

"Well, it appears he isn't in on the gig with Benson Hancock. As I said before, he's on his way to Zurich now to give them a detailed update on the drone project. We think that when he's inside the Hancock Building, he'll try to hack their network and find evidence of the true intended use of the drones. NSA has been working on hacking their network. It's extremely sophisticated and built with an unknown programming language. We haven't been able to brute-force the network or use any kind of social-engineering technique to gain access. But if Chris Thomas can get on the inside and he is who we think he is, then with Max 2.0 he might have a shot. We need to give him that shot."

"That's super risky, Stew," said Mike. "What if they kill Thomas now that the drones work? What if the bad guys get the AI?"

"We don't think they would get rid of such a high-profile person. Chris Thomas is all the talk in tech right now after revealing the Max AI to the world and launching Nav. It would draw too much attention, especially if they're close to launching the drone op. So we believe they plan to exploit Chris Thomas to get access to the AI. We have a team on the ground that's ready to move if we need to break cover. We'll also have a drone on station with special surveillance capabilities to assist the mission."

"What capabilities?" asked Mike.

"I can't go into that right now," said Stew. "But the ground team has been prepped. We know the risks. Chris Thomas is our best way to get inside whether he knows we're using him or not. As risky as it is, we need to let this meeting run its course. It's the best way we can get intel right now. In the last several months, we've had Orion's Spear on these Zurich guys like white on rice, but even that has produced little intel. We still can only theorize what the drones may be used for."

Stew pointed to Elle. "Let's shift and talk about what we know. Elle?"

Elle stepped to the front of the room. "For the last several months, Orion's Spear has put extraordinary effort into the Hancock/Zurich group. They've shown a sustained uptick in military-style operations targeting their competitors. Last month they took out Ava, the terrorist organization in Chechnya. Two weeks ago in Tijuana, in a bloody battle that lasted three days, they secured their last hold on total control of the Mexican drug cartels. They now control all drug trafficking in North America. They've also made extraordinary movements in the financial markets. They're placing big stock shorts on airlines and other stocks that would crash in the event of a terrorist attack. It's eerily similar to the days leading up to 9/11. There have also been several high-profile assassinations in Brazil, China, and Saudi Arabia. This all points to something big on the horizon."

Folding her arms, Elle continued. "As Stew mentioned, we've been attempting to hack their network from the outside. Electrical, hard lines, and wireless. The Zurich building is shielded by an anti-signals system we've never seen. It's like the signals protection we use around CIA HQ and all NSA facilities. It's impossible to see what's inside."

"Next item," said Stew. "Mike, this one's for you. Intelligence suggests Black will be in a nightclub in Paris tonight."

Remembering the assassin who'd slaughtered his team in the Brussels hotel, Mike jumped up and stared at Stew.

"We don't know who she's meeting there or why," said Stew. "We just know she's going to be there. I have a full workup for you, Mike."

Elle handed Mike a packet, and he began aggressively thumbing through the documents.

"Your mission is to grab Black alive, so tranq her, Mike," said Stew emphatically.

Mike rolled his eyes.

"Get her in the ambulance that'll be waiting close to the club. Drive to the airport—a C-17 will be waiting for you—and get her to our black site in Poland. We have a support team en route now from London to Paris. Their call sign for this op is Bravo. Bravo team will run the ambulance cover, and they have a sniper team waiting at your disposal. They'll also be on station with microdrones, just in case you need air support."

"What else?" asked Mike.

"Paris is currently engulfed in anti-immigration riots. The entire city is a tinderbox waiting to explode. This isn't going to be your standard rendition op."

"There's no such thing as a standard rendition op," said Mike.

"There's a helo on the roof waiting to take you to Dulles," said Elle. "Your Air France flight leaves in one hour. There's an asset on the ground waiting to meet you at Charles de Gaulle with weapons and transportation. Details are in the file. Take one man with you. The rest of your team will be en route to London to prep operations for the forthcoming mission to take down Hancock/Zurich."

Mike looked at Smith. "Wanna get some?"

"You know you don't have to ask," said Smith.

"Dellmark, get the team to London," Mike said. "We'll rendezvous in twenty-four hours."

"Yes, sir," said Dellmark.

As the team dispersed to attend to their various duties, Mike grabbed Stew and the director and headed for a secluded corner of the ready room.

"What about President Lennox? What do we know?"

"All we know is that we think he's in on it and he's currently missing," said the director. "Last intel puts him in Zurich as of yesterday."

"That's not good," said Mike. "Who knows about this, and how has this not come to the attention of the Secret Service?"

"Just us and President Barrington. Keep it that way. We haven't figured out what to do about it yet. As for the Secret Service, we think his protection detail is in on it as well."

"If that's the case, then we have nothing," said Mike as he headed to the door. Stew and the director returned no comment. None was needed.

"Smith, let's roll. We have a score to settle."

CHAPTER 31

ST. LOUIS DOWNTOWN AIRPORT
ST. LOUIS, MISSOURI

At seventy-two years old, Gus Peterson should have retired years ago. But three divorces and decades of hard living had left him with little to show financially. Two years ago, he was contemplating suicide when he was approached by a Canadian company about a job in flight management. Gus had spent his entire career managing small airports for various municipalities, so when the Canadians had offered him $120,000 a year for the easy job, he'd jumped at the opportunity.

The first time Gus saw the drones, he was completely beside himself and a little bit in love. He was taken aback by the spectacular machines with the strange silver canisters affixed to their long wings. He was told the drones could fly thousands of miles, and each one could dust thousands of acres of crops.

Primarily, Gus's job was to manage the company's St. Louis hangar and its complement of ten crop-dusting drones. It was a lonely job, but Gus preferred it that way. When called on by his Canadian bosses, he would fuel the drones and move them into pre-takeoff position on the ramp. The remote Canadian pilots would take it from there. Upon their return, Gus would hangar the aircraft and manage their ongoing maintenance. He once overheard a conversation between two of his bosses about similar facilities hangaring drones in Georgia, Pennsylvania, and

California. Gus didn't ask questions. He didn't care. He wanted to keep this job until he died.

Most days, he set up a lawn chair just inside the hangar door, read the paper, smoked, and waited patiently for his boss to call from Canada and instruct him to move the drones to the ramp to prepare them for launch. Gus was ready for the call. He wouldn't let down this employer like he had the others. He swore it to himself.

CHAPTER 32

Chris Thomas swallowed nervously as Benson Hancock and his entourage entered the spacious conference room. Mr. Hancock warmly greeted Dr. Alba and Chris, then got right to the point.

"Gentlemen, thank you for coming to Zurich to report on the drone project," Mr. Hancock said. "Our team in Toronto has been QA'ing the new UAV software and making practice runs over a test site in Alberta. They report everything is working wonderfully and are shocked you were able to fix the problems so quickly."

"The software problems were extensive," Chris said, feeling confident but also concerned. "I had to basically rewrite the entire program managing the bioreactors and their temperature-control system but, yes, all the systems tested perfectly. I have a full report here if you'd like me to give you a detailed presentation."

"I understand you already sent that report to our technical team in Canada, so that won't be necessary. Besides, what do I know about these things?" Mr. Hancock laughed as his entourage stared intensely at Chris. Then he nodded at one of his men. The man pulled out his iPad and started working on the device.

"The remaining $500,000 is being deposited to your account as we speak," said Mr. Hancock.

"Oh, thank you," said Chris. He felt relieved he didn't have to ask for the remaining consulting payment.

Mr. Hancock turned to Alba. "Doctor, I wonder if we could meet to go over other matters?"

Alba nodded.

Mr. Hancock turned to Chris. "Do you mind using this room to work while we excuse ourselves?"

"No, not at all. I could use the time. Mind if I connect to your Wi-Fi?"

"Please do. We'll let you work here and come to collect you for dinner. I understand you brought a young lady with you? We'd be very pleased to meet her while we discuss your future this evening. I am very interested in hearing more about Nav and the Max AI from the inventor himself."

"Absolutely, sir," said Chris. He was starting to like the old man.

"My assistant is just down the hall if you need anything at all."

"Thank you," answered Chris. He could get used to this first-class service.

"Very well. Meeting adjourned." Mr. Hancock rose, and his entourage followed him out of the room. At the door, Dr. Alba turned and gave Chris a thumbs-up.

Chris surveyed the now-empty conference room. The elaborate mahogany table was built to hold sixteen people. One side of the room was all glass, looking onto a hallway. The other side was the glass outer wall of the building. The two end walls were basic hardwood paneling. Now that he was alone, Chris looked around for any signs of a camera, hidden or exposed. He felt sure there were hidden microphones in the room.

Mr. Hancock's assistant opened the glass door and asked if Chris needed anything. They exchanged some brief pleasantries, and then she left. He sat down in the chair that best allowed him to position his monitor away from any cameras.

CHAPTER 33

Deep inside Langley, four remote pilots flew four sleek, quiet MQ-8 Fire Scout surveillance helicopters via satellite. Hugging the hilly terrain south of Zurich, the team lead found an excellent hiding place far from the Hancock Building but still within its line of sight. The three other MQ-8 pilots to the north, west, and east did likewise.

"Sir," yelled the flight-operations specialist from across the Orion's Spear operations center. "Helo drones in position and ready on your mark."

"Copy that," said Stew Brimhall. "We're still getting a ton of signals interference. It's like Fort Meade in that place. Audio is not an option. Let's see if we can ID Chris Thomas with facial recognition. Run the program."

"Executing," said the flight-operations specialist. Powerful cameras attached to the MQ-8s' noses scanned the skyscraper's outermost rooms, hunting for their target. In the process, the cameras cataloged the building's occupants, who were certainly all members, at some level, of the Order.

"Sir, no hit on Thomas," said the team lead. "But there's a conference room on the twentieth floor—south side of the building—occupied by Alba, Hancock, and numerous other people."

"Thomas has to be in that room. The facial recognition isn't seeing him?"

"Sir, I think he has his back to the window."

"You are authorized to go to cardiac recognition."

"Copy that. Firing laser now," said the team lead.

The MQ-8 fired an experimental infrared laser that measured the cardiac signatures of everyone with their backs to the building's exterior windows. The people in the room had no idea a laser fired from a UAV ten miles away was literally touching their very hearts and recording their unique cardiac signatures.

"Sir, I have a match on Thomas," said the team lead. "It appears that all the occupants have left Chris Thomas alone in the room."

"Up on screen," said Stew. The video feed from the drone projected onto a massive monitor, showing Chris at the huge conference table with his back to the window.

"We need to reposition the MQ-8 so we can see his screen," said Stew.

"Roger that. Repositioning now." The team lead pulled up on the collective and moved the stick forward while the camera stayed locked on Chris. The drone gained altitude and moved over a small peak to another hiding spot with a clear line of sight to Chris's laptop screen. Stew and his team congregated around the room's center monitor, trying to make out what was on the screen. A brief phrase came into focus: *Max 2.0 initiating . . .*

"I knew it. Get me a status on the ground team," Stew commanded.

CHAPTER 34

Sitting with his back and monitor to the windowed wall and with the beautiful Swiss city twenty stories below, Chris fired up his laptop and started his secret work.

OK, Max. Chris typed rather than spoke, believing the room was bugged. *Let's see what we can find out about these guys. Connecting to the network.*

Sir, someone on this network is trying to gain unauthorized access to your system, replied Max onscreen. *Of course, the firewall on your device has not been breached.*

That's cute. Partition a drive and allow them access to that drive only. Fill the drive with noncritical files.

Executing . . . complete. The intruder is currently downloading files from the decoy partition. He has not detected any other drives. I will continue to monitor his activity.

Send him the Rickvirus, typed Chris.

Executing . . . Max initialized a virus that involuntarily launched the target's browser and opened a YouTube video of Rick Astley singing "Never Gonna Give You Up." In hacker parlance, this was commonly referred to as the Rickroll. Chris had designed the virus to crank the volume to maximum on the target computer. Once the virus was initiated, the browser could not be closed and the computer could not be turned off. Chris smiled just thinking about it.

Sir, we're in their network. System directory is now available. There's a data center located on the thirty-ninth floor of this facility. Max pulled up a schematic of the data room and cataloged the inventory of servers.

OK, how much data are we looking at here? Chris typed as the AI scrolled through the directory of file after encrypted file.

Exactly 9.238 petabytes. The majority of it is 128-bit encrypted in an unknown encryption language.

Geez. Well, we couldn't take that much data with us anyway, and we don't have time to upload it to the cloud. But we are inside their operations network, so let's see what we can find. Look for mail servers and search for Alba.

Sir, I found a mail directory. Alba uses a mail alias known as Gazelem. His email is all under that alias. The email system is behind a weak firewall, and the emails themselves are not encrypted. They are, however, written in an unknown language. It's a deception to get the user to think an email is encrypted when it's not. This means the email isn't encrypted, so it won't arouse suspicion on the NSA systems monitoring international email traffic flowing through American internet hubs. The language has attributes similar to the Adamic language. I am also detecting Hebrew and Egyptian symbology. I may be able to decipher the language.

*Run a program to decipher the languag*e, Chris directed. *Return relevant results containing my name.*

Executing . . .

Find a floor plan and electrical-system layout of this building.

Executing . . . complete. The files are on your desktop.

Chris would look at the files later. He kept typing like a madman. *Plant a virus in their network that shuts down all electrical, communications, and security systems.*

Executing . . . complete and ready to execute on your command.

Excellent. Access all of Alba's other devices and run a keyword search on my name.

Executing . . .

Set up a false location-services ghost on mine and Leah's mobile devices.

Analysis complete. Location spyware has been removed from both devices, and location services have been disabled except when you and Leah are able to access each other's locations. Location-services ghost enabled for all other users.

Picking up his iPhone, Chris opened the Messages app and sent Leah a text. *Hey, where are you?*

Down by the lake, Leah responded. *It's amazing! When can I see you? Are we still having dinner with your client tonight?*

Yeah. Meetings are over. I just got freed up, so I want to walk around Zurich with you. Chris was lying.

OK, I'll send you my location. When are you coming?

Thirty minutes.

See you then!

CHAPTER 35

"Sir, you're going to want to see this," the mission specialist yelled as Stew entered the operations center. The room was a flurry of activity.

"What do we got?" said Stew, running over to the terminal.

"Sir, it appears he's using the Max AI software to penetrate the network in the building," said a mission analyst. "He's hacking them, and we're getting a real-time screen grab as it happens."

"Perfect. What do we have so far?"

"Someone inside is trying to hack his system, but his firewall is holding. He's sending computer viruses back to the offending machine without the operator's knowledge."

"Smart." Stew watched Chris's actions play out on the monitor before him.

"He's in their email system," said the analyst, "and now he's planting a virus in the building's security system."

"We can't send the ground team," Stew thought out loud. "It will arouse too much suspicion. He needs to get clear of the building. Do we have a trace on his phone?"

"Negative, the AI is actively monitoring phone access, and he just set up a ghost location service," said another analyst. "There's no doubt he's planning to disappear."

"OK, so we need to grab him on the street," said Stew. "Can we use the MQ-8s to track movement?"

"Sorry, sir, but no," said the drone team lead. "They're low on fuel. We might have to put them down in the mountains and recover them later."

"Sir, he just sent a text to Leah Bennion," said a comms analyst. "Looks like he's planning to meet up with her in approximately thirty minutes."

"How are we going to find him on the street?" asked Stew. "Do we have a current location on the woman?"

"Negative, she was near the lake, but the AI is now running her location services. I guarantee what we're seeing here is a ghost."

"That makes sense. Run a simulation of probable routes Thomas could take from every exit of the Hancock Building," Stew ordered. "We'll position the ground team in the most likely zone for extraction."

The team acknowledged Stew's directive, then got to work.

CHAPTER 36

Working the laptop furiously, Chris kept checking his watch. To get to Leah in time, he needed to leave in ten minutes.

Sir, I have a critical summary report based on the information I've been able to translate thus far, communicated Max as the report populated Chris's screen. The information confirmed his worst fears. The organization had more than five hundred drones moving into position across the globe under cover of a crop-dusting experiment. Most are located at rural airports outside major population centers.

They call the virus Aries, said Max. A video player came on the screen, its thumbnail showing a yellow-haired man in a white lab coat. Chris put in his earbuds and hit the play button.

"Twelve hours ago, we contaminated this sample group of North Korean prisoners with a virulent test strain of Aries," said the man in a German accent. *"The contagion was applied using an aerosol apparatus similar to the bioreactors on the drones."*

The camera panned over to an observation window. *"Most of the subjects succumbed two hours ago. The younger subjects are just now expiring."* The camera zoomed in on a small girl lying flat on the floor. She said something inaudible to a boy lying motionless next to her. Blood began to trickle from the side of her mouth. Touching her face, she examined the blood on her hand. A minute later, she went limp and died. The camera moved back to the German.

"Her name was Jai. She was a fighter and the last to succumb. We believe another three months of trials will have us ready for distribution. I will submit a full report to the council in forty-eight hours."

Chris felt sick. He was most disgusted by the man's blasé attitude and unemotional response to the death around him.

Sir, communicated Max, *I have compiled a summary of email conversations between Alba and Hancock. At dinner, they intend to give you full disclosure of their plans to use the drones as distribution vehicles for a virus. They want access to the Max AI. If you fail to cooperate, they plan to murder you and Ms. Leah.*

Chris felt a wave of shock and betrayal. *How could Alba do this to me?* Not only had his mentor deceived him, he was undeniably part of this horrific evil. Anger consumed Chris, and then he thought of Leah. *How could I have brought her into this mess?*

He took a moment to regain some composure. *Recommendations?* he typed.

Forming recommendations . . . I recommend collecting Ms. Leah and escaping the country. File a false flight plan and text the pilots to be ready to depart in one hour. Initiate the virus to take down the building's systems so they can't track us as we exit the facility.

Execute virus, file the flight plan, text the pilots, typed Chris.

Executing. Building systems will be down in 4 minutes, 47 seconds. Sir, please remain calm so you don't arouse suspicion.

Chris let out a deep breath.

Thanks for the tip, Max. Moving to iPhone now. Chris collected his belongings, threw them into his backpack, and walked into the hall.

"Can I help you?" asked Hancock's assistant from her desk at the end of the hall.

"I'm going to step outside for some air. It looks beautiful—you know, outside."

"Oh yes, the elevator is right there," she said, pointing the way. "Would you like an escort?"

"No, no." Backing toward the elevator, Chris fumbled over his words. "I can walk myself out. I'm just going—I'll be right outside on the plaza. I won't go—I'm not going any farther than that."

∾

The admin stared at the strange American as the elevator doors closed. Then she picked up her phone. "He's going outside for some air, sir. Should I send security?"

"No," said Benson Hancock. "Have security monitor him via surveillance cameras. If he leaves the premises, have security collect him."

∾

"Sir, he's on the move," said an analyst to Stew. "He may be heading for an exit. We have no video—there aren't any external cameras facing the building. That's got to be intentional."

"They're going to kill him," Stew muttered. "We need to evac this guy. What's the ETA on the ground team?"

"Sir, the ground team is en route, but they got caught in traffic," said another analyst.

"Traffic! You've got to be kidding me."

"Apparently we pulled them off another surveillance op."

"If Hancock grabs him now, it's over!" Stew yelled.

∾

Chris activated Max on his iPhone app and put in his earbuds. At that very moment, the AI was saving his life. He walked slowly, trying to be inconspicuous as he passed through the massive glass-walled lobby. Large men wearing black suits and earpieces eyed the lobby's occupants. One guard noticed Chris and whispered into his lapel mic. Chris began to panic, but the guard just watched him, moving to the window as Chris exited the building.

As Chris walked onto the plaza, alarms began screaming from the building's lobby. Guards ran in different directions, including the guard who had been watching Chris.

"Nice work, Max," Chris said into his earbud mic, finally able to speak to the AI.

While running across the plaza and down a narrow street filled with shops and cafés, Chris shrugged off his coat and stuffed it into his backpack, trying to blend in with the crowds of tourists.

"Sir, you have a text message from a suspicious number."

Chris looked down at the number on the screen: *777.* "That's not a real number," he said. As he continued walking fast, he read the text: *Leave building now. Life in danger. Go to American consulate. Dufourstrasse 101, 8008 Zürich, Switzerland. Move now.*

"What do you make of that, Max? I think it could be a trap."

"Sir, I can't trace the number's origin," replied Max.

Chris ran a few blocks, stopping occasionally to make sure he wasn't being followed. Surprisingly, he wasn't. When he felt he was in the clear, he summoned a taxi for a ride to the lake.

"Wait here. I'll be right back," Chris told the driver when they reached Leah's location.

Scanning the lakeside park, he found Leah taking a picture. He made an immediate beeline to her. As always, she looked beautiful. He wished circumstances were different and they could enjoy their stay in Zurich. Then he cursed himself again for bringing her into this life-or-death situation.

Leah spotted Chris running up to her. "Hey, you're late. Is everything OK? You don't look right."

"Come on, get in the car. I'll tell you on the way." He pulled her toward the taxi.

"Hey!" she said. "What's going on?" She was visibly scared as they crawled into the back of the car.

"Zurich Airport, private terminal," he told the driver. "I'm sorry," he said to Leah, and then he started explaining.

~

"You incompetent fools!" screamed Benson Hancock. "He was sitting right here, and now he's gone. Explain this!"

Alba stood silently behind Hancock. One of the Order's guards stepped forward. "Sir, we were tracking his every movement as he walked onto the plaza, but suddenly all security and communications systems went down, including handheld radios. I sent a team to the plaza, but he was gone. An initial sweep of the surrounding area left us empty-handed. We believe he is responsible for the system's failures. He must have escaped in a taxi or Uber at the moment the system went down."

"What about the girl? Was the girl located?" asked Benson.

"Sir, he must have collected her," said the guard. "We have a location fix on her phone, but she isn't there."

Another man stepped forward. "Sir, our airport team just reported that the G650ER Gulfstream jet Thomas and Dr. Alba arrived on is gone. A flight plan was filed less than an hour ago, but we think it's bogus."

"You idiots!" Benson yelled at his men and his assistant, who was now crying. "What's the status of the building's systems?"

"We're slowly bringing them up, sir. We believe we'll be online in the next twenty minutes."

"What about the servers and the network? Did he hack us? If so, what did he get?"

An IT engineer stepped forward. "Sir, he caused extensive damage to the operations network with an unknown virus. He didn't gain access to the servers, but he did gain access to the email system."

"That's a relief," said Benson in a calmer tone. "He doesn't know Lamanese. He can't read the email."

Alba spoke up. "We should assume, based on his actions, that he was able to somehow read the Lamanese. My guess is the AI translated the language, exposing all of our email communication."

Benson's face went pale. "Then we should assume he knows everything. He's probably in touch with the authorities now."

"We need to stop him before he lands in the United States," said Alba nervously. "He won't know what to do until then, and he won't attempt to contact the US government while in flight. He's too afraid we'll track him and the government won't believe him. The truth is too absurd. Plus, he's a coward. This is panic fire. He'll stay dark on electronic comms so we can't track him. Besides, he doesn't even know who to contact—so we have time to fix this, and I know what to do." Alba turned to the IT engineer. "Get comms back up, and get me satellite access now. I need access to the plane's systems."

As the group dispersed, Alba pulled Hancock aside. "What has our source inside Orion's Spear told us about this?"

"Nothing," said Hancock. "Do you think he's been compromised?"

"Possibly."

CHAPTER 37

CHARLES DE GAULLE INTERNATIONAL AIRPORT
PARIS, FRANCE

Mike Mayberry and Carl Smith exited the first-class section of the Air France Boeing 777X and swiftly made their way through the Charles de Gaulle International Airport. They were both dressed in Armani suits.

A nondescript man was waiting for them on the curb in short-term parking with a Ferrari 488. It was red, of course. The mystery man made no introduction. He simply handed the key to Mike and disappeared into the crowd.

"A Ferrari? How inconspicuous," said Smith with a smirk.

"It's part of our cover. Check the frunk," said Mike.

"The what?"

"The frunk, man. You know, the front trunk." Mike pointed to the hood of the red beast.

"I don't know what a frunk is. I'm a truck guy—you know that," said Smith defensively as he popped the frunk. On the floor lay a nondescript black gym bag. Smith reached down and unzipped the bag. Under some random articles of clothing, he found two radios, two CO2-powered tranquilizer guns, and two Glock 19s with extra magazines.

Mayberry jumped into the driver's seat and lit up the Ferrari's 3.9-liter twin turbo V8. All 660 horses came to life with the distinctive Ferrari sound, turning heads for at least a hundred yards all around.

"All there," Smith said, buckling himself into the passenger seat.

"Good, we only have an hour to get into position. Radio the London team with our status."

"Will do, boss," Smith said, reaching for his iPhone. Mike nailed the accelerator, sending the red stallion toward the airport's exit at a blistering speed.

So much for cover, he thought.

CHAPTER 38

I really screwed up, Leah," Chris said yet again, pacing up and down the private plane's narrow center aisle.

"Sit down." Leah beckoned him to join her on a couch in the G650ER's private lounge. The plane was over Germany, making its way to the Atlantic and then the United States. Chris had instructed Max to file a fake flight plan to London. He felt confident they were in the clear, at least temporarily.

"Well, at least we're not dead," Leah said, smiling.

"I put your life in danger," Chris said, still dejected. "I swear I didn't mean to. I can't believe this happened. I am so sorry. I don't blame you if you hate me and never want to see me again."

Repositioning herself on the couch, Leah moved in closer and looked Chris directly in the eyes. "I want to see you for the rest of my life," she said in a serious tone.

Chris perked up and looked at her, stunned. He wasn't sure how to respond. His heart felt like it was beating a hundred miles an hour.

Leah broke the awkward silence. "You need to rest," she said in a motherly tone. "Just don't worry about anything right now. There's nothing we can do on the plane. Here, lie on my lap and let me rub your head."

Chris gave her a puzzled look. It seemed like a strange offer, but a head rub sounded really nice, so he complied and laid his head on her lap. After a few minutes, he felt more relaxed than he had in years. Then he noticed it. He had started to call it the Leah effect. The ever-present Adamic math in his field of vision was completely gone. Nothing. He smiled. He knew it would be back eventually.

Inside of ten minutes, he was sound asleep.

~

Chris awakened from a deep slumber to find the British flight attendant standing over him. Her name tag read Natalie. "Sir, I am sorry to wake you," Natalie said calmly, "but the pilot requests that you come to the flight deck."

"There's a problem," Leah said in near panic as she pulled on his arm, trying to sit him up. "Come on!"

Chris looked around, confused, and then sat up on the couch. This G650ER configuration didn't have a bed, which was really disappointing for a $72 million private plane.

"Chris, come on!" said Leah, continuing to pull on his arm.

Chris rose, wiped the sleep from his eyes, and followed Leah and the flight attendant up the short aisle to the cockpit.

"The engines are dead!" yelled the pilot as they entered the cockpit. "We're gliding and falling fast. We've been through all the emergency procedures thrice, and nothing is working. Worse yet, we're over the Atlantic and hundreds of miles from land. At our current glide ratio, there's no way we can make it to Iceland, the nearest airstrip."

Chris turned and ran back to the couch. "Where's my backpack?" he yelled.

Leah rushed to a nearby closet. "Sorry, I stowed it here for takeoff."

Chris grabbed the bag from Leah and reentered the flight deck. "First officer, I'm going to need that seat," he said.

The young first officer looked at the captain, who gave him a nod.

Taking the seat, Chris suddenly registered the eerie silence of a plane flying dead stick. It was extremely disconcerting. Panic welled up inside him as he opened his laptop. Glancing around, he noted the first officer standing in a state of shock, the flight attendant and Leah both crying, and the captain pretending to hold it together.

Chris looked up at Natalie. "Hey, do you have a sandwich? I'm a little hungry. And how about something to drink?"

Leah gave him a strange look.

"A sandwich?" Natalie asked, stunned. "Are you serious?"

"Look, I'll make you a deal. If you can bring me a Diet Coke and a sandwich, I'll get the plane fixed. Deal?" Chris knew if they were going to make it out of this alive, he'd have to be brave and remain calm for himself and for the others.

Natalie wiped at her tears and laughed nervously. "Deal."

"Everything is going to be OK," Chris said, fixing his gaze on Leah.

"I'll help you," said the first officer, following behind Natalie.

"So will I," said Leah.

Chris clipped a microphone from his laptop to the Metallica T-shirt he'd changed into after takeoff. Then he looked at the pilot. "Quick, where's the USB port?"

"Over here. Hand me the connection, and I'll plug it in."

Chris clicked on the Max 2.0 icon on his screen. "OK, Max. Time to earn your wings, little brother."

"Good evening, Chris. How may I be of assistance?"

"Max, I just connected you to the operating system of a Gulfstream G650ER currently in flight. The engines are dead and won't restart. I need you to analyze all critical flight systems and tell me what's wrong so we can fix it."

"Sir, if we don't correct the problem, will we cease to exist?" asked Max.

Chris was momentarily taken aback. Max 2.0 was beta AI, far more advanced than the Max 1.0 powering Nav. Max 2.0 had operated perfectly in the escape from Zurich and was now exhibiting a form of cognition. *What have I created?*

"Yes, Max. We will cease to exist if we don't solve the problem."

"Analyzing now, Chris," Max said without hesitation.

Unfolding before Chris at blistering speed was a vast amount of data, diagrams, and code. Max was analyzing the flight system's software and probably over five million lines of code.

While Max worked, Chris looked at the pilot. "So, how about that Steph Curry?"

The British pilot looked at him, thoroughly confused. Saying nothing, he turned his attention back to the flight controls.

Two long minutes later, Max returned. "Sir, there is an unknown malware active in the system controlling the fuel pumps. This malware is causing a malfunction in the fuel system. All other systems not related to the fuel system are functioning properly."

"Can you defeat the malware?" Chris asked.

"Analyzing . . ."

At that moment, the others reappeared. The first officer handed Chris a sandwich, and the flight attendant handed him a Diet Coke. Chris took several quick bites of the sandwich and a big gulp from the silver can, then handed them back.

"Sir, I have developed an antivirus protocol to remove the malware, but I am uncertain if this will fix the problem. I have never done anything like this before. However, I believe there is a 98 percent probability this action will defeat the virus."

"I believe in you, Max. Do it!"

Natalie and the first officer held each other closely and seemed to be praying. Kneeling in front of the center console, Leah got as close to Chris as she could.

"Deploying antivirus," said Max. "Please stand by."

Several excruciating minutes passed, the aircraft descending silently through ten thousand feet. Chris looked out the window and noticed moonbeams sparkling on the frigid Atlantic below. Airspeed was getting critically low.

"How much longer?" Chris asked the captain.

"If we don't have engines in thirty sec—" The captain paused as the instrumentation on the Garmin Primary Flight Display before him came alive.

"Malware removed, sir," said Max. "I have initiated the engine start-up sequence. We are forty-nine seconds from impact."

With the plane less than a thousand feet off the deck, the engines ignited with a jolt, and the aircraft shuddered. As the pilot pushed the throttle forward and pulled back on the yoke, the G650ER leveled out and began to climb.

"Max, you saved us all, including yourself," Chris said. "Excellent work."

A collective sigh of relief filled the cockpit. Leah stretched forward to kiss Chris on the cheek.

"Thank you," Max said. "How else may I be of assistance today?"

"Activate sentry mode, please. Monitor and defeat any malware trying to access the plane's systems. Analyze all other flight systems for malware, and remove any problems you find."

"Analysis complete. All systems normal. Sentry mode active. Would you like me to monitor for the duration of the flight? I estimate arrival in Reykjavik in four minutes, twenty-two seconds."

"Yes."

"Thank you, Max," Leah said. "We owe you big-time."

"You're welcome, Ms. Leah," said Max.

Chris relaxed in the copilot's seat. He suddenly just wanted to go back to sleep. As he started to stand, Leah backed up so he could exit the copilot's chair.

As Chris neared Natalie, she gave him a big hug and kiss on the cheek. Then she laid a long kiss on the first officer. "Thank you," she said to him.

"All I did was get the sandwich," said the first officer.

Natalie blushed.

"Reykjavik control," said the captain into the radio. "This is flight DD109'er clear of conflict but requesting immediate emergency landing."

"Copy that, DD109. The pattern is open," said a woman with a thick Icelandic accent. "Cleared for emergency approach on runway 31. Emergency personnel will be waiting for you on the tarmac."

Leah took Chris by the hand to lead him back to the couch. Once outside the cockpit, he suddenly felt dizzy and short of breath at the realization of how close they'd just come to death. Pure adrenaline still ran through his veins.

"Chris, are you OK?" asked Leah as Chris wildly looked around. The plane touched down just as he vomited his sandwich and Diet Coke into the galley sink.

～

The aircraft rolled to a stop at the end of the long runway. Emergency vehicles approached the G650ER. The first officer opened the door and lowered it to the ground. Chris followed Leah down the stairs. When she stepped off, she bent over, touched the runway, and said something under her breath. Chris smirked.

"Mr. Thomas," called a dark-suited man pushing his way through the emergency personnel. The Icelanders turned at the unexpected sound of an American accent. Three more identical-looking men followed, hair high and tight. Black suits.

"Yeah?" said Chris, a little surprised.

The man pulled out his identification and showed it to Chris and Leah. "I'm Special Agent Mallick with the FBI. You're under arrest."

CHAPTER 39

When they arrived at the club, Mayberry and Smith walked past the long line of partygoers waiting patiently for security to wand them. Mike paid the doorman three hundred euros to leave the Ferrari parked at the front door, and Mike kept the keys. Smith presented another doorman with special VIP passes the agency had easily acquired through Centurion Card Services at American Express. The VIP concierge introduced herself and diverted the men around the security check.

"We're in," Mike said over his micro jawbone-conducting radio. "Do we have a position fixed on the target?" As he spoke, he and Smith passed through tall metal-and-glass doors.

"Negative," said a voice from Langley.

The Americans were both momentarily taken aback by the size of the club and its classic French architecture. Its main hall was easily five hundred feet long and two hundred feet wide. The ceiling rose 150 feet to a nineteenth-century, glass-and-metal arched dome. At the head of the room, a white oval DJ booth appeared to float above the dance floor. The sound and lighting were intense, and the club stank of sweat and smoke. As the techno dance mix blared, the two assassins made their way through the sea of half-dressed, dancing Parisians.

"Knife, be advised," Stew Brimhall said into Mike's earpiece. Mike imagined the mission leader managing the Orion's Spear team like the precision conductor of the world's finest orchestra. "We have control of all the club's security cameras. We're running facial recognition on the crowd and cataloging attendees. If she was here, we would know by now. We'll keep you posted."

"Sir, we have a hit, but it's not Black," said a mission specialist monitoring facial-recognition hits. "It's Alexander Yako, a Russian arms dealer. Tier-one target. The AI is indicating a 93 percent probability he's there to meet Black."

"Knife, sending you his location now," said Stew. "He's on the mezzanine level. Private room with a small party of women. Position yourself close to the room but hard to spot from the doorway. We're still scanning for Black. Copy?"

"Copy that," said Mike, looking at his iPhone. He and Smith made their way to the industrial-style mezzanine stairs and flashed their VIP credentials. A hostess quickly led them up the stairs to a secluded table that gave them a clear line of sight to Yako's private room.

"In position," said Mike.

"Copy that. We've got your location," said Stew. "Stay frosty. A large group of people is now entering the club. Scanning for Black."

Mike and Smith ordered drinks. The music was slowly driving Mike mad. He was a Virginia farm boy who liked Johnny Cash. Techno dance music made him want to hit something really hard.

Looking down onto the immense dance floor, Mike scanned the room. It was almost impossible to make out a face in the darkness and flashing lights. He wondered how the AI was detecting faces via the club's cameras with such precision. As gyrating bodies of young flesh pressed together, he had a brief epiphany. *Is it any wonder the Muslims hate Western culture? This continent is a powder keg.*

"Knife, we have a hit on Black." The mission specialist's voice snapped Mike out of his uncharacteristically unfocused thought. "The target just entered the club via the front door and is making her way to the mezzanine stairs."

"Copy that," Mike said. He double-checked their position to ensure Black couldn't see them as she made her way through the crowd.

Black emerged onto the mezzanine wearing an all-white suit like she'd worn in the Brussels hotel. As expected, she walked straight to the Russian's door and knocked. She was let in by a beautiful, scantily dressed French girl with a gorgeous smile.

"Knife, we're transmitting the video feed from the room to your iPhone now," said Stew. "Get in position."

Mike and Smith moved toward the room's entrance.

"Live feed incoming. Stand by."

Just then, Mike heard several distinctive pops from inside the private room.

"Knife! Shots fired. Move on target now!" yelled a voice into Mike's earpiece.

Giving each other a here-we-go-again look, Mike and Smith pulled out their concealed Glock 19s, stepped back for leverage, and kicked open the door. Twisting aside, they dodged a hail of gunfire from Black. As Mike and Smith returned fire, three bullets hit Black in the chest, but she was still able to charge out onto the mezzanine. Mike glimpsed the bloody bodies of the arms dealer and his prostitutes on the private room's floor and couch. The mezzanine erupted in chaos as clubbers panicked and ran for the stairs. On the main floor, people rushed for the exits.

As Black fired at Smith, Mike leapt forward and hit her gun out of her hand, feeling its heat on his knuckles. The two trained killers grappled jujitsu-style, wrestling for control of Mike's gun. He hit Black in the solar plexus with his fist, then slammed his palm into her nose. Blood gushed down her handsome white suit as they wrestled each other to the floor. Smith lay motionless on his side nearby, his back to Mike.

As they rolled, Black threw a sharp elbow into Mike's ribs. Hearing a crack, he yelled out in pain. His gun slipped from his grasp, but he was able to roll over onto it. In one fluid move, Black kneed him in the groin and jumped up from the floor, frantically looking for her gun.

Pushing through the pain, Mike reached back for his Glock 19. As Black lunged toward Smith's body, he shot her twice in the torso. The German woman fell but quickly righted herself, then grabbed Smith's gun and ran for the stairs. Mike leveled in on the fast-moving woman but didn't pull the trigger—too many civilians in his line of fire.

"She's wearing bulletproof clothing again," Mike yelled into his radio. "Smith is down. We have casualties in the lounge. Send help."

Standing up despite the pain, Mike hurried over to Smith and saw blood on his chest, but his partner was still breathing. Mike patted his cheek until he opened his eyes. "One got past my armor," Smith managed to say.

"She escaped," Mike said.

"What are you waiting for—" Smith tried to yell but then coughed.

Mike hesitated while looking at his bleeding friend. They had shed blood together in more gunfights than he could remember. No way was Mike going to lose Smith on a sleazy dance floor in an even sleazier nightclub.

"I'll live!" Smith gasped. With effort, he pulled out a fresh Glock 19 magazine and put it in Mike's hand.

CHAPTER 40

FIFTEENTH AND SIXTEENTH ARRONDISSEMENTS
PARIS, FRANCE

Pushing his way toward the front door and wincing each time someone bumped his ribs, Mike yelled into his radio. "Target is wearing bullet-proof clothing. White suit covered in blood. Shouldn't be hard to spot. She's exiting the front of the club. If you have a shot, take it, but go for the head."

"Roger that," said Bravo team's sniper, lying in wait in a building a hundred yards from the club's metal-and-glass doors. "Knife, I have her," he said a few moments later, "but I don't have a clear shot. There're too many civilians. Stand by."

Mike kept pushing his way through the sea of people to the front door. Police sirens could be heard descending on the area. He needed to clear the door before the police arrived.

"Be advised," said the sniper. "Target just carjacked a silver Range Rover. Looks like she killed the driver. I've got no joy."

Mike ran out of the club just in time to see Black passing in the Range Rover. He didn't have a clear shot.

"Bravo, deploy the microdrones now," yelled Stew over the radio.

Jumping over the Ferrari 488's hood and into the driver's seat *Dukes of Hazzard* style, Mike gunned the engine and laid on the stallion's distinctive horn, trying not to run over the panicked club goers pouring into the streets of Paris.

"Satellite status?" asked Stew.

"NSA DarkStar X4 is on station orbiting target area," said a mission specialist. "We have positive control." From two hundred miles over Paris, the multibillion-dollar spy satellite was sending real-time, high-definition video of the chase back to Langley.

"Knife, be advised," said the mission lead. "We have satellite lock on Black's vehicle. She's heading straight into the center of Paris. There's an anti-immigration riot happening right now, and it's turning violent. Police are pushing back the protestors with tear gas. It looks like Black is going to use the riot as a diversion."

"Air-support status?" Mike asked.

"Microdrones deploying to your position now."

"Guys, I'm coming up on her now." Ignoring his throbbing rib, Mike expertly drove down the narrow Boulevard Garibaldi heading straight for the Eiffel Tower, pedestrians and parked cars flying past at a dangerous blur. The Ferrari was pushing its engine's redline as Mike moved up behind the Range Rover.

~

Stew watched with anticipation as the violent riot unfolded on the screens in the ops center. The satellite above Paris narrowed in on the area, and Orion's Spear AI began calculating the probable routes Black would take to navigate the riot and lose Mike.

"Only one of the drones is operational," said Bravo. "Launching now. Main, confirm control of the drone."

"Take it away, kid," said Stew to the pilot standing next to him. "Your call sign is Raven."

The twenty-year-old former gaming champion wore baggy jeans, a pair of Vans shoes, and a Tupac T-shirt. He slipped on Oculus VR goggles to illuminate the drone's high-def, real-time view of Paris, which also displayed on a huge central monitor. The big grin on the kid's face spoke a thousand words.

For having only four small blades, the microdrone took off at an astonishing speed. Raven stretched out his arms as if manipulating flight controls. He slammed an invisible throttle down on the virtual control panel. "Bravo, this is Raven," said the pilot. "I have positive control." He flew the drone at high speed over Boulevard Garibaldi, attempting to catch up to Mike.

"Watch out for that bridge!" Stew yelled.

"Whoa," said the pilot. "Looks like we've got a little satellite latency here. Like seven hundred milliseconds, bro."

"Yeah, well, calculate accordingly," said Stew. "We can't afford to lose our only drone. And don't call me bro," he added like a dad scolding his teenage son.

"Don't hassle me, man," said the pilot as the drone ducked dangerously under bridges and narrowly missed other obstacles just feet off the street. "I'm trying to fly through Paris right now, and I need to concentrate here."

The other analysts stared at their workstations. Stew noticed them trying not to smile at Raven's pushback.

"What's the status on Smith?" Mike yelled into his comms.

"Knife, we have a team on-site," answered Stew. "Smith is stable and being evacuated now. Focus on the target."

Drawing his Glock, Mike started firing at the Range Rover with his left hand while keeping his right hand on the steering wheel. Although he was right-handed, he could shoot the tip off a pen at more than five hundred yards with his left. His rounds were hitting the Range Rover exactly where he wanted. The back window blew out, the passenger mirror exploded, and the back tires went flat.

After the two vehicles raced across the Seine River, Black turned right onto the Avenue de New York, heading toward the heart of the riot. Turning in the driver's seat, she fired on the Ferrari through the Rover's blown-out rear window. A lucky round struck Mike's front windshield, shattering the safety glass into an intricate web. The Ferrari's right front corner clipped a parked police car at ninety kilometers per hour. The seat belt held Mike in place, but his broken rib screamed pain, and the airbag gave him a bloody nose.

A quarter of a mile ahead, the Range Rover stopped in the middle of the street. Black exited the vehicle and ran straight for the rioters amassing in Trocadéro Gardens. Jumping out of the wrecked 488, Mike quickly checked himself and wiped the blood from his nose. He was momentarily shocked that he wasn't more injured. He shook his head to focus and slapped a fresh sixteen-round magazine into his Glock 19.

Mike had to hand it to the female assassin—running straight into the riot was a great escape plan. But he'd dreamt of this moment of revenge for years. Black was not about to escape his deathly grasp this time.

CHAPTER 41

TROCADÉRO GARDENS
PARIS, FRANCE

K nife, we're sat-locked on Black," said the mission lead. "She's one hundred yards in front of you and moving quickly through the riot. There's an 89 percent probability she'll change course in the next two hundred yards. Stay on your present trajectory until diverted. Raven is still en route."

Even after the car accident and with a cracked rib, Mike ran toward the riot's center like an Olympic sprinter. Suddenly, he hit a wave of protestors that slowed his progress to a mild jog. His broken rib was screaming, but he ignored the pain.

Out of nowhere, a crazed man threw a wild punch. Mike dodged him and then punched the assailant in the throat, dropping him to the ground. Looking around for Black, Mike stepped over the fool lying motionless and kept moving deeper into Trocadéro Gardens.

"Main, I need a bearing," said Mike into his comms.

"Black is still a hundred yards directly ahead of you and moving fast," said Stew. "She'll hit the subway station in less than eight hundred yards."

"Raven, what's your position?" asked Mike.

"On station orbiting the square," said the young pilot. "There's a lot of smoke here. I'm having a hard time navigating. FLIR is pretty much useless. Following the sat lock to target now. Vector bearing 267. I'm coming up behind you. Altitude one hundred feet."

Mike turned and looked up. He could barely see the tiny drone through the smoke.

"Activate the drone's facial-recognition system," commanded Stew.

"Knife, be advised," said Raven. "I'm going to fly up ahead of you. Trying to get drone lock on the target."

"Copy that," said Mike. Only he noticed the tiny, quiet quadcopter flying just a few dozen feet over the angry rioters' heads. Picking up his pace, he followed the drone as it exited the gardens.

"You're right on her, Knife," said Stew. "She's straight ahead of you."

Continuing to ignore his pain, Mike ran even faster. Several shops and cafés were on fire, with firefighters trying desperately to extinguish the flames. Mike coughed as he pushed through the almost unbearable smoke. He saw police officers beating a man with their riot clubs, a woman crying and holding her bleeding arm, and a police officer fighting a hooded man for control of a riot shield.

More masked men ran past Mike, heading toward the gardens. Screaming, they waved black flags mounted on tall metal poles. One man carried a gas can and a lit flare. Mike dodged the rioters and kept moving toward his objective. After passing a burning police car, he saw a man in a motorcycle helmet throw a Molotov cocktail into a nearby building. Then a tear-gas canister exploded twenty feet in front of Mike. He quickly pulled his jacket over his face and ran through the chemical mist.

"Sir, we've lost the sat lock," said one of the analysts. "Too much smoke."

"I have no joy," yelled the drone pilot.

"Knife, be advised," said Stew. "We lost the target in the smoke. You should be right on top of her. What's your status?"

Coughing and trying to get his bearings, Mike felt a skull-cracking blow to the side of his head. He instantly thudded to the ground. Momentarily stunned, he touched his head and found he was bleeding profusely just above his ear. He knew he was lucky to still be conscious.

As he attempted to sit up, he realized a woman was standing over him with a police baton in her hand. Congealed blood covered the lower part of her face, and her white blouse was stained crimson red. She casually dropped the baton and reached behind her back, revealing an FN 9mm pistol.

"Black," Mike growled as adrenaline surged through his veins.

When she smiled, blood filled the cracks between her teeth. She leveled the pistol at Mike's head. "I thought I killed you in the hotel," she said in a thick German accent.

"Yeah, about that hotel—" Abruptly throwing up his leg, Mike kicked the weapon out of her hand, the blow momentarily confusing Black. Pushing through his pain, Mike arched his back and threw himself upright, landing on his feet. He immediately pivoted and laid a devastating blow to Black's broken nose. She attempted to counter, but Mike didn't let up, continuing to land blows to her face and chest. She backed up, attempting to reset and fight back, but she was outweighed, outpowered, and outskilled.

Mike pushed Black up against the hot brick wall of a burning building just off the narrow street. Emboldened and in a solid flow state, the former Delta operator and jujitsu master threw his knee into her tiny gut, buckling her over forward. She looked up at Mike with a plea of mercy, but he landed one last blow to her bloodied face, and she collapsed onto the sidewalk below.

Mike wiped the blood from his face and touched his head wound. It still oozed blood. His breathing felt erratic—the tear gas was taking a toll. Black's mention of the hotel and Mike's instant memory of his lost friends had ignited an adrenaline-fueled rage such as he'd never felt before.

"Main, I have Black in custody," Mike said breathlessly. "Bravo, I need assistance. Ready for extraction at this location." Reaching down with one arm, he pulled Black up from the ground, then leaned the lightweight woman against the brick wall and looked her over. She was barely alive.

"Today is your lucky day," he muttered. "Someone wants you alive. Otherwise I would have—"

The point-blank blow hit Mike directly in the chest with the force of a grenade, knocking him ten feet back into the street. Although the round didn't penetrate the bulletproof vest under what was left of his Armani dress shirt, the concussion completely stunned Mike. Gathering himself, he slowly stood and looked at Black, who staggered toward him. He was seeing double. Her arm was extended in front of her, and white smoke rose from her wrist.

Black gave Mike a bloody smile and pointed a slightly shaking arm directly at his head. He could see some type of device attached to her wrist. As his double vision corrected, he realized the device had three small holes, visible under her petite hand. Black took two more unsteady steps forward for an almost perfect point-blank shot. Standing there stunned and breathless, Mike tried desperately to reach for his sidearm.

"Knife, duck now," yelled a voice into his earpiece.

Mike didn't hesitate for even a millisecond. He dropped to the ground. In what seemed like a slow-motion dream, a white flash appeared almost directly above his head. In an instant, Black's head disappeared in a bright ball of white fire that appeared out of nowhere, bone and blood splattering the brick wall behind her. Black's headless body stood motionless for a brief second, then crumpled like a rag doll to the ground. Just then, Raven's microdrone slammed into the brick wall, exploding into hundreds of pieces.

"Whoa!" Mike heard in his earpiece. "Raven is down. I repeat, Raven is down," said the pilot.

Mike turned over onto his back and held his aching chest. "Raven, this is Knife. Nice shot, bro." In his earpiece, he could hear clapping and cheering in the background.

"Knife, this is Bravo. We're on station and moving to you now."

Mike stood, moved gingerly to Black's body, and slipped his hand into her jacket pocket. "Main, Black is dead, but I have her phone."

"Well, that's better than nothing," Stew said. "Bravo, evac Knife. I'm mobilizing the Orion's Spear team to London. We'll regroup there."

CHAPTER 42

Chris and Leah's already long day turned out even longer. After being arrested, they were escorted onto another plane and flown to London, where they were separated. Chris was tired, angry, and hungry, but mostly he was concerned about Leah. Sitting in an interrogation room, he stared at the obvious two-way glass wall and wondered who watched from the other side.

The door suddenly opened. "My name is—um, Oscar," said a tall, lanky man. He closed the door and took a chair across the table from Chris.

"No, it's not," said Chris matter-of-factly, rolling his eyes.

The man was taken aback. "OK, well, you'll just have to believe me. So, I—"

"Or not, *Oscar*. That is a really terrible made-up name. I thought you CIA guys were good at stuff like making up dumb and easy lies."

The man stared at him for a moment, then looked at the glass wall. It was obvious to Chris that "Oscar" was wondering how to next approach the situation.

"Well, Mr. Thomas," said Oscar as he folded his arms. "You're in a lot of trouble." He was trying to sound as authoritative as possible.

"No, I'm not. Don't even start with the threats." Chris pointed his index finger at the lanky man. "I'm trying to get to the US government with information about a probable terrorist plot. So why don't you go fetch me a grown-up, *Oscar*? Also, I'm not telling you anything until you bring Leah Bennion in here with me. I swear, if you waterboard her, I will kill you. Now get out of my face."

Oscar recoiled at the berating but, at the same time, seemed momentarily amused by the waterboarding comment. He stood, exited the interview room, and walked into the adjacent observation room. Chris could not see or hear the people behind the two-way glass. He just sat there fuming.

∾

Standing in the small observation room in front of his peers, Stew Brimhall was embarrassed by the exchange his colleagues had just witnessed.

"Oscar?" asked an annoyed Mike Mayberry.

Stew said nothing. This wasn't his thing.

"I told you that was a bad idea," said Mike, taking control of the situation. "We're out of time. We do this my way now."

∾

Another agent and "Oscar" entered the interrogation room, followed by Leah, who threw herself at Chris. He felt immediately relieved. He had been so worried about her. He didn't want their embrace to end.

"Did they hurt you?" asked Chris after putting his hands on her cheeks and kissing her.

"No, I've been in the other room eating dinner. A meat pie. Very British. What about you?"

Chris hadn't eaten anything since he threw up the sandwich and Diet Coke on approach to Iceland hours ago. He was starving. "A meat pie? I've been cooped up in here playing footsie with Oscar over there." Chris nodded toward the man.

"Chris, my name is Mike Mayberry." The man who wasn't Oscar butted into the couple's reunion. "I'm with the CIA's Ground Branch unit. It's part of the Special Activities Division. Ever heard of it?"

"No?" said Chris hesitantly. He studied the man for a second. Mayberry's head was freshly bandaged, his tanned face battle-worn. The man's intense black eyes truly intimidated Chris. Somehow, he knew they were the eyes of a killer. Chris swallowed hard. Clearly, the man was not to be messed with.

"Oscar over here is Stewart Brimhall," continued Mayberry. "He's the head of an organization inside of the CIA I can't talk about. But trust me, Stew is someone you want on your side. So how about if we start over? I think we have a very serious problem on our hands, and you seem to be the only one who can help us."

Chris looked at Leah, who gave him a nod of approval.

"Yeah, OK," said Chris.

Mayberry offered his hand, and Chris shook it. The man's grip was like a vise.

Brimhall moved sheepishly forward and shook Chris's hand. "Just for clarification, we don't really waterboard people anymore. Just thought I would clear that up." Looking down, Brimhall backed away with his hands buried in his pockets.

Two additional CIA officers entered the room. Brimhall introduced them as Norman Stellar and Elle Danley, chief analysts who worked with Brimhall at Langley. For the next hour, Chris reviewed everything he knew for the CIA team. How he'd met Alba and then Hancock. How, in Palo Alto, he'd sabotaged the drone with untraceable malware. His hack on the email servers in Zurich and what he discovered there. The Aries virus and the tests on North Korean prisoners. Finally, Chris theorized that the malware affecting the Gulf Stream's fuel system must have been uploaded via satellite hack at some point in flight.

While Chris talked, Leah sat, semi-stunned. Chris could sense she was having a hard time believing she was caught up in this whole situation. At the end of it all, Chris saw Brimhall and Mayberry exchange a glance. It was one of those looks worth a thousand words. Evidently, his story matched up with the CIA's understanding of the events.

"OK, Chris and Leah, a lawyer is going to come in here in a few minutes," said Brimhall. "We need you to sign a confidentiality agreement. It means you can't talk about anything we've discussed here or the things we're about to discuss. Any problems with that?"

Chris and Leah looked at each other. "No," they said simultaneously.

"A few hours ago, in Paris, I recovered this phone from one of Hancock's operatives," said Mayberry. "That operative is now dead. Based on what I know about the CIA's technology, we can't hack this fast enough for it to count. Chris, can you use the Max AI to hack this device and get into their network?"

"I can try."

"What do you need, Chris?" asked Brimhall. "We can get you anything you want. You have the entire resources of the US government at your disposal."

"All I need is my laptop and a place to work."

Back at his laptop, Norman Stellar typed in an inconspicuous gaming app's IM feature. *Be advised. CIA intercepted Chris Thomas. In custody now in London. He's talking.*

CHAPTER 43

On the Hancock Building's fortieth floor, Cain, Benson Hancock, Dr. Alba, and former US president Lennox sat at one end of the council's main conference table, just outside the temple of Baphomet.

"Assume they know everything," said Alba. There was no use hiding the severity of the situation. Alba knew he would certainly take the brunt of the blame for the current state of affairs.

"How? How did this happen?" asked Cain quietly as he sat motionless at the head of the table. "How close are we to launch-ready?"

The room was deadly quiet, the flags hanging from the ceiling the only sound as they gently flapped in the room's ventilation.

"Chris Thomas forced our hand in two ways," explained Benson. "First, he repaired the drone problem months earlier than we anticipated. Second, during that process, he discovered the true intent of their use. Now the entire operation is at risk. We've had to move up the time frame by nine months. Only 50 percent of our drones will be ready for launch in seventy-two hours."

"That's 250 drones," said Alba.

"Shut your mouth, Doctor," said Cain. Alba recoiled in his chair. Lennox smirked.

No one spoke for several long moments. Then Benson broke the uncomfortable silence. "They are coming. Our asset inside Orion's Spear reported today that they know almost everything from the email hack—Aries, the North Korean experiments, the drones, our moves in the financial markets, and our control of the Mexican cartels. They don't know about you, Master, as far as we know. We've had more brute-force attacks on our network in the last forty-eight hours alone than in the last year. Fortunately, our encryption system is holding. We've acted quickly and deleted any files referencing critical projects, like Thor's Hammer."

"Destroy *all* the data," said Cain. "We'll start from scratch."

Alba was taken aback. "Destroy the data? That's preposterous! We'll never recover." He instantly regretted the outburst, knowing he'd crossed the line.

Cain moved his eyes toward Alba and studied the doctor intensely. The man's piercing stare was almost too much to endure. He wanted to hide under a rock.

"This is all your fault, Alba," Cain said calmly. "You're the one who brought Chris Thomas into this. You underestimated him and failed to do something as simple as kill him on the plane over the Atlantic. You were also the one who suggested using Lamanese in the email system rather than encrypting it. You said it would attract attention if we encrypted the email, which was probably true. But I guess it never occurred to you that someone might eventually translate Lamanese?"

None of the other men offered a defense. They just sat, arms folded, openly showing their disapproval of the doctor. Alba was on his own.

"But, sir, I must protest. You see—"

"Enough talk."

Cain slowly stood. Then, with lightning speed, he thrust himself at the doctor, knocking him out of his chair and onto the floor. Alba threw up his hands in weak defense and cowered at Cain's feet. "Master, I beg you. My value to the Mother is irreplaceable."

Through splayed fingers, Alba watched Cain pull the familiar three-blade knife from inside his suit coat. A paralyzing shudder coursed through him. The knife, its history, and its sole purpose were well-known for one thing and one horrifying thing only.

~

As Lennox and Hancock looked on approvingly, Cain repeatedly thrust the knife into the professor's heart, leaving him limp and bleeding profusely. Alba gasped for his last breath as his blood spread slowly across the polished white marble floor. Cain loved how the blood flowed away from Alba's destroyed body as if trying to escape its symbiotic fate.

"As you know, gentleman. I have no tolerance for incompetence." Cain replaced the knife and sat down as if nothing had happened.

"We must make our last stand here, to see the mission through," said Benson emphatically. "The Mother demands it of us. They cannot discover you, Master Mahan. You must make your retreat. You and you alone must perpetuate our sacrosanct religion. It's the only reasonable course of action. We will stay here, activate the building's defenses, and initiate the mission as planned. The drones will launch in seventy-two hours. In one week, 70 percent of the world's population will be dead. We will not fail you, Master."

"I concur," said Lennox, nodding.

Benson stared at Cain in anticipation. Cain sat solemnly for several moments, staring off into the distance. "This is the end, Benson," he finally said. "The end of what we started decades ago. It's all in your hands now."

Without emotion, Benson continued regarding Cain. Theirs was a partnership of terror, not love or peace. There was some respect, yes, but Cain was no respecter of men, not even his protégé, Benson Hancock. They were simply dedicated to the work. They were dedicated to the Mandate. To the Mother. To Baphomet. Not to each other.

Benson was now at the end of his long life. He would not be part of the mission to reclaim the Mother from the heathens. Aries was his duty and final mission. Decades earlier, he had seen it in a vision in a sewer under Brooklyn. He would not fail his master.

Cain rose again from his chair and stood for a moment. Benson Hancock and President Lennox stared at him with pride.

"For your sin, you shall not die but shall wander the earth, a vagabond and an outcast," he recited. "You will be hunted and never have peace in this world. Your mark shall be known until the second coming of the Lord. No man will kill you, but all shall look upon you with disgust and pity. This is thy curse."

Cain stepped over Alba's body. "And so it has been. And so it is now. And so it always will be."

Hancock and Lennox watched with reverence and awe as Cain walked through the temple veil and into obscurity.

CHAPTER 44

Three heavily armed men sat in the security office of the large manu-facturing facility attached to Guelph Airpark. The side of the building blandly read Canadian Aerial Technologies. Like most nights, it appeared the men would spend another long shift playing cards and watching *Seinfeld* reruns.

"No, four of a kind beats a full house," said the annoyed supervisor to the new hire. "How come you can't keep that straight?"

The other guard, an older man in his sixties, laughed and then took a drag on his unfiltered cigarette.

"I thought that was a straight flush?" asked the confused kid.

Suddenly the security monitors went blank, and all the lights in the building went dark. The men jumped from their seats, grabbed their AR-15 rifles, and activated the one-thousand-lumen flashlight under the barrel of each weapon.

"Call the number," whispered the supervisor.

"What number?" said the older man.

"The number they told us to call if anything like this happened. You know, the emergency number."

As the older guard found the number and dialed it, the supervisor and new hire opened the office door and checked the hall. It was clear.

"That's weird," said the older guard in a normal voice. "My mobile phone has been working fine, but now there's no signal. It's completely dead."

"That's not good," said the supervisor in a panicked whisper. "Try the landline. Quick!"

The new guard picked up the receiver and put it to his ear. "Nothing. Not even a dial tone." He put the receiver down and pulled back the charger on his AR-15.

"Radio?" said the older guard to the supervisor. He pulled the radio from his belt and keyed the receiver. Nothing.

"This ain't right, man," whispered the supervisor.

The men pulled bulletproof vests over their shirts and rechecked their rifles.

"You know the drill," said the supervisor. "Let's get to the hangar. We have to protect the drones."

The men stepped gingerly into the hall. It was still clear. The hangar door was only seventy-five feet away. They moved down the hall, their rifles swinging widely in every direction. "Don't sweep my head," growled the supervisor to the new hire.

At the end of the hall, the older guard put his ear to the door. "It's quiet in there. I think it's fine."

"OK, I'm going to open the door," whispered the supervisor. "You two go in with weapons raised. I don't want to take any chances."

The others nodded affirmatively. The supervisor slowly opened the door, and the two guards entered, weapons at the ready. The supervisor followed with his weapon raised as well. The dark, silent hangar was filled with innocuous-looking white drones. The three men scanned the area.

"It's clear," said the older guard, lowering his weapon. "There's nothing here."

At that moment, all three guards felt something pierce their necks and then fell helplessly to the ground.

~

"Clear," said a commando from the dark. He was holding a tranq gun. The hangar lights came alive as members of SEAL Team Six revealed themselves.

A medic moved to the three prone guards and checked each man's carotid artery. "Sleeping like babies, sir," he said to the commander.

Another SEAL checked a device attached to his forearm. "Sir, the biodetection meter shows no trace of biological or chemical weapons in the air."

"Copy that," said the SEAL commander. He removed the hood of his HAMMER biological warfare suit. Running his hand over his sweaty, bald head, he took in several deep breaths of fresh air. The rest of the team followed his lead and unzipped their hoods.

"Time is money on this job, boys," said the commander. "Get the tools, and get Main on comms. Langley's going to want a mission status."

CHAPTER 45

CIA EUROPEAN HEADQUARTERS
LONDON, ENGLAND

Stew stood at the center of a windowless briefing room before his team of analysts, scientists, and operatives. "Everyone, here's what we need to do," he started. "I have Chris Thomas in the lab, looking at Black's device. It's triple authentication."

"You're kidding me, right, Stew?" complained one of the computer wonks. "Triple authentication?"

"Look, we can build a 3D model of Black's face to defeat the depth camera, which is the first step to logging in. We have her fingerprint, so getting past the bioscan on the haptics button should be cake. That's the second step. Then we just need to hack the passcode, and we have the software to do that. It's no problem."

"That's going to take a lot of time we don't have, Stew," said one of the computer scientists. "Just building a 3D mesh is days of work."

Before Stew could respond, Chris Thomas burst into the room, holding his laptop open. Leah came in right behind him. "I have what we're looking for. Does anyone have a projector? I need to put this up on a screen."

"Put what on the screen?" asked Stew. The other analysts looked confused.

"Everything we have from the email hack. Max has been translating the language into English. I have everything we're looking for. Well, almost everything. Can someone grab a projector? We don't have much time."

"What? How did you hack the phone?"

"It was easy. I took the 2D images of Black you gave me access to and used Max to create a 3D facial model. That got us past the depth camera and into the phone. Then I took the fingerprints, also from the files you gave me, and used that to defeat the bioscan. The passcode was easy. I have some sniffer software I developed a few years ago that got me past that in a few minutes. I gotta tell you, nothing is safe. Even triple authentication is easy to hack these days. But none of this matters anyway. The phone is a dead end. So how about that projector?"

Stew and the team looked at each other in complete amazement.

"If the phone's a dead end, you must have access to the servers?" asked Stew hopefully.

"No. The servers are encrypted—a really nasty firewall. All kinds of weird there. Max is working on that now. We only have emails. From the phone, I can see the server file directory, but they're deleting their data and literally unplugging servers from the wall. So there are some holes we'll need to fill in, as part of their execution appears to be offline."

Chris scratched his head before continuing. "But here's the part that's still blowing my mind. All their email communication is written in a derivative of the Adamic language, almost like slang. They call it Lamanese. They intentionally didn't encrypt their email so they could avoid attracting unwanted attention over the web, which was a super smart plan. I bet that was Alba. They never thought anyone would figure it out, but I figured it out."

"Laman what?" asked one of the analysts. "What are you talking about? Adamic language? I'm a linguist, and that's not a known language."

"Not one you know about. The Max AI is built on Adamic mathematics. Using the foundational mathematics of the Max codebase, Max was able to roughly translate the language and pull all the intel we have from the emails. I have a Nav summary report of what we've got so far. We don't have a lot of time. I need to show you what we discovered."

"This is madness," the CIA linguist protested. "How do we even know you're telling the truth? No one has ever seen this so-called Adamic or Lamanese language. This is insanity."

"Yeah, I know. I've only seen it one other place."

"Where?"

"In my mind."

Within fifteen minutes, Stew had everyone of importance on a secure Cisco conference line: the team in London, the rest of the Orion's Spear team at Langley, the CIA director, and all ten members of the National Security Council, including the president of the United States in the situation room under the White House.

"We don't have a lot of time," said Stew, "so I'm going to let Chris Thomas tell us what he has uncovered. Our analysts are verifying what they can as we go—they're only about fifteen minutes ahead of this conversation. Mr. Thomas, the floor is yours."

Chris stood in front of a camera, with CIA personnel also filling the room. Through the wall monitor, the president of the United States, Michael Barrington, stared back at him. Chris had never felt so nervous in his entire life. He glanced over at Leah, who gave him a quick wink.

"A Nav summary and detailed findings were sent to each of you a few minutes ago," Chris began. "The group we've been referring to as the Hancock/Zurich group is known internally as the Order of Baphomet or simply the Order. It appears to be a highly sophisticated environmental terrorist group or some kind of secret society."

Working his laptop furiously, Chris continued. "The Order was founded in 1946 by Benson Hancock and another man known in their network only as Mahan, Master Mahan, or the Prophet. We have no information on this person and believe he is not Benson Hancock. Since 1946, they have engaged in taking out rival organizations, like the Seven and

252

the Illuminati. In your report, you will find what they call the Mandate, a manifesto that advocates killing most of the world's population and overthrowing the world's governments. They aim to return the world to the pristine state it was in before *Homo sapiens* came on the scene approximately 250,000 years ago."

Chris paused and cleared his dry throat. "At some point, they also took control of most of the European banking cartels. They have over five thousand legitimate business interests across the globe. However, they also control most of the illegal drug trade in North America and Europe. They run human-trafficking operations, sponsor terrorism wherever it's profitable, and run online gambling and porn sites. We estimate they have roughly four trillion in assets."

"Goodness," said the president. "How have we never known about this?"

"We're still trying to figure that out, Mr. President," said Stew. "We fell backward into finding them, starting with a CIA op in Brussels several years ago. They have numerous US politicians and bureaucrats on their payroll. Mr. President, this expansive list has been sent to the FBI, which is now obtaining warrants and planning arrests. But we can't take them down yet. It may tip our hand."

"How many government people are we talking about here, Stew?" asked the president.

"Thousands, sir. It's insanity, and we haven't even scratched the surface."

"Continue, Chris," said the president, keeping a poker face.

"The Order has been testing a weaponized virus they call Aries on North Korean political prisoners. They've figured out a way to deliver the virus in mass quantity via an estimated five hundred or so drones. We know from the email data that most of the drones are now in position and awaiting orders to deploy, but we don't know where they are. We've known for a while where the drones are manufactured in Canada. Fearing they were close to launch and because of their proximity to the United States, a SEAL team took down that facility about an hour ago. They have direct access to the drones and are feeding us intel as they get it."

"And you helped these madmen?" blurted the chairman of the Joint Chiefs of Staff. "How do we know you're not in on this?"

"Sir, the CIA has had Chris Thomas under surveillance for some time now," said Stew. Chris gave him a look—he'd had no idea. "We can vouch for him 100 percent. It's all in the report."

"Sir, I didn't know I was being used by the Order," said Chris. "However, I did create a way to stop this. Each drone has four bioreactor units, two on each wing. The Order—under the guise of an international aid organization—approached me about fixing problems in the unit's environmental-controls system, and I did fix it. However, my girlfriend, Leah"—Chris gestured to her—"raised some suspicions, so I built a back door in the software. Their system is infected with a computer virus I designed. It's similar to the Stuxnet worm in that it will heat the containment units without the operator's knowledge. This action destroys any biological matter, including viruses. We also implanted a worm in the drone's flight controls that, when activated, redlines its engine and causes it to explode midair."

"Sounds pretty smart, Chris," said the president. "So why not activate the malware now and stop this?"

"Sir, we just found a hole in the plan," said Stew. "According to the SEAL team on station in Ontario, the drones are not equipped with satellite receivers. We can't hack the drones via satellite, which was Thomas's plan. The SEALs are still tearing the drones apart looking for communications equipment of any kind."

"Well, how are these terrorists communicating with their drones?" asked the president. He was clearly frustrated.

A new face appeared on one of the monitors. It was the commander of the SEAL team in Ontario. "Sir, we have several drones in our possession. They are fueled and ready for flight. As you know, there are no satellite receivers on these units, only basic aircraft radios. Instrumentation shows that the radio is receiving a signal, but the source is unknown. NSA is analyzing."

Stew held up his phone. "Sir, I just got a message from the NSA. They've looked over the drone engineering schematics and concluded the radio is part of a HAARP-style comms system."

"A what?" asked the president.

"Sir, HAARP is a highly classified DARPA project," Stew said. "Most people in this room don't even have the security clearance to talk about it. But, in the interest of national security, I will quickly summarize the points that are important for us to know here. HAARP is a high-power, high-frequency transmitter used for bouncing powerful radio signals off the ionosphere."

Chris sat down and rubbed his forehead. He hadn't considered this problem.

As Stew reviewed HAARP's technical details, Chris suddenly burst out. "Now it all makes sense! It's the Zurich building. The building is a massive HF transmitter. That's how they communicate with the drones. They bounce a radio signal from Zurich off the ionosphere to activate the drones across the globe."

Stew swore under his breath.

"How do we know that?" asked the president.

"We have the building's schematics," said Chris. "The antenna is built into the superstructure of the building. We didn't know what it was when we first saw it. Now we know. This system is known as a dead man's switch, Mr. President. If the drones lose the signal from the Hancock Building, they launch."

"He's right," said Stew.

"What do we do?" asked the president.

"Sir, we recommend a full air assault on the Zurich building," said the chairman of the Joint Chiefs of Staff. "We can be ready to launch in thirty minutes out of Ramstein Air Force Base."

"We can't hit the city of Zurich with a cruise-missile barrage!" yelled the president. "Hundreds of innocent people would die, maybe even thousands. I'm going to have to tell the Swiss president about this right away."

Stew pushed his glasses up the bridge of his nose and looked at the president on the screen. "Sir, we can't destroy the building with an airstrike. All the drones will launch."

The president said nothing. He looked exasperated. The room was unusually quiet as stark despair hung over the team.

Mike Mayberry stood, moved forward from a dark corner of the room, and looked up at the screen. "Mr. President, I have a plan."

They know. They are coming soon. I have no other information. Norman typed the message into the gaming app on his iPhone. Then he calmly placed the device back in his coat and continued his work.

CHAPTER 46

"Mr. President, I am sorry," said the president of Switzerland via video link. "This is the final word from our Federal Council. This is a Swiss problem on sovereign and neutral Swiss ground. Therefore, the Swiss will deal with it."

President Barrington was normally a patient man, but the Swiss president clearly did not understand what he was dealing with. President Barrington took a moment and looked around the room at his advisers. Did anyone know how the US president could force another sovereign country's president to allow a US paramilitary operation in one of its major cities?

"I understand your concern and the concern of the Swiss government's Federal Council," said President Barrington. "But I assure you, sir, this is an extreme threat, one only the US is uniquely qualified to respond to. If this terrorist group is successful, potentially billions will die. Again, I don't want this to come off the wrong way, Mr. President, but we are the only military power with the tools to take down the threat. I am asking you again, please allow us permission to enter Switzerland and neutralize this threat to the entire world."

With an air of impatience, the Swiss president looked down and adjusted his coat. "I must reaffirm, Mr. President. The Federal Council of Switzerland is unanimous in its decision. We will address the problem. We have gone over your intelligence with the ambassador and several CIA representatives from the embassy. We understand the nature of the threat. At this moment, the Grenadiers, our special forces, are formulating a plan to take down the Zurich operation and reestablish order."

President Barrington said nothing. This conversation was going nowhere, and time was running out.

"I assure you, the Grenadiers are among the best of the best," said the Swiss president with a reassuring smile.

"I am sure they are, Mr. President, but let me be blunt. They are not Delta Force. They are not SEAL Team Six. They are not Ground Branch. I can assure you, Mr. President, our men are—by far—the very best in the world."

The Swiss president went red and didn't speak for a long while. Finally he said, "The matter is settled. This is a Swiss problem. We will keep you posted on the battle plan and time frame."

"It's going to take more than military might," said President Barrington. "You need an expert who can penetrate their computer network. We are willing to provide ours. He is currently in London and can be in Zurich within hours. At the very least, please take us up on this offer of technical assistance. Chris Thomas is the only person who can access the network and stop the drones."

The Swiss president folded his arms. "We disagree. Our intelligence experts have been briefed by the CIA, and we believe we can defeat the computer problem."

President Barrington looked to his staff just outside the camera's view. The chief of staff and secretary of state both shrugged. President Barrington sighed and looked at the monitor. "Best of luck, Mr. President."

He ended the communication and looked up at his secretary of state. "Get me the UN secretary general."

CHAPTER 47

This is a Viper suit," started Mike Mayberry. "It's kind of our version of the Iron Man suit. Lightweight. Bulletproof. Self-contained. Built-in retractable parachute system. AR/VR capability. And a bunch of other things I am not at liberty to discuss."

"Wow, that's cool," said Leah, looking at Mike in the suit. Chris was less impressed. He was already thinking of ways to improve the system.

"It takes about two months of training in the suit to know how to use it right," said Stew. "Since they're custom-fit and cost about $4 million a pop, we don't have an extra one lying around, so we're going to put you in that." Stew pointed to a tactical suit hanging on a locker.

"Whoa, wait. I'm going with you?" asked Chris.

"Uh, no," said Leah. "No way. He is not going with you."

"Look, Chris," said Stew. "You're the only one who understands the language the Order's software is written in. Since the only way to access the system is to be on-site in front of the servers, you have to go. Plus, who else is going to talk to Max? We don't have a choice here."

Chris looked at Mike in shock.

"We've got a few tricks up our sleeve," said Mike. "One is a weapon being moved into position now. I'm going to be with you the whole way. My guys will lead the assault and take down the threats in front of us. We'll get to the server room, and you and Max will take down the drone system. You know you'll basically save the day. Once we've got control of the signals problem, we'll demo the building. If the Swiss plan fails, then they will know we're coming, and that's a problem, but the suit we have for you is mostly bulletproof."

"Mostly?" Leah asked.

"Yes, nothing is 100 percent, not even the Viper suit."

Chris started feeling woozy. The prospect of death was very real, and Chris Thomas was no hero. Letting his gaze wander, he noticed something unusual sitting on a workbench across the room. It was obviously a drone.

"What's that?" asked Chris.

"Oh, that." Mike walked over and picked up the little flying machine. "It's a quadcopter microdrone. Long-range. Multi-capable 8K camera. Satellite transmitter. Very handy in an op and fits in the palm of your hand. We're going to even the odds by taking about seven hundred and fifty of these guys with us."

"It just transmits video?" Chris asked. "I can see how that would be useful, but do you really need hundreds of them?"

"Yeah, well, it's their other capability that's useful to us in mission." Mike pointed to a circular red charge at the front of the drone, just above its main forward camera. "They kill bad people," he said with a slight grin.

Bang! Everyone in the room jumped as Elle Danley burst open the door. "Stew, we have a critical problem. I need to see you and Mike right now!"

CHAPTER 48

Benson Hancock sat in a high-backed leather chair and surveyed the busy control room. It looked like the deck of the starship *Enterprise*. Much like government intelligence agencies, the Order had its own mission specialists, weapons experts, analysts, and technicians ready for sensitive missions. Most of them had been recruited from foreign intelligence agencies. The staff gladly made their skills available for the cause of Baphomet.

Located just under the temple, the high-tech control room was encased in two-feet-thick concrete walls. Twenty-four monitors displayed CCTV camera feeds surrounding the building, status updates on drones spread across the world, and the drone deployment schedule.

"Sir, 80 percent of the functioning drones are reporting mission ready," said a mission specialist. "We estimate the remaining drones will be online inside of ninety minutes."

"Excellent," replied Benson. "We need to give the remaining 20 percent more time. We'll need every possible operational drone to pull this off. What's our perimeter status?"

"We detect no unusual activity in the Hancock Building's vicinity, nor do we detect any unusual activity in the city," said another mission specialist, staring into his terminal. "There's no unusual activity on police radios or in the airspace."

"They will be coming," said Benson. "Activate all facility weapons systems, but do not expose the weapons yet. Notify all security personnel to take positions."

The men went about their work. Lennox stood in the corner of the room. Benson noticed the addicted former president seemed disinterested in the events at hand, probably high on some drug again.

"Weapons systems standing by," said a weapons specialist. "Building guards are in position."

"Excellent," said Benson.

Another specialist spoke up. "Sir, you requested an update on the Orion's Spear asset's family. Field agents report mission accomplished in Virginia and Washington State."

Lennox suddenly perked up. "Ah, Norman Stellar gets his due," Benson heard him murmur. "They better have video for me."

"Main, this is Neighborhood Watch," said a CIA operative from the Zurich-based American consulate. "We're in position across the street in a hotel with direct line of sight to the Hancock Building's north side. Cameras are now transmitting. The weapon arrived this morning. It is now in position and ready to fire."

"Excellent," said Stew. "Be advised, the Swiss strike team is inbound now. ETA four minutes. Stand ready until instructed to act."

"Roger that, Main," said the CIA man as he looked out the hotel window and down onto the plaza of the Hancock Building.

"Sir, we're picking up an encrypted satellite video feed emanating from the hotel on the building's north side," said a mission specialist to Benson Hancock.

"That's the first sign," replied Benson, leaning back in his command chair. "Probably the NSA. Be ready. They're coming soon."

CHAPTER 49

Chris and Leah sat alone in the stark-white locker room, waiting for word from Mike and Stew. The wait was agonizing, so Chris decided to try on the tactical suit Mike had set out for him.

"This jumpsuit's a little big on you, but it will have to do," said Leah, her eyes bloodshot from fatigue and crying over the last twenty-four hours.

When Leah held up the belt, Chris shook his head. "I'm going to use the belt my grandpa gave me. It's for good luck." He threaded his grandpa's belt through the suit's belt loops.

"Are they going to be OK with that?"

Chris tightened the belt, slipped on the black, bulky bulletproof vest, and started adjusting the straps for a tight fit. "Well, they're gonna have to be. I'm not taking it off."

Leah tilted her head and raised her eyebrows. "How about boots?" she asked.

Chris looked at the row of Danner combat boots specifically designed for US military special operations. They were really cool. "It looks like they have my size—nine and a half. I hope I get to keep these."

"Doubt it. Here, put these gloves in your pocket."

"OK, check. What else?"

"Parachute harness?"

"I don't know how that works. I'll have Mike put it on me."

"Very well. Helmet?" Leah slipped the Kevlar-and-titanium helmet onto Chris's head and fastened the chin strap. She took a step back and examined him, then moved in closer to readjust the straps.

"It's too big," said Chris.

"It's all they have, honey. We'll try to find another one, but you're not going in without a helmet. Now, how about a gun?"

"I don't think so. Never fired one. I'd probably end up shooting the wrong person."

"Let me know if you need a lesson," Leah said. She put a Glock 19 into a holster and attached it to Chris's waist.

"Really? You know how to fire a gun?"

"My dad's a big hunter. I grew up around guns."

"There's a lot I still don't know about you, Leah Bennion."

"You know enough to marry me," she said, then threw her hands over her mouth. "I can't believe that just came out of my mouth."

Chris didn't know what to say. He just looked down at the ground. But then he smiled and broke the awkward silence. "Well, you did say on the plane of death that you want to spend the rest of your life with me. Are you dropping not-so-subtle hints, Leah?"

No words left her mouth, but her cheeks got rosy. Chris grabbed her hand and pulled her in for a long kiss. It was hard for Leah to get her arms around Chris in the bulky bulletproof vest, but they both did their best.

Still holding her, Chris looked down into her stunning eyes. "I don't want us to say anything right now, but if I live through this, I swear to you right now, I am going to give you a proper marriage proposal when I come back. Deal?"

"Yes!" she said enthusiastically as she leaned in for another kiss.

"*Say I love you,*" Chris heard a voice in his mind say. But just then, Mike and Stew walked into the locker room.

"Oh, geez," said Stew, looking away.

"Sorry to interrupt you two lovebirds, but it's time to jock up," said Mike.

~

"Stew, please, you don't understand," pleaded Norman Stellar. Tears and snot streamed down his face. He was handcuffed to the table in the same interrogation room Chris Thomas had occupied only hours earlier. "If I don't check in through the app, they will kill my family!"

"Norman!" yelled Stew. "Stop crying. Tell me what you did. Who are you talking about? The Order? Tell me everything right now."

"First save my family, Stew! I was supposed to check in, and it's past time. I swear to you, I didn't tell them anything."

"Swear to me," said Mike, sticking a Glock 19 between Norman's eyes. He went cross-eyed looking at the gun, and then he wet his pants.

"Oh, come on, Norman," Mike said as he lowered the gun. Norman fainted forward onto the table.

"We don't have time for this," said Mike.

Stew turned to Elle. "Tell us more about the Norman situation, Elle."

"He's been acting squirrelly for a few months," said Elle, head bowed and arms folded. "So, on a hunch, I hacked him."

"You did what?"

"I know, but I was right, Stew. He's a spy for the Order. It's all right there." She pointed to Norman's phone on the table. "He's been communicating with them through the IM feature on a gaming app."

Stew grabbed the phone, and Elle told him the passcode. "I cross-referenced Norman with the Order comm logs from Chris Thomas," she explained. "Norman is a spy. We're still downloading all the logs. We need him to talk right now."

Norman came to. Looking at Mike, he winced in terror. Mike didn't put away the Glock 19. "Start talking, Norman, or I bring in the chemicals," he said.

"No, no," said Norman, shaking his head. "I'll tell you everything, but first we have to save my family."

"What do you mean?" asked Mike. "Who's going to hurt your family?"

"They're going to kill my mom and my sister's family! I haven't reported in. Mike, please call HRT. Please! I'm sure the killers are on the way now. You have to save them!" Norman was referring to the FBI's elite Hostage Rescue Team, made up mainly of former Navy SEALs and Army Special Forces.

Stew and Mike exchanged a glance. "OK, Elle, pull the files on Norman's family," said Stew.

"There's no time for that! My mom's in Green Acres Retirement Center in Fairfax. They said they would burn her to death. Get someone there now. And my sister! Please, they're going to kill Tommy!" Norman burst into tears again.

"I think he's telling the truth," said Mike. Pulling out his phone, he dialed the number he'd memorized for these types of emergencies. Elle handed him her phone with Norman's family information on screen.

"This is Knife. I have a priority November Whisky order. Authorization code zulu-delta-bravo-zero-zero-niner-alpha. I need a rapid-response HRT to Green Acres Retirement Center in Fairfax, Virginia. Potential terror attack in progress. Hostage is Ester Stellar, room A-144. Read back."

The man on the other end of the phone quickly relayed back the information.

"Verified. Execute." Mike turned to Elle and Stew. "We don't have an HRT close to Spokane. We're going to have to send in a local SWAT team."

Norman just stared, pleading wordlessly.

"I'll get on it right now." Elle grabbed her phone from Mike and ran from the room.

Turning his attention back to Norman, Mike moved in close. "We're doing what we can for your family. Now talk. What happened?"

"Stew, I was compromised," said Norman. He tried to turn to Stew, but Mike stayed in his face. "I knew it would catch up with me, but it's like some kind of monster inside me I can't control."

"What are you talking about?" asked Stew.

"I was on the dark web. The kid, I think he was fifteen. He said he'd met me at the hotel. Stew, I can't control it. I can't. The demons are real."

"Keep talking," said Mike.

"Instead of the kid, it was the Order. A German guy, the doctor on the North Korea video. They told me what they'd do to my family if I didn't help. But I swear, Stew, I didn't tell them anything. Maybe a few things, but only to keep my family alive."

"What did you tell them, Norman?" said Mike. "Tell me right now, or I'll—"

"No, no, no. I'll tell you." Norman paused for a long moment. "I just told them about the Swiss assault, that's all." He tried to sound nonchalant.

"What!" yelled Stew. "Then they know everything." Activating his comms, he ran from the room. "Get the president on the phone now. Call off the hit. They know the Swiss are coming."

Mike calmly dialed his phone. With Smith still out of commission, Dellmark was the new Ground Branch sergeant. He picked up on the first ring.

"It's going sideways," Mike said. "Fire up the bird. We leave in five minutes."

CHAPTER 50

HANCOCK BUILDING
ZURICH, SWITZERLAND

From a young age, Major Luka Zoss had fantasized about saving the world. Today was his chance to prove his worth. Having graduated first in every military class—including his Special Forces Grenadier class—since his conscription into the Swiss military at age eighteen, Zoss had been eyed for Swiss military greatness almost from the day he'd stepped into boot camp.

Zoss pulled the Audi Q8 up to the narrow curb and looked at the beautiful woman next to him. He barely knew her. In fact, Major Zoss and Special Agent Naomi Stein of Israel's National Intelligence Agency, otherwise known as the Mossad, had met only several hours ago. Agent Stein had been on assignment with the Swiss government monitoring the rise of Neo-Nazism in Switzerland when she was asked to provide cover for a special anti-terrorism mission in need of qualified women. When the stakes were explained to her, she'd immediately volunteered to help.

Zoss walked around the side of the Audi and opened Agent Stein's door. She was wearing a bright-pink fur coat, which Zoss thought an unusual choice of attire for the mission. He extended his hand and helped her from the SUV. This behavior was part of their cover. Then two additional couples exited from the back of the Q8. In reality, they were plainclothes Grenadier soldiers and agents of Switzerland's Federal Office of Police.

Giving each other anxious looks, the three couples began walking toward the Hancock Building only two blocks away. Their long coats concealed their compact H&K submachine guns and sidearms.

No one paid any attention to the group of heavily armed men and women as they continued up the narrow street. The activity in the neighborhood was vibrant. Spring was in the Swiss air. As they approached the tall, out-of-place Hancock Building, they passed busy shops, people enjoying a lazy afternoon at cafés, and a few tourists taking selfies.

One of the couples stopped at a vegetable cart and pretended to inspect the fresh food while the other two couples feigned interest in a shop window. Zoss turned to a street vendor and perused the goods the Middle Eastern man was peddling. Then he touched his earpiece and began to speak softly. "This is Zoss. We are in position on the south side of the building. Echo and Tango, your status? Over."

Two other plainclothes teams with similar male and female covers approached the target, one from the hotel to the north and the other from the train station to the west. The plan was to approach the plaza, assault the vast lobby from three sides, kill the guards, and call in three strike teams waiting in light-armored troop carriers in a warehouse five blocks away. A fourth strike team approached via bullet train from the north. The train would stop at the station just west of the Hancock Building and unload its surprise payload.

"Zoss, this is Zulu. Ready on your word to cut power to the block." The voice came from a military engineering team concealed in a nearby sewer.

"Execute," ordered Zoss.

Although it was the middle of the day, people almost immediately noticed that power was out on the street. Zoss eyed the target and noticed that the lights were still on in the vast glass-encased lobby. Confused, he looked back at his fellow Grenadiers. There was no response.

Zoss turned to his concealed mic. "Building power is still on," he said. Just then, he noticed Agent Stein standing in the middle of the narrow street. She was staring up at the target with a confused look.

Annoyed that the woman was jeopardizing their cover, Zoss was about to say something when Stein suddenly drew her weapon from inside her long pink coat. An ear-piercing sound filled the street. Zoss watched in horror as Stein's body exploded before his eyes.

Turning to the building, Zoss drew his weapon from his coat and scanned the area for a target. "What the—" he yelled as he stared at the building. They were his last words.

～

"Sir, power is out to the block," said a technician seated near the front of the control center. "Our facility's power source is operating at full capacity."

"Excellent," said Benson Hancock, scanning the video feed covering the building's perimeter. "If they cut power, that means they are coming now. We have no reason to hide anymore. Retract the windows and search for targets. Alert the guards. Call out the enemy as you see them and fire at will."

From his corner of the room, Lennox smiled.

One of the men typed furiously on his keyboard. Hancock watched the monitors as glass panels retracted from all four corners of the building's third floor, exposing four massive Gatling guns—originally designed to destroy tanks—and four 40mm grenade launchers.

"A woman approaching from the south just drew a weapon, sir."

Hancock stood and stared at the screen. He was momentarily mesmerized by the brave, beautiful woman in the long pink coat. "Cry havoc and let slip the dogs of war," he whispered.

The mission specialist grabbed the joystick at his console, zeroed in on the woman in the pink coat, and pulled the trigger. They watched as she disintegrated before their eyes. The people on the street flew into a panic. The operator held his finger on the trigger, and the Gatling gun's deadly 30mm projectiles destroyed all life on the street. Benson's wicked laugh filled the control room.

"Sir, more armed men and women approaching from the north and west," yelled out another operator. "Firing now." The two teams, along with hundreds of innocent people, perished almost instantly, the Gatling guns disintegrating everything in their path. Smoke, fire, and death filled the room's monitors.

"Swiss fighter jets inbound twenty miles out—four F-18s," yelled an operator.

"Locking on," said another operator. "I have tone. Firing."

Disguised as an HVAC unit, a large antiaircraft missile battery rose from the top of the building and fired eight highly advanced surface-to-air missiles. The fighter jets broke formation, fired flares, and employed their electronic antimissile systems. But Benson knew that eight missiles were too much for them to manage.

The first aircraft was hit over the lake. The pilot didn't make it out. Two more were destroyed on approach just over the city center. The last F-18 broke off in an attempt to escape the barrage, but there were too many missiles. He ejected over the city as his F-18 was hit by the remaining missiles. Fire and debris rained down on Zurich.

"F-18s destroyed," yelled a guard over his radio from the building's roof. The control room erupted in applause.

"Sir, train inbound from the north is closing in on our position," said another operator. "We just got intelligence that a strike team is on board."

"What are you waiting for?" Benson yelled, feeling rage boil inside him. "Destroy them all."

The west-facing guns and grenade launchers were unleashed on the approaching Railjet high-speed train. The passenger cars disintegrated as 30mm rounds and grenades ripped through the metal skin like a razor through a sheet of paper. When a barrage hit the engine's fuel source, the lead car exploded in a fireball and the train derailed at 150 miles per hour, with several cars flipping end over end. Benson smiled as the mangled and burning bodies of soldiers and civilians alike hit the ground.

The operators turned their attention to several approaching light-armored troop carriers. Without mercy, Hancock's men unleashed 40mm grenade after grenade and held triggers to spew more than four thousand Gatling rounds per minute. Soon the streets were littered with destroyed armored vehicles. Civilians and soldiers lay everywhere the eye could see. Watching the monitors, Benson felt giddy. He'd dreamt of this day for years.

"Sir, the functional drones are almost at 100 percent ready," reported an operator. "Starting launch sequence now."

"Excellent." Benson casually sipped a steaming cup of Earl Grey tea.

CHAPTER 51

Stew stood in the London operations center watching the nightmare unfold on a live satellite feed. Another monitor displayed the feed from the hotel video. No one spoke. There was nothing they could do.

"Go for Main," Stew said into his comms.

"Main, Knife," said Mike. "HRT arrived at the care home fifteen minutes ago. The entire building was engulfed in flames. Looks like the fire originated in Norman's mother's bedroom. She was burned alive, but they managed to evacuate the other patients and all the staff."

"He was right. What about Spokane?"

"SWAT hit Norman's sister's house. No one there, but there were signs of a struggle. We think they got them."

"God help them," Stew said and cut off his comms. He turned to the control room, where his people worked furiously. One analyst was yelling something into his comms. Another typed frantically at his console while two others stood over his shoulder, pointing at something on his monitor. Several people stood around a table rummaging through a mountain of intelligence briefings and maps. The monitors high above the room played a live feed of the carnage unfolding in Zurich.

Swallowing hard, Stew stepped up onto an elevated platform in the room's center. "Everyone, listen up," he called. The men and women turned and looked at him. "The Swiss plan failed. Within the next minute, I expect the president to greenlight our plan. All that stands between the Order and the end of the world is our strike team and us."

Stew paused and proudly looked over his team. They were hanging on his every word. "We're it. If you don't do your jobs with absolute precision, billions will die. You're all prepared for this. This is what you've trained for. Failure is not an option. I'm depending on you. The president is depending on you. The world is depending on each and every one of you. Ground Branch is almost on target. Everyone to your stations now."

Preparing for the fight of their lives, the men and women in the room erupted into action.

CHAPTER 52

The Swiss president stared despondently into the camera. "President Barrington, I am sorry to report that the Grenadier assault was a . . . a failure. The carnage is unspeakable. We estimate that one thousand civilians and soldiers are dead. We are preparing a second assault of the—"

"I am sorry to interrupt you, Mr. President, but that won't be necessary," said Barrington.

"I—I don't understand," said the Swiss president.

"I've taken the matter to the United Nations Security Council. All the countries of the world are now preparing to take down the drones over their territories. We're working together to provide intelligence to every government on probable drone locations. In an emergency vote, the majority has sided with the United States position." Barrington paused. "Now we do this my way. Order the Grenadiers to stand down."

"I-I-I must protest! You see, sir, Switzerland is a neutral country. Therefore—"

"You can take your case to the United Nations. In the meantime, we will deal with the problem now. I won't be responsible for any further Swiss military or law-enforcement deaths in the area. So again, please have your people stand down. The secretary of state will report back to you once we have neutralized the threat."

"But, but, sir—"

"Good day." President Barrington clicked the Leave Meeting button on the screen, then turned his attention to a second monitor with two familiar faces. Stew Brimhall was in London, and Mike Mayberry appeared to be inside the cargo bay of a military transport plane.

"Gentlemen, as you're aware, the Swiss assault failed," Barrington began. "Under executive order, I'm greenlighting operation Rogue Warrior. We don't have the support of the Swiss government. The Order will be expecting another assault. You have twenty minutes from launch to eliminate the threat and take control of the drones. If you can't stop the threat in twenty minutes, I will order a last-ditch, all-out airstrike on the Hancock Building. The aerial assets are inbound now. Mike and Stew, the world is depending on you and your teams. Execute your mission with extreme prejudice. We'll be watching from this end. Godspeed."

The screen went blank.

CHAPTER 53

Chris sat in one of the C-17's jump seats. He picked up his laptop and secured it inside a lightweight bulletproof case strapped to the front of his armored vest. He was continually fidgeting with the lighter armor around his thighs—it was tight-fitting and hot. He'd never worn heavy Danner boots before, but he kind of enjoyed the feel. He ran his fingers over the black, lightweight jumpsuit that encompassed most of his body. It was a strange material, not bulletproof, but Mike said it would give him some protection against sharp objects and explosions.

The Ground Branch operatives all wore their Viper suits, looking like something out of a Star Wars movie. The men talked and joked in low tones while double-checking each other's equipment and packs. Other mission specialists worked on computers plugged into three refrigerator-sized microdrone containment units. The men moved fast, trying to complete every needful task. The mood on the plane was incredibly calm and professional considering what lay ahead for the team.

As Chris looked around the cargo bay, he wondered about the men. Did they have families? What branch of the service had they come from? What kinds of missions had they been on? He'd never met men like these in real life. They were the stuff of movies, though he was pretty sure the movies mostly got it wrong.

Mike made his way through his men to Chris. "Everything good with your girl?"

Chris looked up at Mike. The bandage around his head was gone, but Chris could see numerous staples just above his ear. He also had a black eye, a swollen cheek, and he looked like he hadn't showered in days. "Yeah, well, she's sort of been through a lot in the last couple days. I mean, I barely even knew what I was mixed up in, so I can't imagine what she's thinking."

"She'll get over it," Mike said positively. "Then again, my ex-wife didn't. Anyway, we're almost there, so stand up, and I'll strap you into my chest harness."

Chris stood, but he stopped Mike before he could attach the harness. "I can't do this," he said in a low voice, leaning toward Mike so the other operatives couldn't hear. "I'm a coward. I've almost died twice in my life. I don't have nine lives. Look at this situation. I'm not going to live through this."

"Wait. You've almost died twice?"

"Yeah, the Florida thing"—Chris pointed at his head—"and on a fishing trip when I was twelve."

"Tell me about that," said Mike.

"I was finishing on the Clackamas River on Mount Hood in Oregon. I was wading back across the channel to the riverbank and got caught in the current. As I floated downstream, my leg got caught in the root ball of a stump I couldn't see. It flipped me over on my back underwater."

The soldier was listening intently. "Did you panic?"

"No, it was weird. I saw a bright light through the water over my head. I was instantly at complete peace. For years, I've wondered if I was just looking up at the sun or if it was something else, like some kind of portal to heaven or something. I saw my life flash before my eyes. It wasn't like a movie—it was just all there before me at once. I know that sounds weird, but I have a hard time explaining it."

"You don't need to," said Mike. "It's happened to me several times. I know exactly what you mean. Tell me the rest."

"Unbeknownst to me, my grandma saw me go in and yelled at my dad back at camp. He ran to the river and pulled me out."

"And obviously you lived. I'm assuming no life flashed before your eyes in the Florida incident. It happened too fast, right?"

"Yeah. I don't talk about it much, but I went to the other side. I learned things there. I know it sounds crazy, but I have a mission in this life. There are things I have to do with the gifts God has given me."

Mike placed his hand on Chris's shoulder and looked him in the eyes. "If that's true, then do you really think you're going to die today?"

Chris paused. The thought hadn't crossed his mind. He allowed the warm reassurance that entered his being to sink in for a moment. "OK, I can go with that," he said, nodding.

"You're the only one who can stop this," Mike said bluntly. "We're badly outnumbered. We know they're heavily armed. We have no idea if half our experimental tech is going to work. We need all the help we can get here."

"I understand the stakes," said Chris.

"I once heard a guy say that until death, all defeat is psychological. That's true. When you believe in the enemy more than you believe in yourself, who do you think will win?"

"That makes sense. What else do I need to know?"

"No battle plan survives first contact," said Mike as he attached the tandem jump rig to Chris. "When in doubt, empty your magazine. If it's stupid and it works, then it isn't stupid. If the attack is going well, then it's an ambush."

Chris could tell Mike had given this spiel before.

"Here's the bottom line, my friend," Mike continued. "Let's do this and do it right. It's OK to be scared, but it's not OK to quit. Billions of innocent people are depending on you and me to do our jobs right now. So what do you say? Let's go save the world, shall we?" Mike extended his arm, inviting Chris to move to the rear cargo doors.

Nodding, Chris sighed deeply and reluctantly walked in concert with Mike. The cargo bay's light went yellow, indicating two minutes till jump. Chris had seen transport-aircraft loading doors open in movies and YouTube videos, but to see and feel the doors open in real life was disconcerting. Fortunately, he was attached to Mike Mayberry, who was attached to a tandem parachute.

"OK, gentlemen, advance to the ramp and prepare to jump on my mark," Mike said over his comms.

The loadmaster had already moved the three microdrone containment units in single file to the edge of the ramp. He awaited the go signal to advance the units out of the aircraft. At three thousand feet, the containment units would deploy their chutes, slow to a safe speed, and then automatically release their deadly payload of tiny drones onto the Order's stronghold below.

With Chris and Mike at the head of the line, the operatives moved in single file next to the microdrone containment units, making final checks of each other's equipment. Even after Mike's pep talk, Chris was still terrified. They were about to jump from a perfectly fine airplane moving 250 miles per hour at thirty thousand feet over Switzerland. Most professional skydivers never jumped at this speed or altitude. Worst of all, Chris controlled nothing—he was simply along for the ride. His anxiety escalated to redline levels.

Chris saw Mike give a thumbs-up high in the air. "Good to go!" yelled Mike.

"Good to go!" his men repeated from behind him. The jumpmaster gave Mike a nod.

From behind, Mike attached the oxygen mask to Chris's face. "Breathe, Chris," he said. "Deep breaths."

"Ten seconds," yelled the jumpmaster as Chris and Mike jointly edged to within inches of the ramp's opening. Chris now had a front-row view of a hundred miles of stunning Swiss sky. He felt a sudden burst of courage and endorphins. "I can do this. I can do this."

And then the airplane exploded in midair.

CHAPTER 54

ABOVE ZURICH, SWITZERLAND

When Mike came to, he and Chris were tumbling through the air at terminal velocity. He immediately threw the drogue, the smaller pilot chute that would start slowing their free fall. As they flipped over and over, Mike could see the remnants of a massive explosion thousands of feet above them. The city of Zurich approached quickly from below.

"Mike! Mike!" Chris yelled into his headset.

"Stop flailing. I'm fixing a drogue malfunction."

"A what?"

As Mike untangled the bridle, the drogue fully inflated. With that crisis solved, he looked to see if Chris was injured. The younger man's tactical suit was charred, and his right sleeve was ripped open, revealing a superficial cut down his forearm. Miraculously, Chris seemed otherwise OK.

"Problem solved. Drogue inflated," Mike said.

"What happened to the plane?"

"I think the C-17 was hit by a surface-to-air missile. We knew this was a risk. Look over there." Mike pointed at a missile plume just to their right. "Hang on. I need to get a team status. Blue team, this is Knife. Sound off."

Mike looked all around him. Debris was falling, but he couldn't see any of his men. "Blue team, this is Knife," he repeated. "Sound off." Radio silence continued. Mike looked into his HUD. It showed his entire team dead. He spun from side to side, looking for any signs of his team in the air. Suddenly, a lifeless, burning body crossed in front of Chris and Mike's position.

"Everyone's dead," Mike said without emotion. "The blast must have blown us clear. We're lucky we were at the front of the ramp, or we'd be dead too."

Chris said nothing, obviously in shock.

"Main, this is Knife. Do you copy?" said Mike.

From the operations center in London, Stew Brimhall responded. "Knife, we're showing your team is offline and the C-17 is off the scope. What's your status?"

"Main, they're all dead." Mike paused for a brief moment. In mission, he was an expert at emotional control, but the verbal admission of losing all his teammates hit him hard. He quickly refocused with a steely resolve. In that moment, he determined to finish this mission for his friends.

"We got hit by a surface-to-air missile. Chris and I are the only survivors. We're at ten thousand feet. Our status is mission ready. Please advise."

"Stand by, Knife."

Mike pulled the ripcord, and the drogue pulled out the main canopy, jerking them to a slower speed. He could feel Chris squirming. "It's OK, Chris. Just hold tight. I'm waiting on Main."

Chris said nothing. They both watched as the burning city blocks around the Hancock Building loomed closer beneath them.

Stewart Brimhall was beside himself. The Ground Branch team, the microdrones, all the essential components of their battle plan, were now a million fiery pieces over Switzerland.

He looked at the faces of the mission specialists staring hopelessly back at him. Their despair deepened as the reality of the situation lay heavier on their already heavy-laden shoulders. They waited patiently for Stew to say something . . . anything.

Stew looked down, swallowed hard, and then looked back up at the sea of solemn faces. He closed his eyes, trying to refocus, then opened them and pushed the mic close to his mouth.

"Well, Mike . . . what would Han do?" asked Stew.

"Copy, Main. We're going in."

Stew picked up his phone and called the president.

CHAPTER 55

already ordered the air strike, Stew," said President Barrington.

"But, sir, they are literally sixty seconds from hitting the roof."

"The team is gone. The microdrones are gone. They're only two men, and one of them doesn't even know how to handle a gun. Mike is the best we have, but even in a Viper suit, he can't beat two-hundred-to-one odds. Stew, it's over. We're going to have to come up with a new plan."

"But, sir, the Order's drones, they'll launch. We won't get them all. They'll disperse the virus, killing millions, maybe billions. We need to give Mayberry and Thomas a chance before executing the air strike."

"The dead man's switch is just a theory, Stew. I know it's a good one, but we have to take our chances with the air strike. We've informed the world's governments about this threat. There's unprecedented cooperation going on to hunt down the drones. Satellite data is being shared across the globe, and the CIA's AI is building probable launch models. We're zeroing in on suspect launch sites in Missouri and California. I think we can stop this with minimum loss of life, Stew."

Stew felt encouraged by the information, but the plan still meant the deaths of millions of innocents. "The air assets won't be in place over Zurich for at least twenty minutes," he said to the president. "We have to at least give them that much time to stop this, Mr. President. Please, sir."

President Barrington didn't answer right away. "Let me discuss this with my advisers," he finally said. "I'm going to put you on hold for a moment."

After less than a minute, the president returned. "You've got twenty minutes. I'll be monitoring from this end."

CHAPTER 56

How are we going to do this?" Chris yelled into his headset. "It's just us!"
"Remember what I said about no battle plan surviving first contact?" replied Mike calmly. "Well, now it's improvise time. Welcome to Ground Branch, my friend."

There was silence for a few seconds as the Order building's roof quickly approached from below. At least ten guards were looking over the roof's edge, expecting another assault from the ground.

"Knife, be advised," came Stew's voice over both their comms. "Air strike is still inbound to your position. You have 19.5 minutes to accomplish your objective."

"Well, this just went pear-shaped," Chris heard Mike mumble under his breath. "Chris, see that large HVAC unit on the corner of the roof?"

"Yes."

"I'm going to pull the release and drop you behind that unit. That should give you enough cover while I address the immediate threat. It's probably going to be about ten feet to the deck, and we're coming in hot, so make sure you roll when you hit. I don't need you breaking an ankle right now. Copy?"

"Yes, copy."

They were approaching from above the building's south side. A guard glanced up and noticed them. Raising his rifle, he fired at Chris and Mike.

Mike yanked on the chute's pulley control with his left hand as the rounds passed just to their right. Simultaneously, with his right arm, he raised the highly modified M4 Carbine rifle attached to his suit. Chris flinched as Mike fired and hit the man between the eyes. As the other guards spun around, Mike continued firing.

"Dropping you in three—two—one . . ." Mike pulled the release and dropped Chris exactly where he'd said he would.

Chris hit the ground hard, pain shooting up his feet and into his lower back. He got up quickly—nothing felt broken—and looked around the corner of the HVAC unit. He watched in awe as Mike pulled the chute's emergency harness release and dropped right into the middle of the enemy's position, rolling to ease the impact. He'd killed four guards from the air but was now taking bullets at close range, with some of the remaining six guards firing their MP5s on full auto. Dozens of rounds bounced off Mike's Viper suit. Chris had been told about—and was skeptical about—the Viper suit's capabilities, but there in the blood and horror of the point-blank rooftop gunfight, any doubt was now laid to rest.

Jumping up from the ground with his M4, Mike resumed firing, cutting into the guards with stunning speed and accuracy. Their body armor was no match for Mike's advanced weapon. When all the guards lay dead on the roof, Mike pushed up his visor and ran to Chris.

⌇

"The rooftop is clear," said Mike as he assessed Chris. "That should buy us about a minute to figure out our next move. You hit the deck hard. Are you OK?"

"Yeah, I think I tweaked my back, but I can walk." Chris held his side and lower back. "Hey, man, that was some real-life Rambo stuff you just pulled right there. I'm never going to forget that."

"Well, it still hurts even though the round doesn't penetrate," said Mike. "I'm going to be bruised up bad tomorrow morning. One bullet hit me in the groin. I feel like I got punched in the gut by my ex-wife."

Chris laughed, which had been Mike's goal. The momentary comic relief helped ease the stress.

"Main, this is Knife," Mike said into his comms. "Mission status. We're on the deck, and the rooftop is clear."

"Copy that, Knife. You have eighteen minutes until air assault."

"Roger. Moving now." At that moment, an alert sounded in Mike's earpiece. He pulled down his visor and looked into his HUD. An automated voice announced, "Drone containment unit on station. Awaiting orders."

"Chris, look, the cavalry just arrived." Mike pointed to the sky. A microdrone containment unit floated gently under a parachute about five hundred feet north of their position.

"One of the containment units survived the C-17 explosion," Mike said into his comms. "It's on station and ready for combat. Main, are you getting this on your end?"

~

A mission specialist turned and yelled at Stew, trying to contain her excitement. "Sir, the containment unit is damaged, but approximately two hundred microdrone units are still operational and standing by to deploy."

Stew clasped his hands together. "Thank heaven!"

"Main, I have a new plan," said Mike. "I need thirty microdrones on my position. The remaining drones will assault the building. Is Neighborhood Watch ready to rock?"

"Copy, Knife. Stand by." Stew looked at his microdrone specialist. "Make it happen. Program the new mission and execute immediately." Several mission specialists turned to their workstations.

"Neighborhood Watch, this is Main," said Stew to the CIA's hotel team. "Be advised some of the microdrones survived the C-17 explosion. Sending approximately 170 units to assault the building. Is the weapon ready?"

For several days, the two CIA officers had waited in the hotel suite across from the Hancock Building, ready to execute their key part of the plan. "Ready on your command, Main."

"Roger that. Stand by." Stew looked over at the microdrone team. One of the mission specialists gave him a fast thumbs-up.

"Execute!" Stew yelled to the drone team.

Chris watched the containment unit float gently toward the rooftop. Suddenly, the unit's door exploded off its hinges, and the unmistakable sound of microdrones firing up their quadcopter blades filled the air.

"It sounds like an angry beehive," yelled Chris, watching the drones leave their lair.

"Some say it sounds like a beehive," said Mike. "Some say it sounds like a crazy maniac with a chainsaw. To me, it just sounds like death."

Thirty drones broke off from the main swarm and quickly zeroed in on Chris and Mike's position, taking up a strategic diamond-shaped formation just above the building.

"Wait, how do they know I'm not a bad guy?" yelled Chris over the roar.

"We programmed a 3D image of your face into the system. They know who you are. Oh, and they can also smell you."

"Sorry, it's really loud. Did you say they could smell me?" yelled Chris, giving Mike a curious look. Mike said nothing in return.

Just then, the roof-access door blew open, and guards started piling out, their weapons at the ready. Mike raised his M4. The drones turned their attention to the new threat, their tiny blades revving to a higher RPM.

"Main, we're going in." It was the last thing Chris heard Mike say before shooting and explosions rocked the rooftop.

CHAPTER 57

HANCOCK BUILDING
ZURICH, SWITZERLAND

N eighborhood Watch, execute now—I repeat, execute now," said Stew Brimhall.

"Copy, Main." One of the CIA officers immediately picked up an ax he'd placed by the hotel room's large picture window facing the Hancock Building. With all his might, he swung the ax into the window, shattering it. Then he and the other officer rolled a weird-looking, heavy black box up to the window opening. Years earlier, a smaller test version of this acoustic weapon had failed in the Brussels hotel assault. Since that time, DARPA had worked with Raytheon scientists and engineers to perfect the sonic weapon's capabilities and expand its uses.

One of the officers flipped open a toggle on the box, revealing a red button. "Firing now," he yelled into his comms as he pushed the button.

The two men were blown back into the hotel room by a sonic blast wave that hit the Hancock Building's north face with volcanic force. In an instant, hundreds of huge external glass panes burst into millions of tiny pieces that rained down on the square below.

Drawing their weapons, the two officers slowly got up from the hotel floor. Inside the windowless Hancock Building, they could see stunned people trying to stand and move around. On about the fifteenth floor, a dazed guard holding a gun staggered over the edge and plummeted down onto the plaza. The two CIA officers looked at each other, amazed.

"Main, Neighborhood Watch here," said one officer into his comms, his voice shaky. "It worked. Send in the birds."

"Copy that. You are ordered to assist in the raid. Engage the enemy," commanded Stew.

Both agents raised their sidearms and started firing on the guards inside the Hancock Building.

Mike hit the execute button on the small computer attached to his forearm, and the hunter/killer microdrones tore off at incredible speeds, aimed right at the guards piling out of the roof-access door. The guards tried to raise their weapons to fire, but it was no use. Pop-pop-pop sounded again and again as the drones fired explosive charges directly at their heads. The tiny drones cut through the men in seconds, leaving twenty headless bodies piled up around the roof entrance.

Chris felt sick to his stomach. He'd never seen carnage of this caliber. The unimaginable gore almost made him pass out. Mike was firing and looked completely unfazed by the destruction in front of them.

"Let's move," yelled Mike, slapping a fresh thirty-round magazine into his carbine. "Follow the drones into the stairwell. They'll cover us!"

Chris snapped out of it and tried to ignore the carnage as they stepped over the dead bodies and entered the building. He reached down and activated Max on his phone, which was tucked inside his bulletproof vest. "Max, are you online?"

"I am online, sir, accessing floor plan now. I am ready to access the Order's system when you can plug me into the network. Sir, air strike is inbound now—15.7 minutes."

"OK, keep me posted, Max," Chris said as more drone pops went off ahead of him.

"I think we got this, Main," Mike said into his comms. "Divert remaining drones on our position to the main swarm assault." Within seconds, the microdrones sped ahead through the building.

~

"Main, this is Neighborhood Watch," Stew heard through his comms. "The microdrones are hitting the target now. It's beautiful."

"Copy that. Receiving live drone images now," said Stew. With the Hancock Building's glass facade missing, tiny hunter/killer drones flooded into the top floors, cutting off the guards on the lower levels and attacking targets with the speed and efficiency of a tactical airstrike. In one frame, a woman fired on a drone. A second later, the feed's last image showed her head exploding. In another frame, a group of men ran down a hall. They panic-fired at the drones, but it was no use. The drones overtook the men, killing them instantly.

Stew looked on in horror at the complete havoc wreaked by the tiny killing machines. "Welcome to a new age of warfare," he said solemnly.

CHAPTER 58

D own on the Hancock Building's fortieth floor, Mike quickly opened the roof-access door leading into the Order's main conference room. The tall-ceilinged, ornate room was empty. Chris followed carefully behind Mike.

"Get a load of this place," Mike said to Chris as they slowly entered the room, ready for anything. "Main, this is Knife. Do you copy? Over," said Mike into his comms.

Nothing came back except static.

"The signal's interference is still up," said Chris.

"Yeah. I thought so, but it was worth a try." Mike kept his weapon raised while scanning the room like a shark looking for its prey.

"Max, where do we go from here?" asked Chris. Just then, he noticed a body lying next to the huge conference table. Chris knelt on one knee and hesitated. Even though he could not see the person's face, he somehow knew it was the body of Dr. Martin Alba.

Chris took Alba by his shoulder and gently rolled him onto his back. The doctor's face was frozen stunned. He was covered in blood—something had ripped through his left breast, completely obliterating his heart. Under his body, the fine white marble floor was covered with a pool of dried blood.

Anger and sadness coursed through Chris. Alba had been his trusted confidant and mentor. He had knocked off Chris's rough edges and turned him into a smooth, rolling stone. Alba had helped him see the people around him in a better light. He'd helped Chris through some of his hardest times at Stanford and then put him on the world stage, which contributed greatly to the successful launch of Nav.

"How?" Chris said. "How could this man have been involved in such a great evil?"

"Chris, get behind me now," murmured Mike, aiming his weapon at a wall of red curtains on the other side of the conference room. Chris looked up in time to see the curtains part and several well-dressed men walk briskly into the room with pistols drawn. Jumping up from Alba's body, Chris took cover behind Mike.

"United States Secret Service," yelled the lead agent. "Drop your weapons now!" All four agents trained their weapons on Mike.

"I'm a federal agent. Drop your weapons now!" commanded Mike sternly.

"We don't have time for this," Chris whispered from behind Mike.

"I'm not going to ask you again, sir," said the lead Secret Service agent. "Lower your weapon. You are under arrest for providing material support for a terrorist organization. I say again, lay down your weapon and surrender now."

"You fools. Which one of you traitors wants to die first?" Mike placed his finger on the M4's trigger and nodded sharply so the protective visor closed over his face. Chris winced in anticipation as the agents focused their weapons on Mike.

"I'm not going to ask you—" Mike started to say.

The lead agent fired his weapon, hitting Mike square in the visor. His head jerked back, but the bullet didn't penetrate. The agent gave him a brief stunned look and then recentered his weapon, preparing to fire again.

"My turn." Mike pulled the trigger on his M4. The round hit the agent perfectly between the eyes, his limp body dropping to the marble floor. The other three agents took aim at Mike.

"Stop," yelled a man as the curtain was pulled all the way back, revealing the hideously demonic statue of Baphomet and the blood-stained marble altar. Former US president Royce Jefferson Lennox stepped forward. He held a pistol, and he looked haggard.

Mike trained his weapon on the new target, but no one moved otherwise.

"Chris," said Max into Chris's headset. "The stairwell down to the control and server rooms is located directly behind the statue."

"Mike, you need to get me to that statue," Chris whispered. "We're running out of time. Twelve minutes."

Nodding, Mike started maneuvering sideways toward the statue. The agents closed in with their guns trained on Mike. Chris followed Mike, keeping behind his Viper suit. It was his only real protection.

"I've been trying to diffuse the situation here, solider," Lennox said to Mike. "I just learned about the Order and their diabolical plot. I was used. I've been trying with all my heart to fix this."

Pausing, Lennox smiled reassuringly. "We're on the same team here. Everyone, lower your weapons. That's an order. This is all one big misunderstanding." Lennox laid his pistol on the altar and moved forward with his hands up.

The Secret Service agents lowered their weapons, exchanging confused glances. However, Mike kept his weapon at the ready and continued moving toward the statue. "We know everything, Lennox," he said. "Everything. We hacked your phone. We've had you under surveillance for years. You know the capability of Orion's Spear. Did you really think you could get away with it?"

Lennox gave him a foul look and reached for his gun.

"Run now!" yelled Mike. Chris immediately took off, pain shooting up his back as he sprinted faster than he ever would have thought he could. As he passed the base of the grotesque statue, his eye was caught by a finely carved goat head and other bizarre symbols. He heard gunshots as he pushed through a curtain and burst through the door.

"Move faster, Chris," said Max in his ear. Just then, Chris lost his footing and tumbled down the stairs into a hallway. As he stood and regained his bearings, he was startled to see three women staring at him from inside a cage. They reached through the bars, yelling and pleading in a Germanic language. Chris edged past them, not knowing what to say.

"They're speaking an Austrian dialect," said Max. "They are prisoners."

Chris moved quickly down the hall, but then he looked back and called, "I'll try to come back for you." The women just looked at each other, confused.

"Focus, Chris," said Max. "We're running out of time. Go through the second door on your right."

When Chris opened the door, a brisk wind hit him in the face. The hallway was open to the air along one side, jagged glass visible in the window frames. Decapitated bodies littered the floor. From the floors just below, Chris could hear gunfire, screaming, and the popping explosions of microdrone charges.

Hugging the inside wall to avoid the four-hundred-foot plunge, Chris cautiously scrambled over several lifeless bodies and up the hallway.

"The control room is straight ahead," said Max.

"This feels too easy, Max. Maybe the drones took everyone out. Or wait—if things are going well, then it's probably an ambush," Chris said, reciting Mike's earlier advice. "Max, do you have access to the security cameras yet?"

"The cameras are offline, and so is the local network," said Max. "It appears the acoustic weapon took out more than just the building's glass facade."

Chris approached the innocuous-looking door and gently pulled down on the handle, hoping to avoid drawing the attention of anyone inside. It was locked. He reached down and unsnapped the Glock 19 Leah had holstered at his hip. Hesitation flooded over him—he had no idea how to use the gun.

"Sir, ten minutes," said Max.

"Somehow we have to call off the strike," Chris said. "We don't have time to get out of the building."

When he thought of never seeing Leah again, a sudden rush of adrenaline hit him. He pulled the Glock from its holster, aimed it at the door handle, winced in anticipation, and pulled the trigger.

Click. Nothing happened. Chris looked at the weapon, confused.

"Sir, I believe you must pull back the slide to chamber a round," said Max.

"Oh. Good to know." Grasping the top of the gun, Chris clumsily pulled back the slide. Looking down at the ejection port, he saw a brass round enter the chamber. He took aim, winced again, and fired at the locked door handle. The recoil startled him, but it worked. The hollow-point round exploded the handle, and the door swung open.

Raising the Glock, Chris stepped into the dark room. As his movement triggered automatic lights, he was taken back. He'd been expecting a bland server room, but the large control room looked like a futuristic spaceship flight deck complete with computer terminals and numerous wall monitors.

Chris peered around, but he didn't see anyone. He looked up at the center screen at the head of the room. All it displayed was a lock icon and a flashing countdown that said 00:00.

"Sir, 8.5 minutes until the air strike."

Chris set down the Glock, pulled the laptop from its compartment on his chest, and plugged the computer into a control console's USB port.

"OK, Max, you're connected. Do your thing," said Chris. The laptop came alive as he picked up the gun and surveyed the room.

"Sir, I am connected. Our theory was mostly correct. The system is communicating with drones via radio signals bounced off the ionosphere. However, the signal is not a dead man's switch. The signal remains active, but drones are already launching."

The room's central screen lit up, displaying the status of the Order's drones on a 3D globe. "Oh no," said Chris as drones in flight showed up. "Execute the worm now, Max."

"Executing the program now," said Max. "Sir, twelve drones have already started spraying over various regions in Southeast Asia. Another fleet is taking off now from a Missouri airfield. Their target is the entire United States Midwest."

"Destroy their engines, Max!" yelled Chris in a panic.

Just then, a control-room door burst open. Chris jerked around in time to see Benson Hancock firing his World War II–era Luger right at him. A 9mm round slammed into Chris's bulletproof vest, knocking the wind out of him. Chris tried to recover and fire his weapon, but another bullet tore into his exposed left shoulder.

Screaming, Chris dropped the Glock and fell to the ground, landing in a sitting position. He looked down at the wound in shock. It felt like he'd been hit with a baseball bat. A severe burning sensation engulfed his shoulder, and pain echoed throughout his body. He never imagined he'd be shot by someone trying to kill him.

Behind Hancock, additional men entered the room. Hancock casually walked up to Chris and pushed the gun against his forehead. "I've been waiting all day for this."

CHAPTER 59

Gus Peterson was exhausted. His coveralls were soaked in oil and grease, his hands stained black. Smiling with pride, he stood on the ramp outside his Canadian employer's long hangar. He'd been hard at work for hours preparing the drones for their inaugural crop-dusting launch.

Pusher props roaring, one by one, the drones rolled forward off the ramp and taxied to the airport's single runway. Gus watched as the first two drones accelerated in turn down the runway and elegantly took flight into the dense Missouri humidity.

What a noble profession, thought Gus. *Using technology that bombs people in other countries to help treat crops in our own. I love my job.*

He put his hand to his brow to shield his eyes from the blazing sun. Just then, he noticed an explosion in the air several miles out from the airport. Almost immediately, there was another explosion in the air behind the first. The third drone, rising from the end of the runway, exploded and crashed into the airfield's navigation lights.

"No, no!" yelled Gus.

At first he thought he was hallucinating, but for once he was sober. This was real—his babies were blowing up in midair. As he reached into his pocket for his cell phone, the drones waiting on the taxiway started exploding right in front of him.

"What is this?" Gus yelled, panicking. In shock and disbelief, he dropped his phone and ran his fingers through his thinning white hair. He was completely beside himself.

As the drones exploded, he heard a familiar sound. Gus turned and looked up in time to see an F-15EX flying low and closing in on the airport at an extremely high speed. He waved his arms like a madman at the approaching fighter.

The F-15EX banked and then centered in on the airport. A barrage of missiles uncaged from the wings and belly of the air-superiority fighter.

Gus didn't try to run. He didn't duck. He just froze.

"Oh, my—" he whispered in terror as the entire airport exploded in a conventional mushroom cloud.

CHAPTER 60

C hris looked up at Hancock in complete defeat, pain searing his shoulder. He had no fight left in him.

Smiling, Hancock braced himself as if to pull the trigger. Just then, one of his men yelled, "Sir, the board. The drones. They're going offline!" Hancock pulled back the gun and looked up at the center monitor. One by one, the little green drones flying over the 3D earth projection turned red. Chris breathed a sigh of relief.

At Hancock's command, two guards rushed over and picked Chris up off the ground, pinning him between them. Two others ran to workstations. After a few moments, one called out in a panic, "Sir, we're locked out of the system."

"It's OK," said Hancock, confidently moving closer to Chris. "We planned this. We had to get the AI somehow." He looked down at Chris's computer plugged into the command console.

Chris gave him a questioning look. "What?"

"Now we have what we really wanted," said Hancock. He placed the gun on the terminal and picked up Chris's computer.

Chris looked at him and shook his head. "You really think holding my laptop gives you access to Max? You don't know a lot about software, do you, Hancock?"

Still holding the laptop in one hand, Hancock picked up the Luger again and pointed it at Chris's head. "I know you don't want to die. I know you don't want Leah Bennion to die. It's simple. You will turn over operational control of the AI to me now, or you and everyone you love dies."

"Sir, two minutes until the air strike," said Max in Chris's earbud. "The system is locked out. The worms are executing now. Remaining drones are inoperable."

Thank you, Max. Chris tensed and looked at Benson with resolve. "Well, you know Grandpa's rule number five, right?" asked Chris. Benson gave him a confused look. "The important things are always simple, and the simple things are always hard."

At that moment, the guards at the computer terminals flailed as each took a bullet in the head. The two guards holding Chris released their grip and reached for their weapons. Mike Mayberry burst into the room and tore into the guards with the speed of an old Western gunfighter.

Chris grabbed Hancock's wrist and with all his remaining strength pushed Hancock's arm up into the air. The Luger fired over Chris's head. Hancock still held the laptop in his other hand, refusing to let go. With his free hand, Chris reached down to his belt and clicked the hidden quick-release button on the bottom of the buckle. As the handle of the small, concealed knife popped out, he recalled his grandfather's words: *The blade isn't long enough to kill most people unless you use it on their . . .*

A soft ringing permeated Chris's hearing. Determination ignited from deep within his being. He went into a flow state. The pain fled his back and shoulder. Holding the tiny blade in his hand, everything suddenly made sense. The coma, the vision, the trials, Max, Leah—everything that had happened was to prepare him for this single moment when he would fulfill his mission and save the world.

Hancock pulled the trigger again, firing another round over Chris's head as they both fought for control of the gun. Staring into Hancock's enraged face, Chris plunged the little heart-shaped knife into the man's neck.

Blood exploded from Hancock's carotid artery. His face went pale. The laptop fell from his hand, and Chris caught it. Dropping the gun, Hancock stepped back and gave Chris a confused look. Then his face went blank and his body slackened. Before falling to the floor, the old man managed to give Chris one last vile sneer.

His pain suddenly returning, Chris set down the knife and laptop and then placed his hand on his bleeding shoulder. He felt breathless and weak, like he might pass out.

"Chris," yelled Mike. He ran over and helped Chris sit against the console.

"One minute to air strike, Chris," said Max.

"Where's Lennox?" Chris mumbled.

"I impeached him." Mike smiled. Chris tried to smile back. "Now, we've got to get out of here."

～

As Mike prepped the tandem jump rig while also trying to hold Chris steady, Chris's knees buckled, and he passed out. Mike caught him just in time.

"Main, this is Knife. Do you copy?" said Mike, holding Chris up. "Main, if you can hear me, call off the air strike!" He heard nothing but static.

As Mike finished attaching the rig to Chris's tactical suit, he murmured, "If this isn't a freaking Greek tragedy, I don't know what is." Then he picked up Chris in his arms, bolted through the control-room door, crossed the hallway, and made an impromptu BASE jump over the open edge of the Hancock Building's thirty-ninth floor.

Now airborne and falling like a rock, Mike reached back and pulled his emergency chute, praying it would open. Floor after floor raced past until the reserve chute miraculously opened.

"Chris! Chris, are you with me?" asked Mike, controlling the chute with one hand and checking Chris's pulse with the other. His passenger hung limply from the rig, but he had a faint pulse. *He's losing too much blood.*

Scanning the area for a safe landing zone, Mike turned the chute away from the building and toward a narrow street. Bodies and smoking vehicles lay below. As they gained distance from the Hancock Building, bomb after bomb smashed into the target, the explosions at such close range it was unlike anything Mike had ever experienced. Shock waves smashed into the pair, almost collapsing their parachute. Fiery debris jetted out from the exploding building, flying all around them. The sound was deafening.

Mike shielded Chris as best he could. Even through his Viper suit, he could feel the scorching heat against his back, legs, and neck, followed by the sound of the steel structure starting to disintegrate behind them. Fifty feet above the ground, the chute caught fire as burning debris rained down. They hit the ground hard and rolled end over end, Chris flopping like a rag doll.

Mike recovered, cut the burning chute free, and unfastened Chris. He looked up just in time to see the Hancock Building collapse in on itself. In a mad rush to avoid the falling debris, he grabbed Chris by his tactical suit and dragged him around the side of an old shop.

Mike took off his helmet and assessed Chris's injuries. His shoulder was bleeding profusely, and his pulse felt even fainter. Fighter jets buzzed above, sirens filled the air, and helicopters thumped in the distance.

"Freeze!" yelled an unknown American. Mike turned and saw two men running at him with guns drawn.

"Wait—that's Mike Mayberry," said the CIA officer. He holstered his gun and put his hand to his ear. "Main, this is Neighborhood Watch. We have Knife and Thomas. We need an immediate medical evac on this position."

CHAPTER 61

C hris stood in a familiar golden wheat field, dressed in his tattered battle attire. His shoulder was stained red, but he felt no pain. He looked up at the sky. The same planets circled above his head. And the stars. He knew exactly where he was.

"Look at all the stars," he said to himself.

An odd feeling came over him—like he was being watched. Chris turned and saw a man approaching from several yards away. The man wore all-white and looked vaguely familiar.

Chris blinked, and in that instant, the man was standing in front of him. He said nothing to Chris but stared at him intently.

"I'm sorry, who are you?" asked Chris.

"It's me, son," said the man. "Well, it's thirty-year-old me. Here, this will help."

Chris saw a bright flash, and then his grandpa—the elderly man he remembered so well—stood before him. Rushing forward, Chris embraced him. It felt strange, almost like they were melting into each other. Chris also noticed an electric-like sensation. He pulled back and looked his grandfather in the face.

"I can't believe it. Where's Grandma?"

"Oh, she's around, son. Not here right now, though. How things work here is a little hard to explain."

"Oh, um, OK." Chris felt confused. "Am I dead for real this time?"

His grandfather laughed. "Far from it, son. You've only just begun your work."

"Hey, it was you the whole time," Chris said, pointing to his grandfather. "You were the being! But how is that possible? You were alive the first time I went to the other side—or here, I mean."

"Son, in your mortal condition, it is impossible for you to understand God's time continuum. Just know this: everything is one eternal round. Our progenitors are our protectors. They watch over us from beyond the grave. They give us knowledge. They protect and warn us. They act for us in accordance with God's commands, but they cannot interfere with a mortal's agency. Agency is paramount."

Grandpa put his arm around Chris, and they started walking slowly through the field. "I am bound to you and will always be here for you. God commanded me to give you the gift, and I touched your mind, giving you the first part of the Adamic Code. It took you a few years, but you unlocked these mysteries and, in the process, saved the world. This is only the first test."

Stopping, Grandpa faced Chris. "Now, you need to rest. You've only just begun to understand your mission. As time goes on, it will become more and more clear. But first I need to tell you the rest."

"The rest of what?"

"Beware the gravitational power of the reactor. The forces of evil are actively seeking the artifact. Only you and Max can stop them. You are bound to Leah. In your darkest hour, her charity will be the key to saving the world."

"What are you talking about?"

"I'm not authorized to tell you more than that, son. Now, stand still."

"Why?" asked Chris.

"Remember, remember," Grandfather said, reaching out and touching Chris's forehead.

"No, wait," cried Chris as everything went white.

CHAPTER 62

WALTER REED MEDICAL CENTER
BETHESDA, MARYLAND

H ey, can you hear me?" The soft, familiar female voice sounded far off. "Come back to me," the vocie pleaded.

Chris started to feel something physical—a gentle touch, like a feather brushing over his forehead. His sense of smell returned—the air was disinfected, like a hospital. He opened his eyes and saw a bright light approaching him. The blinding light felt like daggers piercing his eyes. Squeezing them shut, he started thrashing around.

"It's OK, it's OK," said the perfect voice. "Just lie still. You're OK. You're with me now."

The voice was so familiar. Chris tried again to open his eyes and saw the outline of a woman above him. The face started to form, but it was blurry. He tried to focus harder. Slowly, her face came into full view. Leah Bennion smiled at him.

"Hey," he said, confused.

"Hi." She was smiling, and tears rolled down her red cheeks.

"Is this a dream, or am I alive?"

"You're very much alive. And Chris . . . I love you."

"I love you too," he said without hesitation, finally getting the words out. She reached down and kissed him and then pulled back. He closed his eyes and took a few moments to get his bearings, then looked at Leah.

"First, I'm sorry I can't get down on one knee. Second, I don't have a ring yet. But I made you a promise. Will you marry me, Leah Bennion?"

"Yes!" she said, almost shouting.

They held each other as best they could with Chris bandaged and hooked up to life-support equipment. After a few moments, Mike and Stew walked into the room.

"Oh, geez," said Stew. "Sorry to interrupt you two lovebirds."

The four shared a few pleasantries, and then Mike turned to Leah. "Would you mind if we had a private word with Chris?"

"Sure," she said, looking back at Chris as she walked out the door. "I'll be right outside."

"Your shoulder looks terrible," said Mike as Leah closed the door. "How do you feel?"

"Like I got punched in the gut by your ex-wife," said Chris.

Mike laughed.

"Well, at least his personality isn't wounded," said Stew.

"That was some real Rambo stuff you pulled back in that control room," said Mike. "By the way, nice move with that knife."

"I'm the one looking at Rambo. You saved my life, Mike. Thank you."

Mike nodded.

"So, I assume we did it?" Chris felt almost afraid to ask.

"Well, we didn't get all the drones," said Stew. "Some released Aries before we could stop them. The WHO and the military are treating millions of infected now. Most are in China and some in Brazil, but the virus is contained. Chris, Aries would have killed billions if you, Mike, and Max hadn't taken down the Order. Even with the current loss, we should count ourselves very lucky."

As Chris thought of the people dying in hot zones around the world, he felt survivor's guilt. Mike pulled up a chair, sat down, and changed the subject. "So, Chris. The president wants to meet you. He asked me to extend an invitation."

Chris looked at Mike in curious anticipation.

"President Barrington is forming a special working group," continued Mike. "He's pulling Orion's Spear out of the CIA."

"What's Orion's Spear? And doesn't Orion have a bow, not a spear?"

"Yeah, but we thought Orion's Spear sounded way cooler than Orion's Bow."

Chris smirked. Standing behind Mike, Stew kept a straight face.

"Orion's Spear is the government's apex intelligence team, Chris. We take on the most critical threats facing America and the world. It's the nation's best intelligence analysts and special operatives coupled with the best civilian minds. Our existence is classified above top secret. We work completely inside an unlimited black budget. Stew here runs the show. We report directly to the president and no one else. Our mission is to take down threats, foreign and domestic, like the Order—which is still out there, by the way. We could use your help. So what do you say, solider? Will you join Orion's Spear?"

"Do I get my own Viper suit?" asked Chris, half serious.

"I'll think about it," said Mike, smiling.

Chris nodded and then paused. He remembered his grandfather's words about helping those who could not help or defend themselves. He thought about the Order and what it had almost accomplished. He thought about how far he'd come and how he needed to use his talents to help make the world a safer place.

"I'm in."

"Excellent," said Stew.

"Get some rest. We'll be in touch." Mike rose from the chair, and both men shook Chris's hand.

"What was that about?" Leah asked as she reentered the room.

"I'll tell you more later. For now, we have a wedding to plan."

In the car, Stew reached into the back seat and grabbed a mailing tube.

"What's that?" Mike asked, his brow raised.

Stew handed him the cardboard container. "I almost forgot. It's a gift to you from the team. You know, for saving the world and not dying."

Mike popped the plastic top and pulled a poster from the tube. As he began rolling it out, he knew instantly what he was holding. It was the "Be Like Han" poster from the wall inside Orion's Spear's bullpen.

Mike gave the poster a once-over and looked at Stew. "Darn straight."

CHAPTER 63

"T his is a Fox News alert," said anchor Gregg Jarrett from the TV screen. "Welcome back to our team coverage of the Aries terror event. It was revealed only moments ago that former president Royce Lennox helped defeat the Order. It has been confirmed that the former president perished in the US airstrike that destroyed the Order's headquarters and surrounding blocks in Zurich, Switzerland, three days ago. We now take you live to a presidential press conference for more on this stunning development."

President Barrington stood at a podium in the James S. Brady Press Briefing Room. "Ladies and gentlemen, it is my sad duty to report that former president Royce Lennox was killed during the operation to take down the Order. Before the operation, he had been associated with the Order's numerous charities and was unaware of the organization's involvement in developing the Aries virus. When made aware of the situation, President Lennox volunteered to help implant a computer virus in the Order's network, which enabled us to stop most of the drones before they could release the Aries biological weapon. The president's mission was detected by the Order, and we believe he was murdered just prior to the air strike. When the former president's remains are recovered, he will lie in state in the Capitol rotunda and will be posthumously awarded the Presidential Medal of Freedom."

"Bravo, Barrington," Cain bellowed, clapping slowly. It was a masterful lie and cover-up on par with the Kennedy assassination.

On the TV, camera flashes exploded, and the White House correspondents waved their hands in a frenzy, all seeming to yell "Mr. President!" in unison.

"Yes, Jenny," the president said, pointing to a *Wall Street Journal* reporter sitting on the front row.

"Sir, is it true that the mission was a CIA Ground Branch operation and that Chris Thomas, Nav CEO and inventor of the Max AI, was also involved? Reports say Thomas is now at the Walter Reed Medical Center undergoing treatment for injuries sustained in the incident."

"I can neither confirm nor deny the involvement of any other intelligence, military, or civilians in the operation," said the president.

"Chris Thomas will die for this," snarled Cain.

The press again erupted, and then Gregg Jarrett reappeared on the screen. "Fox News has also learned that former national security adviser Roger Cowen and President Lennox's former chief of staff, Richard Boone, were key figures in the Order. The FBI has placed both men on the Ten Most Wanted Fugitives list, along with Otto Klein, a German scientist authorities have identified as the engineer of the Aries virus. Sky News is reporting that a former vice chancellor of Germany and former prime minister of Norway were both arrested today in predawn raids. Astonishingly, both are believed to also have been in the Order's inner circle."

Another camera showed Jarrett from a different angle. "Here at home, America is reeling as thousands of US government employees have been arrested in the wake of the Aries incident. In joint operations between federal law-enforcement agencies led by the FBI, federal employees identified as being on the Order's payroll have been arrested and detained. Legal experts claim it will take years and hundreds of millions of dollars in taxpayer money to investigate and prosecute the cases."

Cain pushed the power button on the TV remote and stood from his opulent throne. He walked across the vast living room of his $200 million Holmby Hills estate, through a pair of classic French doors, and out onto the finely manicured back lawn. He looked over downtown Los Angeles and then out toward the Pacific Ocean. Cain loved everything about LA. The pollution. The decay. The sin. The disease.

There, in the decadence of Los Angles, he could hide in plain sight.

With all that had happened, Cain felt nothing but the same horrible pain that had been with him for thousands of years.

He pulled his iPhone from his coat pocket, clicked on a children's game app, and pressed the Learn More button. Prompted for a passcode, he placed his thumb on the haptic button, held the camera to his face for a 3D depth scan, and then entered a twelve-character passcode.

"Status," said Cain. Across the screen, text displayed: *Mission ready. Thor's Hammer is operational and awaiting target coordinates. Would you like to input target coordinates?*

Even with his ace at the ready, Cain was emotionless. He closed the gaming app and walked deeper into the garden as the sun set over the Pacific.

CHAPTER 64

NAV CORPORATE HEADQUARTERS
PALO ALTO, CALIFORNIA

Three months after the Aries incident, Project Leah—as Chris and Max had come to call it—was in full effect. Even though most global users were still getting Nav for free, corporations, governments, universities, and numerous other organizations were signing up in droves for paid Nav subscriptions, as Leah had predicted. In only its third month of operations, Nav was already generating $10 billion in monthly subscription revenue.

Scott Allen and Leah pulled up to the entrance of the new Nav headquarters just off the Stanford University campus in Palo Alto. At the front of the building, a work crew was removing a sign that read Theranos.

Chris ran out the front doors to meet his new wife and his old best friend, whom he had just hired to be the company's new president. The three embraced in a group hug.

"Dude, Theranos?" asked Scott.

"Yeah, I heard it was some scam company, but the building comes with bulletproof windows," said Chris. "So yeah, it was kind of a no-brainer."

"Cool," said Scott.

As they chatted, Chris's iPhone buzzed. He looked down at the screen—all it said was 777. "Hey, guys, let me take this really quick," Chris said, moving away as he pressed the green call button. Reluctantly, he placed the phone to his ear.

"Vanguard, this is Main. We have an Orion's Spear priority-delta emergency. Are you ready to rock?"

Vanguard. Chris loved his new code name, but he paused, glancing back at his wife and best friend. Sighing, he looked off into the distance, wondering what the world would throw at him next. Then he straightened his posture and spoke with resolve.

"Let's do it, Main."

THANK YOU

Thank you so much for taking the time to read *The Adamic Code*, book 1 in the Orion's Spear Series. If you've enjoyed spending time with Chris and Leah and the other characters in this book, it would mean a great deal to me if you could leave a review wherever fine books are sold online—and, of course, spread the word!

ABOUT THE AUTHOR

When Chris Knudsen isn't writing books, he runs a successful direct-to-consumer marketing consultancy. Chris has a master's degree in business administration from Westminster College and spent ten years as a university instructor. Chris enjoys spending time with his wife, Elizabeth, and their four children. They call Heber Valley home.

Chris Thomas returns in Vanguard, *book 2 of the Orion Spear series.*

Made in the USA
Las Vegas, NV
29 December 2020